1932: A ... n ... ne ... nks ... Great Depression. The ranks of the unemployed have increased by 11 million in the two years since the spring of 1930. Later the same year Americans elect Franklin Delano Roosevelt president, with his promise of a New Deal. *(The Detroit News)*

1935: Controversial Louisiana senator Huey Long launches a campaign to win the presidency from FDR. The Kingfish is so certain of victory that he even writes a book titled *My First Days in the White House.* On September 8 an assassin's bullet ends Huey Long's campaign—and his life. (The Louisiana State Museum)

1936: Playwright Eugene O'Neill wins the Nobel Prize for Literature. O'Neill began writing plays in 1912, when a bout of tuberculosis confined him to a sanitorium for a year. Such plays as *Anna Christie*, *Strange Interlude*, and *Desire Under the Elms* brought new themes of high seriousness to the American stage. (Culver Pictures, Inc.)

1937: After only three years as a professional boxer, Joe Louis—the Brown Bomber—wins the heavyweight championship title after knocking out James J. Braddock in eight rounds in Chicago. At age twenty-three, Louis is the youngest champion ever. He would successfully defend his title twenty-five times until his retirement in 1949. (Culver Pictures, Inc.)

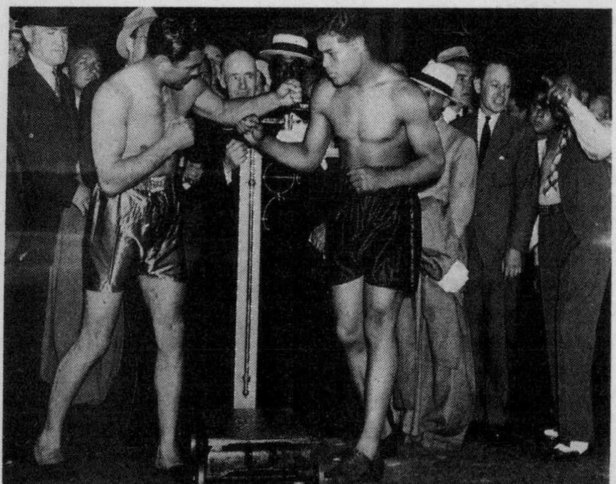

1938: Halloween night. Millions of Americans listen in terror as a voice on the radio describes how Martians armed with death rays have landed near Princeton, New Jersey. What many don't know is that the voice belongs to Orson Welles and the broadcast is a Mercury Theater of the Air production of the science fiction classic *The War of the Worlds* by H. G. Wells. (Culver Pictures, Inc.)

1939: Mickey Rooney (with Judy Garland) reigns as Hollywood's number one box-office attraction. Rooney endears himself to the moviegoing public as the bumbling but likable teenager Andy Hardy in a long-running series of MGM comedies. (The Museum of Modern Art/Film Stills Archive)

The American Chronicles by Robert Vaughan
Ask your bookseller for the books you have missed

DAWN OF THE CENTURY
OVER THERE
THE LOST GENERATION

THE AMERICAN CHRONICLES
VOLUME IV

HARD TIMES

ROBERT VAUGHAN

DOMAIN™

BANTAM BOOKS

NEW YORK • TORONTO • LONDON • SYDNEY • AUCKLAND

HARD TIMES

A Bantam Domain Book / March 1993

ISBN 0-553-56238-X

Published simultaneously in the United States and Canada

Bantam Books are published by Bantam Books, a division of Bantam Doubleday Dell Publishing Group, Inc. Its trademark, consisting of the words "Bantam Books" and the portrayal of a rooster, is Registered in U.S. Patent and Trademark Office and in other countries. Marca Registrada. Bantam Books, 666 Fifth Avenue, New York, New York 10103.

PRINTED IN THE UNITED STATES OF AMERICA

OPM 0 9 8 7 6 5 4 3 2 1

This book is respectfully dedicated
to Greg Tobin

CHAPTER ONE

JULY 28, 1932, WASHINGTON, D.C.

The rain falling on Washington, D.C., that night wasn't a hard, cleansing rain. It was a soft, gentle spray, carrying trapped within its fine mist some of the ash from the burned buildings along Pennsylvania Avenue.

As John Canfield rode in a taxicab en route to the Willard Hotel, where the National Democratic Committee kept a suite of rooms for visiting members of Franklin Delano Roosevelt's presidential campaign staff, he stared out the window in disbelief. The older son of St. Louis industrialist Robert Canfield—majority owner and CEO of Canfield-Puritex Corporation, one of the wealthiest and most powerful corporations in America—John was in Washington at Roosevelt's request so that he might render a firsthand report on the unrest being caused by the Bonus Marchers.

Twenty-five, handsome, with the same dark hair and blue eyes that his father had and the runner's body that his father once had, John Canfield was on everybody's most-eligible-bachelor list. He was bright, energetic, and ambitious, and he was also a young man of great personal convictions. A member of Canfield-Puritex's board of directors and an active officer in the company, John had asked his father for an extended leave of absence from the family business to do what he could to alleviate the suffering of those caught up in the Great Depression, as it was universally known.

Like many other wealthy and compassionate young men, John's earliest efforts had been well intended but ineffectual. He had toured the country, making large donations of food, clothing, and money to various relief agencies. He had provided food to sharecroppers in Arkansas and had provided money to renovate buildings for the homeless in Detroit. He had distributed clothes in Cleveland and helped stock soup kitchens in New York.

But he had seen all that as nothing more than patchwork. What he really wanted was to get involved in some movement, some "great crusade," as he put it, that would find the cause of the depression, eliminate it, and restore America to economic greatness. When he had stated those aspirations to Champ Dawson, the senior senator from John's home state of Missouri, Senator Dawson convinced him that the best way to accomplish his goal would be to get Franklin D. Roosevelt elected president. John had met the governor, listened to what he had to say, then undertook the task of getting Roosevelt elected with all the unbridled zeal a twenty-five-year-old could muster.

Now, shifting around in his seat, John leaned forward to talk to the taxi driver.

"Did you see any of the riot today?"

"Yeah, I seen it," the hackie replied.

"What happened?"

"The veterans and the police fought it out."

John nodded. "Yes, that much I know. What I mean is, what caused the trouble? I thought their stay here had been peaceful."

"Used to be. Ain't no more. 'Course, them that's camped down on the Anacostia mud flats still ain't causin' nobody no trouble. But there was bunches of 'em in those abandoned buildings down on Pennsylvania Avenue, and they was gettin' pretty bad. You know. Harassin' people. The police tried to move 'em out, make 'em get back across the river with the others, but they didn't want to go, so they started fightin'. The veterans used bottles and bricks, the cops used bullets and tear gas."

"How did the fires start?"

"Don't nobody really know. Some say the veterans did it, some say the police did it themselves. Could'a been from the tear gas and smoke grenades, too."

"Yes, I suppose so," John said grimly, deeply troubled that things had gone so far. "Tell me, what do you think of them?"

"You mean the veterans?"

"Yes."

"They got no business here."

"I see."

"Don't get me wrong; I'm all for the veterans. I mean, my oldest brother was killed in France. But when you got this many people just hangin' around the city like this all the time . . . Well, most folks here ain't too happy about it. Why don't they just all go home?"

John shook his head. "Many of them don't have a home to go to."

"Well, they came from somewhere, didn't they?"

"I suppose they did."

"Then they should go back to where they came from. They should go back and go to work. You can't tell me there ain't jobs out there to be had. Maybe a fella can't get the kind of job he feels he should have, but there's work to be had. Hell, I know there is."

"If there are jobs out there, I can't find them," John said. "And I've been all over the country looking for them."

The cab driver gave John a piercing look in his rearview mirror. "You'll excuse me for sayin' so, mister, but it sure don't look to me like you're hurtin' none. That's a nice suit you're wearin', that's a good haircut you got, and you ain't hungry in your eyes. I've seen enough hungry people to know what it looks like to be hungry in the eyes."

"I'm sorry," John said. He smiled apologetically. "I didn't make myself clear. I mean, I've been looking for work for others."

"Oh. You're one of them do-gooders, are you?"

John chuckled. "You might say that."

"Yeah, well, I still say there's work out there. A well-dressed, well-fed man like you just don't know where to look, is all."

"Perhaps you're right," John said, not wanting to argue any longer. "Oh, let me out here, will you?"

"What do you want out here for? It's still four or five blocks to the hotel."

"I know, but I'd like to walk."

"Okay, it's your shoe leather," the hackie replied with a shrug, pulling over to the curb.

John paid the fare, then began to walk. Despite the rain some of the buildings continued to burn, and flames licked at the night sky, lighting the low-hanging clouds from below with a diffused, orange glow. From far off John could hear the echoing wail of sirens, the sporadic rattle of gunfire, and the occasional muffled thump of a tear-gas bomb. He cringed internally, thinking that America wasn't supposed to be like this.

The crimson light of the night glow disclosed a pile of charred, smoking timbers—a building that had burned earlier in the day. As John walked by the rubble, the falling rain hissed and popped on the still-smoldering fire, making it sound like the sputtering fuse of a live grenade. Scattered pockets of tear gas hung in visible clouds, and here and there John saw people scurrying about with handkerchiefs clutched against their noses and mouths.

For several weeks the city of Washington had been under siege by an army of twenty thousand souls, and though the invading army wasn't foreign, tensions among the residents were as high as if it had been. When twenty thousand hungry men gathered together in one spot and for one common purpose, it tended to make those around the gathering place very nervous.

When Roosevelt had decided several days earlier to

send John to observe the Bonus March, the young campaign staffer immediately did thorough background work. He was now well informed about the history of the Bonus Army; he was also in the Bonus Marchers' corner.

Along with many others in the country, the veterans had suffered severe deprivations as a result of the Great Depression that held the nation in its grip. Congress had voted a war bonus to be paid to everyone who fought in the Great War, but it had also voted that the bonus wasn't to be paid until 1945—which to the veterans was like giving someone a can of food without a can opener. Finally their frustration came to a head, and a small group of veterans from Portland, Oregon, decided to go to Washington to pressure Congress into paying them now. As that little group traveled across the country, news of what they were doing spread to other desperate veterans, and by freight train, car, truck, and on foot, new marchers found their way to the advancing column. The group began to grow exponentially, gathering a platoon-strength number of followers in Montana, swelling by a company in Nebraska, growing by a battalion in Missouri, adding a regiment in Ohio, picking up a division in Pennsylvania, until they reached Washington with the strength of an entire army.

They had stayed in Washington for several weeks, standing on street corners and milling around by the thousands on the Capitol grounds. They had lobbied for their cause with emaciated bodies, gaunt faces, and soul-scarred eyes. When the House finally passed the bill that authorized immediate payment of the bonus, the veterans had declared a victory and congratulated each other, talking about the tough campaign they had just come through as if it had been one of the battles they had fought in France. They had waved and cheered at passing motorists, some of them smiling for the first time in over a year.

Then word came that the Senate had voted the bill down. The veterans were stunned, watching victory snatched from their grasp. Their laughter turned to ashes in their mouths, and for several days they had milled about without direction, resorting to the old military axiom of waiting until someone told them what to do.

The leaders of the Bonus Army—some self-appointed, others elected—finally decided to hold a "death march," a slow, shuffling, elliptical march directly in front of the Capitol steps. Working in relays, the veterans had kept the march going twenty-four hours a day for several days, each marcher keeping his dead eyes fastened on the back of the neck of the man in front of him. It had made quite an unnerving sight to the legislators and federal employees as they arrived for work each morning and left each evening. Most of those who worked in the Capitol began going in through side doors so they wouldn't have to see the group of haggard, physically and emotionally exhausted men shuffling around in a slow, mind-numbing track.

Congress adjourned without bringing the bill up for reconsideration, the lawmakers sneaking out through underground tunnels to avoid seeing the veterans. The battle was lost. When the veterans learned what had happened, the peaceful lobbying turned ugly. Washington police ordered the veterans to disperse, and when the protesters hadn't moved quickly enough, the police began to move in on them.

It was like dipping sand out of a bucket. As soon as one group of veterans was moved, another group flowed in to take its place. The police accomplished nothing, and finally, that morning, rioting began in the streets. One veteran was killed, several were wounded, and hundreds of veterans and Washingtonians had to suffer through the effects of tear gas.

Fear and tension gripped the entire city, and those responsible for President Hoover's safety ordered the White House to be guarded at all times. Now, everywhere John looked he saw soldiers fully armed and staring out over the smoldering city. Great banks of spotlights lit up the Ellipse, painting it a stark scene of harsh white and featureless black.

Then John saw something that made his blood run cold: an army on the move. Not the ragtag army of World War veterans, but well-disciplined, uniformed, Regular Army soldiers. Some were riding in the backs of trucks; others, with drawn sabers, were mounted on horses; still others manned a dozen or more light tanks.

John spotted a taxi standing empty along the curb, and he hurried over to it.

"Follow them!" he told the driver, pointing to the soldiers on the move.

"Are you crazy, mister?" the man replied. "Those boys look like they're about ready to hand out some trouble, and I don't want to be any part of it."

"You can stay a safe distance behind them," John argued. "When they stop, you stop. I'll go the rest of the way on foot."

"That's not a very good idea," the driver protested.

"I'll pay double what's on the meter."

Smiling broadly, the driver reached back to open the door of his cab. "Get in, mister. You just hired yourself a hack."

John climbed into the taxi, watching anxiously out the window as they proceeded along behind the military force. When the trucks and horses and tanks abruptly came to a halt, the cab did likewise. John paid the driver double as he had agreed, then got out and quickly walked foward to see what was going on. Soldiers poured out of the trucks and deployed, along with the tanks, around the bridge that crossed the Anacostia River. Officers and noncommissioned officers barked orders, bayonets were fixed to the ends of rifles, and bolts were worked, slamming cartridges home with metallic clicks. Huge, truck-mounted spotlights were turned on, their beams sweeping back and forth over the ramshackle village that had grown up across the river on the mud flats.

John knew of this "Hooverville," as all such shantytowns were called, but this was the first time he had seen this one. It was huge, consisting of thousands of shelters made from cardboard, tin, scrap lumber, and even bits of paper and cloth. Most were so meager that they looked as if they would come down with a good sneeze, but a few of the shanties had been reasonably well constructed and decorated. John even saw one that looked like a perfect, tiny bungalow. It was painted white and had green shutters and a neat picket fence.

There were nearly as many signs as there were shelters:

BONUS NOW! MOST OF US WILL BE DEAD BY 1945!
WE WILL NOT STARVE TO DEATH IN THE LAND OF PLENTY!
WE FOUGHT FOR THIS COUNTRY. DON'T DESERT US NOW!
HOOVER, WHERE IS YOUR COMPASSION?
GIVE US OUR BONUS! GIVE US WORK!

Even more dramatic than the signs and shanties were the people. They were frozen into immobility by the sweeping beams of light, like animals on the road sometimes freeze when caught in the headlights of a car. There were many, many women in the village and an even greater number of children. Those children small enough to be held were in their mothers' arms; the rest were clustered around their mothers' legs, hanging on to their skirts and peering around from behind.

What affected John most was the look on the villagers' faces. To a soul they were wan and drawn, their eyes dull. They didn't appear frightened, despite the fact that an army was assembling just across the river. They didn't show any defiance, either. They just looked on with an almost detached curiosity.

John recognized an imposing figure among the military men. General MacArthur, impeccably dressed in a beribboned, dark-brown blouse, khaki riding breeches, and highly polished boots, strolled around behind his soldiers, slapping a riding quirt against his leg as he watched his army move into position. Then, responding to a subtle signal of the quirt, the soldiers began to sweep forward.

A couple of hundred veterans were on the city side of the river, and they stood defiantly at the bridge as the army swept forward.

"You don't want to come after us, do you now, lads?" one of the veterans yelled. "We were soldiers, just like you!"

"We fought in the war!" another shouted.

But most of the uniformed soldiers were too young to have fought in the war and seemed impervious to the cries for pity from the old veterans. The young army moved inexorably forward, bowling over the old, hungry, emaciated veterans with the weight of their horses, slashing at them with their sabers, and knocking them down with wicked strokes from their rifle butts.

"My ear! My ear!" one veteran screamed, slapping his hand to the side of his head after a cavalryman slashed with his saber. Bright-red blood spilled through the veteran's fingers.

Several shots were fired into the air, and the veterans, realizing they were beaten, turned and ran back across the bridge to the safety of their makeshift village.

"That's it. The soldiers won't go any further," John heard someone say, and he turned toward the voice with some surprise. He had been so transfixed by the tragic spectacle in front of him, he hadn't noticed that other civilian bystanders were observing the scene with him. Most were newspaper and radio reporters, including newsreel cameramen grinding away as they recorded the terrible scene.

"What makes you think they won't go on?" one of the other newsmen asked.

"Because I heard it from the top. MacArthur has orders not to go across the bridge."

John felt his body relax slightly, unaware until that moment just how tense he had been. The thought that the army would cross the bridge and terrorize the women and children as they had the men had been almost too horrible a thought to contemplate. At least that worry was over.

Then, to John's outrage and the voiced outrage of the other observers, General MacArthur *did* order his men across the bridge. The horses galloped across first, their clattering hooves raising a thunder from the bridge planking. They were followed by the tanks, then by the infantrymen. The Bonus Marchers, clearly shocked that they had been chased all the way into their sanctuary, shouted out in fury and frustration. The women screamed in fear, the children began crying in terror. Here and there a veteran would try to defend his pitiful shelter, rushing forward with a rock or bottle or brick—only to be beaten back with grim efficacy.

Fires began breaking out throughout the village, and

John was puzzled as to their origin. Then he saw soldiers running from structure to structure, setting them alight. Fires licked at the night sky, and, silhouetted against the orange flames, soldiers could be seen shoving, herding, crushing the final, futile efforts of resistance.

Soon flames covered the entire mud flat, creating a huge glowing circle in the blackness. Just beyond the wavering flames the bloodied veterans and their terrified families gathered, weeping silently as they stood in the protective cloak of darkness.

John spotted an army officer hurrying toward his commander, and he walked closer to eavesdrop.

"General, the village is secure," the officer reported to MacArthur with a crisp salute.

"Good. We'll keep our people here overnight," MacArthur replied. "Tomorrow we'll bring in the bulldozers and knock down anything that might still be standing. I don't want two sticks left together."

"Yes, sir," the officer replied, again saluting crisply, then hurrying back in the direction he had come.

John Canfield hurried away, too, to report to *his* commander: Governor Franklin D. Roosevelt.

As soon as he had dismissed the bellhop and closed the door of his hotel room, John had flung his travel case onto the bed and placed a long-distance call to the governor's mansion in Albany, New York, impatiently waiting for the connection to be made.

It then took him some thirty minutes to describe what he had seen, his minutely detailed depiction interrupted frequently by the governor's questions.

"Yes," Roosevelt now said on the other end of the line, when John had concluded his eyewitness account, "we listened to a radio broadcast of the event, which said essentially what you have. Though, I must say, your having been there adds a great deal of insight and immediacy to it."

"It was awful, Governor," John said quietly. "I never thought I'd live to see the day when American soldiers turned against their own people."

"You know what this means, don't you, John?" Roosevelt asked, his voice a mixture of sadness and anticipation.

"What's that, sir?"

"Herbert Hoover has just handed me the election on a silver platter."

BERLIN, GERMANY

Simon Blumberg sat in the back of the taxi, holding his crutches across one leg and scratching absentmindedly at the stump of the other. His empty trouser leg was tucked in just above what used to be his left knee. For almost ten years after the World War's end he had worn an artificial leg to replace the one lost in battle. He had worn it simply as a matter of vanity and finally stopped wearing it when he realized he could get around better without it.

"The war?" the driver asked.

"I beg your pardon?" Simon asked, turning his dark-eyed gaze from the view out the window to meet the driver's own in the rearview mirror. A breeze from the open window ruffled his dark hair, and he smoothed it back into place.

"Your leg," the driver said. "Did you lose it in the war?"

"Yes."

"Then you are a veteran."

"Yes."

"You should wear your medals," the hackie said, his tone making it more a command than a suggestion. "You should wear them proudly to show that you fought for the fatherland."

"This is my medal," Simon said, indicating the empty trouser leg.

"Yes, yes, but you must display your pride in your homeland. Don't you understand? The Jews and the Communists and the rest of the world have tried to keep us down for too long, but we have suffered enough. Soon we will suffer no more."

"I'm glad you think the suffering will soon be over," Simon said dryly.

"It won't end by itself, of course," the driver continued,

either ignorant of or ignoring the sarcasm in Simon's voice. "We must take control of our own destiny."

"Yes. That is an admirable thought." Simon said the words by rote and without conviction. Berlin, indeed all of Germany, seethed with political unrest. Everyone had a political agenda, and Simon avoided them all with an equal lack of enthusiasm. At thirty-seven, he was world-weary and cynical, making no bones about the fact that he didn't give a damn about anything—least of all himself.

"That's why I am a Nazi," the hackie said resolutely. He held out his lapel, proudly displaying the swastika pin he was wearing.

"And you think Adolf Hitler has the answers?" Simon asked.

"Yes, of course. Do you know anyone who is better qualified to lead the new Germany?"

"Actually, I rather like the ideas of Fritz Nagel."

"Who?"

"Fritz Nagel. He believes all the troubles of the world could be eliminated if everyone would just go about naked and there were no capital letters in the alphabet."

"You are making jokes," the driver snorted angrily. "This is no time for jokes. This is a time for action. This is a time for all true sons of Germany to join the National Socialists and stand together."

"I am not a true son of Germany," Simon said. "I am Austrian."

"Yes, yes, but Austrians, Germans, we are the same, no? Even Adolf Hitler is from Austria."

Simon smirked. "Yes, I know."

"And when Hitler is elected president, Germany and Austria will be united. We will be the greatest country in Europe. The greatest in the world."

"And you really believe Corporal Hitler can do all this for you?"

"He is a corporal no longer," the hackie said. He stared hard at Simon's reflection in the mirror. "Why is it that you aren't for Hitler?"

"I'm afraid that would be a bit difficult, under the circumstances."

"But I don't understand. You are Austrian. You are a veteran of the war. There is no reason why you should not be for Adolf Hitler."

"I am a Jew."

The driver slammed on the brakes so hard that Simon had to put his hand up to keep from being thrown against the seat back in front of him.

The hackie turned to glare at Simon. "You should have told me you are a Jew!" he snapped

"But isn't that what I just said? I am a Jew."

"I would not have taken you in my cab."

"Why not? I'm paying for the ride."

"Jews shouldn't have the right to ride in taxis—or on trolleys or buses."

"I see," Simon said. He stared at the cab driver. "That's what you believe, is it?"

"Yes," the hackie said defiantly. "That is what I believe."

"And just what value do you place on your political convictions?" Simon asked. "After all, these are difficult times, are they not? And money is hard to come by. By the way, did I mention that I will be paying in marks, not shekels?"

The driver briefly scowled at Simon, then turned back around, put the car in gear, and continued the journey.

Simon leaned back in his seat. "I'm glad to see that we understand one another," he said dryly.

When the cab driver reached Simon's destination a few moments later, he jerked the car to a stop, a clearly deliberate move that made Simon's head snap back. Hauling his slender body out of the car before paying the fare, Simon leaned on his crutches outside the driver's window. With very measured movements, he pulled out a roll of money so large that the cab driver's eyes bulged.

"How does a Jew come by such money?" the hackie demanded.

"Haven't you heard?" Simon replied. "We are all money changers. We are the ones your Christ threw out of the temple." He paid the exact fare, omitting the tip.

The driver looked at the money, then shoved it in his pocket. "Filthy Jew," he spat as he drove away.

Smirking, Simon crossed the sidewalk on Unter den Linden Strasse to his apartment building. As he was about to enter, the front door of the apartment building next door was suddenly thrown open and several Brownshirts came rushing outside, laughing and pushing before them a terrified man and an even more terrified woman. The man was wearing a placard around his neck with the words: I AM A JEW. I DEFILED AN ARYAN WOMAN. The placard hanging from the woman's neck read: I DISGRACED MY RACE. I SLEPT WITH A JEW.

"Wouldn't you like to sleep with this filthy slut, Hans?" one of the Brownshirts shouted to a fellow SA recruit, pointing to the woman.

"Are you crazy? She has been with a Jew. If you stuck your cock in her, it would probably fall off!"

"How about the Jew? Did his cock fall off?" a third SA man asked.

"I don't know. Let's see. Show us your cock, Jew! Take out your cock for all to see!"

"Please," the terrified man whimpered.

The Brownshirt named Hans slapped him so hard that his nose began to bleed.

"I said, take out your cock!"

With trembling hands, the man began to unbutton his trousers.

"Look at it, Hans. Doesn't it look like one of those fat white worms you turn up under a piece of decaying wood?"

"No," Hans answered. "It looks like a maggot. A disgusting, white maggot." He turned to the woman. "And you, you slut! You let this maggot cock inside of you!" He struck the woman as hard as he had struck the man a moment earlier, and almost instantly the woman's left eye began to swell shut.

"Come," another of the SA men suggested. "We'll take them down to the corner for all to see. *She slept with a Jew!*" he shouted, and he motioned for the others to shout with him.

"She slept with a Jew!"
"She slept with a Jew!"
"She slept with a Jew!"

Simon stood back along with the other passersby who had been drawn to the scene, watching the Brownshirts push and pummel the couple all the way down to the corner of the block. He felt a myriad of emotions: anger, impotence, frustration, and shame.

He didn't feel fear, but it was hardly odd that he didn't. To feel fear one had to be concerned for his life—and on that particular issue Simon had long ago crossed the Rubicon. The war had destroyed more than his left leg; it had destroyed his spirit. He no longer cared whether he lived or died.

Turning back to his apartment building, he awkwardly climbed the steps and went inside, shutting the door tightly and blotting out the taunts and cries that echoed from down the street.

CHAPTER TWO

JANUARY 30, 1933, BERLIN

Unter den Linden Strasse was a ribbon of fire as more than one hundred thousand Brownshirts, all carrying torches and singing the "Horst Wessel" song, marched in a massive victory celebration. The walls of the buildings lining the street echoed with their singing, the vibrating boom of muffled drums, and the metered thump of jackbooted feet against cobblestones. It was after eight o'clock in the evening, and the celebration had been going on all day, having started the moment President Hindenburg agreed to name Adolf Hitler chancellor of Germany.

From the window of his darkened apartment, which overlooked Unter den Linden Strasse, Simon Blumberg had an excellent view not only of the flowing river of fire, but also of the new chancellor. Hitler, illuminated by the dancing fingers of a half-dozen spotlights, was standing in the window of the Chancellery Building, saluting the marching throng. But his salute didn't take the approved Nazi form of the right arm held straight out; rather, it was bent in at the elbow, much as when one takes an oath.

Simon shifted his weight on his crutches to find a more comfortable position, then studied the new chancellor—a man who had, in fact, once been his comrade in arms. Though Austrian by birth, Simon preferred Germany and had chosen to be educated in Germany. During the war he had fought in a German regiment, serving in the very same squad as his fellow Austrian who had just been appointed Germany's chancellor.

Adolf Hitler was anti-Semitic even then and had made no effort to conceal his feelings, often strutting about the bunker giving long harangues against the Jews. However, when it came to things like stealing extra food rations—the soldiers called it "organizing"—Hitler, who was very good at it, would frequently pass over new replacements to share his booty with those veterans who had been in the war with him from the very beginning. On such occasions Simon, though a Jew, happened to be one of those veterans and would benefit from Hitler's organizing efforts, while non-Jew replacements would be left out.

Hitler had been a dedicated warrior, and he respected other soldiers who showed courage and a willingness to perform their duty. Simon was just such a soldier. Therefore, during the war, even though Hitler continued his diatribe against Jews in general, he never harassed Simon in particular.

Simon hadn't seen Hitler since the war and didn't have any desire to do so. If he were to encounter him, he was sure it would not be a friendly reunion, for Hitler had risen to power on the strength of his Jew hating. Under Hitler's leadership, Nazis boycotted Jewish shops and stores, often going so far as to post thugs by their entrances to enforce the boycott. As a result, Jewish businesses were disappearing with alarming regularity, and it was getting increasingly difficult for Jews in Germany to make a living. There were dark hints that the situation was going to get even worse, and now that Hitler and the Nazis were in power, Simon was sure of it.

Fortunately he didn't need to earn money in Germany in order to make a living. Once a month he received an exceptionally generous stipend from his cousin, David Gelbman, who was the owner of Blumberg's, a large department store in Vienna that had originally been owned by Simon's father. Ostensibly, Simon was David's German liaison, making arrangements for any purchases Blumberg's Department Store might make in Germany and for any sales the store made to Germany. However, the ever-increasing anti-Semitism being shown by the government, businesses, and ordinary citizenry of Germany made Simon's job a job in name only, for he was finding that he had less and less to do.

As the situation for Jews worsened, David repeatedly tried to convince Simon to come back to Vienna. So far Simon had resisted.

"I don't care if people don't like me because I'm a Jew," Simon had recently told his cousin. "Why should I care? Hell, I don't like people, and I don't even *need* a reason."

Now, finally satiated with the spectacle outside his window, Simon turned away and crossed the room to his bed. He stretched out and turned on the radio to hear Hitler's address to the nation, the first in his capacity as chancellor.

Hitler was introduced by Rudolf Hess. The introduction was short and pithy.

"Hitler ist Deutschland! Deutschland ist Hitler! Ich gebe Sie Adolf Hitler!"

After the crowd noise died down, Hitler began to speak, and as his words filled the darkness of Simon's apartment, Simon thought how odd it was to be listening now to the same voice he used to hear in the trenches on the Western Front. Then Hitler's speeches had been addressed to an audience of seven or eight men who hadn't particularly cared what he said. Now he was being heard not only by the throng outside the Chancellery, but by millions of radio listeners across Germany, all of them hanging on every word.

"All the world is suffering from economic chaos, and none have suffered more than the German people. Our suffering is unique because it has been imposed upon us by those criminal nations who would hold down our spirit and the natural triumph of our will.

"The suffering of the German people has been all the greater as a result of a series of weak and ineffectual governments, dominated by Communists and tainted by the demoralizing, bloodsucking Jews. All over Germany, whenever a business has failed or a family has gone without food, one has only to turn on the light of truth to find the Jews, preying on that misfortune like maggots on a corpse.

"All this, I promise you, has ended!"

Hitler's speech was interrupted by hysterical cheering and applause, then by the chants of "*Sieg heil! Sieg heil! Sieg heil!*"

When the crowd noise died down, Hitler began to speak again.

"The world must now be made to understand that Germany did not die of its defeat in the World War. Germany will again take the place she deserves among the nations!"

There was more cheering.

"I pledge to you a Germany that will never surrender and will never again sign a treaty that cannot be fulfilled!"

Again the multitude interrupted his speech with their cheers.

"I will do this by making Germany strong again. And Germany's strength will again come, as it has in the past, from the strength of its industrial might.

"We have seen the failed policies of the weak governments that have plagued our nation since the war. Now we shall see the result of a strong government. My government!"

The throng erupted in a frenzy. Hitler waited, the pause in his delivery serving only to underscore the crowd's adulation of him. Then he continued.

"Private enterprise cannot be maintained by the false promise of democracy. Private enterprise is conceivable only if the people have a sound idea of the personality and authority of a powerful leader.

"All the worldly goods we possess we owe to the struggle of the chosen. We must not forget that all the benefits of culture must be introduced with an iron fist; therefore, it is my intention to restore the German Army to its former position of glory."

Once more the crowd began shouting "*Sieg heil,*" and once more Hitler waited a long moment before going on.

"I also make this promise to you. It will be my policy to eliminate the Marxists from our government and to remove—forever—the corrupting influence of the Jews from our lives. In order that I accomplish all this for Germany, I pledge to you that I will allow no divisive elections to disturb the order I have restored. There will be no retreat from this position. I will stay in power by whatever means, by whatever weapons are necessary. The election we have just come through will be the last election, perhaps for as many as one hundred years.

"Behind us lies Germany! Before us marches Germany! Our future is Germany!"

When the multitude began cheering again, Simon reached over to turn off the radio. Turning off the radio did not, however, turn off the crowd, and even through the closed window Simon could hear the roaring from the street below.

The thousands of torches carried by the frenzied Nazis cast an eerie glow on the night sky and caused a flickering, sulfurous light to wash across the walls of Simon's apartment. He shuddered. It was like a glimpse into hell.

MARCH 4, 1933, WASHINGTON, D.C.

The car bearing Champ Dawson, the senior senator from Missouri, his wife, Gloria, daughter, Faith, and aide, John Canfield, drove alongside the Anacostia River, past the mud flats. John was surreptitiously watching the senator's beautiful twenty-one-year-old daughter when she suddenly shivered in revulsion.

"Oh!" Faith exclaimed. "How disgusting!"

"What is it?" John asked, peering past her out the window.

"There are huge rats out there, crawling around on that rubble. Do you see them?"

"No, I don't," he answered. He faced back inside. "But it doesn't surprise me that they're there."

"What is all that mess out there, anyway? Why don't they get it cleaned up?" Faith asked.

"That's what's left of the shantytown the Bonus Marchers built here last summer," John explained. "You remember reading in my report about how President Hoover ordered General MacArthur to destroy it."

"So that's where it was," Faith said. "Yes, I remember. And I know that Governor Roosevelt believes that did as much as anything to get him elected."

Senator Dawson smiled. "We'll have to remember that it isn't Governor Roosevelt anymore," he said. "It's *President* Roosevelt now."

"*President* Roosevelt. I like the sound of that, don't you?" John asked, grinning.

"Yes, it does have a certain ring to it," Champ replied with a chuckle.

Tall and rail thin, Champ was well known in Washington for his behind-the-scenes maneuvering. An early supporter of Franklin Roosevelt, Champ had stuck by him even after the disastrous 1920 election in which Roosevelt, running for Vice President on the Democratic ticket with Governor James Cox, was soundly defeated. Now, with Roosevelt's political comeback complete, Champ Dawson was one of the President's closest confidants and a key figure in his fight to bring America out of the Great Depression.

Three blocks away from Anacostia flats the senator's car passed a long line of defeated men and downtrodden women shuffling slowly along the street, waiting for their handout of a loaf of bread and a small amount of cheese. Washington was a city that depended upon the federal government for employment, and, as such, its residents barely experienced the depression. But the city had drawn hundreds, even thousands, of out-of-work, starving people from around the country, some as a part of the Bonus March who had never left, others in a futile effort to go somewhere and do something—anything—to improve their lot.

"Oh, look at those poor people," Gloria Dawson said sadly. "My heart just goes out to them. I wish we could do something to help."

"That's what this new administration will try to do, Mrs. Dawson," John said.

"Did any of you see the article in the paper this morning?" Champ asked, his voice filled with anger. "The idiot who wrote it called upon the D.C. police to shut down all the breadlines and soup kitchens for the day. He said it created a bad image for the city of Washington to have visitors see so many hungry and destitute people." Champ shook his head with disgust. "Can you imagine?"

"I didn't see the article," John replied, "but I'm glad the police didn't pay any attention to it. What a heartless idea."

"That's what I thought," the senator said. "I called the newspaper and reminded them that Washington certainly isn't the only city in the country that's undergoing such turmoil. It's happening in hundreds of cities and towns all across America, and in many cases the breadlines are all that stand between these poor people and starvation."

John knew the senator was right. Whenever a soup kitchen or breadline was set up, no matter where it was, the needy would find out about it through their own grapevine and gather quickly, until the line stretched out for several blocks.

There had always been charitable food programs, John knew, most of them operated by some religious group hoping to exchange a slice of bread for someone's soul. In those cases the customers were predominantly men, along with a few women, who had known a lifetime of destitution. They were the alcoholics and the mentally deficient to be found in all societies, pathetically struggling people whose lot could never be improved.

But now the bread- and soup lines of 1933 were different. They were filled with men who had been bankers, electricians, stockbrokers, welders, business managers, and mechanics, all desperate for even this meager sustenance. There were women in the lines as well, former store clerks and schoolteachers and housewives, many of whom carried one baby and clutched the hand of another.

Forty million Americans were either unemployed or a

member of a family in which the principal breadwinner was unemployed. And it wasn't just town and city dwellers who were suffering. More and more farmers who had grown up on land their fathers and grandfathers and great-grandfathers had worked before them were finding sheriffs' foreclosure documents plastered on the doors of their homes and barns and on the fences around their fields, notices informing the public that the buildings, land, equipment, heritage, and dreams of these farmers were to be sold at public auction.

Aside from those unlucky enough to face unemployment, the Great Depression affected hundreds of wealthy families as well. With the collapse of the financial institutions they kept all their money in, people who had been enjoying a third generation of affluence were thrust into instant bankruptcy. Men and women who but a short time before had been millionaires now found themselves standing in breadlines with the same men and women who had been their servants.

John Canfield was luckier; his family fortune had not been affected by the depression. Perhaps because he had so much in the midst of so many who had so little, he had felt compelled to work for Roosevelt's election in an attempt to turn the situation around. Today John was reaping the reward of his efforts. Along with Champ Dawson and his family, the young aide was to be one of the special guests allowed to sit on the terrace of the Capitol's east plaza during the inauguration ceremony. He would be no more than fifty feet away from the podium where Franklin D. Roosevelt would be sworn in as the thirty-second president of the United States.

Just a few minutes after passing gloomy breadlines, the senator's limousine turned onto the Capitol grounds. Thousands of citizens had already gathered there for the milestone, and most were waving small American flags and smiling, uplifted by the event and hopeful that the new president would find a way for the country to get out of its economic crisis. The senator's car, with its VIP markings, was passed through by Capitol police until it reached the unloading point, where the passengers were helped out and then escorted to their seats of honor.

Because Roosevelt had suffered an attack of polio some years earlier, he was prevented from making a grand entrance onto the porch. As John took his own seat, he wasn't surprised to see the President-elect already seated behind a podium, which was sprouting numerous microphones—a way to conceal his condition from the nearly one-hundred-thousand-strong crowd that had gathered outside the east plaza to witness the event.

During the long and arduous campaign, John had seen how difficult it was for Roosevelt to do the most ordinary things. He knew how painful the leg braces were when they had to be snapped into place just so Roosevelt could maintain a standing position. And though beads of sweat often broke out on Roosevelt's face and his eyes occasionally registered pain, the President-elect had never complained.

"Governor," John had asked when he had first met him, "doesn't the idea of being the president of the United States during such terrible times ever seem overwhelming to you?"

Roosevelt had chuckled. "John, old sport, when you have spent two years in bed just trying to wiggle your big toe, everything else seems easy."

John had decided at that moment that Franklin Delano Roosevelt was one of the most courageous men he had ever known.

The seating arrangement on the VIP platform put John right next to Faith, and as FDR began taking his oath of office, Faith slid her hand over John's and held it. He knew that it was nothing more than her reaction to the excitement of the moment, but the physical contact was very pleasant, and it added to his appreciation of the experience. In fact, having just learned that Faith planned to work in her father's office during the coming summer, John had hopes of seeing much more of her.

After President Roosevelt completed his oath of office, he turned—painfully, it was clear—to face the crowd, resolutely gripping the podium. John found his words stirring.

"Let me assert my firm belief that the only thing we have to fear is fear itself. Nameless, unreasoning, unjustified terror,

which paralyzes needed effort to convert retreat into advance.

"Only a foolish optimist can deny the dark realities of the moment. Values have shrunk to fantastic levels, our ability to pay has fallen. The withered leaves of industrial enterprise lie on every side, and the savings of many years and thousands of families are gone. More important, a host of unemployed citizens face the grim problem of existence, and an equally great number toil with little return."

This was it, John thought. This was what needed to be said. It was a clear and concise understanding of the situation. Surely a man with such a grasp and such compassion would be able to save the country.

John thought of the millions of people all across America who were, at that very moment, glued to their radios—men and women in the row houses and apartment buildings of the big cities, families in their homes in the towns and villages, farmers and ranchers in their isolated houses out in the country, and sailors gathered around the wireless sets on ships at sea. The lives of all who heard this speech would be forever changed as a result. This would be one of those times about which, years later, people would ask, "Where were you when you heard Roosevelt say, 'The only thing we have to fear is fear itself'?"

John turned his attention back to the President.

"I shall ask the Congress for broad executive power to wage a war against the emergency as great as the power that would be given to me if we were, in fact, invaded by a foreign foe.

"This nation is asking for action—and action now!"

The conclusion of the speech was met with tumultuous cheering and applause. Someone helped the President sit down, and he smiled broadly, then reached up from his seat to shake the hands and accept the congratulations of his well-wishers.

"It's amazing," Faith said.

"What's that?"

"That a man like that, a man who can't even walk from here to the car by himself, could evoke such confidence. Oh,

John, I believe he's going to be the most wonderful president we've ever had!"

"I hope you're right," John said. "Because certainly no president since Abraham Lincoln has ever faced a crisis as great as the one facing us now."

CHAPTER THREE

JUNE 15, 1934, ST. LOUIS, MISSOURI

When the cab driver went to turn off Market onto Eleventh Street, he found his way blocked by a wooden barricade. The policeman guarding the intersection waved him on, but the driver started going around the obstruction anyway. He was immediately stopped by an even more vigorous arm movement and a series of short, loud blasts from the policeman's whistle.

"Keep it moving! Keep it moving!" the policeman shouted, walking toward the taxi. "You can't come this way!"

The hackie stuck his head out the window and yelled back at the policeman, "How'm I supposed to get to where I'm goin'? Every damned street in this part of town is blocked off! What the hell is goin' on here?"

"They're having a wedding in Christ Church Cathedral," the policeman explained. "You can cross over when you get down to Fifteenth Street."

"Fifteenth Street! You mean to tell me I've got to go all the way down to Fifteenth just 'cause of a wedding? Who the hell is gettin' married, anyway? The King of England?"

"Could be," the harried policeman replied. "All I know is the governor and the mayor are both here, along with a bunch of U.S. senators and congressmen. And if you ain't somebody, I got orders to keep you away."

A long, black Packard limousine glided silently up to the wooden barricade and rolled to a stop, its motor purring. Starting back toward the Packard, the policeman said to the hackie over his shoulder, "Now, be a good man and move on, will you, buddy?"

"Yeah, yeah, I'm goin', I'm goin'," the cab driver growled disgustedly. He shifted into reverse with a grinding clank of the gears, backed up, shifted again, then continued west on Market Street as he had been directed.

The chauffeur of the Packard rolled down his window and displayed a cream-colored envelope to the policeman. The policeman touched his cap in an informal salute, then moved the road barrier aside. After the car had passed through, the barrier was replaced, and the policeman returned to his task of keeping all other traffic away.

A moment later the Packard rolled to a smooth stop in front of Christ Church Cathedral, the huge, gray-stone Gothic that served as the see for the Protestant Episcopal Church of the diocese of Missouri. A radio announcer standing on the sidewalk in front of the cathedral clutched the base of his microphone, the upper portion of which was a round, black disk surmounted by the letters KSLM.

Standing a short distance down the curb was a yellow panel truck with the same call letters emblazoned in red on its side. This was the station's remote truck, an ordinary panel truck converted for remote broadcasting with myriad batteries, vacuum tubes, oscillators, potentiometers, dials, gauges, control board, and a transmitter. The truck itself then became a broadcast studio, pushing its signal out through a thirty-foot-tall, three-piece portable antenna that had to be assembled and disassembled on site. Behind the truck a sound engineer sat at a table, twisting the mixing dials of his control board to transmit the signal from the truck's antenna back to the main studio downtown, where it would be broadcast to KSLM's radio listeners all across the region.

The radio announcer standing curbside was a slim, thin-faced man with high cheekbones, dark brown hair, and an intense light in his gunmetal-gray eyes.

"This is Floyd Stoner, broadcasting to you from just outside Christ Church Cathedral in downtown St. Louis. In front of the cathedral, and for several blocks in every direction, uniformed chauffeurs are standing alongside shining limousines. These automobiles belong to the most affluent and influential men and women in the country, for, indeed, America's elite have gathered in St. Louis today.

"The reason for this gathering, ladies and gentlemen, is a wedding. And, as you have no doubt surmised by now, it isn't just any *wedding. It's what* The St. Louis Chronicle *has called 'the wedding of the year.' In just a few minutes, inside this very church, Bishop William Scarlet, Episcopal Bishop of Missouri, will perform the rites that will unite in marriage John Henry Canfield and Faith Elizabeth Dawson.*

"John Canfield is the son of Mr. and Mrs. Robert Canfield of this city. A graduate of Jefferson University, he is vice president and a member of the board of directors of the Canfield-Puritex Corporation. For the past two years Mr. Canfield has spent a great deal of time in Washington as a consultant to Senator Champ Dawson and the Economic Recovery Advisory Board.

"The lovely bride, Faith Dawson, is the daughter of Senator and Mrs. Champ Dawson. A graduate of Stephen College, Miss Dawson made her debut in St. Louis four years ago, and some listeners may remember that she was one of the Handmaidens to the Veiled Prophet for 1930 and First Runner-up to the Goddess of Love and Beauty. For the past year she has worked as a volunteer in her father's Washington office.

"Ladies and gentlemen, another guest has just arrived in a black Packard limousine. I don't know who this might be, but given the nature of this auspicious occasion, if he's even here today, we can only assume that it's someone important."

Behind the great red doors of the cathedral, inside the

flower-filled narthex, ushers greeted the guests, examined their invitations to determine the pecking order, then escorted them to their seats. Those already seated were being entranced by a Bach prelude. Sometimes the music was as soft as the flutter of angels' wings, while at other times the great organ filled the cathedral with its grandeur, the music reverberating off the walls, then crashing over the enraptured listeners like melodious thunder.

Behind the elaborately carved reredos, in the rear of the cathedral, was a small anteroom, just off the bishop's office. In that room Robert Canfield sat on a leather sofa, smoking a cigar and listening to one side of a telephone conversation going on between Senator Champ Dawson and the President of the United States.

The father of the groom, Bob Canfield, was fifty-two years old, with completely gray hair and a considerably thickened waist. There was little in his appearance to suggest the champion long-distance runner for Jefferson University he had been some thirty years before.

Bob was founder and chairman of the board of Canfield-Puritex, the third-largest food processing company in America and the largest that was privately held. In addition to Canfield-Puritex, Bob also owned vast tracts of farmland in southeast Missouri, a ranch in Arizona, and another in Argentina. He had other interests as well, including substantial holdings in Rockwell-McPheeters Aviation Company and Mid-America Transport, an airline serving Chicago, New Orleans, Tulsa, Cleveland, Omaha, Nashville, and all the cities in between.

Senator Champ Dawson, the father of the bride, was sitting in an over-stuffed chair beside the telephone table. Though two years older than Bob, Champ's hair was still more brown than gray and he had retained a lifelong slimness. The senator was Chairman of the Economic Recovery Advisory Board, which consisted of members from the legislative and executive branch of government as well as members from business and academia. Rewarded by the President for unflagging loyalty, Senator Dawson's mandate was so sweeping that he was involved in one way or another in all aspects of Roosevelt's "New Deal."

Even Hugh Johnson, head of the National Recovery Administration, had to coordinate all his activities with Champ, as did the head of all the other "alphabet agencies" —the CCC, PWA, and WPA. Of Champ Dawson, *Time* magazine said, "The senior senator from Missouri is, without doubt, the most powerful man in Washington outside the President himself."

Bob saw Champ slip a cigarette into his mouth, then pat his pockets for a light. Bob pulled out his own lighter, snapped it, and held it under Champ's cigarette. Champ nodded his thanks.

"Yes, Mr. President, the package arrived yesterday," the senator said into the phone, blowing out a cloud of smoke. "I've checked it very carefully, so I can assure you it's undamaged. And I'm sure they will be delighted with your gift. It was most thoughtful of you. . . . Yes, of course I will pass along your best wishes."

There was a much longer pause while the President spoke at some length.

"The Reciprocal Trade Agreement Act?" Champ finally said. "Franklin, I'm shocked that you would bring up business on my daughter's wedding day." After a brief silence, Champ laughed. "Why did I invite Senators Dennis and McConnel to the wedding?" he responded. "I guess you know me pretty well after all, don't you, Mr. President? You're right; I am going to work on them. And I'm sure I'll be able to sell them on it. It's just a matter of a twisted arm here and a pat on the back there. The problem is they think the Reciprocal Trade Agreement Act gives too much power to the president. They are saying it moves you one step closer to becoming a dictator. I'm sure you realize that they aren't the only ones who think this."

There was another pause for the President's response; then Champ laughed again, this time more vigorously than before.

"Oh, so you promise to be a benevolent dictator, do you? Ho, now, wouldn't the Hearst newspapers like to get hold of *that*? They're already calling the NRA 'No Recovery Allowed.' But, not to worry, Franklin. Your secret is safe with me."

The President spoke again, then Champ turned and smiled at Bob. "Bob Canfield?" the senator said into the receiver. "Of course. He's right here. I'll put him on." Champ held the phone out toward Bob, saying, somewhat unnecessarily, "He wants to talk to you."

Bob got up from the sofa and walked over to take the receiver.

"Hello, Mr. President."

"Hello, Bob. Did you wake up to Corn Toasties?" the President asked, referring to the radio advertising slogan for the breakfast cereal Canfield-Puritex was best known for. Though the company now produced myriad food products, from assorted breakfast cereals to baking products to canned meats, it was, and would always be, best known for the one product that changed a tiny animal-feed processing company into a multinational food giant.

Bob chuckled. "The truth, Mr. President? I don't care much for *any* cereal. I prefer bacon and eggs."

President Roosevelt laughed heartily. "You'd better not let your advertising boys hear you say that." Then, mimicking the radio commercial, the President sang the jingle. The words sounded even more ludicrous when rendered in his upper-class, Harvard accent.

"Wake up, wake up,
wake up to Corn Toasties.
It's the breakfast, the breakfast,
the breakfast with the mosties."

Laughing, the President said, "Terrible poetry, old sport. But then, what word *does* one find to rhyme with toasties?"

"That was our problem," Bob admitted, also laughing.

"Well, now," Roosevelt said, changing the subject, "so John is about to get married. He couldn't have selected a finer young woman for his bride. I've known Faith since the Democratic convention in San Francisco, when Champ convinced Governor Cox to select me as his running mate. She was still quite young then, but she was already as bright as a new penny. And I don't have to tell you what I think of John, not only for his efforts in helping me get elected, but also for the work he is doing now for Champ. And doing it all for a salary of one dollar per year, I might add. That certainly speaks volumes about his patriotism. You should be very proud of him, Bob."

"I am, Mr. President. I'm very proud of *both* my sons."

"Oh, yes, I've heard all about Willie," the President said with a chuckle. "John thinks his younger brother hung the moon. Almost literally, I think, since Willie is such a fine aviator. Anyway, I know you would like to have John back in St. Louis with you, helping you run Canfield-Puritex." His sense of humor bubbling over again, Roosevelt laughed and added, "I mean, I'm sure a bright young man like John could certainly come up with a better jingle than 'Toasties with the Mosties.' But the senator needs him, I need him, and our country needs him. And I hope that you, in a true altruistic spirit, will allow him to stay on a while longer."

"Both of my sons are their own men, Mr. President, and I have little to say in what they do. I'm sure John has no plans to quit. He is absolutely dedicated to doing everything he can do to help you get this country on its feet again."

"That's good to hear. I tell you, Bob, if I had a thousand young men just like John, I could mount a crusade. I could send them out across the nation, armed with sweeping powers to root out the incompetent, deal out instant and harsh justice to the corrupt, and restore confidence, pride, and jobs to our people. We'd have this depression whipped in ninety days." The President sighed. "But, of course, the Supreme Court, those nine doddering old men, would never let me do such a thing. So there is nothing to do but muddle onward and upward."

"You have set a good course for recovery, Mr. President," Bob said. "I think in the long run the results will silence a lot of the naysayers."

"I pray that you are right," Roosevelt replied. "Now, tell me about this man Truman who is running for senator from your state. Does he have any real chance of winning the primary? I know your Governor Stark doesn't care much for him. What is your opinion?"

"To be honest with you, Mr. President, I don't know

him personally," Bob said. "He's from the other side of the state. But I have learned quite a bit about him."

"Then you know he's mixed up with Tom Pendergast and that bunch of crooks from Kansas City."

"Well, I know the *Post-Dispatch* is trying hard to paint him with that brush. They're calling him 'Tom's errand boy.' *The Chronicle*, however, is being a bit more circumspect," Bob said.

"How can they be circumspect?" Roosevelt asked. "It is either true or it isn't true. I guess what I'm asking is, if he does win the primary and becomes the Democratic candidate for senator, can the Republicans make anything out of Mr. Truman's connection with Tom Pendergast?"

"No, sir, I don't think they can."

"Why not?"

"He's been a county judge over there for some time now. That's like a county commissioner in any other state. And in that position he's had to administer several million dollars. In all that time, and with all that money, there hasn't been the slightest breath of a scandal. No one has gotten a contract who didn't deserve it, the taxpayers have received a dollar's worth of goods and services for every dollar spent, and not one penny has been unaccounted for. The Pendergast machine may have sponsored him, but they sure don't own him."

"Is that a fact?"

"Yes, sir."

"You sound like Truman actually has a chance to win the primary."

"Not only do I think he has a chance, I think he'll *win.* Milligan and Cochran will split the opposition between them, and Truman, with solid support from Kansas City and from the state's farmers, will win."

"And in Missouri, whoever wins the Democratic primary will win the general election," Roosevelt said. It wasn't a question; it was a statement of fact that Roosevelt well understood. "So, what you are telling me is Harry Truman is going to be the next senator from Missouri."

"That's my belief, yes, sir," Bob said.

"Will he be good for the Democratic party?"

"Mr. President, he'll be good for America," Bob replied firmly.

Roosevelt laughed. "We can't ask for any more than that, can we? Well, listen to us prattling on about politics when you have a wedding to attend. I'd better let you go. Please extend my best wishes to the bride and groom and especially to your lovely wife, Connie. My people tell me that in my election I had a higher percentage of support from the women voters than I did from the men. Since Connie is one of the people most responsible for getting the vote for women, I feel I owe her as great a debt as I owe John."

"Don't tell her that; she'll try to collect on it," Bob quipped.

The President laughed again. "Then she has already learned the first order of politics. Now, put Champ back on, if you would. The esteemed senator and I still have some business to conduct. Even though it his daughter who's getting married, I can't let him off the hook quite as easily as I can you. You aren't an elected official."

Bob chuckled and handed the telephone back to Champ, and as the senator became involved in his conversation, Bob silently excused himself and slipped out of the room.

Just a few doors down was the cathedral's library, which was where Bob's two sons were waiting. He stepped in to see them and found John pacing back and forth nervously, while Willie, the best man, was sitting at the library table, drumming his fingers. Both were dressed in formal attire of morning coats and striped trousers; both were handsome and vigorous. At twenty-six John was a year older and slightly taller, slimmer, and darker than Willie. Hardworking, ambitious, and pragmatic, he most resembled his father, both in appearance and in personality.

Willie was of a more muscular build and much more like his mother, not only in his features and his coloring—he, too, had auburn hair and hazel eyes—but in his personality. A hard worker like his brother, Willie's outlook on life tended more to the romantic than the pragmatic. He had very little to do with the family's food-processing business or with politics, preferring instead to spend his time with Mid-

America Transport, the airline he had helped establish—an idea his father and brother thought ill-advised. Even though both John and Bob had substantial investments in the airline, they often tried to convince Willie that an airline was the worst possible venture in these difficult times. But Willie wasn't a businessman to the degree that his father and brother were. Debentures, cross collateralization, profit-and-loss sheets meant little to him. All he knew was that he was going to stick it out. As he repeatedly explained to his father and brother, flying wasn't his business; flying was his life.

"Hi, Pop," Willie said, looking up from the table when his father came in. "How's it goin'?"

"So far, so good," Bob replied. "I was just speaking to the President. John, have you seen the gift Mr. Roosevelt sent you?"

"No, not yet," John said.

"Champ showed it to me. It's really something. A model of the clipper ship *Flying Cloud* built by Donald McKay himself to use as a guide in constructing the actual ship."

John's eyes widened. "I know that model, and I know how fond the President is of it. That's quite an impressive gift, isn't it?"

"Yes, it is," Bob agreed. "It shows just how much the President thinks of you. By the way, Willie, your mother wanted me to check. You do have the ring, don't you?"

"The ring! Oh my God! The ring!" Willie exclaimed, making a big show of frantically slapping all his pockets.

"You don't have the ring?" Bob gasped in surprise.

"He has it, Pop," John said, laughing. "He's just having fun with you, that's all."

Willie produced the ring and held it up, smiling broadly. "Would this be it?"

"Very funny," Bob grumbled. He looked back at John. "Are you nervous?"

"A little," John admitted.

"You shouldn't be. Faith is a wonderful girl. I'm sure you'll have a very good marriage."

"Oh, I'm not nervous about that. It's all *this,*" he said with a broad sweep of his arm. "I mean, we're being married in Christ Church Cathedral by the Bishop of Missouri. All of

St. Louis and half of Washington are here for the wedding, and if that isn't enough, the damn thing is being broadcast over the radio."

Bob chuckled. "Well, the wedding itself isn't being broadcast. I refused to let Floyd Stoner come into the church. They're having to do the whole thing from the front sidewalk."

"That must have been quite a setback for the 'Voice of St. Louis,'" John said dryly. "I had visions of old Floyd standing right up there between Faith and me, shoving his microphone in my face, in Faith's face, probably knocking off the bishop's cap. . . ."

Willie laughed.

"That's miter," Bob explained.

"What?"

"It's not a cap, it's a miter."

"Well, whatever it is, I wish we had just run off somewhere and gotten married," John groused.

"Hey, I offered," Willie said, holding his hands up. "If you remember, I told you I'd fly you anywhere you wanted to go."

"I should have taken you up on it."

"You don't mean that," Bob interjected, putting a hand on John's shoulder. "Something like this is important to the women. Your mom and Faith's mother are in seventh heaven right now. And if you could see Faith, you wouldn't think of denying her this wedding. Her eyes are shining like diamonds. I've never seen her so excited—or beautiful."

"Yeah, well, that's just it. I tried to see her, but you'd think that brigade of bridesmaids were guarding the pass at Thermopylae."

Willie laughed. "That's their job. You're not supposed to see her before the ceremony," he explained. "That would be bad luck."

The door to the library abruptly opened, and the bishop stuck his head in. He was wearing his cope and miter.

"It is time, gentlemen," he announced.

"Couldn't you just do it back here?" John asked with a groan.

The bishop grinned. "And disappoint all those folks out

there? Why, if we did that, we'd be run out of town on a rail."

John took a deep breath, then let it out slowly. "Okay," he said. "I'm ready."

"Into the breach," Willie quipped, standing up and thrusting his arm forward as if he were a cavalry officer leading a charge.

BENTON, MISSOURI

A rusting, fender-flapping 1923 Oakland wheezed and rattled to a stop in front of the Scott County courthouse. With crates tied on the top and bundles strapped onto the rear, the old car was straining under its load. In addition, the inside of the car was so full that there was barely room for the driver and the woman sitting beside him.

The driver, Del Murtaugh, was a tall, gangly man with a pleasant, easygoing face that featured pale-blue eyes that were quick and alert and a prominent Adam's apple. It had been a long time since his sandy hair had been cut by a real barber, and the irregular trim looked it.

His passenger was Rubye Parker, an exceptionally pretty young woman who had light-brown hair shot through with gold so that in certain light it appeared almost blond, skin that was smooth and clear, and hazel eyes flecked with silver. Those eyes now gazed at Del with loving adoration.

Del gripped the wooden steering wheel with both hands and stared out across the faded hood of his car. A wisp of steam curled up from the radiator cap, and Del could smell hot oil and burnt rubber and hear tiny pinging sounds from the overheated engine block. It had been only a fourteen-mile drive up from Sikeston, yet already the engine was showing the effects. Del knew that if they made it all the way to Oklahoma it would be a miracle, but he wasn't going to give voice to his doubts because he didn't want to worry Rubye.

He pointed to the courthouse. "There it is," he said.

"I don't see anyone around. Do you think we're too late?" Rubye asked anxiously.

"No, I don't think so. They aren't supposed to close until five," Del replied. He let go of the steering wheel and covered Rubye's small, delicate hand with his large, callused one. "Are you scared?"

"A little," Rubye admitted.

"Of me?"

Rubye smiled shyly. "No, not of you. I love you. But this is a big step, Del. I mean, us getting married and leaving, all at the same time. I've never been more than a hundred miles away from home, and here we are about to leave for Oklahoma."

"Well, that's where our farm is."

"A farm that we've never seen."

"What difference does it make that we've never seen it? I've farmed hill country, bottomland, sand, clay, and rock. Whatever it is, it'll be fine. And it'll be ours."

"Ours," Rubye repeated. "That sounds nice, doesn't it?"

"Yes, but not as nice as Mr. and Mrs. Del Murtaugh. What do you say we go in now?"

"All right." Rubye looked back at the courthouse. "I just hope the judge is still here."

They climbed out of the beat-up car and hurried along the cement walk to the courthouse steps. Skipping up the weathered steps, they entered the foyer and found it deserted. A sign that depicted a pointing hand directed them to the judge's chambers, and as they walked down the long corridor, their footsteps echoed hollowly on the polished concrete floor. At the far end of the hall they found a door with a sign on the frosted glass reading JUSTICE OF THE PEACE. Del pushed it open and they went inside.

Just inside the room was a long counter that separated customers from court employees. Two of the court employees, both women, were sitting at their desks, listening to a radio report. Del was about to ask for help when one of the ladies turned up the volume:

"And here they come, ladies and gentlemen," the commentator was saying in an excited voice. *"The bride and groom are leaving the church right now, ducking under a shower of rice. And what a handsome couple they are, ladies and gentlemen! The bride's dress, which would appear to be*

white silk, is covered with pearls and trailing a long train. A lovelier picture this reporter has never seen. Oh, and now she has paused to hold aloft the bridal bouquet. All the other young ladies are gathered around . . . and here is the toss!"

Del thought it sounded more like a sporting event than a wedding—an impression enhanced by the squeals and shouts that could be heard over the radio.

"And the bouquet was caught by a lovely young lady with dark hair and blue eyes. This reporter will try to get the young lady's name and, if possible, an interview. But for now, this is Floyd Stoner, returning you to our studios at KSLM."

The almost breathless, live-action report by the reporter was followed by the silky-smooth voice of a studio announcer:

"Instead of eating between meals . . . instead of fattening sweets . . . beautiful women keep their youthful slenderness these days by smoking LUCKIES. *The smartest and loveliest women of the modern stage take this means of keeping slender; when others nibble fattening sweets, they light a* LUCKY!"

One of the women snapped the radio off.

"Oh, don't you know that that was just the most beautiful wedding there ever was?" she asked her coworker.

"Wouldn't you love to have been there?" the other woman replied.

"Ahem," Del finally interrupted.

"Yes?" the first woman asked, glancing up when Del cleared his throat and looking almost astonished to find someone there. "What is it? May I help you?"

"My name is Del Murtaugh. This is Rubye Parker. We want to get married."

The woman took a paper from one of the drawers of a file cabinet and handed it to Del with a friendly smile. "Well, we can certainly handle that for you. If the two of you would just fill out this application form, then bring it back on Monday, the judge will marry you."

"Monday?" Del said, feeling his stomach drop with anxiety. "But can't he marry us today?"

"It's Friday, and it's almost five o'clock. You'll have to come back Monday."

"Please," Rubye said. "We have to get married today."

Another door at the back of the office opened at just that moment. An overweight, red-faced man, chewing on the stub of a cigar, took a step through the doorway and stood there, looking on. His hand was stuck under his shirt, idly scratching his belly.

"What is it, Doris? What do these people want?" he asked.

"They want to be married, Judge," Doris said. "I told them to come back on Monday."

"You're the judge?" Del asked.

The man nodded. "Judge Joe Cain. That's what it says on the office door."

"Judge, is there any way we could get married now?"

"Why the big hurry? You're going to be married for the rest of your life. One more weekend shouldn't hurt."

"We have to be in Oklahoma by Tuesday to sign the papers for our farm," Del explained. "My old car . . . Well, the truth is, if we don't get started right away, we'll never make it."

"Young folks always seem to be in a hurry nowadays," Judge Cain grumbled. Suddenly he took the cigar from his mouth and squinted at Del. "Say, wait a minute. I know you, don't I? Have you ever come before my bench?"

"No, sir," Del said. "I've never been in a speck of trouble."

"What's your name?"

"Murtaugh. Del Murtaugh."

The judge broke into a big smile. "Well, of course it is! That explains why I know you. I'm a big baseball fan, Mr. Murtaugh, and you used to play baseball for the Sikeston Stags, didn't you? You were the catcher."

"Yes, sir, I played some."

"As a matter of fact, you were a pretty good ball player," the judge said. "You and Lenny Puckett."

"Oh, I wasn't nowhere near as good as Swampwater," Del demurred.

"Who *was* as good as that boy? Who *is* as good?" the judge replied. "He's made this part of Missouri real proud since he went up to the majors. 'Course they say ol'

Swampwater Puckett's comin' up on the end of his career. Not too many years left. Too bad he never got to play in a World Series."

"The St. Louis Grays never had any hitting behind him," Del said. "It don't matter how good a pitcher you are; if you can't score no runs, you can't win no ball games."

"That's the truth of it, Del, that's purely the truth of it. Say, you were a pretty good hitter, as I recall. It's a wonder *you* never went up to the majors."

"I always figured baseball was somethin' I did for fun," Del explained. "Farmin' was how I made my livin'."

"You farmed here, did you?"

"Yes, sir. I've farmed for the Canfields, the Byrds, the Colemans, and the Allens. I always had to farm on shares, though; never had nothin' of my own. But now I've bought me a little piece of land."

"In Oklahoma?"

"In Oklahoma."

"That's a long ways from home."

"Land's cheap there," Del explained.

Judge Cain stuck his cigar back in his mouth. "Well, I wish you good luck, boy. Doris, you and Alice stand up for them as witnesses. I'll just go get my book, and we'll have ourselves a weddin' just as nice as that one y'all been listenin' to."

As the judge started back into his office, Rubye squeezed Del's arm. "I sure wish Mama and Papa could have lived long enough to see this," she said.

Del took her hand. "Old L.E. might not've approved of me," he said. "Him bein' Mr. Canfield's farm manager and all, he was pretty particular."

"Papa would have approved," Rubye said. "All he'd have to do is see how happy you make me, and he would have approved."

"Still, your papa was a man of means for all his life," Del said. "He provided real good for your mama and for you and Richard Edward. And I don't want to do no less for you. That's why I want to go to Oklahoma and farm my own land. You do understand that, don't you, Rubye?"

"I understand," she replied. "And since Mama died last

year, there's really nothing to hold me here anymore. Except Richard Edward. But with him driving that truck for Mr. Foster, he's gone all the time anyway. I haven't been seeing him more than once every couple of weeks." She sighed. "I wish he could've been here to stand up for us at our wedding."

"I know, darlin'," Del said, taking Rubye's hand and patting it. "But seeing as how he's down in Mississippi, we don't have time to wait for him to come back. He'll just have to understand, that's all."

"Okay, folks," the judge said, returning with his book. "Why don't you two just step over here, and I'll tie the knot for you?"

Del smiled and led Rubye across the room. "Sounds real good to me, Judge."

CHAPTER FOUR

JUNE 15, 1934, ST. LOUIS, MISSOURI

When the broadcast of the wedding was over and all the chauffeured limousines had gone or were leaving, the bright-yellow truck with the red letters KSLM painted on the side remained behind. Just as it took several minutes to set up the truck to begin remote broadcasting, it took just as long to strike it—take it down.

Setting up and striking the remote unit was the task of the engineer, Neil Goodman. He was on his knees, disassembling the base of the antenna, when Floyd Stoner stepped out of the back of the truck and handed him a wrench.

"Is this what you want?" Floyd asked.

"Yeah, the spanner, that's it," Neil answered. "Thanks. Oh, and thanks for helping me, too. You know, most of the other announcers won't lift a finger. They figure all they have to do is say a few words into the microphone and that's it."

"Well, I do it because I like to keep you sound guys happy," Floyd explained. "I figure if you wanted to, you could make me sound like I've got a voice of gold—or like I just gargled with glass. I want to keep you on my side."

Neil laughed. "You really are different from all the other announcers," he said. "You've got some sense."

Floyd laughed with him. "Listen, Neil, I've got the board stowed. You want me to roll this up?" He pointed to a heavy cable that ran from the base of the antenna to some point inside the truck.

"No, leave the coax. I'll have to take care of that myself."

"You sure?"

"Yeah, it goes with the antenna."

"Okay," Floyd said. "Well, I guess I've done about all I can do here."

"See you at the station," Neil offered.

"Not tonight you won't," Floyd replied. "I'm going to go have my dinner, then go to bed. I have to be on the air at four in the morning."

"Well, then I guess I'll see you when I see you," Neil quipped.

Waving good-bye, Floyd walked down Locust, the side street where he had parked his car. He was proud of his snappy little maroon Ford roadster. It had a V-8 engine and could run nearly one hundred miles per hour on a good road. Sometimes, though, he felt almost self-conscious about driving it. Floyd had a job, a good-paying job, in an economy where a significant part of the work force was unemployed.

There was, Floyd thought, a peculiar irony to this age. It was a time when automobiles were more dependable and more luxurious than ever before. Vacuum cleaners, washing machines, and a dozen other appliances offered the housewife an opportunity to be relieved from a millennium of household slavery. The future held so much bright promise —but for too many it was all a cruel hoax.

Like deprived children with their noses pressed to the glass of a candy store, most could only look longingly at the wondrous new inventions. The shining advertisements in the slick magazines and on the nation's billboards taunted the people, for the nation was in the grip of the most devastating depression in its history.

Yet despite all that, or perhaps because of it, there was an almost universal fascination with the rich. The most successful movies were stories about glamorous people in posh settings, with never the slightest mention of economic hardship. The public devoured the day-to-day comings and goings of the nation's affluent, and Floyd had read the surveys that showed many more people would be listening to the broadcast of the Canfield wedding than would listen to a news story about layoffs in Detroit.

Oddly enough there was very little envy or jealousy involved in this fascination with the wealthy. It was almost as if the people wanted such lifestyles to continue, not only to elevate them from their own miserable circumstances, but also to keep the hope alive, however small the glimmer, that the rags-to-riches dream of the American people was still possible.

Ironically, the envy and jealousy that *were* displayed weren't directed toward the very rich, but toward what the economists called the upper-middle class. As Floyd understood it, that was because great wealth had never been more than a golden dream to most people, whereas before the depression upper-middle class had been attainable. In fact, many of those suffering most from the current economic condition had been members of that stratum of society, and they felt an intense bitterness over having been deprived of what they felt was their rightful station in life. The self-consciousness Floyd sometimes felt around the unemployed occurred when he encountered this particular kind of bitterness.

As Floyd approached his car he suddenly stopped, then leaned forward slightly to look more closely.

Someone was in his car!

Spotting a fist-sized rock lying on the sidewalk near the curb, he picked it up and, holding it down by his trouser leg, continued to walk toward the car. He slowly approached it from the right side, carefully staying at just the angle he knew would keep him out of the mirror and unobserved by whoever was inside. Finally reaching the door, he grabbed the handle, then jerked it open.

The sudden opening of the door badly startled the young woman in the passenger seat, and she gave a brief shout of alarm, though she recovered quickly. Floyd recognized her at once.

"Shaylin McKay!"

"What are you trying to do, give a girl a heart attack?" Shaylin asked, putting her hand to her breast. "My goodness, something like that could give a person the vapors."

Floyd laughed, and tossed the rock away. "The *vapors?* What in hell are the vapors, anyway?"

"I'm sure I don't have the foggiest," Shaylin admitted with a grin. "All I know is that my aunt Millicent used to get them at the slightest provocation." She turned back toward the front of the car and twisted the rearview mirror around so that she could see herself in it. A reporter for *The St. Louis Chronicle,* twenty-four-year-old Shaylin had red hair, green eyes, and a light spray of freckles across her nose, and although probably no one would describe her as beautiful, she was pretty and effervescent. She patted her hair as she examined herself in the mirror.

"What are you doing with my mirror?" Floyd asked. "For that matter, what are you doing in my car?"

"Waiting for you. I thought perhaps you might want to take me out to dinner tonight. We could discuss the big story. You know, reporter to reporter?"

Floyd walked around to the driver's side of the roadster and slipped in behind the wheel. He readjusted the mirror, shoved in the key, then stepped on the starter.

"Big story," he scoffed. "Some story. A wedding. I can't believe they sent me down here to do a wedding." He checked the mirror, then pulled away from the curb.

"I can. This is just the kind of material radio should be doing. What is radio, anyway, but whipped cream and cake icing? If anyone has a right to gripe, it is I. I'm a serious newspaper reporter. I mean, we've got people writing for the society page who are supposed to do this sort of thing. What are they sending me down here for?"

"There is no such thing as a serious woman reporter," Floyd replied.

It was a running joke between them—Shaylin belittling radio as a genuine news medium and Floyd insisting that a woman could not be taken seriously as a reporter.

"Tell that to our boss," Shaylin replied. "She started out as a reporter, remember?" Though Shaylin worked for *The Chronicle* and Floyd for KSLM, they had the same boss because Kendra Petzold owned both.

"Yeah, what a rags-to-riches story that is," Floyd replied sarcastically. "It's the great American dream. Anyone who works hard and keeps their nose clean can rise to the very top." He paused. "Of course, it helps to marry the boss, then have the boss die."

"Mrs. Petzold is all right," Shaylin said. "She's a sharp lady, and she knows the business."

"Newspaper business, maybe," Floyd said. "But she has a lot to learn about radio. I believe that radio is going to make a bigger impact on society than the automobile." Floyd stuck his arm out the window to signal a left turn.

"That's asking a lot from a box that plays music and touts soapsuds," Shaylin scoffed. "Where are you taking me, anyway?"

"Where do you want to go?"

"Well, for sure, not to the White Castle. After seeing all these rich folks today, I don't want to get stuck with greasy hamburgers. I feel like something elegant."

Floyd chuckled. "I see. *You* feel like something elegant, so you ask *me* to take you out."

"Sure," Shaylin replied. "Who am I, anyway, but an anonymous newspaper reporter? You, on the other hand, are 'The Mouth of St. Louis.' You're making a lot more money than I."

"That's as it should be," Floyd insisted.

"And when a man and woman go out for dinner together, the man pays. That, too, is as it should be."

"Is the Chase all right?"

"Sure, the Chase is fine. I'm going to order lobster."

"What a surprise *that* is," Floyd said dryly.

It took but a few minutes to reach the Chase Hotel,

which aside from having an excellent dining room also had the distinction of being Floyd Stoner's residence, and when he drove under the portico, a uniformed doorman came toward the car.

"Good evening, Mr. Stoner," the doorman said, touching the bill of his cap. "And will you require the use of your car again tonight?"

"No, I don't think so," Floyd replied.

"Very good, sir. I'll have it parked in the garage for you."

"Thank you," Floyd said, helping Shaylin out of the car.

"So, you won't be needing the car again tonight, will you?" Shaylin asked as they started toward the restaurant. "You're pretty sure of yourself, aren't you?"

"You can always take a taxi back," Floyd suggested.

"I reserve the right to keep that option open," Shaylin said.

Just inside the restaurant they were greeted by the maître d'.

"Good evening, Mr. Stoner. And, Miss McKay, it is good to see you again. There will be two for dinner?"

"Yes," Floyd said.

"Very good, sir. Right this way."

He led them to their table, and after he had handed them their menus and retreated, Shaylin said sotto voce, "I don't know if I like that guy. He seems altogether too familiar. I mean, you live here, so he's expected to greet you by name. But you'd think he'd show a little more discretion in greeting me. It's almost as if he is saying, 'Spending the night with Mr. Stoner again, are you, hussy?' "

Floyd laughed. "Well, he does know you, after all. And he's just trying to be friendly."

"Why doesn't he just put a big, red A on my forehead and be done with it?" Shaylin grumbled.

"Have you ever thought that he might know you from the articles you write for the paper?"

"Yeah, I'm sure that's it," she said dryly. She opened the oversized menu she had been handed and began examining it. "Ah, here it is. Lobster. A dollar and a quarter."

"Has anyone ever told you you're an expensive date?"

"Yes. And in the same breath they admitted to me that I was damn well worth it."

Their waiter came and took their order, which halted the bantering between the pair. As soon as the man left, Floyd told Shaylin, "Oh, I read your story on the Senate race."

"What did you think of it?"

"I thought it was courageous," Floyd replied.

"Courageous?"

"Your article came out solidly for Truman," Floyd said.

"But I didn't endorse him."

"You all but did. Everyone else has been painting him with the tar brush of Tom Pendergast's dirty political machine, but you made him look like a knight in shining armor."

"I just reported the truth about him, that's all," Shaylin said, shrugging. "He's an honest man who has done a good job. Why do you think reporting the truth is so courageous?"

"Because Harry Truman doesn't have a chance of winning that primary," Floyd said. "And whoever *does* win is going to remember the story that you wrote. And look at who you're making an enemy of. Truman is running against Congressman Jacob Milligan, who has been in Congress for fourteen years, and John Cochran, who last year was voted by the Washington newspapers as one of the six most useful members of the House. Yes, I would call your story courageous."

She smiled. "What if Truman wins? Then what I wrote would be prophetic and I would be smart, wouldn't I?"

"Believe me, Shaylin, he doesn't have a snowball's chance in hell of winning," Floyd said as their dinner arrived.

They said little during their meal, focusing most of their attention on their food. As soon as they had finished eating, they went up to Floyd's apartment, which was located on the top floor of the Chase Apartments, directly behind the Chase Hotel.

"I need to use your telephone," Shaylin said when they entered.

"You know where it is," Floyd said. He walked over to

the radio. "Want some music?" Enough ambient light was coming in through the window that he didn't bother switching on any lamps.

"If you can find something nice," Shaylin said, taking off her earring and cradling the phone in her neck. "Remember, I don't like hillbilly."

"Who the hell does?" Floyd said with a snort, bending to the level of the radio. The soft yellow light from the dial seemed bright in the relative darkness as he turned the tuning knob, working through a series of buzzes, whistles, and static before the station he was looking for came in clear. Someone was singing "Brother, Can You Spare a Dime?"

"Not that, please," Shaylin said over the receiver as she dialed the number.

"Calling your brother?" Floyd asked as he continued twisting the dial. He picked up "Someone to Watch Over Me."

"Yes," Shaylin answered, listening to the rings on the other end of the line. "Oh, that's a good song. Leave it there."

Floyd covertly watched Shaylin, admiring the young woman's sense of responsibility. He knew that her mother had died two years before, leaving Shaylin responsible for a thirteen-year-old brother. Kevin was fifteen now, and since he was still in school, he was dependent upon his big sister for food, clothing, and housing. Otherwise he was pretty self-sufficient.

"Hi, Kevin, how are you doing?" Shaylin abruptly said, making it clear that her brother had answered. "Have you eaten? . . . No, go ahead and eat it all, if you want. I've had my dinner. Uh, listen, I'm going out with some of my friends and will probably spend the night with one of them, so I won't be in tonight. I just thought I'd tell you so you wouldn't be worried. . . . What? . . . No, Kevin, I am not going to sign for you. If they found out we lied, we'd *both* go to jail. When you're seventeen . . . When you're seventeen, Kevin, and I don't want to hear any more about it. Be sure and lock the doors. I love you. . . . No, it isn't mushy, it's real. I love you. I'll see you tomorrow."

"Is he still talking about joining the Navy?" Floyd asked as Shaylin hung up the phone.

She sighed. "That's *all* he talks about. You know, he's so big for his age. He's already over six feet tall. I'm afraid he's going to just up and enlist someday while I'm gone."

"There could be worse places for him than the U.S. Navy," Floyd said.

"I suppose so," Shaylin admitted. "But he's still so young. I'd hate to think about him off who knows where until he gets a little more mature." She gazed beyond Floyd through the window. "Look at that view," she breathed. "I never get tired of it."

She walked over to the window, and Floyd joined her. The lights of the city were spread beneath them like thousands of brilliant diamonds displayed on velvet. Here and there, great slabs of buildings thrust up from the velvet depths, each displaying glowing windows in intricate patterns. Also visible were the graceful arches and trusses of the railroad and highway bridges that spanned the Mississippi River. Across the river the community of East St. Louis was lighted as well, but beyond the metropolitan complex of the two cities, out into the countryside, there was nothing but a vast blackness, punctuated here and there with tiny flickers of light marking a few isolated farmhouses.

"Yeah, I like the view, too," Floyd said. "That's why I took this apartment. But, do you know the *best* way to see it?"

"How?"

"Naked."

Shaylin laughed.

"What is it?"

"I have this mental picture of everyone in St. Louis taking off all their clothes and standing out on the streets, looking up at us, just so we can see the entire city naked."

Floyd laughed with her. "Well, that would work, I suppose," he said. "Or, we could do it the other way around. We could get naked, then stand up here and look down at the city."

"Who are you kidding?" Shaylin asked seductively as

she started unbuttoning her blouse. "If we get naked, we aren't going to stand here and look at the city."

"Yeah, I guess you're right. So, you think it's a bad idea, then?"

Shaylin turned toward him and put her arms around his neck. "It isn't all bad," she purred, smiling up at him. She pressed herself against him. "The getting naked part, I like."

VAN BUREN, MISSOURI

When Del Murtaugh came back inside the unassuming little tourist cabin, his new bride was already under the covers in bed. After getting married in Benton, they had made it as far as Van Buren that night before Del decided the old Oakland badly needed a rest.

"Is everything all right with the car?" Rubye asked.

"Yes," Del answered. "I filled the radiator, put in a quart of oil, aired the tires, and checked all the tie-down ropes. We're ready to go again."

"I'll bet this is a pretty place," Rubye said. "Of course, I couldn't see it very well in the dark. I guess I'll have to wait until morning to get a good look at it."

Del sat down on the edge of the bed and began removing his shoes. "Won't be able to see it in the mornin' either," he said. "We need to get away before daylight. I'm afraid to drive this old car too fast, so that means what we can't do in speed, we got to make up for in time on the road. I'm sorry, darlin'."

"Whatever you say, Del. But if you want to get up that early, maybe we should dig around in our things for the alarm clock."

"We won't need no alarm clock. I'm pretty good at wakin' myself up whenever I want." By now, Del had slipped out of his shirt and trousers and was beginning to pull off his undershorts.

"Del!" Rubye gasped. "What are you doing?"

Del stopped, then looked at her. Though no lights were on inside the cabin, a bright streetlamp just outside the cabin window threw enough light inside to allow them to see each other quite clearly. Rubye sat up, pulling the sheet to her chin.

"What do you mean what am I doin'? I'm gettin' ready for bed," Del replied matter-of-factly.

"You're getting naked!"

"Of course I'm gettin' naked. That's how I sleep. That's how I've always slept. I hadn't figured on changin' it none."

"I've . . . I've never seen a man naked," Rubye said.

"That's 'cause you've always been a good girl. But me and you are married now, Rubye, and there ain't nothin' at all wrong with you seein' me naked or me seein' you the same way. We'll be lyin' side by side in the same bed for the rest of our lives."

Del slipped out of his shorts, then stood there for a moment. At first she looked away; then curiosity got the best of her, and she turned to look right at him. Under her direct and unabashed gaze Del began to get erect.

"It's . . . it's growing!" Rubye said in quiet awe.

"Yes, it is. That's the way of it," Del explained. "Darlin'," he then asked in a husky voice, "are you wearin' a nightgown?"

"Yes."

"I'm goin' to ask you to take it off."

Working behind the sheet, Rubye removed her nightgown, putting it on top of the sheet to show him she had removed it. Then, gently but firmly, Del reached for the bed sheet and pulled it down, exposing Rubye's own nudity. As he so often did, Del found himself marveling that such a beautiful woman would be his.

"What . . . what now?" she asked, her voice a whisper.

"Shhh!" Del said gently. "You just lie back and let me show you."

Del stretched out on the bed beside her, pulling her to him. They were naked flesh to naked flesh, from the tips of their toes to their thighs to their chests to their mouths. Through her breast pressed against his Del could feel the rapid beat of Rubye's heart, and in her neck under his fingertips the flutter of her pulse. It was as if he had captured a wild bird and was holding it in his hand. She was hesitant and unsure of herself, but she offered no resistance to anything he did and was compliant to his slightest wish.

She cried out briefly and he could feel her wincing slightly when he entered her virginal body, but soon she was caught up in the rhythm of their intimate dance and was mewling with pleasure.

"I love you, darlin'!" Del cried as he climaxed, riding a wave of almost intolerable ecstasy. Then the wave subsided, and he sank with it into torpor.

Listening to Del snoring softly beside her, Rubye lay on her back, staring at the shadows cast onto the ceiling by the outside light. She smiled, thinking to herself that now she was really a woman. Her vagina was slick with the wetness of Del's lovemaking and still tingling. She had had no idea what lovemaking would be like and was very pleasantly surprised by the experience.

Rubye snuggled against her new husband and clutched his hand. She didn't care that all their worldly possessions were stacked up on an old car that might not last another day. She didn't care that they were going to work a farm that neither of them had ever seen, to live in a place where they knew no one. As long as they had each other there was absolutely nothing in their future that couldn't be overcome.

CHAPTER FIVE

JUNE 16, 1934, NEW YORK CITY

The trimotored airplane circling Manhattan was a Rockwell-McPheeters Tri-Star, which competed with the Trimotor Ford and the Curtis Condor for recognition as the most popular airplane in use by the airlines. This particular craft, however, was a private one belonging to the Canfield-Puritex Corporation. It was painted white with a blue band at the window line, and its tail was a series of alternating white-and-blue diagonal stripes, a stylized duplication of the company's logo found on every box, bottle, and can of Canfield-Puritex products.

On this bright, sunny morning, Willie Canfield was at the controls. An accomplished aviator, in addition to being president of Mid-America Transport, he was also chief pilot for the airline. He rarely flew this particular airplane because Canfield-Puritex had its own corporate pilots, but he had volunteered to fly his brother, John, and John's new wife, Faith, to New York where they would board an ocean liner for their honeymoon trip to Europe.

When configured for airline use, the Tri-Star's cabin was designed to carry fourteen passengers. In the corporate model the cabin housed a couch, a couple of overstuffed easy chairs, a galley, and a wet bar. During the flight from St. Louis, John and Faith had had lots of room to stretch out in the customized blue-and-white-leather interior of the airplane, for they were the only passengers on board.

"By the way, the couch makes down into a bed, if you're interested," Willie had told them just before they had taken off from Lambert Field.

"Willie, you're *awful*!" Faith had replied, blushing furiously. "What makes you think we would want a bed?"

"I was thinking you might want to go to sleep," Willie had said, feigning innocence. "What were *you* thinking?"

"Don't be insolent," John had quipped.

Willie's remark was all the more cogent since John and Faith had not as yet had their wedding night. Directly after the wedding there had been a large reception followed by a joint-family dinner, and then they had to take off at one o'clock in the morning to reach New York in time to meet the ship before it sailed.

John and Faith had not made the white leather couch down into a bed. However, once during the night Willie happened to glance into the darkened cabin and saw that they were both sleeping sitting up, with Faith's head resting snugly against John's shoulder.

Just after dawn the airplane had set down in Columbus, Ohio, for fuel and breakfast. There they had the unexpected and unpleasant experience of facing a horde of newspaper and magazine photographers anxious for pictures of the handsome young couple. After hurrying through breakfast, they dashed back out to the plane, trying to avoid the press—though one particularly enterprising photographer had driven his car at breakneck speed alongside the runway to get a picture of them in the plane as they were taking off. They had been glad to leave that mania behind.

Now they were minutes away from their final landing at La Guardia Airport, and Willie was circling Manhattan to give John and Faith a spectacular view of the towering skyscrapers.

"There's the Empire State Building," Faith shouted above the clattering noise of the three engines. "Can you believe how tall it is?"

"You don't see any big monkeys climbing up the outside, do you?" John quipped.

"Don't be silly," Faith said with a laugh. "Anyway, I think it was the Chrysler Building the poor beast was crawling around on."

"No, it was definitely the Empire State Building. I recognize the radio tower."

Willie came back into the cabin to join them.

"Enjoying the view?" he called.

"Yeah, thanks," John shouted back.

"I thought you might be."

"Willie! Who's flying the airplane?" Faith asked.

"Oh, don't worry about it. I just put out an anchor," Willie teased. "It'll be all right till I get back."

"Really? I didn't know you could do that."

"The copilot is flying," John explained, laughing.

"Well, how am I supposed to know?" Faith asked, pouting. "I don't understand anything about airplanes."

Willie smiled gently at his new sister-in-law. "Oh, don't worry. Most folks would've wondered the same thing. Anyway, I just came back here to tell you folks good-bye and wish you a good trip. Soon as we drop you off, we've got to immediately get started back. A weather front is moving down from the north, and I want to be gone before it arrives. By the way, I radioed ahead. They'll have a limousine waiting for you at the airport to take you straight to the pier."

"Thanks, little brother," John said. "I don't know what we would have done without you."

"I just hope the steamer trunk got there all right," Faith said.

"It did," John assured her. "I called yesterday."

Willie smiled. "Faith, you never have to worry about things like that with John. He's Mr. Efficiency."

"Willie!" the copilot suddenly called back through the opening that separated the cabin from the pilot's compartment. "You'd better get back up here! La Guardia wants us to land now!"

"Okay, I'll be right there!" Willie called back. He shook his brother's hand, then hugged Faith. "See you when you get back," he said.

John and Faith fastened their seat belts, then held hands as the airplane began its descent, which was smooth and fast.

True to Willie's word, a Cadillac limousine was waiting for the newlyweds and whisked them from Queens to the west side of Manhattan, where the thousand-foot-long passenger liner *Valkyrie* lay at berth alongside Pier 92 in the Hudson River. The porthole-dotted steel sides of the ship lifted high above the cobblestoned street. A red flag flying from the stern hung so limply in the breezeless day that except for the color there was nothing to identify its nationality. However, the large black letters curving across the back of the ship gave its port of origin as Hamburg, and another means of identification was the red band painted around the middle smokestack. In the middle of the band was a white circle, and in the middle of the white circle, a black swastika.

"There it is," John Canfield said as the limousine turned off Fifty-second Street, then pulled to a stop near the first-class passenger entrance. "That's our ship, the *Valkyrie.*"

"Oh, John, isn't this exciting?" Faith asked, clutching her husband's arm and staring at the ship through the car window. "Just think, in six days we'll be in Europe. I wish the six days were behind us and we were already there, don't you?"

"Well, there are five nights with those six days," John said, squeezing Faith's hand. He looked at her and smiled. "And since we missed last night, I'm sort of looking forward to them, if you get my meaning."

"John!" Faith gasped, and she glanced toward the limo driver as her face flushed red. But despite her chagrin at John's boldness in front of the driver, she squeezed his hand back, making it clear that she agreed with him.

The driver stopped the car by the first-class boarding

ramp, then hurried around to open the door. "Here you are, folks. I hope you have a nice trip."

"Thank you. I'm sure we will," John replied, sticking his hand out to help Faith from the car. Arm in arm, the handsome young couple strolled across the sidewalk and up the long, red-carpeted ramp. At the top of the ramp they were stopped by a red velvet rope attached by a shining brass clip to an equally shining brass eye. Just on the other side of the barricade stood a young, slim, very crisp officer, wearing a red armband around the left jacket sleeve of his white uniform. He raised his clipboard importantly as the two approached.

"Welcome aboard the *Valkyrie,*" he said in a thick German accent. "May I have your name, please?"

"We are Mr. and Mrs. John Canfield."

The officer examined his clipboard, then looked up at them. "I'm sorry. I see no Canfield listed here."

"Look again," John said easily. "You must have made a mistake."

"Perhaps it is you who made the mistake," the German officer replied with clipped courtesy. "You are aware, are you not, that this is the first-class gate?"

"Yes, of course I am aware," John replied dryly.

"The reason I asked is that sometimes people don't understand," the boarding officer explained. "On the other hand, sometimes people do know that they aren't authorized to board through this gate, but they try to do so anyway. You can understand, I'm sure, that it is my job to prevent such people from boarding."

"Yes," John said. "The question is, why are you preventing *us* from boarding?"

"I have explained that to you, sir. You are not booked first class."

"And I have explained to *you,* sir, that we are," John insisted. He spotted one of the ship's porters passing by, pulling a luggage wagon. Several steamer trunks were piled high on the cart, and among them John recognized his own. All were appropriately marked with first-class tags, and he smiled.

"Well, at least someone got it right," he said, pointing to

the cart. "That's our steamer trunk. If we aren't booked first class, perhaps you could tell me why it is here."

"I have no idea, sir."

John was losing patience with the smartly uniformed automaton. "Indulge me," he said testily. "Check one more time?"

"If you insist," the German officer said. "You said your name is Canfield?"

"Yes, Canfield, John Canfield." For Faith's sake he had tried not to become so irritated, but the officer was being insufferable.

Trying to control his temper while the German carefully rechecked his list, John glanced around. At the bottom of the boarding ramp he saw a middle-aged couple just starting up. The man was greatly overweight and wore a monocle and a large, walrus-type mustache. The elegant, rail-thin woman with him had her hair pulled back and held in place by a pair of diamond-encrusted, tortoiseshell combs.

"I'm very sorry," the officer said after examining his clipboard again. "But I'm afraid we have no Mr. and Mrs. John Canfield."

"Come now, where is that famous German efficiency we have all been hearing about?" John asked.

"It is *not* German efficiency being questioned here," the officer replied sharply. "*You* are the one being questioned here. You are attempting to gain entry into an area where you are not authorized."

"But that is ridiculous," Faith said, finally speaking up. "Didn't you see our steamer trunk? It should be very obvious to you that we are supposed to be here."

The heavyset man and his rail-thin wife reached the top of the boarding ramp at that moment.

"What is obvious to me is that your name is not on this list," the boarding officer replied to Faith. "Now, if you would be so kind, please step aside so that I may continue boarding the passengers who are authorized to be here."

"Look here, officer," the heavyset passenger said, speaking with an upper-class British accent. "Why don't you let this gentleman and his wife pass through? You can get to the bottom of it later."

"If their name is not on my boarding list, I have no authority to let them pass," the officer insisted. "And if they do not step aside immediately, I shall be forced to summon the purser."

"Well, now, that's the first sensible thing you've said," John rejoined. "I should have thought of it myself. Summon the purser."

The officer snapped his fingers at a nearby sailor, then barked a short, gruff order that sent the sailor scurrying on his mission.

"While we are waiting to clear this matter up, I will be happy to board you," the officer said to the British couple.

"Oh, no. It wouldn't be proper for me to move ahead of this gentleman and his wife," the Englishman protested. "We'll just wait until all this is resolved." He smiled broadly and stuck his hand out to John. "Whitehead is the name. Brigadier Thackery Whitehead. This is my wife, Margaret."

"Please call me Maggie," the woman said, extending her own, bony hand. "Everyone does."

"John Canfield."

"Faith Daw—" Faith stopped and smiled. "I mean, Faith Canfield."

"Oh, heavens, newlyweds, are you?" Maggie said. "How delightful!"

Just then the sailor returned, leading another officer. This officer's uniform had more buttons, brass, and braid than that of the boarding officer. He, too, was wearing a swastika armband.

The newly arrived officer eyed John. "Now, sir, what seems to be your problem?"

"The only problem I have is with the bungling inefficiency and loutish behavior of the unpleasant person you have greeting arriving passengers," John said coolly. "My steamer trunk has received more courteous treatment."

"Would you care to explain this, Schmidtt?" the purser asked the other officer.

"He is trying to board as a first-class passenger," Schmidtt replied. He showed his clipboard to the purser. "His name is Canfield, and as you can see, he is not on my list."

The purser took the clipboard, lifted up the top pages, and examined a page underneath.

"Canfield?" the purser asked. He looked at John. "Would that be John Canfield?"

"Yes, it is," John replied.

"Schmidtt, you are an ignorant swine!" the purser snapped. "Herr Canfield booked passage after the original list was completed, as you would know if you had bothered to check the supplementary list!" He pointed to a listing on another page on the clipboard.

"I did not think to check the supplementary list," Schmidtt replied meekly.

"That is the problem with you, Schmidtt. You do not think," the purser said. The entire exchange had been in English so that John would understand and appreciate the fact that the boarding officer was being severely reprimanded. Then the purser continued his tirade in German, giving Schmidtt a thorough dressing-down, the gist of which was understandable in any language.

Schmidtt came to attention, uttered *"jawohl"* several times, and turned crimson under the blistering attack. Finally the purser turned his attention back to John.

"Please forgive us, Herr Canfield," he said, clicking his heels together sharply and bowing slightly. "My name is Klaus Reinhardt, and I will personally escort you and your wife to your cabin."

"Thank you, Herr Reinhardt," John said. The velvet rope was still barring his way, so he looked pointedly at Schmidtt. Quickly, the junior officer leaned over and unhooked the barrier.

John kept his hand protectively on Faith's back as they followed Reinhardt across the deck, into the ship's interior, and along a corridor. They finally stopped at a stateroom door, and Reinhardt opened it with a flourish.

They were just stepping inside the cabin when a steward came hurrying down the corridor toward them.

"Excuse me, sir," the steward said somewhat breathlessly. "You are Herr Canfield?"

"Yes."

"You have a telephone call, Herr Canfield," the steward

said. "It is the President of the United States!" he added in an awestruck voice.

"Thank you," John replied. He looked at Reinhardt. "Will I be able to take the President's call in my stateroom, or must I go to the radio room?"

"While we are at the dock we are connected to the city telephone system," Reinhardt answered. "I'll have the call switched here." He picked up the phone on the bedside table and spoke a few brusque words in German. After a few seconds he handed the telephone over to John. "The connection has been made," he said.

John took the receiver. "Hello?" he said tentatively.

"Mr. Canfield?" a woman operator's voice asked.

"Yes."

"Please hold the line, sir, for President Roosevelt."

"Hello, John, old sport!" the President's cheery voice came on and declared a moment later. "I just wanted to call before you left and wish you bon voyage!"

"Thank you, Mr. President."

"Of course, I have to tell you that I'm concerned with how Senator Dawson is going to get along with you two gone," Roosevelt said, laughing. "I'll do all that I can to keep the old rascal in line, but without you two around to keep him on the proper course, it's going to be a hard job. I hope you don't become so enraptured with what Europe has to offer that you forget to come back home."

"You needn't worry about that, Mr. President. But I'm not sure the senator shares your sentiment. He said he was glad to see us go, that we were just getting underfoot," John said with a laugh.

"Oh, he did, did he? Well, we'll just see what sort of song he sings about a week from now when all the bureaucratic red tape starts entangling him and he has no one to turn to to get things unsnarled. In the meantime, as far as I'm concerned, the only redeeming factor in your being gone is the fact that you will be my personal ambassador over there. I want you to take a good close look at this 'miracle' Mr. Hitler is supposed to be working in Germany. If you see anything he's doing that I can use, report it back to me."

"I'll do that, Mr. President."

"I guess I'd better let you go," Roosevelt said. "I know how it is when you're just checking on board. You and Faith probably have a million things to do. Have a good time, old sport, and do come in and see me as soon as you get back."

"I will, Mr. President, and thank you for your call," John said. He hung up the receiver, then turned back to the room.

"Will there be anything else I can do for you, Herr Canfield?" Reinhardt asked solicitously.

It was very obvious to John that the officer was greatly impressed by John's having received a personal call from the President of the United States. In fact, John decided, that was probably the reason the President had called him in the first place. And as for the business of John being the President's personal envoy, that had never even been discussed before, so John knew it was solely for the benefit of the Germans who would undoubtedly be listening in on the call.

"No, thank you," John replied to the purser's question. "We'll do very nicely now."

The officer clicked his heels together and made a slight bow, then departed the stateroom.

Soon after, three loud blasts sounded from the ship's horn, signaling that departure was imminent. Moments later the pier girders began sliding by just outside the stateroom's port-side window as the ship got under way.

"Oh, John, can we go out on deck and watch?" Faith asked eagerly.

"Sure," John replied. "Let's go have a look."

They scurried down the corridor to the first outside door, joining the dozens of other passengers lining the boat deck, some waving, some just watching the action intently. There were even a few who were looking on with what could only be described as bored detachment.

With tugs pulling at the bow and pushing at the stern, the *Valkyrie* was eased away from the pier and turned south in the Hudson River. When the ship was well clear, the tugs squealed high-pitched toots on their whistles and were answered by a stomach-shaking blast from the ship's horn. The connecting hawsers fell away, the tugs dropped back, and the deck began vibrating underfoot as the *Valkyrie* started moving under its own power.

"Look! There's the Statue of Liberty," John said, pointing to the tall, green sculpture at the entrance of the harbor.

"Have you ever seen anything more beautiful?" Faith breathed.

"Yeah," John said, turning to look at her. "You."

"Flattery will get you everywhere," Faith answered with a giggle.

"Really? Is that merely a platitude, or may I put it to the test?" John asked, smiling.

"What do you mean?"

"I mean, we do have a private room, a big bed, and several hours before dinner. That is," he added, "if you aren't afraid."

Faith looked up at him, her large blue eyes filled with trust. "You are my husband, John Canfield," she said. "I'm not afraid."

Putting his arm around her and escorting her back toward the corridor, he felt her shudder. "Cold?"

"No," she replied softly. "Not cold."

Once in their room, John took his bride into his arms and kissed her passionately. Breaking off the kiss with great effort, he turned and locked the door behind them. When he turned back, Faith was taking out her blue-silk nightgown from the steamer trunk. Smiling self-consciously at him, she disappeared into the bathroom.

As soon as she was gone, John began slipping out of his own clothes. He folded them fastidiously and put them on a chair beside the bed, then donned his new black-and-gold-silk pajamas. Walking over to the bed, he turned down the sheets, then slipped into bed, his anticipation—among other things—rising.

A moment later Faith reappeared, and John caught his breath. She looked astonishingly beautiful—and astonishingly sexy. Over her nightgown was a matching blue-silk negligee, held closed by blue ribbons. She glided across the room and stood at the edge of the bed, looking down at John for a moment. Then—agonizingly slowly, it seemed to John—she untied the ribbons and let the dressing gown fall to the floor. Her nightgown clung to her body, and her nipples protruded boldly through the whisper-thin fabric.

"I . . . I hadn't planned to wear this during the day," she said. "I hope you don't think it's too brazen."

"I think it's wonderful," John said, finding his voice with some difficulty. He turned down the corner of the bedcovers, inviting her in.

John kissed her as she slid into bed alongside him. The kiss was urgent and demanding, and after a moment he left her lips and began kissing her throat, her bare shoulders, and then with a simple rearrangement of her nightgown, his mouth found her breast.

John had touched Faith's breast many times before, always with an aching urgency that promised what couldn't be delivered. But now it promised fulfilled pleasure, and under his loving, tender caresses, he felt Faith responding to him.

His hands, his lips, his tongue explored her body. At first Faith seemed shy, but soon she began learning his body in turn—tentatively at first, then with growing ardor. Her touch excited John even more until all the nerve endings in his body seemed to be on fire. When she gave herself to him, moving to facilitate his entry, touching him with her fingers, guiding him when necessary, he felt an ecstasy more wonderful than his most erotic fantasies. It was a piece of eternity, shared in an instant.

Later, much later, when they were completely sated, John rolled off Faith, then slid his arm under her so that her head rested upon his shoulder. There was no self-consciousness to their nakedness. It was as if this room on this ship in the middle of this ocean was their own private world. In this world, which no one else could enter or even touch, they belonged in such a primal state.

Finally, but only after several minutes of contented silence, Faith spoke.

"Promise me," she said.

"I promise."

Faith laughed and raised up on one elbow to look down at him. "You don't even know what I want you to promise."

"It doesn't matter," John replied, playing with her nipple. "I promise anyway."

"I want you to promise never to forget this moment," Faith said. "I want you to lock it up in a part of your heart, to keep forever."

John moved his finger from her nipple to her mouth. Tracing her lips, he said softly, "I promise. I will never forget this moment."

Faith started to lean over to kiss him, then sat up, a startled look on her face. "Oh! How did that get here?"

Following her gaze, John saw a cream-colored envelope lying on the floor just inside the door. He rolled over and looked at it for a moment, then got up and padded over to retrieve it, not bothering to cover himself. "It must have been slipped under the door," he told her.

"What is it?"

Opening the envelope, he read the card inside. "It's from the captain. He has invited us to dine at his table tonight."

"Isn't that nice?"

John smiled broadly. "The invitation is for *Ambassador* and Mrs. John Canfield."

"Ambassador? But you aren't an ambassador. What does that mean?"

"That means they piked the telephone call," John said, chuckling. "Thanks to President Roosevelt, I believe we are going to get the royal treatment for the entire voyage."

When John and Faith Canfield were shown to the captain's table that evening, they were pleased to find that Brigadier Whitehead and his wife, Maggie, were among their fellow diners. The brigadier was in the uniform known as "dress mess," which, except for the gold epaulets, dark-blue sash, and spray of medals across his chest, was remarkably like the dinner jacket John was wearing.

In addition to the British couple, there was Marcel Aubron, an unaccompanied restaurateur from Paris, a very fat German businessman named Heinrich Pfaf and his wife, Elga, from Hamburg, and, of course, the captain of the ship, a full-bearded man named Gustav Streicher. The captain commanded not only the ship, but the table, for it required only the slightest movement of his finger to send one of the stewards off, barking orders at waiters.

An orchid sat at the plate of each female guest, and an obliging young crewman pinned the flowers to the women's dresses. The wife of the German businessman was wearing a very low-cut gown that exposed the top halves of large, creamy breasts, and she made some guttural remark as the steward was pinning on her orchid. The remark brought peals of laughter from her husband, but it caused the face of the young crewman to redden in embarrassment.

"You are the proprietor of Marcel's Café in Paris?" Brigadier Whitehead asked the Frenchman, after meals had been ordered and introductions made.

"*Oui.*"

"Well, I am delighted to make your acquaintance," Whitehead said with a warm smile. "Your place is quite famous for the writers and artists who gather there."

"*Oui,* it is that," Marcel said proudly. "Years ago, before the American writers Ernest Hemingway and Eric Twainbough became famous, they were regular patrons at my café. They would come in midmorning and sit for hours at their respective tables, writing on big yellow pads and drinking wine and saying nothing to each other. Then, when each had finished with his work for the day, they would visit and laugh, and sometimes they would sing. Others would come too: Ford Madox Ford, Sherwood Anderson, Marcel Proust, and Gertrude Stein."

"Gertrude Stein? Isn't she a Jew?" the German businessman interrupted.

Their dinners suddenly arrived, and Marcel stared coolly at the German businessman while the dishes were laid. As soon as the waiters departed, the restaurateur finally answered, "Yes, she is a Jew. And she is also somewhat overweight."

"Overweight? What does that have to do with it?" the German asked, holding his fork over his plate and clearly bewildered by Marcel's response.

"Precisely," Marcel answered.

John laughed loudly.

"I do not see the humor in this," Pfaf sputtered.

"Perhaps, gentlemen, we could steer the conversation onto less controversial grounds," the captain suggested diplomatically. He turned to John. "Herr Canfield, you seem quite young to be an ambassador. You must be a man of superior ability."

John laughed again. "I'm not really an ambassador," he said. "When President Roosevelt used that expression in our *private* telephone conversation, he just meant that he wanted me to give him my impression of Europe when I return."

The captain coughed in embarrassment, and Marcel chuckled appreciatively.

"Even so," Brigadier Whitehead said. "For the President to request a personal report from you is quite an honor. You must be a remarkable young man to have come to his attention."

John smiled self-deprecatingly. "The most remarkable thing I did was be born the son of my father," he said.

"Canfield," the German businessman said, mulling over the name. "Yes, I know who you are. Your father owns Canfield-Puritex, does he not?"

"Yes. And through my father I met Senator Champ Dawson. Senator Dawson is now the head of President Roosevelt's Economic Recovery Advisory Board, and I have been working for him." He reached over and took Faith's hand. "While in that capacity I met, fell in love with, and have married his daughter."

"Ah, then Senator Dawson is your father?" the brigadier said to Faith.

"Yes."

"And you, Herr Pfaf, are the head of Pfaf Industries, I believe?" Whitehead said.

"Yes. We manufacture heavy industrial equipment," Herr Pfaf said proudly.

"I am indeed honored, gentlemen, to be dining with such notables," the Englishman announced, digging into his food.

"You belittle your own accomplishments, Brigadier

Whitehead," the captain said, smiling. "You commanded the York Brigade at the Battle of Ypres, did you not? And didn't you succeed where Generals Gough and Plummer failed?"

"I had the break of good weather during my show," Whitehead replied modestly.

"Are you returning to England, or will you be visiting Germany?" the captain asked.

"I'll be returning to England."

"And you, Herr Canfield. You'll be visiting Germany?"

"That is on our itinerary, yes," John said. "We will visit France first, then Germany, and after Germany, Austria. My father has friends in Vienna."

"What, no friends in Germany?" Pfaf put in.

"As a matter of fact, we do have a family friend who lives in Hamburg," John said. "Perhaps you've heard of him. His name is Tannenhower. Karl Tannenhower."

"The Gauleiter of Hamburg?" Pfaf asked, impressed by this piece of news.

John chuckled. "To tell you the truth, I only know he's some sort of official. I don't know exactly what kind."

"A most important kind," Pfaf replied. "Your friend Herr Tannenhower is a very influential man."

"You seem to move in very powerful company, Herr Canfield," the captain added.

"Don't be overly impressed with my acquaintanceship with Herr Tannenhower," John replied. "I haven't seen him for many years. When he attended school in America, he was a friend of my uncle's. Classmates, in fact. But Herr Tannenhower returned to Germany before the war, and he fought for Germany. My uncle fought for the Allies, of course."

"And now they are friends again, eh? Just like our two countries," Pfaf said somewhat smugly.

John picked up his glass of wine and took a swallow before he answered. Finally he replied, "My uncle was killed during the war."

"Unfortunately, many good young men of both sides died in that war," the captain said. He suddenly smiled. "But, of course, that is all behind us now. Adolf Hitler is forging a new Europe, and all is being put right."

"A new Europe?" Marcel asked. "What about France? Is Adolf Hitler including France in his new Europe?"

"The new Europe I'm referring to is the one that is emerging now that Germany is, once again, assuming her rightful position," the captain explained.

"And the Jewish problem being addressed," Herr Pfaf added.

"Why have you people such an obsession with the Jews?" John asked.

"Surely you, an American, should not have to ask such a question," Pfaf replied. "Haven't you had your own racial problems with the Negro?"

"It's not the same thing," John said. "I agree, racial prejudice is very strong in our country, especially in the South. But our government is moving gradually toward a system of *including* the Negro in our society, whereas your government is moving in the direction of exclusion."

"But it *is* the same thing," Pfaf insisted. "The only difference is, our government reflects the will of the people and your government doesn't."

"No, Herr Pfaf," the captain put in, "I can see what Herr Canfield is saying. But there is one important point I think you are both overlooking, one which, when I explain, will make things very clear to each of you." The captain turned toward John. "You see, Herr Canfield, our problem with the Jew is much more acute than your problem with the Negro. The difference is that the Jew is very smart and mean-spirited, whereas the Negro is simpleminded and good-natured. Everyone knows it is much easier to deal with someone who is uncomplicated and easygoing than with someone who is clever and diabolical. Also, because of his color, the Negro is very easy to identify, whereas Jews can, and quite often do, hide among us. That is the social problem facing us today. And not only Germans, but all men of western European stock, which means also most Americans. Does that make it easier for you to understand our 'obsession with Jews,' as you put it?"

"No, it doesn't make it easier at all," John said. "You see, to accept that, I'd have to accept your premise that all Jews are smart and mean-spirited and all Negroes are simpleminded and good-natured. Well, I'm sorry, I don't buy that at all."

Pfaf laughed. "And so now, I suppose, you are going to tell us you know a dumb Jew and a smart Negro?"

John smiled. "Well, I wouldn't exactly call Max Baer a genius or mean-spirited."

"And can you also find a smart Negro to champion?" Pfaf asked.

"A person like myself is hardly adequate to the task of defending someone like Professor Loomis Booker," John said. "And even if I were, he would need no defense from me." He stood up, then pulled Faith's chair out for her. "Captain, I appreciate the invitation to your table," he said. "It was an interesting experience, but we really must be going now."

"You are leaving before dessert?" the captain asked, clearly surprised at the abrupt departure.

"Yes," John said. He patted his flat stomach. "I'm beginning to put on a little weight, so I believe a turn around the deck would be preferable to dessert. If I don't see any of you again during the trip, I wish you all bon voyage." He smiled down at Faith. "Darling, are you ready?"

She smiled back and stood up. "Quite."

The other men politely got to their feet as John and Faith made their departure, and John caught a slight wink from Marcel Aubron.

"I hope you aren't angry with me for being so rude as to walk away like that," John said as they headed out of the dining room toward the deck. "But if I had stayed, I'm afraid I might have done something even more undiplomatic."

"Angry with you?" Faith replied, squeezing John's arm. "I thought you were magnificent. I've never been more excited."

John looked at her quizzically. "Excited?"

She gave him a come-hither look. "You know. Sexually aroused."

"You don't say?" John replied, wagging his eyebrows lewdly.

Faith laughed. "I do say. If we had stayed for dessert, I might well have attacked you right there on the table."

John cleared his throat noisily. "Well, then, my little kumquat, instead of taking a turn around the deck, what would you say to just going back to our room?"

"I say that would be a wonderful idea. Unless you want to do it in one of the lifeboats," Faith added jokingly.

"Do it? Heavens, you mean you actually want to *do* it?"

"Yes, damn you, yes," Faith said, stretching up to nibble on his earlobe. "Now, where is it going to be? In the lifeboat, or do we go to our room?"

"I don't know. A lifeboat *would* be kinda fun . . . except for one little thing."

"What's that?"

"You might get splinters in your ass."

CHAPTER SIX

JUNE 1934, BOSTON, MASSACHUSETTS

When a capped-and-gowned Andrew Booker followed the other graduates down from the stage, he was clutching his medical degree in his hand. His wife, LaTonya, met him at the bottom of the stairs with open arms, where they kissed and embraced.

"You know, I've been wanting to kiss a doctor for a long, long time," LaTonya quipped, laughing happily. "I'm glad you finally got your degree. Otherwise, I would've had to go out and find a medicine man somewhere."

"It's funny you should say that. Because all this time I've had an overwhelming urge to snuggle up in bed with a doctor's wife," the new Dr. Andrew Booker replied.

"Will I fill the bill?"

"You might say you are just what the doctor ordered," Andy said, and they laughed again. He looked around. "Say, where's Pop?"

"I don't know," LaTonya replied, looking around as well. "He and Mama were standing just over there a few minutes ago. I don't know what happened to them."

"You know, with my pop married to your mom, I guess we'd better be careful how we refer to them," Andy suggested. "Otherwise people might get to thinking that people from Missouri are sort of, well, strange . . . like sisters marrying brothers, that sort of thing."

LaTonya laughed. "Maybe down in the Ozarks, some of those hillbilly white folks marry cousins. But I don't know of any colored folks who do it."

"Shh," Andy warned. "Here comes Dean Moyers."

"Ah, Dr. Booker," Dean Moyers said, extending his hand. "I want to offer you my most heartfelt congratulations."

"Thank you, Dean Moyers."

"I was telling your father a few moments ago how proud we are of you. I mean, here you are, a colored man, yet you are an honors student and in the top two percent of the class. Not only that, you have an invitation to join the staff of the Schillingberg Institute of Medical Research. What a bright and glorious future you have before you, young man. And what an outstanding representative you are of your race."

A quick cloud passed over Andy's heart, but he quickly willed it aside.

"But, of course, no one is surprised. I mean you are, after all, Professor Loomis Booker's son, one of the most, if not the most, illustrious colored educators in America."

"I prefer to think of him as one of the most illustrious educators in America, regardless of his color," Andy said, unable to keep all of the sting out of his words.

Dean Moyer's eyes showed a moment of confusion; then his good humor returned. "I'm sorry. Of course you are right," he said. "I guess I just wasn't paying any attention to the way I sounded. I came across as somewhat of a bigot, didn't I? Will you forgive me, Doctor? I am extremely proud and happy for you, and in my enthusiasm I was just prattling on."

Now Andy felt a bit ashamed over his quick flash of

anger and he, too, smiled warmly. "Don't worry about it, Dean Moyers. You couldn't have knocked the chip off if I hadn't had it on my shoulder in the first place. Oh, would you excuse me? There's Pop. I haven't seen him since the ceremony."

"Of course," Dean Moyers said. "I know this is an important moment for both of you."

"There's Mama with him," LaTonya said.

Loomis Booker, a tall, distinguished-looking man with a wide face and a head of silver hair, smiled broadly at Andy as they approached each other. Every bit as tall as his father, Andy wasn't as broad-shouldered or as heavy-limbed. When seen together, however, the family resemblance between the two was evident.

Andy's mother, Pearl, Loomis Booker's first wife, had died during the great flu epidemic of 1918. Eight years later Loomis married Della Welles, the mother of Andy's high-school sweetheart, LaTonya.

Della was only fifteen years older than LaTonya, and she looked more like a beautiful older sister than LaTonya's mother. She had never married LaTonya's father. In fact, she never even saw him again after the weekend her child was conceived. As a result, Loomis was not only LaTonya's father-in-law and stepfather, he was the only father she had ever really known. Though confusing, it had worked out very well.

"So this is my son, the doctor," Loomis said, embracing his son happily.

"I didn't think this day would ever get here," Andy confessed.

"Dean Moyers tells me you've been offered a position with the Schillingberg Medical Research Institute. He said the director of the Institute was quite impressed and offered you a very good position."

"Yes, he did, Pop. Isn't it great? I was going to tell you tonight, at dinner. He read my paper on the acquisition and storage of blood for subsequent transfusion. He even wants to publish it." Andy shook his head. "Can you believe it?" he asked with disbelief.

Loomis proudly patted his son's shoulder. "Of course I

can believe it. I've always known you could do anything you wanted to do. I've always hoped you would want to do the *right* thing."

"This *is* the right thing, Pop, I'm sure of it," Andy said. "I mean, this is what I set out for in the beginning, remember? I wanted to specialize in medical research, and now I'm going to do it. And at one of the most prestigious medical research facilities in the United States. In the world, even."

"If you accepted that position, that would mean you would stay here in Boston, I assume."

"Yes," Andy answered. "And that's another good part about it," he added. "Here they let me be me. There's no prejudice in Boston. Here people are much more interested in the working of my brain than in the color of my skin."

"Is that the truth? Well, that's wonderful." Loomis looked pointedly at his son, then asked, "So, tell me, Andy, are you and LaTonya going to buy a house on Beacon Hill?"

"Well, no," Andy replied defensively. "Come on, Pop, what are you saying? You know I couldn't buy a house on Beacon Hill, even if I could afford it."

"Oh. You mean because they won't allow Negroes there?" Loomis asked.

"That's what I mean," Andy admitted, somewhat crestfallen.

Loomis bowed his head and pinched the bridge of his nose. "Forgive me, son," he said. "I had no right to do that to you, just to make my point. The truth is, you don't even have to be Negro to encounter prejudice here. You could be as white as snow and be Irish Catholic, and the prejudice would be just as damning. Not only in Boston, but anywhere you go. I just want you to have your eyes open, that's all."

"I'm not blind, Pop."

"I'm glad that you aren't. But now, what do you say we let that distasteful subject drop? There's someone here I want you to meet."

"Who?"

"A friend of mine," Loomis said. "His name is Professor Henry Jackson, and he was one of my students the first year I taught at Lincoln University. In fact, Professor Jackson is a schoolteacher himself now. Well, actually, he's a school principal, and one of the leaders of his community. That's why he came."

"What does he want?"

"All he wants to do is talk to you."

"What about?"

"He'll tell you."

"Something is going on here, Pop," Andy said, peering at his father through narrowed eyes. "And I'm not sure I like it."

Loomis put his hand on his son's shoulder. "Andy, I promised Professor Jackson you would listen to him and give him a fair hearing. That's all I promised. After you listen to him, you make up your own mind. I don't intend to say a word that would sway you in one direction or the other."

"I don't even know what you're talking about when you say 'give him a fair hearing.' A fair hearing about what? Where is your friend from?" Andy asked.

"He's from Delta, Mississippi," Loomis said. "It's a little town on the Sunflower River. Andy, the people down there—*our* people—are in desperate need of a doctor."

"Pop," Andy said in a quiet, pained voice, "Pop, no. What are you saying? Please, don't do this to me. Not now. Not when everything is going my way."

"I'm not going to do anything to you, Andy," Loomis insisted. "I told you, it's your decision to make."

"I've made my decision," Andy said. "I'm going into medical research."

"I'm sure you believe that's the right thing to do," Loomis said.

"Yes, I do, Pop, and I don't feel I should have to apologize for that."

"No, of course not," Loomis agreed. "All I ask is that you talk to him. And, when you turn him down, please show some compassion for his needs and leave him with a bit of dignity."

"Well, of course I'd do that, Pop. You know I wouldn't want to do anything to hurt anyone's feelings. And I do want to do the right thing. I think you know that."

"Yes, I do know it. I'm very proud of you, Andy. There is nothing on God's green earth you could ever do that would diminish my pride in you by one iota. If you accept my friend's offer, there's no doubt in my mind you'll be the best general practitioner in the state of Mississippi. Just as if you accept the offer of the Schillingberg Medical Research Institute, you will be the best medical researcher in the country. Now, how could I not be proud of either one of those choices?"

Andy laughed. "Okay, Pop, okay. I give in. I'll talk to your friend. You missed your calling, you know that? You should have been a lawyer."

Loomis chuckled. "I *am* a lawyer, don't you remember? I passed the bar three years ago."

At Loomis Booker's request, the dean made his office available for the meeting between Andy and Henry Jackson. Andy insisted that LaTonya attend the meeting as well, since whatever he decided was going to affect her as much as it did him.

Professor Jackson was already waiting in the dean's elegant, wood-paneled office when Andy opened the door. He stood as Andy and LaTonya entered, and when he did, Andy recognized him at once.

"I remember you!" Andy said, smiling broadly. "You're Pickpocket Jackson."

Professor Jackson smiled. "That's me," he said.

"Pickpocket?" LaTonya asked, clearly startled. "You mean he's a thief?"

"Oh, LaTonya, he's not just *any* thief. He's the best damn thief I ever saw," Andy said. Noting the thoroughly confused look on LaTonya's face, he laughed. "At stealing the basketball," he explained. "He played on the Lincoln University basketball team. I was just a kid then, but I can sure remember watching his plays."

The professor chuckled. "I'll tell you the truth, I remember you, too. You used to come out during practices and sit there under the goal, wearing that way-too-big purple basketball shirt and watching every move we made. We players used to kid each other that you might be spying for the coach. We figured that if one of us made a mistake and the coach didn't see it, you'd tell him about it."

"I *did* tell him," Andy said, laughing. "But I'm not sure he ever listened to me."

"Your pop tells me you were quite a good basketball player yourself," Jackson said.

"I enjoyed it," Andy said casually. He indicated the sofa and chairs. "Well, if we're going to have this little chat, we may as well sit."

"This is quite an office," Jackson said as he sat on the dark-green leather couch and looked briefly around, clearly impressed. He smiled sheepishly. "I have to confess, I'm not used to being in places this grand."

"So, you're a schoolteacher now," Andy said. "No, wait, Pop said you were a school principal."

"I am the principal, but I still teach. English and history. And I coach basketball," he added. "We went undefeated this year." There was a twinkle in his eye. "But before you get too awestruck by how important I am, I probably should tell you that when all the kids and other teachers are gone, I get out the push broom and sweep the halls."

"High school?" Andy asked.

Jackson grinned. "You really don't understand, do you? We're talking about a colored school in Mississippi. We don't have grade schools and high schools. We just have schools. From the first grade through the twelfth."

"I hope you're well paid for all that."

"Forty dollars a month during the school year," the professor said. "Nothing in the summer. And the truth is, the school board doesn't always come up with the money during the school year."

"Forty dollars a month?" Andy gasped. "That's all you make? My God! How do you live?"

"My wife, Doney, and I have a garden. And we have chickens for eggs and a cow for milk. We raised a couple of hogs last year, and that helped. But there's a depression on, after all, so I suppose that when you compare us to how a lot of other people are living, black or white, we're probably doing quite well."

"Yes, if you put it that way, I guess you're right," Andy agreed, nodding.

"Of course, there's more to it than money," Jackson said.

Andy laughed softly. "And so here comes the pitch," he said.

Jackson smiled. "You are an astute young man, Dr. Andrew Booker," he said. "And you're right. This is the pitch."

Andy leaned back in his chair, holding up his hands as if to catch a baseball. "All right, Professor, throw it in here. I'm ready."

Professor Jackson wordlessly assessed Andy at some length. Finally he said, "Well, I'll tell you, Dr. Booker, at this point I have to decide whether I'm going to continue with this meeting or get up and walk out."

Andy looked at him quizzically but said nothing, waiting for the professor to continue.

"You see, if I think you're hearing me out simply because your father asked you to or simply out of politeness, I'll just thank you and take my leave. If, however, I believe that you are genuinely interested and really want to hear what I have to say, then I will stay."

"And what do you believe?" Andy asked.

Jackson shook his head. "You call it."

Andy smiled. "I'd like you to stay, Professor. I want to hear your proposal."

Professor Jackson nodded, then leaned forward to rest his arms on his long legs and clasp his hands. "As I told you, Dr. Booker, I teach history. So I'll use that to make my point. Now, if you consider the history of mankind, there are certain people whose names simply jump out at you: Socrates, Julius Caesar, Jesus Christ, Joan of Arc, Christopher Columbus, Benjamin Franklin, and, in our own race, Crispus Attucks, Frederick Douglass, Sojourner Truth, and George Washington Carver, to name a few. Why is it that we remember some men and women for as long as four thousand years after their passing, while others are nothing but dust motes in the corridors of time, immediately forgotten? I'll tell you why," he went on, not waiting for an answer. "We remember them because they rose above the masses, they seized the moment, and by their actions they changed the course of the world."

Jackson sat back on the couch and let the information sink in for a moment, studying Andy's face closely, measuring the effect of his words. After a moment he continued.

"I have seized the moment," he said. He pointed toward the south. "Last year there were three hundred fifteen students in my school. Fifteen years from now those three hundred fifteen will have roughly seven hundred children. Thirty years from now the number of their descendants will have grown to some two thousand, and forty-five years from now there will be more than ten thousand, and they will touch upon the lives of *one hundred thousand more.*"

Professor Jackson's voice rose to a crescendo, and he let his last words hang in the room at length. Then, more quietly, he continued.

"And somewhere, Dr. Booker, somewhere in that future multitude there may be someone who takes a rocket ship to the stars . . . or discovers a cure for polio . . . or leads our people to the promised land of racial equality. What I do today can set all that in motion."

Andy nodded. "I admit, there is more than money involved," he said thoughtfully.

"You can be a part of this too, Dr. Booker," Jackson said. "You can seize the moment."

"Professor Jackson, in your scenario you suggested that one of the people in your future might discover a cure for polio. How do you know that I won't be that person? I have been offered an opportunity here—a very rare opportunity for a Negro. Perhaps you've heard. I've been recommended for a position at the Schillingberg Medical Research Institute."

"Yes, I have heard, and I extend my heartfelt congratulations. It's quite an honor"—Jackson smiled wryly—"and I suppose it pays very well."

"Yes. It pays extremely well. But, like you, I'm not motivated by just the money. You must believe that."

"Oh, I *do* believe it, Doctor," Professor Jackson said. "I don't think any person sets out to be a doctor unless he's imbued with a sense of compassion and concern for his fellow man. Clearly you have that sense. That's why I think you would find appealing the idea of coming to a community where there are thousands of souls who would be dependent upon you. Doctor, a baby who dies at the age of two because he was denied medical care will never fulfill the promise God had for him."

"Yes, but I can't save every two-year-old baby in the world," Andy protested.

"No. But you could save one. Or twenty. Perhaps five hundred," Professor Jackson responded. "You have lived a charmed life, Dr. Booker. You were raised by parents who not only loved you, but who were always able to provide for you. You have never wanted for creature comforts. You don't know what it's like to go to bed hungry or cold. You've accepted an education as if it were your due. However, your skin is black, therefore I assume you have encountered some prejudice. Someone may have called you a nigger at one time or another. And I'm sure there have been places you wanted to see but were denied entry to because of your race. Am I right?"

"Yes, of course."

"You have encountered all those things, my boy, and yet you are the cream of the crop. You enjoy a life at the extreme upper echelon of our race. You are privileged, moneyed, and educated."

"Yes, sir," Andy admitted. "I suppose that's true."

"Then tell me. Do you feel that you owe *nothing* to your fellow man? Do you think God handed all this to you on a silver plate and expects no repayment whatever?"

"I guess I've never really thought of it that way," Andy replied.

Jackson's face softened. "It may be," he said, "that you *are* the one who is destined to find the cure to polio . . . or to make some other great medical discovery. That may be the repayment expected of you, and, if so, that is what you should do, for who am I to question God?" He held up his hands in supplication.

"Professor Jackson, would you give me a little time to consider your offer?" Andy asked. He reached over to take LaTonya's hand, and when he looked at her, he saw with surprise that she was silently crying. He looked back at Jackson. "How soon do I have to let you know?"

"I'm taking the train back tonight," the professor said.

"I'll give you my answer before you leave," Andy promised.

"You haven't asked about the money," Jackson said, his face breaking into a large smile.

"No, I haven't. But, as we both said, there are some things more important than money. Whatever my decision may be, money will play no part."

"I'm glad to hear you say that," Professor Jackson said, chuckling, "because there isn't any money."

Loomis Booker, who was the chancellor of Lincoln University in Jefferson City, the only state-supported black university in Missouri, had missed spring graduation at Lincoln University this year so that he could attend his son's graduation from medical school. Having driven up from Jefferson City to Boston, he and Della had stayed with Andy and LaTonya in the small house Andy had rented. In celebration not only of the graduation, but also of the visit of their family, LaTonya had prepared a big dinner for them.

They had laughed and joked and talked all during the meal, but it was readily apparent that Andy was distracted and deep in thought. He had said nothing to his father about the meeting with Professor Jackson, and Loomis didn't ask about it. But the professor may as well have been a fifth guest, for his presence hung over them throughout the evening.

"Oh, by the way, Andy, I noticed that you have all four of Eric's books on your shelf," Loomis said as they were drinking coffee after the meal. It was clear that he was looking for something to talk about that would avoid the obvious. "Have you read all of them?"

"Not yet," Andy replied.

"Why not?"

"School, study, that sort of thing. I haven't really had the time."

"They're very good books," Loomis insisted.

"I'm sure they are," Andy said. "I read *A Time for All Things* and *Stillness in the Line*. They were both very good. But, as I said, I haven't had time to read the others."

"Andrew, Eric is almost like your older brother," Loomis said reproachfully. "You should make the time."

As a child Andy had repeatedly enjoyed hearing the story of how when the well-known novelist had been a fourteen-year-old orphan out on his own, circumstances had contrived to drop him almost literally into Loomis's lap, more dead than alive. Loomis and Andy's mother, Pearl, had taken the injured boy in, nursed him back to health, fed, clothed, and subsequently educated him. Loomis took no small amount of pride in the fact that though he and Eric Twainbough were of different races, Eric had essentially regarded Loomis as his father. Although not often seeing each other over the past thirty years, the two men had kept up a constant exchange of letters.

"I'll get around to reading them, Pop, I promise," Andy said, knowing how much it meant to his father. He looked across the table at his wife. "LaTonya, I know you're probably about ready to do the dishes, but leave them for a while, would you? I'd like you to take a walk with me."

"Sure, sweetheart," LaTonya said. It was evident that Andy wanted to discuss his decision, and the young woman quickly got up from the table to honor his request. "Would you excuse us?" she asked her mother and stepfather.

"Of course we will, honey," Della said for both of them. "And don't you worry any about the dishes. Loomis and I will do them."

"Wait just a minute, woman!" Loomis declared in mock protest. "What gives you the right to volunteer my services?"

"I was hoping you would volunteer yourself," Della replied in a sugary voice. "You know, just to keep me from being angry with you for the next twenty-four hours?"

"In that case I concede," Loomis said with a laugh. "Okay, you wash, I'll dry."

Thanking them, Andy and LaTonya stepped out of the house into the warm June night. A few doors down the street a group of kids were playing a game, and the squeals of their happy laughter filled the air.

They walked on for several blocks, passing a house that had a radio playing loudly enough for it to be heard through the open window.

"Here in Boston, Swampwater Puckett and the St. Louis Grays held the Sox to just two hits as the Grays won, two to nothing. Meanwhile in St. Louis, our Braves took the measure of the Cardinals, four to one.

"We'll be back with more scores, after this message from our sponsor."

The message was in the form of a jingle:

> *"Pepsi-Cola hits the spot.*
> *Twelve full ounces, that's a a lot.*
> *Refreshing without filling, too.*
> *Pepsi-Cola is the drink for you."*

"I wish I had one," LaTonya said with a sigh, speaking for the first time since they had left the house. She patted the perspiration on the back of her neck with a lacy white handkerchief.

"That's what they want you to wish," Andy pointed out. He reached over and took LaTonya's hand in his. "Sweetheart, earlier, when we were in Dean Moyer's office, I noticed that you were crying," he said softly.

"Yes."

"Why?"

"I don't know. I guess I was touched by what Professor Jackson had to say."

"So was I," Andy admitted.

"You've decided, haven't you?"

"Yes."

"You want to go to Mississippi, don't you?"

Andy looked at her with a pained expression on his face. "I don't know, LaTonya. It's not so much that I want to go as it is that I feel I *should* go. It's as if there were something deep inside me telling me that this is what I'm supposed to do." He sighed and shrugged, holding up his hands. "God only knows why. But I want you to know that I won't go unless you are a hundred percent with me on this. I mean, you have to say yes, and you have to mean it. *Really* mean it."

"Yes."

"I know it probably doesn't make any sense to you. And it'll be hard, no doubt about it. But it will only be for a year or so."

"Yes."

"I won't give up on my research. I'll still— What did you say?"

"Yes," LaTonya repeated a third time, smiling up at him.

"You mean, you're saying that we can go to Mississippi?"

"Yes. If you feel that's what you should do, then you must do it," LaTonya said. She was smiling happily though there were tears in her eyes. "I agree with you. That's where God wants you to go, and, as Professor Jackson said, who are we to argue with God?"

BIMINI ISLANDS, THE BAHAMAS

Eric Twainbough had had his house built on the northern island, at the highest point on the tongue of land at the eastern tip. From the sea it appeared old and abandoned, for it was gray and weathered whereas most of the other houses on the island were painted glistening white. But it was sturdily built, well maintained, and very comfortable—all of which Eric's New York-based editor, Sam Hamilton, who was visiting for the first time, had quickly discovered upon his arrival.

As Sam now stood on the white-sand beach, a solitary figure staring out over the blue-green vastness of the sea, he noticed several commercial fishing boats working about a mile or so offshore. The boats were little more than dots on the horizon, and Sam peered at them for a while, wondering what it must be like to go to sea every day in such small craft, completely at the mercy of the elements.

Sam briefly glanced over his shoulder at the weathered

house behind him. He pictured Eric Twainbough in his second-floor office, seated at his desk facing a window that had a panoramic view of the sea and working on his latest book. This would be the fifth one that Eric had written for Pendarrow House, and Sam had been the editor for all of them.

Eric was one of the most successful authors in America. All four of his previous books—*A Time for All Things, Stillness in the Line, Fire on the Northern Ice,* and *Then Came the Gladiators*—had climbed to the top of *The New York Times* best-seller list. *Stillness in the Line* had also won the Petzold Prize for fiction, a feat not diminished by the fact that Eric had once worked for the late publisher of The *St. Louis Chronicle,* Thomas Petzold, for whom the prize was named.

Now Eric was nearly finished with his fifth novel, *The Corruptible Dead.* He had invited Sam down from New York to "be in on the finish and get a feel of the island." In a spirit of adventure, Sam had accepted the invitation.

The editor turned and started walking down the beach, following the line separating wet sand from dry. As he fastidiously avoided the jellyfish, seaweed, and other deposits from the Gulf Stream, he thought about the set of circumstances that had brought him to this spit of sand.

Sam Hamilton was a fifty-five-year-old bachelor who was completely at home in New York. He liked being able to step out of his apartment and have a dozen exceptional restaurants within walking distance. He liked having a newsstand on his corner that gave him a choice of newspapers from every major city in the world. He liked telephones and taxicabs and plays and nightclubs. He even liked the hurly-burly of millions of people and city traffic.

So why was he here, where there were none of those things? Because he was, above all else, a man of books.

He was a Harvard graduate who undoubtedly could have had a higher-paying job in another profession but wouldn't trade positions with anybody for any amount. He loved what he did. He had a sense of destiny, an awareness that the books he honed and polished and shaped today were destined to live beyond him, projecting his signature far into the future.

On some cold day in the twenty-first century, long after he was gone, someone was going to go to a library and select a book written by one of Sam's authors. That someone would curl up by an open fire and begin reading (of course, Sam thought, that was assuming there would still be cold days and open fires in the twenty-first century; surely science wouldn't eliminate them, even if it could), and the images conjured up in that reader's mind far in the future would be the same images in the author's mind when he had written the words and the same ones in Sam's mind when he had edited the manuscript. His authors' books were Sam's shot at immortality.

That shot at immortality had brought him here. Though he had frequently discussed story lines with authors and had exchanged letters of encouragement and help during the writing of books, he had never been physically present at that magic moment when a manuscript was actually finished. The idea held great appeal for him.

When Sam had arrived by ship from the mainland the evening before, Eric had met him and almost immediately had explained his writing schedule. He wrote from seven in the morning until two in the afternoon. At two he stopped for lunch, then took the afternoon off. After dinner he went back to work for a couple more hours.

"We'll have a good time during my afternoons off," Eric had said. "Later this week we'll go fishing, but tomorrow we'll go down to Miguel's and get drunk, then bust up all the tables and chairs and break out all the windows."

Sam smiled wanly at Eric's proposal and tried to draw comfort from the fact that he was sure the writer was kidding—but he couldn't be one hundred percent sure. Eric was a powerfully built man who had lived a life of adventure and was now without the civilizing influence of his wife, Tanner, for Eric lived in Bimini while Tanner lived in St. Louis.

Tanner, whose real name was Brunhilde Winifred Tannenhower, was an heiress. Her grandfather had founded Tannenhower Brewery in St. Louis, the largest brewery in America, and when her parents were killed in a plane crash in southwestern Kansas three years earlier—a tragedy that took the life of Knute Rockne, the famed football coach, as well—she became the beneficiary not only of the brewery, but of her father's beloved St. Louis Grays baseball team as well.

Tanner's rather unusual name came from her own mispronunciation of her surname when she was a very small child. It had stuck, and now few people knew her given name. That suited Tanner fine, for she had no love for the Teutonic names her parents had bestowed upon her.

She had met Eric in Paris in the spring of 1921, right after her college graduation, while making the kind of grand tour of the Continent that had become traditional among the sons and daughters of the wealthy. Eric was a veteran of the World War, living in Paris at the time and struggling to keep body and soul together. He was an expatriate, one of the brash young literati that Gertrude Stein had called "the lost generation."

Eric and Tanner fell in love, had a whirlwind courtship, were married, and had continued to live in Paris until the air crash that killed her parents. They were still married, but though Eric had wanted his wife to place the day-to-day operation of the brewery in someone else's hands, she had refused. Tanner felt strongly that a member of the Tannenhower family should run the company her grandfather founded, and since the only relative she had was a cousin in Germany who had no interest in the company, she chose to live in St. Louis, where the brewery headquarters was located.

Eric had tried living in St. Louis for a while but found it too confining. As he had explained to Tanner, experiences were his stock-in-trade. He needed freedom and stimulation for his inventory the way a greengrocer needed fresh vegetables for his. Above all else he was a writer and a highly successful one—even though his income, as good as it was, couldn't approach the amount of money that Tanner realized from the brewery.

Two years ago they had bought the house on Bimini, which was where Eric now spent most of his time. He would occasionally visit St. Louis, and Tanner would occasionally visit Bimini, but by now they were maintaining wholly separate residences. Sometimes their twelve-year-old son, Hamilton, whom they both called Ham and who was named after Sam Hamilton, would visit Eric alone. It was as if Eric and Tanner were divorced, and Ham's visits were a part of the visitation agreement.

Sam was thinking about all this and watching a pair of dolphins rolling through the surf when he heard the screen door slap shut behind him. He turned around to see Eric walking down the slope of white sand toward the water. Sam studied his old friend, and a smile tugged at the corner of his mouth. Eric was clothed several degrees beyond casual in a pair of khaki shorts that had once been a pair of khaki trousers, a faded-yellow shirt worn loose over the shorts, and soft, leather moccasins worn with the heels mashed beneath his feet, turning them into slip-ons. He had a full beard, and though he was only forty-four, his beard and hair were already liberally streaked with gray. His face and massive forearms were deeply tanned, though his legs were much lighter in tone, almost as if they had been shaded by the overhang of his considerable belly. He was the picture of the quintessential beachcomber, Sam thought to himself.

Sam was much smaller than Eric, both in height and weight. And ever the Manhattan office worker, he was wearing a suit—though it was a tropical worsted and he had made, to him, the rather daring concession of removing his tie.

"Get dressed," Eric said, "and we'll go down to Miguel's bar."

"Get dressed? You mean I should put on a tie?"

"No, goddammit, I mean take off at least half of what you're wearing," Eric grumbled. He reached for Sam's suit coat. "Get out of this jacket," he ordered.

Sam removed his jacket.

"And the shirt."

"My goodness, Eric, I can't do that! I can't appear in public in my undershirt!"

"Well, you can't wear that," Eric insisted. "And I don't have anything that will fit you." He sighed. "All right. That shirt will have to do, I suppose, but we'll have to take care of the sleeves."

He produced a pocketknife and, before Sam could even protest, began cutting into the shirtsleeve about halfway between the elbow and shoulder.

"What are you doing?" Sam yelped. "This is a Hathaway shirt!"

"Yeah, but it's a *long-sleeved* Hathaway shirt," Eric retorted. "And that's no good down here."

Sam groaned in protest but made no attempt to stop Eric as he cut off first one sleeve, then the other.

"There you go," Eric said, smiling broadly at his handiwork. "Now all you have to do is roll them up to even them off." He held up the sleeve ends, dangling them in front of Sam's face. "You want to keep these cuff links?"

"Yes, of course," Sam snapped.

"Okay. I'll stuff them in the jacket pocket," Eric offered. "Hey, Charley!" he yelled. "Charley, get out here!"

A young black man appeared on the porch of Eric's house. Charley, Sam had learned immediately upon arrival, was Eric's housekeeper, cook, and helmsman for the author's thirty-five-foot cabin cruiser, *Katya.* "Best damned helmsman on the island," Eric had insisted. "He can actually read the wave patterns and know where the fish are going before the fish know."

Eric held the jacket up, indicating that Charley should take it, and the young man hurried down for it.

"You want some lunch?" Charley asked as he took the proferred garment. "I can make some nice sandwiches."

"No. We're going down to Miguel's."

"You told me once don't ever let you go down there without something in your belly," Charley protested. "You go down there and drink too much and you'll get very sick."

"We'll eat some shrimp," Eric promised.

"How about dinner? Should I make dinner?"

"What do you have in mind?"

"I can make a nice fish chowder. I can keep it warm so it won't matter when you come back."

"Yeah, that's a good idea, Charley. Come on, Sam. No doubt there's some son of a bitch down at Miguel's who already has a head start on us. We'd better get there before he drinks up all the liquor."

Miguel's was just a short walk down the road that paralleled the beach. It was cool in the bar and, after the brightness of the coral road, so dark that it took a moment for Sam's eyes to adjust. Miguel, the owner, was behind the bar, and he smiled broadly at Eric and Sam when they stepped inside and the author hailed him.

"I know what you want, Eric," Miguel said as they took a couple of barstools. "You want daiquiris. What does your friend want?"

"A daiquiri will be fine," Sam said.

Miguel walked to the end of the bar and began mixing the drinks. Sam glanced around. Some half-dozen other drinkers were at the bar, while from behind came the click of billiard balls as a couple of men played pool.

"And all of your girls," Miguel called as he tossed ingredients into a cocktail shaker, looking at Sam, "do they drink daiquiris as well? Or do you make them drink only absinthe? I have heard that absinthe is an aphrodisiac, but I have never tried it out."

"All of my girls?" Sam asked, completely confused. He eyed Eric. "What is he talking about?"

"I told everyone that you own the biggest brothel in New York," Eric explained matter-of-factly, grabbing a handful of boiled shrimp from a large bowl on the bar. He began peeling them, dropping the shells into one of the many smaller bowls put on the bar for that purpose.

"Why did you tell everyone *that*?" Sam demanded.

"What the hell is Pendarrow House if it isn't a brothel?" Eric asked with a shrug. "I mean, it's a good comparison when you think about it. All the editors are pimps, all the writers are whores." He popped a shrimp into his mouth. "Hemingway doesn't peel them."

"What?" Sam asked. He was having a difficult time following Eric's train of thought.

"The shrimp," Eric explained. "Hem makes a point to eat the shrimp whole: skin, head, tail, and legs. He pretends he enjoys them that way, but you know what a pretentious bastard he is."

Miguel returned and put a couple of large daiquiris in front of Eric and Sam. "Someday when a very beautiful woman comes in here alone, if I can get some absinthe, I am going to try it," he said, continuing his discussion as if it had not been interrupted. " 'Have this nice drink,' I will suggest as I put the absinthe in front of her. And afterward, when she is dizzy and flushed and sexually aroused, I will say, 'Would you like to go upstairs and lie down? I have a nice bed in a cool room, and I think you would be very comfortable there.' And she will say, 'Yes,' and I will close the bar and go upstairs with her. 'Don't you think you would be more comfortable if you took off your dress,' I will say. And, of course, the absinthe will be working on her and she'll do it, because by now she will be so hot for me that she can no longer control herself. Her breasts will be round and hard like oranges, and the nipples will be like cherries."

"The last time they were like strawberries," Eric reminded him.

"Yes, I know, but I think cherries are better. They are a brighter red. Don't you think cherries are better?"

"Absolutely," Eric agreed, nodding sagely. "Cherries are better."

"And, at the belly button, here"—Miguel put his finger on his own belly button—"there will be a tiny line of hair, very light, very fine, you see, going down the lower part of her belly, pointing like a finger to the great mystery. Do you know what the great mystery is?" he asked Sam.

"Yes, I think so," Sam said.

"It is better, don't you think, to use such words as 'great mystery' than to use the vulgar name for it?"

Sam indulged the man. "Yes, I agree. It is better."

Miguel smiled, then continued with his story. "I will look at this line of very light, very fine hair, going down the lower part of her belly and pointing like a finger to the great mystery, and then I will not be able to take it any more, so I will remove all my clothes and climb into bed with her and spend the entire afternoon making love to her."

Eric clapped Sam on the back. "Congratulations," he said, then peeled another shrimp and popped it into his mouth.

"Congratulations?" Sam replied, frowning. "What for?"

"That's Miguel's favorite fantasy, and he doesn't ordinarily share that with anyone until after they've had five or six drinks. You got it on your first drink . . . before your first sip, even."

"Gee. Why was I so honored?" Sam asked dryly.

"Because you are a professional whoremonger," Miguel explained. "You know women like this, and you can appreciate them. So, tell me, Sam. Did you like the story?"

"Uh, yes," Sam replied, not knowing what else to say. "I liked it very much."

Miguel grinned proudly. "Everyone likes it," he said. "I have told Eric he should write it. He should put it in one of his books. Eric and I could become very rich if he would just listen to me. I have a lot of ideas for books. Really good books. Books people would like to read, not the kind of books he writes."

"But people already read the books he writes," Sam pointed out. "They regularly make the best-seller list."

"Who reads the books on the best-seller list? Only the high-toned people, that's who," Miguel protested. "Men who sit in overstuffed chairs in oak-paneled clubs and women who wear sunbonnets to keep out the sun and sit in wicker chairs beside the swimming pools while their maids keep an eye on the children. And they go to literary teas and talk about such books over aperitifs, because they want the other high-toned people to know that they read them because they were on the best-seller list.

"But who writes books for the truck drivers and the beauty shop operators?" he went on. "*These* are the books that are really important. Many more men go to bars than go to oak-paneled clubs. Many more women go to the five-and-dime than go to literary teas. If Eric would listen to me, I could make him rich."

"I'm already rich," Eric said, sliding his empty glass across the bar for a refill.

"Yes, but I could make you richer," Miguel insisted, taking the glass. He turned and walked down to the other end of the bar to make some more daiquiris.

Shaking his head with amusement, Eric turned to Sam. He seemed pensive as he briefly studied the editor. "I didn't think you'd come down," he then said.

"Why not?"

"I don't know. I thought maybe you were a permanent fixture up there. I was afraid you were mounted in concrete, like Mr. Melchoir, and like him, you could never leave."

"What do you know about Mr. Melchoir?" Sam asked, feeling his face reddening slightly.

"I know he's the gargoyle on the building across the street from your own. I know you've made him your pet and talk to him every day." Eric flashed a grin. "I *don't* know if he answers."

"You know all this about me and still you trust my editorial judgment?" Sam asked wryly.

"Maybe that's *why* I trust your editorial judgment," Eric quipped. "Anyway, I'm glad you're here." When Miguel returned with Eric's second drink, he took one look at his good customer and went back to the far end of the bar, sensing that his presence wasn't wanted.

Sam looked down at his glass and ran his finger around the rim for a moment, deciding whether he should keep up the pretext of the reason for his visit. He opted for the truth. Looking up again, he asked, "Eric, it wasn't just so I could be in on the finish of your book that you invited me here, was it?"

"No," Eric said, shaking his head.

"What is it? Why did you ask me down here?"

"I needed someone around for the next few days," Eric replied. He raised the glass to take a drink, and Sam was shocked to see a sheen of tears in his old friend's eyes. Eric took a swallow, then put the glass down. In a pained, husky voice, he said, "Sam, I don't know what I'm going to do. Tanner wants a divorce."

CHAPTER SEVEN

JUNE 18, 1934, NORTHEAST OKLAHOMA

Two other cars were sitting in front of the combination service station/general store when Del Murtaugh pulled in. As was his, they were piled high with the personal belongings of the occupants. One vehicle had a rocking chair tied to the luggage carrier in the rear; the other had an old grandfather clock lashed facedown to the roof.

It was funny, Del thought, what families decided to take with them when they moved. And there were a lot of people on the move now. The Great Depression had reawakened America's pioneer spirit, but instead of long trains of Conestoga wagons plodding along at ten miles per day on rutted, muddy trails, today's pioneers moved west in automobiles on ribbons of crushed gravel and cement, sometimes at speeds of up to fifty miles per hour.

Steam was hissing from the radiator of Del's Oakland when he braked to a stop in front of the gas pumps. He got out of the car and, using a short length of pipe he carried just for that purpose, poked at the radiator cap, turning it until air and steam began gushing out. After the air and steam came the water, surging up like a geyser and then raining back down on the dirty hood of the car.

Rubye, who had been leaning against the half-closed car window, asleep, suddenly sat up, rubbed her eyes, and looked around, wakened by the spewing, rushing sound. Del smiled at her and walked back to the window.

"Hello, sleepyhead," he teased gently.

"Where are we?" she asked, stretching.

Del looked over at the front of the service station. Hanging from the eaves of the front porch of the small, unpainted clapboard building was a hand-lettered sign reading BUSHYHEAD. Just below the sign, tacked to one of the wooden pillars holding up the porch roof, was a large thermometer with an illustration of a smiling, towheaded youngster wearing a Coca-Cola bottle cap as a hat, peering around the gauge. The slogan over the thermometer declared: *"Coca-Cola. The pause that refreshes!"*

Looking back at his new bride, Del admitted, "I don't really know where we are. That there sign says Bushyhead, but if it's supposed to be a town, this gas station's all I see of it."

"It's awfully hot, isn't it?" Rubye said. She pulled the top of her dress away from her sweating body and fanned herself, the only breeze obtainable in the stagnant air.

"Yeah, it's pretty hot, all right," Del said. "But we can take the heat. It's the car I'm worried about."

"What's wrong with the car?"

"The thermostat keeps sticking, and the engine's overheating. If this keeps up, we're goin' to burn out a bearing. Then we'll really be in trouble."

A man dressed in a pair of denim trousers, a red shirt, and a billed cap came out of the building. He shoved the match clamped in his teeth over to one corner of his mouth and asked, "You needin' gas, mister, or are you just after the free water?"

"I need about ten gallons of gas," Del said. "But I'll be wantin' some water, too, if you don't mind."

The man smiled. "Mister, I don't mind a bit givin' water to my payin' customers. What gets my goat is them deadbeats comin' through wantin' free water an' air an' the use of the bathroom, then goin' on their way without ever spendin' so much as one red cent. Ten gallons you say?"

Del nodded.

The attendant began working a handle back and forth on the gasoline pump, and the large glass cylinder at the top of the pump started filling with red-brown liquid. The man pumped until the gasoline in the cylinder was even with the ten-gallon mark, and then he took the hose and stretched it to the Oakland's gas tank. Fumes rose in shimmering waves from the open cap.

A group of people abruptly emerged from the service station bathrooms and started for the other two cars. There were three men in work overalls, seven children of various ages and gender, and three women who looked much older than it was likely they really were.

"Them's the kind I was talkin' about," the attendant said derisively to Del. "They used my soap, towels, and toilet paper, but they didn't buy one blessed thing."

"Seems like I been seein' lots of folks like that," Del said as the people piled uncomfortably into the two cars, which then pulled away with rattling frames and clanking engines. "Where are they all goin'?"

The service station owner looked at Del in surprise. "Are you kiddin' me, mister? What do you mean, 'Where are they all goin'?' You're one of 'em, ain't you?"

"I don't know. I reckon so. But I won't be on the road much longer. I bought me a farm."

"You bought a farm? What? You mean here in Oklahoma?"

"Yeah. I bought the Crawford place down near Langston in Logan County. You ever heard of it?"

The man slowly shook his head. "Can't say as I have." He flashed a crooked grin. "I take it all back, mister. You ain't like all the rest of them. They're all runnin' away from Oklahoma, you're runnin' *to* it."

"I reckon I am," Del agreed.

"Tell me this, mister. What you plannin' on *doin'* with that farm you bought?"

"Why, I'm plannin' on raisin' crops," Del replied, wondering why the man had just asked such a dumb question. Hell, he thought to himself, what else would a person do with a farm but raise crops?

"You know anythin' that'll grow in dust?" the man asked.

Del stared at him. "What are you talkin' about?"

"That's all there is left of Oklahoma farms now. Like as not the farm you bought is actually up in Kansas now or out in Wyoming or maybe even in Oregon or some such place. The topsoil's all blown away, mister. You ask these folks, they'll tell you they ain't leavin' their farms; they're just tryin' to chase 'em down." He laughed gruffly at his own joke.

"I don't reckon it can be as bad as all that," Del muttered.

"It's worse than that." By now the last of the gas was out of the glass, and the station owner screwed the gas cap back on.

"Maybe the problem with the folks in Oklahoma is that they just don't know how to farm," Del challenged.

For a moment the attendant's eyes flashed combatively as if he were going to accept Del's challenge. Then they changed, softening, and the combativeness was replaced by something that could almost be pity. Del liked the combativeness better, and he wished the attendant would have kept up the argument. Instead, the man returned the hose to the gas pump.

"Let's see, you had ten gallons. That'll be a dollar sixty-nine." He hooked the hose back into its holder on the side of the pump.

Del pulled his billfold from his pocket. "Whew," he said, handing over two dollars. "Gasoline sure is dear."

"I reckon that's why them folks that own oil wells is all rich," the man replied. He motioned toward the car. "Your lady looks awful hot, mister. We got some ice-cold sodies in there. There's Coke, Orange Crush, Grapette, Squirt, Spur

Cola, and RC. Just about whatever you'd want, we got, and they're all packed in ice water."

Del leaned down to the window. "You want somethin' to drink, Rubye?"

"Can we afford it?"

Del smiled. "I reckon we can. We're near about there now. Leastwise, we're in Oklahoma."

"A Coke would be nice," Rubye said.

Standing up, Del told the station owner, "All right. Bring her a Coke and bring me a . . . oh, bring me a Spur Cola, I guess. That's about the biggest, ain't it?"

"It and RC are about the same," the attendant said. He pulled out two dimes and a penny. "Here's your change, takin' out for the sodies. I ain't chargin' you no deposit on the bottles, so don't leave with them."

"We won't," Del promised. He walked over and looked at his radiator. "The engine has probably cooled down enough to put water in now," he said.

"Like I said, help yourself to the water. I'll bring the drinks out to you."

"No need for you to do that," Rubye called, getting out of the car. "I want to stretch my legs a bit, anyway. I'll come get them." She followed the man into the building.

Del pumped water into a bucket that had a long, flexible spout, then carried the full bucket around to the front of the car and began pouring the water into his radiator. The radiator hissed and snapped as the water hit the hot metal.

Del thought about what the station owner had said about the topsoil blowing away. He hadn't wanted to say anything to Rubye, but he had been fearing that same thing ever since they had reached Oklahoma. Yesterday he had seen in the distance a great black cloud of dust that rolled and billowed until the sky itself was turned a sulphur yellow. Was the man right? Was the farm he had bought worthless?

No, it couldn't be. He wouldn't *let* it be! He had been farming since he was old enough to walk behind a plow. There wasn't anything about dirt and seed and crops he didn't know. He would bring in a crop if he had to put each seed in the ground by hand and spit on it for the moisture.

He had done the right thing by leaving Missouri. He believed that . . . he *had* to believe that.

"Here's your Spur Cola," Rubye said, coming back to the car and handing it to him. A tiny piece of ice was clinging to its side. "Don't know why you like that better than a Coke."

" 'Cause it's bigger'n a Coke."

"Bigger isn't better," Rubye countered.

"Anyway it's good and cold."

"I'll say," Rubye agreed. "I had to stick my arm way down in the water to get these. It was so cold that it hurt."

"Yeah?" Del remarked, turning his own bottle up and taking several swallows, his Adam's apple bobbing. When he lowered the drink, he smiled at her. "I thought you was complainin' of bein' too hot."

"I was hot," Rubye said. "I'm still hot. Only my arm is cold."

"Maybe I should take you back in there and dunk you all over," Del teased, taking a step toward her. "Then you'd quit complainin' about being hot."

"Del, you wouldn't really, would you?" Rubye asked, taking a couple of steps back, not entirely sure he wouldn't do it.

"I might," Del said.

"If you do, I'll never speak to you again," Rubye warned.

"Well," Del retorted, "that might make it all worth it."

Rubye danced away from him, putting the car between them. Del lunged toward her, laughing. Then, tiring of the game, he turned and looked out toward the highway. It was supposed to be a gravel road, but there was very little gravel left. As a result, a constant cloud of dust lay over it, lifted into the air by the passing of each car. The cloud hung in the shimmering Oklahoma heat, rising and falling over a series of small hills and disappearing in the distance.

Rubye walked around to stand beside Del. Both drank their pop quietly for a moment.

"Is the gas station owner right, Del?" she finally asked, putting into words what Del was also thinking. "When we get there, will the only thing we find be a big pile of sand like what I saw drifted up against that barn we passed yesterday?"

Del eyed her in surprise. He had also seen that barn, and it had bothered him terribly, but he had thought Rubye was asleep when they drove by.

"You saw that?" he asked.

"Yes."

He started to lie to her, started to tell her that everything would be all right. Then he thought better of it. She was a part of it now, and she deserved to know his doubts and fears as well as his hopes and ambitions. He put his arm around her and pulled her to him.

"I don't know, darlin'," he said, sighing. "I just don't know."

"Don't worry, Del," Rubye replied, the tables turned now as she comforted him. "It'll be all right. Whatever happens, it'll be all right."

ST. LOUIS, MISSOURI

Kendra Petzold stood in the door of her office of *The St. Louis Chronicle* and looked out over the large, nearly empty newsroom. There were forty-five desks in the newsroom, though to conserve money the staff had been cut back to only twenty reporters. Since the overhead lights were left off where unnecessary, more than half the city room sat in perpetual shadow.

Kendra had listened to the debate as to whether or not she should have the extra desks removed. Her business manager had been in favor of getting rid of them; her managing editor had argued to keep them.

"It's like being in the military," the business manager had explained. "When a soldier is killed, the first thing the Army does is get rid of all his personal effects so that the other soldiers aren't oppressed by an empty bunk."

"Yeah, well, our reporters weren't killed," the managing editor had responded. "They were just laid off."

"It's pretty much the same thing, isn't it?" the business

manager had asked. "Besides, think how much money we could raise by selling the desks and chairs and typewriters."

"And think how much it would cost to replace them when business picks up again," the managing editor had countered.

"We aren't in any position to be thinking about business picking up," the business manager had said. "What we're more concerned with here is survival."

"But we can't think only of survival," the managing editor had insisted. "We have to believe that things are going to get better. You remember what Roosevelt said in his inaugural address. 'The only thing we have to fear is fear itself.' "

Kendra had listened to both sides of the argument, then made the decision. She would keep the desks, no matter how gloomy they made the newsroom look.

Kendra was only thirty-two years old, but widowhood had conferred upon her sole ownership of *The St. Louis Chronicle* as well as KSLM, one of St. Louis's first commercial radio stations. Though Kendra had achieved this position of authority by marrying Thomas Petzold, the founder of *The Chronicle* and KSLM, she did bring qualifications of her own to the job. She had studied journalism at Jefferson University and, before marrying Petzold, had been a very successful investigative reporter for the paper.

Since its founding over thirty years before, *The Chronicle* had grown into the city's biggest—and one of the nation's most influential—newspapers, and KSLM, though much younger, was already rivaling the newspaper in importance. But the depression was now jeopardizing all that Thomas Petzold had accomplished in his life. When St. Louis's retailers, hurting because their customers were, started trimming back their budgets, their first and largest cuts were made in advertising. When families began tightening their belts, they canceled their subscriptions to cut expenses. This loss in circulation further cut into the advertising so that over the past three years *The Chronicle*'s circulation was down by thirty percent, and its advertising revenue had eroded by over forty percent.

Though Thomas Petzold had fought hard to save his paper, its health seemed to be failing—ironically partly because it had grown so large that it now needed a great deal to support it. Another factor had been Petzold's own failing health. Early in 1932 he had collapsed and was hospitalized for three weeks with a serious heart condition. He had recovered from that attack, but six months later, as he was standing on the floor beside the huge web press and watching the print run of his ever-smaller paper whip through the ink drums, he collapsed again. An ambulance was called, but it was too late. Thomas Petzold lay dead on the pressroom floor. The chief press operator, who had been with Petzold from issue one of *The Chronicle,* stopped the presses on his own authority. He rethreaded the issue of October 13, 1932, and started it through again, printing it with a black border.

Kendra Petzold, who had quit working at the newspaper to raise their son, Tommy, then five years old, suddenly found herself saddled with sole responsibility for a struggling newspaper and a growing radio station. A number of people had advised Kendra to sell both immediately while there was still some value to the properties. After all, she didn't need the businesses to survive. Thomas Petzold had been personally a very frugal man, and he had left enough money for his wife and child to be quite comfortable. But Kendra had refused to give up, not only because she felt she had an obligation to her employees, but also because she knew how much the newspaper had meant to her husband. She intended that *The Chronicle* would continue to publish for as long as she could raise enough money to buy ink and paper.

Thinking back on all that now, Kendra wondered for a brief moment if she had made a terrible mistake. Then she squared her shoulders, shook off the pessimism, and stepped into the city room. Just as she did, Shaylin McKay, carrying a piece of paper in her hand, came in. Shaylin smiled at Kendra and called to her.

"Hello, Mrs. Petzold. Want a cup of coffee?"

"Sure," Kendra replied. "Why not?"

Shaylin walked over to the large, commercial coffee urn, filled two white porcelain cups, and walked over to Kendra, handing her one cup and keeping the other for herself.

"Shaylin, have you seen Tommy?" Kendra asked as she accepted the cup of coffee.

"I think he's down in the pressroom."

Thomas Amon Petzold, Tommy to one and all, was Kendra's seven-year-old pride and joy.

"I hope he's staying out of everyone's way."

Shaylin laughed. "You don't need to worry about him. Tommy knows his way around the pressroom better than I do."

"What are you working on?" Kendra asked, pointing to the paper the reporter was carrying.

"Oh, this isn't mine," Shaylin replied. "This is the Babs Benedict column."

Babs Benedict, a Hollywood columnist, wrote fascinating—some said scandalous—gossip pieces about movie stars and the motion picture industry. Her column was syndicated in more than one hundred fifty newspapers across the country, *The Chronicle* being one.

"I thought you didn't like her style," Kendra said. "Why the interest?"

"This particular column is about Demaris Hunter. I thought I might see if I could come up with a local angle."

"I see. Does Miss Benedict have some new scandal to report?" Kendra asked dryly.

"Of course she does. Would she even bother to write her article otherwise?" Shaylin quipped.

"Who does she have Demaris connected with now? Dick Powell? Clark Gable?"

"That's yesterday's news," Shaylin said with a wave of her hand. "The big love in her life now is Ian McCarty. Haven't you heard? They're about to get married."

The news took Kendra aback. "Is that a fact? I thought Demaris was married to Ken Allen, the cowboy star."

"She is," Shaylin said. "But she's getting a Reno divorce. That's what makes this romance so juicy. Anyway, with all the interest in her, I just thought I'd see if I could come up with something local to remind our readers that she's one of our own. I think she won some sort of beauty contest here, didn't she?"

"She was the Goddess of Love and Beauty for the

Veiled Prophet Ball," Kendra said. She reached for the article and Shaylin handed it to her.

"Oh, right. That was it. Anyway, I thought I might try to find some relative to interview."

"She has no family here anymore," Kendra said.

"No one?" Shaylin asked. "I mean, I know her father was one of those stockbrokers who committed suicide back in '29. But I thought I might be able to find *someone*."

"He died in 1930," Kendra corrected. "Then her mother died in '32. She has no brothers or sisters. Her mother has a sister who lives in Memphis."

Shaylin's eyebrows rose. "You must really be a fan to know all that. I'm impressed. Okay, if she has no family, maybe she's got some friends here."

"I know she has one," Kendra said quietly.

Shaylin sipped her coffee and studied Kendra's face over the rim of the cup. "You mean you, don't you?" she asked after a moment. "Mrs. Petzold, do you know her? I mean, did you know her before?"

"We were roommates in college."

Shaylin's mouth dropped open. "You *were*? I never knew that."

Kendra smiled. "There's no reason you should have known."

Shaylin took the column back and read it for moment, then looked up at Kendra. "You know, Mrs. Petzold," she said in a quiet voice, "if you'd rather we not run this story, if you'd rather I not try to do a local interest piece . . ." She let the sentence hang.

"No, no, run it," Kendra said. "Demaris chose this life for herself. Besides, our readers might find it interesting. That is, what readers we have left. And we need another human interest story, now that the Canfield-Dawson wedding is over."

"I, for one, am glad that it's over," Shaylin groaned.

Kendra laughed. "I know how you feel. I haven't forgotten what it's like to be on the hunt for a real story, but times are hard, and my circulation manager and advertising director tell me that that's the kind of stuff people like, so we have to give it to them."

"Well, we did," Shaylin said. "About the only way we could have given a wedding any more coverage would be if the Pope decided to marry Greta Garbo."

Kendra laughed. "Now that *would* be a scoop," she said.

"We could always start the rumor," Shaylin suggested, laughing with her boss. "We could run it for, oh, two or three days, then print a retraction." She held up her hands. "I can see the headline right now: *'Pope to marry Garbo.'* "

" *'To retire to desert island,'* " Kendra added.

" *'They want to be alone,'* " Shaylin put in.

" *'Garbo to quit acting; will make grass skirts instead.'* "

With every additonal subheadline they came up with, Kendra and Shaylin laughed harder until they were almost shrieking. Suddenly Kendra noticed a man standing by one of the deserted desks in the part of the city room kept in darkness. He was standing so quietly that she almost didn't see him, but his glasses caught a reflection from the lighted part of the room, and it was that flash that caught Kendra's eye.

Composing herself with great effort as quickly as she could, Kendra called, "Yes? Is there something I can help you with, sir?"

"You are Mrs. Petzold?" the man asked in a flat twang.

"Yes."

"I know you haven't endorsed my candidacy, Mrs. Petzold, but you have played square with me in your newspaper, and I want to thank you for that."

He stepped forward from the shadows, and Kendra immediately recognized him from pictures she had seen of him.

"You're Harry Truman, aren't you?" she asked, somewhat unnecessarily.

"Yes, I am."

Kendra gestured to the redhead beside her. "This is one of my reporters, Mr. Truman. Shaylin McKay."

Truman smiled broadly. "You wrote the article."

"Yes, I did."

"To be honest with you, I wasn't sure, by the name, if you were a man or a woman. I guess I just assumed you were a man."

Shaylin grinned. "I must confess that the ambiguity of my name sometimes works to my advantage."

"At any rate, it was a fine article," Truman said. "Aside from the fact that I obviously appreciated the content of the story, I also thought it was exceptionally well written."

"Thank you," Shaylin said.

"Would you like a cup of coffee, Mr. Truman?" Kendra asked.

"Don't mind if I do," Truman replied.

"I'll get it," Shaylin offered.

"Please, have a seat." Kendra gestured to a chair behind one of the empty desks. "That is, if you can find a place to sit in this busy establishment," she added wryly.

Truman's eyes widened in question for just an instant until he realized that Kendra was joking with him. He chuckled appreciatively as he pulled out a chair and sat down. Kendra pulled up another of the chairs, setting down her coffee cup on the empty desk that separated them.

"I guess being a big, important newspaper is no guarantee against feeling the effects of the depression," Truman noted.

"Would that it were," Kendra replied with a sigh.

"This depression can't last forever," Truman said. "And I think President Roosevelt is on the right track. I've been a big supporter of his."

"So I've heard," Kendra said. "The question is, does he support you?"

"Who supports me isn't important. It's more important that I support the President and his policies."

"Unfortunately, that isn't entirely true, Mr. Truman," Kendra said. Shaylin returned at that moment, carrying the cup of coffee. As Truman accepted it, Kendra added, "A great many people are very concerned over who is supporting you."

"You're talking about Tom Pendergast," Truman said.

"Yes."

"Tom Pendergast may support me, Mrs. Petzold. He doesn't own me."

"That seems to be true, Mr. Truman, and that's why our newspaper refused to join with the *Post-Dispatch* in calling you 'Tom's Boy.' Before Shaylin did her article, she examined the books very closely and found no evidence of any wrongdoing."

Truman nodded. "I'd be very surprised if she had, since I haven't done anything wrong."

"But," Kendra continued, "the fact that you haven't publicly denounced Tom Pendergast could make someone question your judgment."

"They might question my judgment, but they can never question my loyalty," Truman said with a smile.

"Is loyalty that important to you?"

"Yes, of course."

"What if loyalty and judgment come into conflict? What then?"

Truman took a swallow of his coffee and studied Kendra for a long moment.

"I'm a Democrat, Mrs. Petzold. And I come from an area of 'Yellow Dog' Democrats. Do you know what a Yellow Dog Democrat is?"

"I can't say that I do," Kendra replied with a shake of her head.

"A Yellow Dog Democrat is—and no pun is intended here—the most dogmatic Democrat you can be. A Yellow Dog Democrat would vote for a yellow dog if that was what the Democrats put up for election. But several years ago I voted for a Republican. Then two years ago when I ran in the Democratic primary for county judge of Jackson County, the fact that I had once voted for a Republican was brought out by my opponent."

Truman took another swallow of his coffee before continuing.

"I'm not sure if you fully understand the implications of that. To the Yellow Dog Democrats of Jackson County, what I had done was heinous, unforgivable. Of course, I had cast my Republican vote in the general election, which meant that it was a secret ballot. I could have denied it, and no one would have known the better."

"But you didn't deny it?"

"No, Mrs. Petzold, I didn't deny it," Truman said. "You see, that Republican and I, we served together during the war, sometimes in places that would make hell look like a playground. He was one of the most effective and dependable battery commanders I ever knew. He once kept his guns firing in the face of a fierce enemy attack when all the other batteries were pulling back. His battery single-handedly broke the German attack. He was a decent man and a loyal officer. I was proud of him. Proud of his courage and proud of his friendship. And I have no apology to make. Now, how could I deny that I voted for a man like that? I would have felt like Peter denying our Lord."

"So what did you do?"

"I went around and talked to those Yellow Dog Democrats," Truman said. "A lot of them were veterans, and the ones who weren't knew people who were. I told the veterans that I knew they understood what loyalty to a fellow soldier was. I figured if they knew the why of it, they wouldn't be so down on the what of it."

Kendra was impressed. "You obviously figured right. You were elected."

"By a wide margin," Truman said, smiling broadly.

"And you figure that same loyalty will serve you in this election?"

"If you're asking if I think it will get me elected, I don't know. But if you're asking if I figure loyalty to be a virtue worth standing up for, the answer is yes. I've got Tom Pendergast in my camp, Mrs. Petzold. I'll either be elected with him, or I'll go down with him. But he is my friend, and I'll not turn against him just because it's getting a little hot. My mother always said, 'If you can't stand the heat, get out of the kitchen.'"

"Mr. Truman, it's quite a step, isn't it, from being a county judge to being a United States senator?" Shaylin asked.

"I suppose it is," Truman admitted.

"And you feel that you're competent for the job?"

"It's a job, Miss McKay, and I've always handled whatever job I tackled. But to be honest with you, I figure that for about the first six months I'm going to wonder how the hell I ever made it into the U.S. Senate." A wide grin split his face as he set his coffee cup on the desk. "After that," he added, "why, I reckon I'll be wondering how the hell all the *rest* of them got there."

Kendra and Shaylin both laughed; then Kendra stood up and extended her hand.

"Mr. Truman, I truly hope you do get there," she said as they shook hands. "And, for what it's worth, you'll have the endorsement of this newspaper."

CHAPTER EIGHT

JUNE 29, 1934, NÜRNBERG, GERMANY

Frau Uta Tannenhower, still strikingly beautiful, flaxen-haired, and slender at thirty-seven, was enjoying the view out the window of the train whisking her and her family from Hamburg to Nürnberg when a knock sounded on the door of their private compartment. Responding, Uta found the porter standing there, bearing a silver tray laden with coffee and sweet cakes.

"Oh, but there must be some mistake," she said. "We didn't order anything."

"No mistake, Frau Tannenhower," the porter replied with a click of his heels. "This is with the compliments of the conductor. We will be arriving in Nürnberg soon, but before we do, Herr Helgen wished to express his admiration for Herr Gauleiter Tannenhower."

"Well, then, you must give the Gauleiter's thanks to

Herr Helgen," Uta said, reaching out for the tray. "And our thanks to you for delivering it."

"It was my pleasure, Frau Tannenhower." The porter clicked his heels again, bowed, then withdrew.

Uta brought the tray over to the table where her husband, Karl, the Gauleiter—party district leader—of whom the porter spoke, sat writing on a lined tablet. Now forty, Karl had achieved prominence and prestige that men twenty years older would envy. Uta thought her husband looked incredibly dashing—as dashing as he had when she had first met him some nineteen years before. Of medium height with blond hair and light-blue eyes, he had maintained a taut wrestler's build throughout his adult life—though Uta would have preferred him to be less muscular. He was meticulous in his appearance as well as his body, and his tan riding breeches were creased just so where they tucked into his tall, highly polished hobnail boots. The red armband on the left sleeve of his matching jacket, which was on a hanger behind him, had gold wreaths embroidered in the white background that encircled the black swastika, and the jacket's black collar tabs depicting golden eagles clutching a wreathed swastika in their talons also identified his rank within the party. A gold Sam Browne belt holding an officer's pistol completed the uniform.

Uta was pleased that Karl would be in full-dress uniform today, for that meant he got to wear, suspended from a narrow ribbon around his neck, the Blue Max. Uta felt immensely proud whenever her husband wore the medal. It was Germany's highest military award, and Karl, who had been the captain of an airship during the Great War, had earned it for acts of bravery. He also wore the Knight's Cross with Diamonds and the Iron Cross First Class. In that these were medals given for genuine valor, they set Karl apart from many other gauleiters. Their uniforms also bristled with medals, but Uta knew that they were generally for such things as "twelve-year member" and commemorative badges for various rallies.

Though Karl was not actually a member of the military, his position within the party called for him to wear a military-type uniform and authorized him to wear whatever awards and decorations he had won while in the service. As party leader of a major city, Karl was roughly equivalent in rank and prestige to a major general in the regular army.

"What have we here?" Karl asked Uta as she set the tray down.

"Coffee and sweets," she replied. She gave a small cake to Max, their sixteen-year-old son, and another to Liesl, their eight-year-old daughter. She started to give one to Karl, but he held up his hand.

"None for me," he said. "Just coffee."

"Why do you starve yourself so, Karl?" Uta scolded gently. "You exercise and lift weights as if you were still playing the American game of football. It's embarrassing. You have so many muscles that if someone saw you without your uniform, they might think you were nothing but a common dock worker."

As a young man, Karl had spent some time in America, attending Jefferson University in St. Louis, where he became a star football player. But after accidentally killing an opposing player during a game, he quit school and returned to Germany to fight in the war. He joined the Navy and was assigned to zeppelin duty, eventually commanding his own airship and leading several zeppelin raids over London.

"I've always followed good health practices, you know that," Karl said. "Besides, why should you be embarrassed if I am taken for a dock worker? Working on the docks is honest employment."

"But you are *not* a dock worker. You are a high official in the government."

"I am not a government official," Karl reminded her.

"Perhaps not, but you are a high official in the National Socialist party," Uta insisted. "And the National Socialist party is the government. Besides, the conductor gave us these sweets to honor you. It would hurt his feelings if you didn't eat at least one little piece."

"All right," Karl said, giving in to her persuasion. "But just one. I don't want to become as fat as Göring."

"Why not? Being fat certainly hasn't hurt him. He's now prime minister of Prussia."

"Not because he eats cake," Karl joked.

"The Führer eats cake," Max put in. "Lots of it. Funny. He eats cake, but he won't eat sausages."

"Why won't the Führer eat sausages, Papa?" Liesl asked. A dribble of chocolate had decorated her chin. Uta pointed it out, and the girl wiped it with a napkin.

"Because he is a vegetarian."

"What is a vegetarian?" Liesl asked, the words slightly muffled by the cake in her mouth.

"Someone who won't eat meat," Karl answered. "Now, will everyone please quit talking to me? I have to finish this speech. Though I don't know why I worry about it since no one will even hear it."

"No one will hear it? Why, how can you say such a thing?" Uta asked. "You will be speaking from the very podium the Führer will speak from. It's National Party Day, and hundreds of thousands of people will be there."

"Yes, but I will be speaking tomorrow afternoon, not tomorrow night when the real festivities begin," Karl explained. "The sun will be high, and people will be hot and confused and milling around, still trying to find their places. No one will be paying attention to anyone on the speaker's dais, believe me. I've been to enough of these things to know what it's like in those first few hours."

"My brigade will be out on the parade ground," Max said proudly. "*We* will listen to you, Papa."

Max, too, was in uniform, one that consisted of a tan shirt, dark-brown short pants, knee-length socks, and brown shoes. A Sam Browne belt, red armband, and garrison cap completed the uniform of the Hitler Youth. Collar tabs identified Max as a member of the Eric Dietzel Brigade of that organization.

"Very good, Max," Karl said dryly. "That means that out of two hundred thousand people, I can count on at least one hundred boys listening to me."

"And two girls," Liesl chimed in. "Mama and I will listen, too, won't we, Mama?"

Uta laughed. "That we will, dear. That we will."

"Papa," Max said, pointing at the window, "I think we must be coming into Nürnberg now."

"So soon?" Karl turned and looked out. "So we are. And I didn't even get to finish revising my speech."

"Your speech will be wonderful, dear. I know it," Uta said. "But you should be in uniform before we arrive. I want everyone who sees you to know that you are someone important."

Karl stood up and began putting on his jacket. "Paul Maas is going to meet me at the station and take me to the luncheon with Hitler," he said. "The Führer has asked that I sit next to him at the table—though for the life of me I don't know why."

Uta's heart leapt. "I am so proud of you, Karl," she said, her eyes gleaming with excitement. She checked his jacket and began removing minute pieces of lint, grooming him in a ritualistic validation of her position and blissfully unaware that an anthropologist could have pointed out the similarity between this and the ritual as practiced among the lower primates—though Uta would have bristled at any such comparison. "To think, you will be sitting right next to the Führer."

"You can get to the hotel by yourself?" Karl asked, reaching for his hat.

"But of course," Uta replied. "Don't you worry about us."

"I won't be going to the hotel, Papa," Max said. "I must take a bus directly to the stadium. My brigade will be camping in tents on the parade ground."

"You have to sleep outside?" Liesl asked, making a face. "I wouldn't want to do that."

"Oh, but it'll be great fun," Max said. "All the other brigades will be there, too."

The train abruptly stopped, then started backing up onto another track. A moment later the sky disappeared as the train slid under the roof of the great car shed at the Nürnberg Bahnhof. The Tannenhowers gave the compartment a final check to make sure they weren't leaving anything behind, then stepped down off the train.

"Karl! Karl, I'm over here!"

Karl turned toward the voice, spotted the source, and

waved. Turning back to Uta, he asked, "You're sure you and Liesl will be all right by yourselves?"

"Of course," Uta replied. "We'll take a taxi directly to the hotel. Don't worry. Now, go on. You mustn't keep the Führer waiting. I can't wait for you to get back to tell me all about the luncheon."

Giving his wife a quick kiss on the cheek, Karl hurried off, working his way through the crowd of travelers to reach his friend.

"Hello, Paul," he said when he had reached him. Noticing that Paul was in the black-and-silver uniform of an Obergruppenführer of the SS, Karl was puzzled. "Why aren't you in an SA uniform?"

"I have switched from the Sturmabteilung to the Schutzstaffel," Paul said.

"But why would you do such a thing?"

Paul smiled. "You'll understand it all later. I have a car outside. Are you ready to meet the Führer for lunch?"

"Yes, of course."

Karl was led by his old friend out of the station to a waiting car, a Mercedes convertible whose top was down. The driver, also wearing an SS uniform, stood at stiff attention as he held the door open for his two high-ranking passengers.

"Do you remember the early days?" Paul asked as they seated themselves. "The days of our struggle?"

"I remember."

"Many was the day we couldn't even afford carfare. And now look at us. We can ride through the city like this," Paul said. He beamed. "It's nice to be in power, isn't it?"

Karl chuckled. "Oh, I agree. It is much better to be *in* power than *out* of power."

"Look," Paul said enthusiastically, gesturing at the thoroughfare. "Look how the city has been decorated for our Party Day rally."

Indeed, Nürnberg was an absolute orgy of red. The red flags with the white-circled black swastika in the center flew from every building, from every pillar and post, and hung suspended from wires over all the streets. Once only the flag of the Nazi party, it was now by the decree of Chancellor Adolf Hitler the national standard.

From a distance the combined effect of all the flags was one of powerful physical substance. As the car drew closer to them, however, Karl could see that they were actually made of almost gauze-thin muslin. "Why, you can see right through the flags!" Karl exclaimed, surprised.

"Of course you can. That's by design," Paul replied.

"By design? Why?"

"Do you see how even the most gentle breeze lifts them? It allows them to float overhead so that they appear to cover Germany. It is most symbolic."

"Symbolic?"

"Yes. Symbolism is the Führer's greatest talent. He is absolutely brilliant at garnering the maximum effect from symbols. The flag, for example. He designed it himself, you know."

"Yes, I know. And it's very dramatic," Karl noted.

"Oh, it's much more than dramatic. It's dynamic. Consider the swastika. For twenty centuries the most powerful symbol of all mankind has been the cross of Christianity. But the Führer has managed to take that powerful symbol and make it even more powerful. He has turned a static symbol of acceptance and defeat—after all, it does symbolize a man dying on the cross, does it not?—into an angry, aggressive symbol. 'No man can be crucified on *this* cross,' the symbol says."

"I guess I hadn't considered that," Karl admitted.

"And that isn't all," Paul said. "Have you noticed that the swastika is always tilted, never straight up and down? That gives it forward motion. And the thickness of the arms is significant, too. If they were any thinner, they would look weak. If they were any fatter, they would look stagnant. So the swastika must be at just the right angle and dimension to achieve the maximum effect. Further, the red must be the exact shade. Not with a touch of yellow, like the red of the Communists, mind you, but with a touch of blue—the color of a patriot's blood."

"You seem to have made quite a study of this," Karl said.

Paul chuckled. "I guess I have. I find it all fascinating. Adolf Hitler is a man who charted his course from the very beginning. He rose from nothing to become the most powerful man in Germany—probably in all Europe and possibly in the world. And he did it by his own sheer genius with symbolism and showmanship. He hasn't made one mistake."

Karl didn't feel quite that certain. "What about the book burning?"

Paul frowned slightly. "What about it?" he asked.

"I've had friends in other countries tell me that they can't understand why we've done this."

"And what do you say to them?"

"I say nothing," Karl replied. "I don't know how to answer such accusations."

"You should tell those who ask such questions that it's yet another symbol, a ritualistic purging of the perfidious writings of all the false prophets who came before the Führer. By burning these books we're sending a message to our people to be loyal to the one, true way—the way of National Socialism."

"But don't you believe it could also be a symbol of fear?"

"Fear? In what way?"

"Fear of comparison. If all Germans believed, as I believe, that National Socialism is correct, then they would welcome comparison with other ideologies. In that way, you see, National Socialism would prove its superiority with each challenge."

"That may be fine for people like you and me, Karl," Paul replied. "We are thinking men, and we can discern the difference between the truth and cleverly disguised fiction. But so many of our people are unable to make this distinction. They are like sheep, easily led. It's our responsibility to see that they're led to the truth, and the easiest way to do that is to eliminate all ideas and dogmas other than those espoused by, or approved by, the guardians of National Socialism."

Karl gazed out the window. He supposed Paul was right. Certainly National Socialism was the salvation of Germany. Still, he did wonder slightly whether the people shouldn't be given the opportunity to reach that conclusion themselves.

During the course of their conversation, the car had passed through the labyrinthine streets of the medieval city and was now rolling down a broad, shaded avenue. The car suddenly slowed, turning off the street and through a guarded gate. It followed a long gravel driveway that wound through a beautifully landscaped formal garden.

"This estate belongs to Count Albert Kaufmann," Paul said just before the car drew to a stop in front of a great stone mansion.

A young man in black trousers and a white uniform jacket opened the car door for them. His uniform, too, had the stylized SS emblem that resembled twin lightning flashes.

"This is quite a place," Karl said, gazing out over the grounds.

"Yes, it is. The Führer will be staying here during the entire week of the rally and ceremonies. You know, there was a time when someone like the count wouldn't even look at Adolf Hitler. Now such men are falling all over themselves to make their homes available for his use."

Two more uniformed men, also wearing the runic markings of the SS, pulled open the great carved-oak doors, and a third escorted Karl and Paul inside. He led them down a long hallway lined on each side by suits of armor to a huge dining hall. The room was dark with stained-glass windows and heavy velvet hangings and furnished with massive Renaissance pieces, and it took a huge crystal chandelier and numerous electric wall sconces to overcome the gloom. Karl, who had expected to be one of at least a score of gauleiters present at the luncheon, was surprised to see that only ten places were set.

Hitler was over to one side of the room, talking to Prussian Prime Minister Göring, SS Reichsführer Himmler, and five other uniformed men. He spotted Karl and smiled broadly, then left the others and hurried over with his hand extended.

"Tannenhower," he said. "It is good to see you again.

And your beautiful wife, Uta, and your lovely children? Have they come to Nürnberg as well?"

"Yes, my Führer," Karl said. "Uta and my daughter, Liesl, are at the hotel. Max has gone to the campground to be with his comrades."

"Max is in the Hitler Youth, then?"

"Yes."

Hitler beamed. "That is wonderful. I am very proud of young men such as your Max. No other ruler in history has understood the youth as I do. All that I have done I have done for the youth, and when fate separates me from my duties, I will have left a corps of young people welded together by bands of iron."

"Fate will not call you for another fifty years, my Führer," Himmler put in reassuringly.

"Himmler reads the stars," Hitler said with a bemused smile. "So what he says must be true. Now, you know Himmler and Göring."

Both men nodded at Karl, who nodded back, though it wasn't easy to be so nonchalant. Göring, dressed in full uniform, was wearing face powder, rouge, eyeliner, eye shadow, and lipstick. Karl had first met Göring eleven years ago, and though even then Göring was making elaborate alterations to his party uniform, he hadn't yet gone so far as to wear makeup. When Karl first heard that the prime minister had taken up that practice, he hadn't believed it. Now that he saw it, he was hard-pressed to keep from staring—or laughing.

"You know how often I have spoken of the gallant young man who carried our standard during that ordeal of fire in Munich when first we thrust National Socialism onto the world scene," Hitler said to the others gathered. "Well, I am pleased to introduce you to that very man. Herr Tannenhower used our flag in a way that many might think disrespectful. When the Army opened fire on those of us who had linked arms for our march to glory, cutting us down with their machine guns from point-blank range, Karl Tannenhower went from man to man, tending to their injuries, using our flag to wipe away the blood from their wounds. The flag he carried that day is now the most sacred flag in all of Germany, for it is stained with the blood of those who became martyrs to our cause. One thousand years from now citizens of National Socialist Germany will draw inspiration from that flag and especially from the martyrs' blood with which that flag is stained. And I am proud to say that some of the blood on that flag is my own."

"What an inspiring story, my Führer!" one of the men gushed.

It might have been an inspiring story, Karl thought, but it wasn't entirely true. Hitler was right when he said that Karl had been carrying the flag and had used it to clean away the blood from some of the wounded. But since Hitler's injury was *not* an open wound, none of the blood was his. But recalling the conversation he had just had with Paul, Karl supposed that it didn't really matter whether any of the blood was actually Hitler's. It was *symbolically* his blood, and that was all that was important.

"And now, Obergrupenführer Maas, have you the medal?" Hitler asked.

"Yes, my Führer," Paul answered. He stuck his hand into his jacket pocket and pulled out a small box, which he handed to Hitler.

"Gentlemen, would all of you please come to attention?" Hitler asked. "You too, please, Gauleiter Tannenhower."

There was a clicking of heels as every man present, including Karl, came to rigid attention. Hitler opened the box and looked at its contents for a second. He then looked at Karl, and his eyes flashed with a kinetic power so strong that it almost seemed as if they could hold Karl prisoner.

"Gauleiter Tannenhower," Hitler said, removing the contents of the box, "I designed this medal myself. I had it struck for you alone, then had the mold destroyed. Therefore, this medal in my hand is the only one of its kind, and by my orders no other party medal will ever supercede it in importance. I am awarding it to you in honor of the bravery you displayed in Munich on November 9, 1923, at twelve-thirty in the afternoon, in front of the courtyard of the former War Ministry. Like the sacred blood on the flag you carried, may this medal be forever a glowing example to the people of the Reich."

The medal was a gold medallion with a bas-relief arm, the hand of which was clutching a flag. It was suspended from a V-shaped ribbon of red, white, and black.

"Thank you, my Führer," Karl said as Hitler pinned the medal to his tunic and the others applauded.

The ceremony thus concluded, Hitler suggested, "Well, then, shall we have lunch?"

"A very good idea, my Führer," Göring replied, hurrying to his place at the table. The others soon found their own places, then stood behind their chairs, waiting for Hitler. Göring, who had already sat down, realized at the last moment that he had committed a faux pas and quickly stood up again. He visibly relaxed when Hitler finally sat.

"Now," Hitler said, rubbing his hands together as he looked out over the table. "What have we for lunch?"

"My Führer," Göring said, snapping his fingers at one of the white-jacketed waiters who stood by, "I've taken the liberty of bringing some *Wurst von einem Wildschwein*."

A plate of sausages was put on the table. Smoking hot and aromatic, their rich, spicy aroma filled the room.

"I see," Hitler said disdainfully, looking at the sausages. "And tell me, Hermann, are we to understand that you murdered the poor beast yourself?"

"I took him in a hunt, yes," Göring replied.

Hitler sighed and looked at the rest of his lunch guests. "I am a tolerant man and so do not apply my dietary habits to others," he said. "Therefore, if any of you wish to become corpse eaters, eating the flesh of this dead animal Prime Minister Göring has murdered, you have my permission to do so."

"Thank you, my Führer," Göring said, oblivious to the disparagement, and he signaled to a waiter. The prime minister leaned back in his chair with his hands laced across his large belly, watching appreciatively as the waiter transferred a generous portion of the sausages to Göring's plate, then asked Karl, "Are you a hunter, Gauleiter Tannenhower?"

"No, I'm afraid not," Karl answered.

"I myself have hunted all sorts of game," Göring said. "I find the sport most invigorating."

"There is nothing to excite one about hunting," Hitler put in, accepting a bowl of cabbage soup. "How can one get excited about hunting when even someone with a fat belly can shoot any animal from a safe distance?"

"Hunting is as old as mankind, my Führer," Göring protested.

"Precisely my point," Hitler replied. "Perhaps in the days of the cave dwellers man's only means of survival was to eat the animals that didn't eat him. But he eventually discovered agriculture, a discovery that liberated him for all time. Man can grow his own food, which is more healthful and supplies his every need. And freed from the necessity of hunting animals just to stay alive, man has been able to develop in other ways. Ideas were born and culture was begun. Yet there are still some who cling to the prehistoric barbarism of murdering animals and eating dead flesh."

Hitler's monologue was persuasive enough to cause many of the others to stop eating the sausage, but Göring continued to relish the meat, totally unaffected by Hitler's disapproval.

Throughout lunch Hitler continued to dominate the conversation, which turned from diet to religion.

"Do you realize that the Moslems attempted to capture all of Europe but were driven back after the battle of Tours in the eighth century?" Hitler asked. "If they had won that battle, the entire world would be Islamic today."

"How so, my Führer?" someone asked dutifully.

"It's quite simple, really. You see, the Arabs would have remained in Europe just long enough to convert all of Germany to their religion. But ultimately the Arabs would have had to withdraw, leaving behind an Islamic Germany. And we Germans would have then spread the religion throughout the rest of the world. How much better off we would be if that were the case."

"Better, my Führer? You would prefer the Islamic religion to Christianity?" someone asked.

"Yes. Anything would be better than Christianity. It has been our misfortune to have the wrong religion. Better, even, that we had the religion of the Japanese, for they regard sacrifice for the fatherland as the highest good. Or that we would be Muslims with Islam's emphasis on spreading the faith by the sword, rather than Christianity with its meekness and flabbiness."

The conversation ebbed and flowed for a while longer; then Hitler looked over at Karl.

"Captain Tannenhower," he said, reverting to the title Karl had held at the conclusion of the war, "I didn't invite you here today merely to confer a special award upon you. You see, as I have elevated you, I have also elevated the flag you carried. It has become our sacred 'Blood Banner,' and with it I shall soon be performing a most important ritual."

He paused and shook his head slowly. "It is my sad duty to report that His Excellency, President von Hindenburg, is near the end. His doctors tell me that death could come at any time. When President von Hindenburg dies, it is crucial that we hold our country together, and I believe that that can best be done if I assume the office of president and chancellor."

"I agree, my Führer!" Göring said quickly, wiping sausage grease from his lips.

"As do I," Himmler added just as quickly. The others around the table, including Karl, were swift to add their own endorsement.

"There are some who would want us to return to a monarchy," Hitler went on, "or at least to a constitutional monarchy, similar to the government of the British."

Himmler snorted. "Fine for the British, perhaps, but not for Germany."

"I am glad everyone agrees with me," Hitler said, smiling. "But in order to make certain that everything goes smoothly, it is imperative that I have the support of the Army General Staff."

"They will support you," one of the other gauleiters said. "Surely they see how good you have been for the fatherland."

"They will support me," Hitler said, holding up his finger, "but only if I can guarantee them that the SA will not be in competition with the Army. Therefore, at the rally tomorrow night, I will officially make the Army the nation's only armed military force. And that is where you come in," he said, pointing to Karl.

"I am honored, my Führer, but I must confess that I don't know what role you may have for me," Karl said.

"That will be made clear to you tomorrow night," Hitler said with an air of mystery. "Of course, you understand that after tomorrow night there will no longer be an SA," he continued. "At least, not as we have known it. And as there are some functions that cannot be attended to by the Army, the SS will have to be greatly enlarged. I have left that up to Reichsführer Himmler."

Himmler beamed proudly, and Karl now understood why Paul Maas was wearing an SS uniform instead of the SA uniform he had worn for the past eleven years.

"And what of Ernst Röhm?" Karl asked. "Is he to become a general in the Army?"

"No," Hitler said, without elaboration. He bowed his head for a long moment and plucked at the bridge of his nose in silence.

"Allow me, my Führer, to speak for you," Göring put in. "Gentlemen," he said somewhat imperiously, addressing Karl and the other gauleiters, "we have recently learned most disturbing news. Röhm and the others of his staff are planning, and have been planning for some time, an insurrection."

Gasps of surprise were uttered from all around the table. "An insurrection? Röhm? No," one of the gauleiters insisted, "that can't be. He is the most loyal man in the entire country. He is devoted to the Führer."

"It is difficult to believe, I admit," Himmler interjected. "But the information I have gleaned on my own supports that of Göring. Röhm is planning a coup, perhaps as early as tomorrow."

"What . . . what is to be done about this . . . this treachery?" another of the gauleiters asked.

Hitler raised his head. He brushed the fall of hair out of his eyes and looked around the table at his guests, his gaze lingering on each man. Karl studied him in turn and saw a deep, profound sadness in Hitler's eyes. What he didn't know was whether it was genuine sorrow or sadness for effect—and he had the strange, rather disquieting feeling that Hitler didn't know either.

"As many of you are aware," Hitler said, "I have considered Ernst Röhm my oldest and dearest friend. He is the only man with whom I use the affectionate *'du.'* And yet the sense of obligation I feel to Germany and to the German people is such that I have no choice but to put friendship aside in order to see that the evil Röhm has planned does not happen. I promise you, before morning all will be set right."

When Karl returned to the hotel later that afternoon, Uta was aglow with excitement. She had bought a new dress for the ceremonies the next day and was trying it on, modeling and posturing before the mirror. As the wife of a high-ranking party official, she would have the privilege of sitting in the VIP section. Since more than one thousand other people would also be in that section, it wasn't exactly intimate, but there would be more than two hundred thousand spectators in the quarter-mile-long seating area, and there would be another hundred thousand or so, including Max, out on the parade grounds, taking part in the actual ceremony.

"How was your lunch with the chancellor?" Uta asked the moment Karl stepped into the room.

"It was most interesting," Karl replied. He smiled. "Incidentally, he asked about my beautiful wife, Uta."

"By name?" Uta asked, astonished. *"He remembered my name?"*

Karl chuckled. "Yes, of course he remembered your name."

"Oh," Uta said, fanning herself in excitement, "think of that. It takes my breath away to know that of all the women in Germany, the Führer actually remembers me and my name." She whirled once again before the mirror. "I bought red. The Führer likes red."

"And me, Papa?" Liesl wanted to know, jumping down

off the bed and running over to her father. "Did he ask about me?"

"Well, he did ask about my lovely children," Karl said, putting his hand on Liesl's head.

"That has to be me," Liesl said, squealing in delight. "Max isn't lovely."

Uta and Karl laughed. "You're right, dear," Uta said. "It has to be you."

Pointing to his uniform jacket, Karl asked, "What do you think of this? The Führer awarded me this medal today —which he says will be the only one of its kind." After describing its significance, he said, "I believe we ought to celebrate. What do my two favorite females say to being tourists for the remainder of the day?"

He decided not to tell Uta anything about the sweeping changes that were about to occur. She would find out soon enough, he thought. For now they should just enjoy themselves.

"Karl! Karl, wake up!"

Karl opened one eye. Judging by the light, it was still very early in the morning—much earlier than he had planned on waking.

"Wake up!" Uta repeated urgently.

Groaning, Karl turned over and looked at Uta, who was sitting on the side of the bed and staring at him anxiously. She was wearing a white-silk dressing gown, and it was dazzlingly bright in the beam of sun that poured in through the window. The gown gaped open at the top, revealing one breast all the way to the nipple. It was an arousing sight and a pleasant way to start a new day.

"Good morning," he said, reaching for her with a smile.

"Karl, I'm frightened," Uta said, pulling the dressing gown closed. "Something is happening."

The fear on Uta's face and the tremor in her voice cooled Karl's ardor. He sat up and ran his hand through his hair.

"What is it?"

"I'm . . . I'm not sure," Uta replied. "When I turned

the radio on this morning, the newscaster was reporting it. There has been a putsch of some kind, a revolution."

"Hand me my robe," Karl said.

Uta took a wine-colored robe from the closet and handed it to him; then both moved into the sitting room to listen to the news broadcast, given by an excited announcer in breathless fashion.

". . . *According to Reichminister Goebbels, Chancellor Hitler, Prussian Prime Minister Göring, and Reichsführer Himmler flew to Munich, then drove to the Hotel Hanselmayer in Bad Wiessee, where they surprised the plotters in their lair. There, the chancellor dealt personally with the treachery of Captain Ernst Röhm, Chief of Staff of the SA, and with Karl Ernst, leader of the Berlin SA. Before dawn this morning Captain Röhm was summarily tried before an honor council, found guilty of treason, and offered the opportunity to take his own life. In the cowardly manner of a traitor, he refused and was executed for his crimes. Karl Ernst was killed while attempting to escape.*

"The SA leadership was not acting alone in their treachery, for former Chancellor Kurt von Schleicher was also involved. Von Schleicher and his wife were killed while making an armed resistance against the arrest.

"In addition to the treasonous plotting that was taking place in the hotel where the SA leadership was arrested, Röhm and other members of his staff were engaged in deviant and immoral behavior too perverted to be mentioned here—although their hedonistic activities could perhaps be appreciated from the menus of the meals the revolutionaries consumed during the debaucherous days they spent while plotting the revolution. The meals included such non-German fare as frogs' legs, birds' tongues, shark fins, sea gulls' eggs, and vintage French wines and champagnes.

"President von Hindenburg issued a statement today, praising Chancellor Hitler and Prussian Prime Minister Göring for their quick and decisive action in stamping out the revolution that would have endangered the entire German people.

" 'When circumstances require it, one must not shrink

from the most extreme action,' President von Hindenburg stated. 'One must be able to spill blood, also.' "

"Oh, Karl, I'm frightened," Uta said, her voice barely above a whisper. "What does all this mean?"

Karl turned off the radio. "It means Hitler has just won over the Army," he said flatly.

The telephone rang, and Uta, who was closest, picked it up.

"Frau Tannenhower here," she said. She then gasped. "Yes! Yes, at once!" She covered the mouthpiece of the phone and looked at Karl with eyes wide with alarm. *"It's the Führer!"*

Karl took the phone. *"Jawohl, mein Führer."*

"You've heard?" Hitler asked.

"On the radio. Just now."

"But you didn't hear everything," Hitler said. "You can never imagine what we found when we went into Röhm's room at two o'clock this morning, Tannenhower. He was in bed with another man! They were together, naked! And not just Röhm! In all the rooms we found naked young men sharing beds. Even if he had not been plotting to overthrow my government—even if he had not been plotting to kill me—he could have been found guilty on perversion alone."

"I am glad the plot was discovered and the revolution broken," Karl said.

"Yes. I must say, it was a dangerous night. I suppose there are some leaders who would not have taken the risk I did, but I felt it was necessary, even though I didn't know whether they would have armed guards to use against us. Did you hear? I offered to allow Röhm the honorable way out, but he refused. To think that someone who had been awarded the Blue Max for bravery would refuse to take his own life. 'If Adolf wants me dead, let Adolf kill me,' is what he said. Well, he wouldn't do the honorable thing, and I wouldn't give him the satisfaction. I had him executed like any other common prisoner."

"I'm sure it was difficult for you, my Führer," Karl remarked, not knowing what else to say. He wondered why Hitler had called him.

"Tannenhower, you remember I told you yesterday that

you would play an important part in bringing the Army under my control?"

"Yes, I remember. You didn't tell me what I was to do, however."

"You will be my flag bearer," Hitler said. "Tonight you will stand beside me, holding the flag you carried on that fateful day in Munich."

Carrying a flag was something normally reserved for a private, Karl thought. He didn't know why Hitler wanted him to perform such a mundane task, but if that was what his Führer wanted, that was what he would do.

"I shall be honored," he said.

"You should be very honored, Obergrupenführer Tannenhower. When the history of this glorious event is recorded, it will be recorded that the one who carried the flag when it was first stained with the blood of heroes was the same man who carried it for the sacred ceremony to bring the Army under my command."

"Excuse me, my Führer, but what did you call me?"

"Obergrupenführer. I have decided that you are not only to be Gauleiter of Hamburg, you are also to be a major general in the SS. I instructed Himmler to put your name on the rolls this morning. I shall want you in that uniform tonight. You will, of course, be drawing pay for both positions." Hitler chuckled. "It's a little way I have of rewarding loyalty."

"Thank you, my Führer," Karl said.

Hitler broke the connection, and Karl lowered the receiver.

"What is it?" Uta asked as Karl hung up the phone.

"Hitler plans some ceremony whereby the SA will be placed subordinate to the Army. During this ceremony I am to stand beside him."

"You will be standing beside the Führer? Oh, Karl, all eyes will be on you! How proud I am of you!"

"Yes, well, I'll have to get another uniform ready."

Uta shook her head in confusion. "But you had a new one made just for this rally."

"It's the wrong uniform," Karl said. "I've just been appointed a major general in the SS."

"*A major general!*" Uta exclaimed, barely able to contain herself. "Karl, can you imagine? Oh, what a wonderful time we are living in! Who would not love Adolf Hitler?"

"Some of Röhm's friends might have a hard time," Karl suggested dryly. "Well, I had better get dressed if I'm going to go buy a uniform."

"Why go out?" Uta asked. "I can call a tailor and have him come to you. You are much too important a man to do your own shopping."

She fussed over him for a few moments, then began making telephone calls. Karl listened briefly to her conversation, then walked over to the window and looked out across the wide plaza that separated the hotel from the railroad station.

Scores of Nazi flags flew for as far as he could see. He had to admire Hitler. After tonight, the man's power would be all but absolute. With the Army behind him it would be a simple thing to consolidate the offices of chancellor and president into one. And why not? In England the power was with the prime minister, and in the United States the power was with the president. It was ridiculous to divide the duties of head of state between two men.

Politically, Karl could agree with Hitler. But something was nagging at him, and though he wouldn't speak of it, he couldn't keep the unflattering thought from surfacing. Hitler was making a big thing about Röhm's homosexuality—as if it were something he had just learned. In fact, Hitler and everyone else of any consequence already knew about Röhm's sexual preference and had known about it for many years. Why now was Hitler finding it so disturbing?

Karl tried to imagine what it must have been like for Röhm to be suddenly and rudely awakened in the wee hours of the morning by having someone kick open the door and rush in. It had to be both terrifying and humiliating. Karl had never particularly liked Röhm, had always thought him to be mean and a bully. Nevertheless, he couldn't help but feel a little sorry for him.

Still, it was necessary that there be major political change if Germany and her people were to regain their former strength. And turbulent events were to be expected.

BERLIN

"You don't seriously think anything will change, do you?" Simon Blumberg asked. He picked up an empty laboratory beaker and idly fingered it.

"Yes, I do," Dr. Sigmund Rosen replied firmly. He ran his hand across his forehead as if brushing back a shock of hair, but he had such a high forehead that there was nothing to brush back. His liquid brown eyes were slightly drooping and vaguely Oriental, while his ruddy cheeks looked as if he had just come in from a cold, brisk wind—though, in truth, they looked that way all the time.

"You are much too naive, Sigmund. You have spent too much time with test tubes and microscopes."

"But things must improve now," Dr. Rosen insisted. "Hitler has eliminated Röhm and the Brownshirts, and they are the ones who've been causing all the trouble. They are the ones who've been beating up Jews on the street and breaking out the windows of Jewish homes and shops and desecrating the temples."

"They couldn't have done all that without Hitler's approval."

"But he didn't approve, don't you see? He didn't approve at all, and last night he took action. I think that period is over, thank God."

"What Hitler did last night was purely political," Simon insisted. "The SA was becoming an embarrassment to him, but it had nothing to do with any change in his beliefs. Don't forget, I once knew him."

"Yes, many years ago you knew him, when the two of you were in the war together. But you have said yourself that the Hitler you know today is not the Hitler you knew then."

Simon replaced the beaker and looked directly at his companion. "Herr Doctor Rosen, my good friend, some things never change. Hitler was anti-Semitic then, and he is anti-Semitic now. The only difference is, then all he could do was rant and rave. Now he is the chancellor of Germany with the power to do more—much, much more—than rant and rave."

"And yet he did eliminate the SA, and that gives me

hope," Rosen said. He looked at Simon with eyes that were almost pleading. "Surely, Simon, you don't wish to deny me the tiniest ray of hope?"

Simon sighed, then smiled condescendingly. "No, Sigmund, I would not want to do that."

"Good. Now, would you like some more coffee?" Rosen held a china coffeepot over Simon's cup.

"Yes, thank you."

"No, it is I who should be thanking you, Simon, for the wonderful gift of a pound of coffee. I didn't realize how much I had missed it until I smelled it brewing. But its cost is so dear, and ever since the university reduced my salary, I have had to be extremely parsimonious about what I spend."

"It is unbelievable that they cut your salary," Simon said. "Why, you are one of the most respected physicists in all of Europe."

"Thank you for your kind words." Rosen poured himself a second cup of coffee and took a sip with obvious appreciation. "The problem, of course, is that the university has introduced all those new courses, and new courses mean additional instructors who also must be paid, and yet the total amount of money available to the staff and faculty has remained the same. Therefore, the rest of us have had our salary reduced."

"And you have taken the biggest reduction of all."

"Yes," Rosen admitted.

"Racial Theory . . . Aryan Principles . . . German Purity . . ." Simon said, scowling over each subject. "All quack subjects taught by imbecilic Nazis at high salaries, while the real teachers and scientists suffer."

Rosen sighed. "Simon, I'm just glad I still have a job. Do you have any idea how many Jews remain at work in a university environment?"

"Not many, I'm sure."

"Practically none. And if it weren't for the nature of my work, I might not even have my job."

"Yes, well, you'd better be careful or before you know it, they'll want you to start teaching Aryan Physics," Simon scoffed.

Rosen laughed too. "You don't know how close to the

truth that statement is. However, I do no teaching at all now." He grimaced. "The authorities don't want German minds contaminated by Jewish ideas. But I'm just as glad. That gives me more time to work on my project."

"What exactly is this project you're working on?"

"It has to do with matter and energy and Dr. Einstein's equation, $E = MC^2$," Rosen explained. "Right now I'm working on isotope enhancement."

Simon chuckled. "You are way over my head, Sigmund. I don't even know what you're talking about. But tell me, is this research for the sake of research? I mean, if you're successful, will knowledge be its own reward?"

"Yes, of course."

"It's no wonder you're so naive about other things. You spend your entire lifetime working in a world that few others even know exist and fewer still can understand. And all for the intangible sake of knowledge."

"That is the nature of academia." Rosen shrugged. "Of course, to say it's all intangible is a misstatement. There's practically no limit to the amount of energy that would be released if a controlled atomic reaction could be generated. Which is understandable when you realize that this is precisely the energy that causes stars to explode," he concluded, holding up his hands.

"What?" Simon asked. "You've lost me again."

"Atomic energy," Rosen replied. "Scientists now believe that the stars that are sometimes seen to explode do so because of a runaway reaction from splitting atoms."

"And that's what you are trying to do?"

"Yes. No."

"Which is it? Yes or no?"

"I am working on a concept that would prove the theory of atomic energy. I do *not* intend to actually bring about an atomic reaction."

"If you could, what would you have?"

Rosen chuckled. "If I couldn't control it, I would have an exploding star. Only the star would be the planet Earth."

"And if you *could* control it?" Simon suddenly had a very ominous feeling about all this.

"A device for releasing energy."

"Like a bomb?"

"A bomb? Yes, I suppose you could call it a bomb. Though it would be very difficult to think of it in those terms. Besides, I never think of such things when I'm working."

"Someone has," Simon said grimly, "or you wouldn't still be working."

NÜRNBERG

The scene at the parade grounds that evening took Karl Tannenhower's breath away. Architect Albert Speer had created the spectacle, and the centerpiece of his design was a gigantic, stylized eagle clutching a swastika in its talons and spiked to a timber framework, much like a butterfly in a collection. As the wingspread of the eagle was over one hundred feet from tip to tip, it dominated the scene and gave the effect of taking everyone in Germany under its huge wings.

Then at a precise signal there came from each corner of the parade ground thousands upon thousands of uniformed marchers, moving toward each other in four long columns. All the marchers were carrying torches so that it appeared as if four rivers of fire were flowing together.

Around the perimeter of the parade ground one hundred and thirty searchlights spaced at forty-foot intervals sent sharply defined beams of light some twenty-five hundred feet into the air, where they merged into a general glow. The overall illusion was one of an enormous shimmering dome held up by towering pillars of light. The effect was both solemn and beautiful.

From a high concrete wall very near the VIP stand fifteen uniformed trumpeters appeared in a flood of light. Their long, thin, highly polished ceremonial trumpets reflected shimmery glints from the searchlights and the torches, making the brass instruments look as though they were alive. From the bell to the mouthpiece of each horn there hung a large red banner with the ubiquitous Nazi emblem. The trumpeters raised the instruments to their lips, then played the first four notes of a stirring fanfare.

From nearby the notes echoed.

Then they echoed again from somewhat farther away.

Finally there was a third echo, the music faint but clearly audible and hauntingly beautiful.

At the conclusion of the fanfare a battery of one hundred timpani took up a steady drumming. The pulsating rhythm of the kettledrums moved into the bloodstream and heartbeat of everyone present, not only the marchers on the field, but the spectators in the stands and the dignitaries in the VIP section. As the drums throbbed, the four rivers of fire came together, joined, then bent sharply, shaping into a flaming swastika.

Karl waited for his signal. When it came, he took the bloodstained flag and followed Hitler down a long flight of torchlighted stairs, then stood in the center of the parade ground. The flag bearers from all the major Army units then began marching by, and as each flag bearer passed Hitler, the soldier would stop and dip his colors. At first Karl thought the colors were merely being dipped in a salute. Then he saw what Hitler had in mind. The Führer would touch the "Blood Banner" to the flag of the Army unit, the idea being to pass on to the Army flags the "spirit" of the Blood Banner. Those Army flags would later anoint other unit flags, thus infusing the spirit of National Socialism into every flag in the entire Army.

After the flag ceremony came the oath. One hundred thousand officers and soldiers chanted as one, swearing allegiance not to Germany, but to Adolf Hitler personally:

"I swear by God this sacred oath that I will render unconditional obedience to Adolf Hitler, the Führer of the German Reich and people, Supreme Commander of the armed forces, and will be ready as a brave soldier to risk my life at any time for this oath."

When the oath was completed, Karl Tannenhower felt a chill run down his spine. He was witnessing history being made, witnessing an event that was surely destined to be long remembered. Though President von Hindenburg was not yet dead, Karl knew that Adolf Hitler's control of Germany was complete and ironclad, and his destiny and that of his people were now inexorably linked.

CHAPTER NINE

JULY 1934, FRANCE AND GERMANY

When John and Faith Canfield finally stepped onto European soil after completing their trans-Atlantic crossing, they motored up through France to the small port town of Dunkerque—or Dunkirk, as the English insisted on spelling it. There they spent a week in a room in a tiny hotel overlooking the English Channel.

For the whole of that time they were completely self-absorbed, talking only to each other except when it was necessary to speak with the desk clerk or to order meals. They slept late every morning, woke up in each other's arms, and made love before getting out of bed. Most of the time they did nothing more than stroll around town arm in arm, taking lunch at one of the many sidewalk cafés—though oftentimes they went no farther than the hotel dining room so they could then hurry back up to their room and make love again.

In the evening they walked hand in hand along the

beach, watching the bloodred orb of the setting sun as it dropped slowly into the channel. Sometimes after dark they visited one of the many small bistros, where a band might be playing. But most of the time they hurried immediately back to their room, where they made love with the window open and listened to the night sounds drifting in. Then, naked, they stood at the window, just looking at the rippling moonlight on the channel. Finally they made love one last time so they could wake up the next morning in each other's arms.

After their stay in Dunkirk they went to Paris, accepting the invitation Marcel Aubron had issued on the *Valkyrie* during the crossing. Marcel was justifiably proud of the role his café had played in the literary output from the expatriate Americans during the decade just after the war, and barely had John and Faith walked in the door when the restaurateur showed his guests the respective tables used by Eric Twainbough and Ernest Hemingway when Marcel's Café had been their hangout. Marcel had hung a shelf on the wall above each of the two tables, displaying the books the writers had personally autographed to him. There were also autographed photographs of Twainbough and Hemingway, and Faith quipped that they looked so much alike that she believed she could switch the pictures in the frames and many might never know.

The inscription on Hemingway's photograph was written in bold, aggressive script across the bottom.

> When the weather was cold and raining, the writing here was always good. When the weather was clear and fine, the writing was good too.
>
> Hem

The words on Twainbough's portrait seemed somewhat less aggressive, perhaps because they were written in cursive letters.

> There may be other books. There may be better books. But there will always be only one first book, and it was written here.
>
> With warm regards,
> Eric

The honeymooners stayed for a week in Paris, enjoying having their own personal tour guides in the forms of Marcel, his wife, Denise, and their charming fourteen-year-old daughter, Chantal. But finally—and reluctantly—they had to leave the City of Light and continue on with their itinerary.

They arrived in Nürnberg in time to witness the giant Party Day rally and were suitably impressed with all the pomp and pageantry. John's father had made arrangements for them to have dinner with Karl Tannenhower and his family, and this they did. However, despite their connection—Karl had been a good friend of John's late uncle Willie at Jefferson University—John found that Karl was now so high up in the Nazi party that the visit was actually quite uncomfortable, for he and Faith had to walk on eggs to avoid saying something controversial. Skirting taboo subjects like politics and economics, they were left with small talk about such things as American football. Karl was surprised to learn that his picture hung in the Jefferson University Bears' locker room for having been named to the All Decade team for the 1911 to 1920 period.

In contrast to their visit with the Aubrons, John and Faith felt no reluctance about saying good-bye to the Tannenhowers, and they returned to their hotel feeling much more lighthearted. Relieved that their obligatory visit with Obergrupenführer Karl Tannenhower was over, the young couple looked forward to continuing on with the rest of their European tour.

Though they had had reservations for first-class train travel and accommodations in the finest hotels while they were in Germany, they decided at the last minute to do something different. John rented bicycles for them, and they pedaled through the countryside, staying in the hostels and *Gasthäuse* of the small villages they found along the way. John figured that it would be a good way to get a firsthand feel as to how things really were in the country—as opposed to how Karl Tannenhower and the Nazi-dominated press said things were. He was sure he'd be taking back to America an account of an oppressed people just waiting for the opportunity to throw Hitler out. To his complete surprise he learned that quite the opposite was the case. Karl had been right when he had insisted that the vast majority of Germans were enthusiastic supporters of Adolf Hitler. In fact, from what John was able to determine, Adolf Hitler probably enjoyed a broader base of support from his people than Franklin D. Roosevelt did from his.

"The inescapable conclusion," John wrote in the letters he sent back to his father and father-in-law, "is that the average German citizen has willingly traded his freedom for a full lunch bucket."

The honeymooners' next scheduled stop was Vienna, and they arrived there by train on the morning of July 29, their itinerary calling for a week's visit to Austria before finally returning home. Their Viennese host would be David Gelbman, formerly of St. Louis, who after graduating in the same class at Jefferson University as Bob Canfield had come to Vienna to help a relative with a financially troubled department store. What was supposed to be a temporary stay had turned permanent when David met and fell in love with Anna Rosenstein, a beautiful young Viennese and an ardent Zionist. He had married her and, except for a couple of rare visits back to St. Louis, had been in Vienna ever since. That was thirty years earlier, and David now considered himself more Viennese than St. Louisian.

David and Anna had had two children. Their daughter, Miriam, had just turned twenty-two; their son, Leo, would have been sixteen, but he had died six years earlier after contracting pneumonia. From a letter David had written recently to Bob Canfield, John knew that though the Gelbmans' would always mourn their lost child, the passage of time had served to mollify their pain to an underlying sadness. So as not to aggrieve David and Anna, John and Faith had decided to avoid any mention of Leo during their visit.

Stepping off their train in the Westbahnhof depot, John and Faith Canfield were met with the almost overpowering smells of coal smoke, steam, and teeming humanity along with various aromas of bratwurst, kraut, and freshly baked bread emitted by the many kitchens of the huge depot. The shed was a symphony of sound—steel wheels rolling on steel tracks, clanging bells, chugging pistons, rattling cars, shouted orders, and the murmur of hundreds of conversations.

They had just started toward the entrance when Faith pointed to a man holding up a chalkboard on the end of a long pole. On the chalkboard was written: JOHN CANFIELD.

"John, look," Faith said. "He must have been sent by Mr. Gelbman."

John called and waved to the man. "Hello! Hello, sir! I'm John Canfield!"

The man with the sign signaled that they should follow him, and he led the young couple through the crowd to a middle-aged, well-dressed, pleasant-looking man who started coming toward them, smiling broadly as he approached.

"Welcome to Vienna, folks. I'm David Gelbman," he said in slightly accented American English. "So, you are Bob's oldest, are you? I met your brother, Willie, seven years ago when he made that wonderful flight from New York to Vienna, and I've been looking forward to meeting you as well." David shook John's hand heartily.

"It's a pleasure, Mr. Gelbman."

"Please, please. Call me David."

John smiled. "David. And this is my wife, Faith."

"Well, what a pleasure this is. John, I see you've inherited your father's eye for beauty," David said admiringly. "Faith, you are every bit as beautiful as John's mother—and that is saying a lot. Now, give me your luggage tags and I'll have the cases brought to my car, which is just outside the entrance."

John handed over the baggage claims, and David secured the services of a porter, who scurried to collect the suitcases.

"Come along," David said, leading the way. "My wife, Anna, and my daughter, Miriam, are at home, getting things ready for your visit. They've been as anxious for you to arrive as I."

"Thank you," John said as they started weaving through the crowd toward the street door. "We've been looking forward to meeting all of you as well. Oh, and before I forget, my parents send their kindest regards, and they're wondering when *you* will come for a visit."

David pushed through the entrance door and ushered them to his waiting car, a sleek, black Mercedes. He waited until the luggage was loaded and they had all piled inside before responding to John's question.

"I can't really answer that," David said as they pulled into traffic. "I know I should come sometime, but since both of my parents are now gone and I no longer have any financial interest in the St. Louis store, there really isn't much to bring me back."

John smiled. "That's exactly what Pop told me you'd say. So he told me to ask you, 'What do you mean you have nothing to bring you? What are your friends? Chopped liver?' "

David laughed loudly as he shifted gears and turned a corner. "That sounds just like *your* father trying to sound like *my* father." He sighed. "Seeing as how Bob and I are the only Quad Quad members left, I suppose we really should get together sometime." He briefly turned his head toward John, then asked, "Do I need to explain the Quad Quad, or has he told you about it?"

"Are you kidding?" John replied. "You and Pop are two of the most honored alumni of the university. You were founders of the Quad Quad."

David's expression was one of confusion. "Founders? What do you mean, founders? There was nothing to found. We were just four people who used to hang out around the Spengeman statue in the middle of the quadrangle. Four in the quad. That's why we started calling ourselves the Quad Quad. It was nothing more than that."

"Maybe so, but nowadays being elected to the Quad Quad is the highest honor that can come to any Jefferson University student," John explained.

"*What?* You mean it's still going on?"

"Yes, sir, very much so. At the beginning of each academic year four people are selected by the faculty and student body. They are inducted into the Quad Quad in a very solemn ceremony."

"John was a Quad Quad," Faith said proudly, putting her hand on her husband's shoulder.

"Well, I'll be," David said in a bemused voice. "Who would have thought that something we dreamed up for fun would one day be an honored institution? Tell me, what is the purpose of the Quad Quad?"

"Well, one of our charges is to tend to the monument of Jefferson's founder. We're the only ones authorized to touch the statue, so keeping it clean is our responsibility. But of course, it goes beyond that."

David smiled. "You want to know something interesting? A few years ago I bought a book on sculpture and sculptors, and of course it had a section on Rodin. And there, right alongside 'The Thinker,' was our Professor Henry Spengeman. It made me feel good."

"The Spengeman statue is one of the first things prospective students want to see when they tour the campus," Faith put in.

Chuckling, David mused, "It's nice to know that some things, at least, don't change. It was that way when I attended Jefferson, too." He downshifted then, and said, "We're almost there. Just a few more blocks."

He turned a corner and suddenly slammed on the brakes as a large mob of unruly men wearing uniforms and Nazi armbands came rushing out into the street. They were shouting and cursing, and as they passed right in front of David's Mercedes, one of them leaned across the grille of the car and looked in through the windshield. His face was twisted into an expression of hate and anger.

"Verräter Dollfuss! Verräter Dollfuss!" he screamed, banging on the hood of the car. Grasping the three-pointed star that was the radiator ornament, he wrenched it off, held it up, spit on it, then threw it down.

"What the hell is that crazy fool doing?" John shouted. "He's tearing up your car!"

John started to get out, but David reached across the seat and grabbed him and pulled him back.

"John, no, stay here!" he warned.

"Ein Volk! Ein Reich! Ein Führer!" the rabble-rouser shouted, and he left the car to join his cohorts. It was only

then that John realized the others were shouting the same thing—a hundred or more guttural voices screaming in unison, *"Ein Volk! Ein Reich! Ein Führer!"*

Just then a number of uniformed policemen arrived on the scene. Some rode in on horseback, others on truck beds. Wielding clubs, they plunged into the mob, striking out left and right with their weapons until at last the mob was broken up and scattered in all directions. Within a few moments order was restored and the street clear of men, though the automobile traffic that had been brought to a standstill by the sudden uprising was now hopelessly snarled. One of the policemen, equipped with a whistle, stepped to the middle of the street and with several short, staccato bleats of his whistle and exaggerated arm and hand motions managed to get the traffic flowing again.

"See," David said. "Now it's all over. Nothing to worry about."

"Those were Nazis, weren't they?" John asked.

"Yes."

"What did he yell?" Faith asked. "Something about Chancellor Dollfuss?"

"He called Dollfuss a traitor," David translated. "The others were all shouting, 'One people, one nation, one leader.' "

John was extremely surprised by that. "Really? Then you mean there *are* people in Austria who want to unite with Germany? We kept hearing that all over Germany, but I thought it was just Nazi propaganda."

"There are some who would like to see Austria submit to Germany," David replied. "And the Nazi party has more members here than I would like to admit. But, thank God, they are in the minority. And luckily Chancellor Dollfuss is very much an anti-Nazi."

"That's why they were calling him a traitor?"

"Yes. But as you can see, the police broke up the demonstration quickly enough. And as long as Dollfuss is running things, the Nazis will never get out of hand. Ah, here is my street," he said. "That's my house, right over—"

David stopped in midsentence, and John saw why. Painted on the front of the fence was a huge, misshapen Star of David. Beside it was the word JUDE. Just as the car turned into the driveway, two women came out of the house, carrying buckets and brushes.

"Oh, those bastards," David growled. He stopped the car and leapt out, hurrying over to the women. "When did it happen?"

"I'm not sure," the older of the two women replied. "Miriam just noticed it. We were hoping to get it taken care of before our guests arrived. We didn't want them to have to see it." She looked at John and Faith as they approached and smiled. "I apologize for all this. I'm David's wife, Anna," she said. "This is our daughter, Miriam."

Anna was tall, and her chin-length dark-brown hair was shot through with gray, but her amber eyes sparkled with youthfulness, and her features were still quite delicate. And Miriam, at twenty-two, looked so much like her mother that John was pretty sure he might well be looking at Anna at that age. Miriam, too, was very pretty, with an oval face, very dark eyes and hair, high cheekbones, and an olive complexion. Like her mother, she was heavy-breasted enough that it took a second look to see that she was actually quite slender. She nervously brushed a strand of hair from her face, then set the bucket down and held out her hand.

"Welcome to our home," she said.

They shook hands all around, and then John picked up one of the brushes and started toward the fence.

"No, no," Anna admonished. "You mustn't do that."

"But I want to help," John insisted. "And I won't be dissuaded."

Smiling sadly, Anna relented.

It took several minutes to clean the fence. While they were working, two young boys in brown uniforms and Nazi armbands rode by on bicycles and shouted, *"Dreckige Juden!"* The Gelbmans ignored the taunt.

The fence scrubbed back to its original state, they all went inside the spacious, beautifully decorated house and got John and Faith settled in. Later, the hosts and their visitors sat around the dinner table, entertaining each other. David had them laughing so hard with stories about the days when he and Bob Canfield were classmates that they were almost able to forget about the earlier unpleasantness.

"What do you miss most about America?" Faith asked her host.

"Baseball," David replied.

"Baseball?"

"The St. Louis Grays," he explained. "My father had box seats at the ballpark, and when the Grays were home, I hardly missed a game. The blue sky, the green grass, the white ball, the smell of the sun on the wooden seats, the sound of the vendors selling their wares, the crack of a bat against the ball . . ." David sighed. "Yes, I would have to say that I miss that a great deal."

John laughed. "You'd have to be a dyed-in-the-wool fan to miss the Grays nowadays," he said. "They're awful."

"And yet in the papers I get from the States, I've read that one of their pitchers is really quite remarkable."

"You're talking about Swampwater Puckett. I'll admit that he is good, but I don't know how much longer he's going to be able to hold up. He's about the only asset the Grays have, and they're working him to death."

"Swampwater?" Miriam asked with a little laugh. "Is there really someone named Swampwater?"

"No," John answered, laughing with her. "His real name is Lenny. They just call him Swampwater because he comes from an area that used to be swamp. I think the newspapers hung it on him. They like the subjects of their stories to be colorful—or at least colorful sounding."

"Well, we don't have baseball and such colorful names as Swampwater," Anna said. "But we *do* have the opera in Vienna. And the Vienna Boys' Choir. Perhaps you would like to take in one of the performances?"

"I'd love to," Faith said enthusiastically. "Especially the Boys' Choir."

"I'm glad you chose that," Anna said. "The opera is doing Wagner, and I must confess to being a bit tired of Wagner. He can be so bombastic . . . among other things."

"I understand he's Hitler's favorite composer," Faith remarked.

"Yes, he is," Anna said. She chuckled. "I imagine Hitler

can afford slightly better seating now that he is such an important man than he could the last time we saw him."

Faith's eyes widened. "You mean you knew him from before?"

"We didn't exactly know him. He was just a boy then. An insolent, unpleasant, wild-eyed boy. Who could have known then that . . . ?" She let the words trail off, leaving the question unasked.

"When I first arrived in Vienna, Adolf Hitler was carrying bags at the depot," David explained. "He carried my bags, in fact." He laughed. "I must say, I sometimes get a kick out of thinking about that—the great world-leader, Jew-hater Hitler . . . carrying a Jew's luggage. He was also trying to sell a few of his paintings at the time."

"Oh, yes. I'd heard he was an artist," John said. "Was he any good?"

David snorted. "He was *terrible.* But his paintings served some purpose when I discovered that putting a picture in a frame—*any* kind of picture—would help to sell the frame. I bought a dozen or so of Herr Hitler's artistic creations. He was pretty upset when he learned why I actually wanted them, and he stopped selling them to me."

"I find this all fascinating," John said. "I mean, the fact that you knew Hitler before he became so famous and powerful."

"Well, I didn't actually know him," David corrected. "Except for the time he carried my bags and once when Anna and I saw him at the opera, where he was sitting in the so-called penny seats, I never had any encounters with him or even saw him, for that matter. I bought his art from someone else who was acting as his agent."

"Simon knew him," Miriam volunteered. "He knew him very well. They were in the same squad during the war."

"Who is Simon?" John asked.

"My cousin," Miriam said.

"And what does Simon think of him?"

"You ask the wrong question," David replied. "You should ask, 'Does Simon think?' "

"David, don't be cruel," Anna scolded.

David reached out to put his hand on his wife's. "I'm sorry, my love," he said. "I know we are all the family he has left. But you have to admit, Anna, there is something not quite right about a Jew who stays in Germany with the way things are now."

"Here," Miriam said, getting up and stepping over to the sideboard and reaching into a drawer. "Here's a picture of him." She held open a photograph album between John and Faith, pointing to a picture of a sullen-looking man leaning on a cane and staring morosely at the camera. "He lost his leg during the war," she explained.

"And you say he's still in Germany?" John asked.

"Yes. In Berlin," David answered. "Though in God's name I'll never know why."

John was thoughtful for a moment, then said quietly, "You know, David, there are those who think that Jews who live in Austria may also be in danger."

"Not really," David said. "I'll admit there are a handful of Nazis around who are all excited because Hitler was able to worm his way into power in Germany. And, of course, they take some sort of perverse pride in the fact that he was born in Austria. But Germany was a mess, just ready for someone to walk in and start grabbing power. And Hindenburg is an old, sick man, unable to fight back. Our mighty midget is neither old nor sick—and he has Mussolini in his back pocket. As long as Mussolini is guaranteeing Austria's independence, we don't have anything to worry about."

"Why do you call Dollfuss a mighty midget?" Faith asked.

"Have you ever seen him?"

"Just pictures."

"You can't really tell from the pictures . . . he always manages to be photographed alone, or else in a position where it's difficult to judge. But he is very short. Less than five feet tall."

"Really?" John said. "I had no idea he was that small."

"He may be small, but he isn't afraid to stand up to Hitler," David insisted. "And as long as we have him around, the Jews in Austria have nothing to worry about."

"Could we please talk about something other than politics?" Anna asked. She smiled at Faith. "Tell us about America."

"Yes," Miriam said. "Tell me about people my age in America. What kind of clothes do they wear? What kind of music do they like? Do all young Americans drive fast cars?"

Faith laughed and was about to respond when the Gelbmans' cook, a rotund, middle-aged woman, appeared in the doorway between the dining room and the kitchen. She had a shocked look on her face.

"Frau Franck, what is it?" David asked.

"The radio," Frau Franck said, her voice so choked that she could scarcely be heard. "It is on the radio."

"What? What's on the radio?" David prompted.

"Herr Chancellor Dollfuss. The Nazis . . . they have killed him."

SOLOVETSKY ISLANDS LABOR CAMP, U.S.S.R.

In the dreary community meeting room of the Solovetsky labor camp, Valentina Lvovna sat bolt upright in the straight-backed wooden chair, staring at the unpainted pine coffin. The only concession to long-accepted form that the carpenter had made in constructing the box was to put a slight flare at the shoulder. Otherwise it would have looked no different from a crate holding farm implements.

The coffin, which was closed, sat upon two sawhorses, and a small bouquet of wildflowers that Valentina had picked rested on the lid. The carpenter had apologized quietly to Valentina for not putting a cross on the coffin, but the camp officials disapproved of such things, and the carpenter had not wanted to get into trouble. Valentina had thanked him for the thought, telling him a cross wasn't necessary.

She was not a believer, and a cross on the outside of the coffin would have meant nothing to her. Her mother, Katya, had been a believer though, so when Valentina had prepared her for burial, she had slipped Katya's small crucifix into her folded hands. Valentina felt it a foolish thing to have done, but she also knew that her mother would have appreciated it.

Just seventeen, Valentina had never been outside the Solovetsky work camp. For as far back as she could remember she and her mother had shared a dingy one-room apartment in one of the camp's barracks. Valentina was tall and willowy, with long blond hair, ice-blue eyes, a delicate nose, high cheekbones, and a beautiful complexion. Many people told her she was a beautiful young woman, and those who had known her mother in her youth often compared the two of them. Since so many people had told her that her mother was beautiful as a young woman, Valentina assumed it was so. But there were no surviving pictures of the young Princess Katya Lvovna, and Valentina had never known her mother as anything but the prematurely aged, drawn, and haggard old woman she had become in the work camp.

The camps had been created to readjust the thinking of those considered enemies—or, for that matter, even potential enemies—of the state, the idea being that when their thinking was readjusted and they were no longer a threat to the republic, they would be released.

Katya had been pregnant with Valentina when the Communist revolution overthrew the czarist government in 1917. The father of Katya's baby was an American journalist sent by his newspaper to cover the tumultuous struggle. They had been living together and had planned to marry, but events had conspired against them. An old law—still on the books after the revolution because the new government was ponderously slow to change some of the less-important civil laws—decreed that the marriage of any member of the royal family needed the czar's official permission to take place. It was a classic conundrum: Though the czar was dead, the civil authority installed by the Bolshevik government wouldn't grant Katya a marriage license without the approval of the very monarch they had just killed.

Katya's American lover had had no better luck when he had asked for help at the American embassy. He had been told that since there was no international marriage agreement, the United States and its personnel had no jurisdiction to perform a valid marriage in another country. When the

American journalist then sought permission for Katya to emigrate to America, an embassy official had discovered Katya's name on a list published by the State Department of people to whom no asylum would be offered. Katya was a Royalist, and the United States government hadn't wanted to side with either the Royalists or the Bolsheviks until after conditions had settled.

Katya and her American journalist had been left adrift in a sea of red tape. But despite the fact that they weren't married, they had continued to live together as man and wife, waiting for the birth of their child. Then one day while her lover was gone, the secret police had come for Katya. She was a princess and as such, they had said, she might be a rallying point for the White Russians harboring the idea of a counterrevolution. Katya had been spirited away to the Siberian labor camp, never to see or hear from her American journalist again.

Katya Lvovna had been a prisoner of the state when she gave birth to her daughter, and she had been a prisoner of the state, seventeen years later, when she died. There would be no funeral, no priest to exhort God to receive Katya into His Kingdom or to say a few comforting words to Valentina. Colonel Viktor Cherensky, the current commandant of the camp, believed that funerals were counterproductive, a barbaric custom designed to wring the last tear from the grieving survivors. And certainly in the early days there had been so many people dying that if funerals had been allowed, there would have been time for nothing else.

One of the older residents of the camp, a woman who had known the princess when she was young and beautiful, had commented to Valentina about how terrible it was that Katya Lvovna would be denied a traditional burial.

"This is a traditional burial," Valentina had responded dryly. "Throughout my entire life all the burials I have witnessed have been exactly like this."

"You poor, deprived child."

"I do not feel deprived," Valentina had answered with a shrug.

There was no funeral, but Colonel Cherensky had told

Valentina she could sit—alone—with her mother's coffin for as long as she wished. That was what she was doing now.

"Mama," Valentina said quietly, "many times I heard you say prayers for those you loved after they were dead. I wish I could say a prayer for you now. I think you would like it if I could . . . but I cannot. I don't know who to pray to. For your sake I hope there is a God and a Jesus and a heaven. If it's true, I know you will go there. I hope it's as beautiful as the houses and palaces in St. Petersburg that you often told me about."

Behind her the door to the small room opened and closed. Valentina glanced over her shoulder and saw Lieutenant Yakov Kosior. Yakov was a very nice-looking young medical officer, just a few years older than Valentina. He was from Moscow and had been assigned to Solovetsky six months before as a member of the hospital staff.

"My captain gave me permission to come sit with you for a while," Yakov said softly. "I hope you don't mind."

"I don't mind," Valentina said. "I'm glad you could come."

He pulled up a chair and sat beside her. They were silent briefly, then Yakov spoke.

"What will you do now?"

"I don't know. Why do you ask?"

"Colonel Cherensky says you aren't an inmate here."

Valentina looked at Yakov in surprise.

Yakov nodded. "He says your mother was the prisoner, not you. You were here only because you were your mother's child, but now that she is dead, you must leave."

Valentina felt her stomach lurch. "I must *leave*?"

"That's what Colonel Cherensky says."

She was stunned. "I had no idea."

"Where will you go?"

"I don't know," Valentina replied. She shook her head. "I've never given it any thought."

"I'd like you to go to Moscow," Yakov said.

"With you?"

"Not with me. I must stay here for one more year, after

which I'll be posted somewhere else. But you could go to Moscow and wait for me."

"What would I do? Where would I stay? I don't know anyone in Moscow." Her anxiety was rising with every passing moment. The Solovetsky labor camp was her home. Despite all the terrible things that the inmates said about it, she knew nothing and no one else.

"You could go to my parents' house," Yakov suggested. "My father is a doctor in a hospital there."

"Yes, I can see it now," Valentina said sarcastically. "I will knock on the door, and when your father or your mother answers, I will say my name is Valentina Lvovna. I was a lifelong resident at the Solovetsky Camp for many years—I thought I was a prisoner, but apparently not—and now I am free, and I was wondering if you would take me in."

Yakov grinned. "Yes, that's exactly what you should say," he said. "My mother and father know all about you. I've written them. And I have another letter for you to give them." He pulled an cnvelope from his pocket and handed it to her.

"What have you told them?" Valentina asked.

"Essentially what you just said. That you aren't really an inmate here, just a victim of circumstance. And also that I like you very, very much."

Valentina smiled. "Do you now?" she asked. She looked toward the door. No one was there. She turned back to Yakov and kissed him passionately, feeling a thrill both from the contact and the danger of it. Any type of romantic fraternization between the inmates and the soldiers was strictly forbidden. But, then, Yakov had just told her that she wasn't really an inmate—so they weren't violating the rules after all.

"Is that *all* you told them?" she asked. "Did you tell them about that evening down by the soccer field? Did you tell them what we did?"

Yakov's cheeks flushed. "I have never told anyone about that night," he said. He looked at her intently. "Did *you* tell anyone?"

"I told my mother."

He looked astonished. "You . . . you told your *mother?* But I thought girls never told such things. How could you have told your mother?"

"I had no secrets from my mother. I told her everything. Are you angry with me?"

"No," Yakov said. "I would have been angry only if she had said you could never see me again."

"She would never have done that. She could see how I felt about you, and she was happy for me."

"Even though I am a soldier?"

"You are a doctor," Valentina said firmly.

"I am a doctor-trainee. But I am also a soldier."

"I know. But my mother said there are good soldiers and bad soldiers. She thought you were a good soldier."

Yakov smiled. "Your mother was a wise woman."

"Yes, she was."

He took her hand in his. "You're going to miss her, aren't you?" he asked softly.

"Very much."

"I am very sorry that she died so young," Yakov said. "Now you have no mother or father."

"No, that isn't true. I have a father."

Yakov's eyebrows shot up. "You have a father?"

"Yes."

"I am astonished! But where is he? Why has he never come for you? Is he an enemy of the state?"

Valentina's expression hardened. "He isn't an enemy of the state, but he is *my* enemy," she said in a cold voice.

Yakov's own expression turned stern. "How can you say such a thing about your own father?"

"Because it's true. For seventeen years I watched my mother cling to the pathetic hope that someday my father would come for us and take us away from here. She looked for him every day. She actually *expected* him every day. I think that on the very day she died, she would not have been surprised if he had suddenly shown up to liberate her."

"But your mother was an enemy of the state. Your father couldn't have freed her, even if he had come."

"Yes, he could have," Valentina countered. "You see, my

father is an American. And many years ago my mother received a letter from our government stating that it would let her leave the country if my father would come for her and marry her. Oh, how she clung to that letter! It was her most precious possession. Once, when I was young, our barracks caught on fire. Neighbors pulled us outside, but my mother broke free and rushed back in through the flames. When she came back out a few minutes later, she was blackened with soot and coughing from the smoke she had inhaled. But she was clutching that letter."

"It was evidently very important to her," Yakov said.

"You don't know how important. She would read that letter when she was tired, cold, dispirited, or hungry. And when she was dying she had me read it to her. How I hated that accursed letter!"

"Where is it now?" Yakov asked.

Valentina pointed to her mother's coffin. "In there," she said. "At first I wanted to burn it. I took it from the envelope and held up a lit match, ready to set fire to it . . . but in the end I couldn't do it. So I'm burying it with her."

"Did your father know that the government would let her go free if he came for her?"

"Yes, he knew. He just didn't want to come," Valentina said bitterly.

"And yet your mother still clung to the hope that he would?"

"Yes. Oh, she made many excuses for him. At first she said he had no idea where we were or even if we were alive or dead. For many years my mother didn't know where he was or how to reach him. Then she found out and wrote to him, telling him that we were alive and he could come for us. She wrote him many times, but of course he never came. That didn't stop her from hoping, though. Every morning of her life she believed with all her heart that he would come for us that day."

"Did your father ever give your mother a reason why he wouldn't come?"

"He never even answered her letters," Valentina said harshly.

"Maybe he didn't receive them. Maybe the letters couldn't find him," Yakov suggested.

"No, they found him all right. I am certain of that. He'd be very easy to find because my father is a very important man in America. He's a very famous novelist. His name is Eric Twainbough."

CHAPTER TEN

JULY 23, 1934, ST. LOUIS, MISSOURI

"By God, I don't give a damn if Emerson Electric and Canfield-Puritex *did* cave in to those Communist bastards! I'm not going to. And I'm not doing this just for MC Motors either, by God. No, sir, I honestly believe I'm defending the American way of life. I mean, *someone* has to stand up to the goddamn unions, or they're going to ruin this nation's economy. And if nobody else will do it, then, by God, I will!"

Jason Carlew, a cigar clenched firmly between his teeth, got up from his desk and stalked over to the window to look down on the entry gate of his factory. The company he headed, Mid-Coastal Motors, manufactured automobile components for some of the largest automobile producers in the country. But MC Motors was currently in a great deal of difficulty because they were two weeks behind in their delivery schedule to Studebaker and Hudson Motors. To ensure timely delivery of critical parts, those two auto manufacturers had written penalty clauses into their contracts, so now in addition to the revenue they were losing from not shipping the parts, MC Motors was also being penalized ten thousand dollars per day, per company, for every day it was late. So far the deal with Studebaker and Hudson had cost the company a total of $140,000 in penalty charges alone. Within another week they were going to have to start paying Nash Motors as well.

From his office window Carlew could see his uniformed guards standing nervously just inside the front gate. On the other side of the gate a handful of men were milling around, carrying picket signs.

JOB SECURITY, one sign read.

ONE MONTH'S SALARY FOR MC PRESIDENT = FIFTY YEARS' SALARY FOR AN MC WORKER, read another.

AN HONEST DAY'S PAY FOR AN HONEST DAY'S WORK, read a third.

Carlew pulled his handkerchief out and wiped his forehead. "Goddamn, it's hot," he said to the dark-haired, tough-looking man sitting on the other side of his desk, not turning away from the window. "I wonder how hot it is, anyway."

"Matter of fact, I looked at the thermometer when I came through the gate," Kerry O'Braugh replied. "It was a hundred and four."

"One hundred and four! Jesus, when it gets that hot in St. Louis, these damn brick buildings turn into baking ovens. What did it say in the paper this morning? Ninety-six people have died already from the heat?"

"Yeah, somethin' like that. Maybe the heat's cookin' their brains."

Carlew slowly shook his head. "Look at those ungrateful bastards down there," he muttered, ignoring Kerry's remark. "By God, I feel like I've been stabbed in the back. I've worked as many of them as I could all this time, and this is the thanks I get. You know, there are plenty of men out of work who would welcome the opportunity to earn a little money for their families. Tomorrow we'll bring them in and let them work. We'll see just how much grit those striking bastards have when they see their jobs going to hell in a hand basket."

"How many replacement workers do you have lined up for tomorrow?" Kerry asked.

"Just over three hundred, I think," Carlew answered. Finally turning around, he pulled his cigar out of his mouth and pointed the chewed end of it at Kerry. "You *will* be able to get them through the picket lines, won't you?"

"You don't have to worry about that," Kerry assured him. "I'll get 'em through."

Carlew stuck the cigar back into his mouth, then turned and looked out the window again. "It's not enough that I've got those striking bastards to worry about, I've also got Senator Dawson to contend with. He wants me to end the strike by . . . *negotiation*." He twisted his mouth into a sneer as he said the word, showing his contempt not only for the concept, but also for the senator. "He says our country can't afford labor unrest in these troubled times."

Kerry smiled. "I'm afraid I can't help you there," he said. "I'm not exactly one of Dawson's favorite people."

"You let me handle Dawson. All the money I've contributed to that son of a bitch's campaigns over the years ought to buy me a little understanding."

Kerry smirked. "It always helps to have the right people obligated to you. I've sure learned that in my business over the years."

"Yes, I imagine you have. By the way, you do understand, don't you, that I'm not hiring you to break any laws? I want that clearly understood. I'm a legitimate businessman and a loyal American trying to keep my factory open for the sake of the country. And I'm willing to go the extra mile to see that it does stay open. But I will not be a party to the violation of any laws."

"We won't be breakin' any laws, Mr. Carlew," Kerry said easily. "It's the men on the picket lines who're breakin' the laws. The law says you can hire part-time replacement workers durin' a strike, but the strikers have put up a picket line to prevent anyone from gettin' through. All I'm goin' to do is see to it that the law is obeyed so the replacement workers *can* get through. Besides, look what the police did up in Minneapolis last Friday. Accordin' to the paper, they opened fire on a bunch of strikin' truck drivers and shot about fifty of 'em. And they *are* the law."

Carlew ground his cigar out in the highly polished brass ashtray on his desk, then studied Kerry through narrowed eyes. Finally he said, "I guess it must be some change for you. I mean, being on the same side as the law."

"Are you talkin' about the liquor business I was engaged in durin' Prohibition?" Kerry asked.

"I suppose I am. Hell, it's no secret, is it, that you were the biggest bootlegger in St. Louis?"

Kerry smiled easily. "No, it's no secret. I freely admit that I was a bootlegger. But now the law allows traffickin' in whiskey, so me and the law, we're on the same side." He grinned, and his blue eyes danced with mischief. "I just happened to arrive at this side sooner than the law did, that's all."

Carlew laughed heartily. "You arrived sooner, huh? That's pretty good, O'Braugh. Yes, sir, that's pretty damn good." He sat in the swivel chair behind his desk and stared up at Kerry. "All right. Those replacement workers have to get through the picket line tomorrow, so I suppose you have a deal."

"On my terms?"

"Yes, Mr. O'Braugh, on your terms. Just get the job done."

"Your production line will be fully manned tomorrow," Kerry promised, standing up and shaking the executive's hand.

Kerry O'Braugh quickly left Jason Carlew's office and stepped outside into the sweltering air. Looking through the high chain-link fence that separated the picketers from the company grounds, he could see heat waves rising up from the ground and radiating away from the brick buildings, distorting the picketers so that their wavering images were ghostlike in appearance. The strikers who weren't actually walking the picket line were across the street, staying close to the sides of the buildings so that they could take advantage of what little shade there was on this blistering-hot day.

A huge billboard on top of the building across the street caught Kerry's eyes. The picture on the billboard was of a father, a mother, a little girl, and a boy, all smiling brightly through the windshield of a red automobile. Only the windshield and a small part of a red hood were visible in the illustration, making the make and model of the automobile anonymous. The billboard proclaimed:

> THE AMERICAN DREAM CAN BE YOURS WITH A NEW AUTOMOBILE, BUILT WITH COMPONENTS SUPPLIED BY MID-COASTAL MOTORS. SEE YOUR CAR DEALER TODAY. WHEN YOU BUY A NEW CAR, YOU MAKE JOBS FOR FELLOW ST. LOUISIANS!

A chauffeured Cadillac, provided for Kerry by MC Motors, was just inside the gate, and the driver was standing by the rear door, holding it open. Kerry nodded his thanks as he slipped onto the back seat. As soon as the driver started the car, Kerry told him, "Turn on the radio, will you?"

"Sure thing, Mr. O'Braugh."

The driver reached over and twisted a knob, and music filled the big auto's interior. The song playing was "Brother, Can You Spare a Dime?" and Kerry smiled at the irony of it.

As Jason Carlew had intimated, Kerry O'Braugh had been St. Louis's leading bootlegger throughout the era of Prohibition. Kerry had fought hard for the position, emerging victorious after a series of brutal gangland wars and killings. Today he was the top man in organized crime not only in St. Louis, but throughout the Midwest.

Kerry O'Braugh was a sworn member of the Mafia. Non-Italians weren't normally "made," so people were always surprised to learn about Kerry's membership. But Kerry had been born in Sicily to a Sicilian mother, thanks to the fact that his father had fled there from Ireland to avoid a murder charge, married a local girl, and became a trusted enforcer in the Mafia family headed by his bride, Maria's, father—Kerry's grandfather. Thus Kerry O'Braugh considered himself first, last, and always Sicilian.

While Kerry was still very young, his father and grandfather were killed in a vendetta. The elders of the village decided that in the interest of future peace, it might be better to get Kerry out of Sicily before he came of age and started seeking revenge. A collection was taken up in the village to raise enough money to send Kerry and his mother to America, where they could start a new life with a new husband arranged for Maria.

The boy and his stepfather had hated each other. When the twelve-year-old Kerry committed a petty theft, his stepfather turned him in to the police. Kerry was sent to reform school, his ties to "home" broken forever.

It took a while, but Kerry finally escaped from the brutal reform school, finding work with underworld boss Big Jim Colossimo. He soon "made his bones," which is to say he committed his first gangland killing, for Johnny Torrio and Al Capone.

But that had been over fourteen years ago, and several drastic changes had taken place in the underworld. Big Jim Colossimo was now dead, Johnny Torrio had been deported back to Sicily, and Al Capone was in federal prison. Prohibition had been repealed, the "Roaring Twenties" were over, and America was deep in the throes of a devastating depression.

Many of the very wealthy and powerful racketeers who had built their empires upon Prohibition were gone, and the criminals making news today were the likes of John Dillinger and Bonnie and Clyde. The latter pair, nickel-and-dime holdup artists made popular by the press simply because they were a couple, had been killed two months before, ambushed by a posse just beyond Shreveport, Louisiana.

Though he had heretofore operated outside the law, Kerry O'Braugh wasn't interested in making money by robbing banks or gas stations. He was the type of man who could find opportunity in chaos and now saw his fortune in the constant unrest that existed between labor and management. The field of labor negotiations was particularly lucrative for someone like Kerry because he was a man who brought no social attitudes of his own to the negotiation table. He cared nothing about the inherent rights of labor; neither was he concerned with the logic of efficient operation beloved by management. Kerry's only concern was with what he personally stood to gain. As a result he could play either side of a labor dispute with equal enthusiasm.

Kerry had been very successful in getting his people into key positions in several of the union locals within the city. And in those places of business where the unions had resisted his efforts, Kerry offered his services to management.

When Kerry approached the Congress of Auto Workers, Local 381, to put forth his services in negotiating with MC Motors, they turned him down cold. So Kerry felt no compunction in offering those same negotiation services to Jason Carlew, Chairman of the Board for Mid-Coastal Motors. For Kerry it was a win-win proposition: Carlew would pay him handsomely to break the strike. Breaking the strike would also break the union. And once the union was broken, Kerry could move in and pick up the pieces.

But the truth was, Kerry thought, if ever employees had just cause for a strike, automobile workers did. While the average yearly wage of the chief executive officers of the major auto plants was over three hundred thousand dollars per year, and their top twenty executives were all earning more than one hundred and fifty thousand dollars a year, the average yearly wage of any auto worker in any of the plants was less than five hundred dollars. And yet for every man who was ready to strike, there were two more who were eager to take his job.

The limousine deposited Kerry before a storefront office on Olive Street. A sign on the window identified the office as that of the Missouri Labor Negotiations Commission. It was a very ordinary-looking place, not much different from the spaghetti house on the left side of it or the laundry on the right. Two flags hung by the front door, one the Stars and Stripes, the other the Missouri tricolor, which looked just like the French national flag, differing only in that it had at its center the state seal.

Very few people knew that this innocuous office was actually the headquarters of all organized crime in the city. In fact, because of the official-sounding name and the flags, many believed that it was in some way connected with the state or the federal government. And given that several state officials were receiving kickbacks of one sort or another from Kerry O'Braugh, those who thought that the Missouri Labor Negotiations Commission was associated with the state government weren't that far wrong.

When Kerry returned from his meeting with Jason Carlew, Vinnie Todaro was sitting at a desk reading a newspaper while Carmine Brazzi was drinking a beer and playing a pinball machine that sat incongruously amidst the businesslike atmosphere created by the desks. Vinnie and Carmine had been with Kerry since he had left Chicago and moved down to St. Louis to start a "branch" of the Chicago mob for Johnny Torrio. The branch quickly became Kerry's own personal operation, and Vinnie and Carmine were Kerry's chief henchmen.

"Did you see this?" Vinnie asked, holding up the front page of the newspaper.

**G-MEN GUN DOWN DILLINGER
AS HE LEAVES CHICAGO THEATER**

Betrayed by Woman in Red
Last Picture was Manhattan Melodrama

"They got him, huh?" Kerry said. He smirked. "And they got Bonnie and Clyde a couple of weeks ago. This'll teach the amateurs not to play in the streets with the big boys."

Vinnie laughed. "Or, at least, not to play with women in red."

"Tilt?" Carmine shouted angrily, banging on the side of the machine. "Don't you go tilting on me, you son of a bitch!" He kicked the leg, setting off a series of noisy bings and dings. Grinning, Carmine picked up his beer and turned toward Kerry. "Well?" he asked expectantly.

"Well what?" Kerry answered.

"Well what," Carmine grumbled. He affected a mincing voice and asked, "Well, gee, is it rainin' outside?" He grimaced. "Christ, you know damn well 'well what.' How'd it go? Is Carlew going to meet our price or what?"

Kerry grinned. "He didn't even quibble."

Carmine rubbed his hands together and chuckled. "Damn. I gotta hand it to you, boss. You've come up with one sweet deal. I mean, this sure beats the hell out of robbin' banks like that dumb-assed Dillinger." He pointed to the paper Vinnie had been reading.

"What's the catch?" Vinnie asked, eyeing Kerry carefully over the top of his newspaper.

"What makes you think there's a catch?"

"I know you," Vinnie said. "I know the look on your face."

Kerry rubbed his chin. "Well, for one thing, it's going to be rough," he said. "There are probably a thousand or so men who gather outside the gate every day."

"Yeah, well, you know how any mob is," Vinnie said, folding the paper and setting it aside. "I mean, show 'em a little blood and ninety percent of 'em are ready to shit in their pants. Besides which, don't forget that we got us a pretty good crew of muscle. There's ten men with us who've been through all this before."

"You ain't nervous, are you, boss?" Carmine asked.

Kerry smiled. "No. It's nothin' we can't handle."

"Damn right we can handle it," Carmine said, feeding another nickel into the pinball machine.

Kerry, Vinnie, and Carmine got down to the plant gates shortly after six the next morning. Because Jason Carlew had made arrangements with the police, the three mobsters were provided with security guards' licenses, which authorized them to carry pistols—and all three of them were doing so.

They were accompanied by ten of their toughs, all of whom had fought with them in previous confrontations on picket lines. The battlers were carrying the weapon of choice for such encounters: sawed-off hoe handles.

Kerry had purposely chosen early morning to make his move when, in contrast to the thousand or so strikers who would swell the line during the day, only about a hundred strikers would be present, having volunteered to spend the night and keep their presence felt. And those few men who had stayed would be tired and dispirited from having slept poorly outside on the damp ground, fighting off the mosquitoes that were particularly bad at this time of year.

Several women were present with the strikers. Using commodities made available to them by the Congress of Automobile Workers' national headquarters, the women had made coffee and biscuits at a makeshift camp stove fashioned from welded oil drums. Most of the men were already standing in line for their morning handout. For some, Kerry knew, this meager handout from the CAW would be the only food they'd have for the entire day. In fact, that was the incentive that had kept them through the night.

"Here they come," Carmine said, excitement in his voice.

Kerry looked down the block and saw Jason Carlew's big Cadillac slowly leading a convoy of about fifteen trucks. The backs of the trucks were loaded with men who had agreed to cross the picket line.

Kerry took a deep breath. "All right, men," he said quietly, "get ready. The fun's about to begin."

The strikers hadn't noticed Kerry and his men until the trucks began arriving. Then, as the trucks stopped and one by one the replacement workers began climbing out, the strikers realized that something was afoot. Kerry could see the nervousness spreading through them as they quickly clustered around the gate.

Carlew got out of his car and hurried over to Kerry. "Is everything ready?"

"We're all set."

Carlew looked at Kerry and the men with him, then demanded, "Hey, what is this? Are you trying to tell me I paid you all that money for just a dozen or so men? Don't you understand what this is all about? I intend to bust this goddamned strike wide open! How the hell are you going to do it with just these few men?"

"Watch and you'll find out," Kerry replied. He signaled to the strikebreakers, many holding lunch buckets, who were now waiting beside the trucks. Kerry assumed that this situation was no different from other strikes he had helped bust, which meant that a number of these scabs had worked with the men walking the picket line and considered them their friends. Probably some were even related by blood or by marriage, and only desperation had driven them to this point. The replacement workers looked down sheepishly, unable to meet the gazes of those who had been their friends or were kin.

"Let's go!" Kerry called.

As the newcomers gathered into a group, the strikers started shouting angrily at them.

"Scabs! Dirty scabs!"

"What are you doing here? You're sticking a knife in our backs!"

"Get out of here, you bastards!"

Kerry, Carmine, Vinnie, and their henchmen formed a V with Kerry at the point. The workers fell in behind them as they started toward the plant entrance, walking slowly and quietly across the street. The shouts of the strikers died away, and they watched in silent, seething anger as Kerry and his men led the strikebreakers toward the gate.

From a distance came the sounds of a freight train, its whistle giving a mournful alarm and its steam engine chugging heavily. But here there was an almost unearthly silence, broken only by heavy breathing and the clomping of feet against concrete.

"Here they come!" one of the strikers shouted, the quaver in his voice betraying his fear and anger. *"Here the sons of bitches come!"*

"Get the women out of here!" another striker yelled, and out of the corner of his eye Kerry saw the women being hustled to the rear as the strikers readied themselves for action.

The strikers, armed with clubs, crowbars, car axles, and anything else they had managed to put their hands on, waited tensely as Kerry and his men advanced on them. Kerry studied each striker's face, able to tell from the expression who would fight and who at the last minute would turn and run. He knew who would be dangerous and whom he could ignore. He had learned to survive by being a good judge.

The validity of his judgment was borne out when one of

those he had already discounted threw down his club and ran when Kerry's group was still ninety feet away.

"Jensen, you yellow bastard, get back here! Stand your ground!" one of the strikers screamed, but Jensen didn't return. His rapid departure was infectious; four more men threw down their clubs and ran to join him.

When Kerry and his men were no more than twenty feet away from the strikers, he called to them, "You fellas step away and no one'll be hurt. We're here to see to it that these new workers can get through."

"Like hell they'll get through!" one of the strikers answered, and the two groups were instantly on each other, fists and clubs flying.

It was the job of Kerry and his men to keep the strikers occupied so that the new workers could get through the gate, and this they were able to do quite easily. Kerry glanced toward the gate to see how many scabs were left outside. Suddenly he felt an excruciating pain in his left knee, and the next thing he knew he was lying on his back on the pavement.

A striker with a baseball bat had swung at Kerry's kneecap as if he were hitting a ball over the center-field fence. Kerry's knee felt as if someone were holding a red-hot poker to it. He knew that it was shattered and wondered, almost with a sense of detachment, if he'd ever walk again.

"Boss! Boss, are you all right?" Carmine shouted, coming to help him.

"Yeah," Kerry muttered, grimacing. "Yeah, I'm all right. Help me to my feet."

He had been in a dozen of these battles, but this was the first time he had ever sustained more than a minor cut or bruise. Nevertheless, he was determined to get up.

Helped to his feet, Kerry was barely standing when he saw Vinnie go down, pummeled by a striker. The striker then began raising an ax over Vinnie's head. Kerry took a step toward Vinnie, but he found that he couldn't walk.

"Carmine, help Vinnie!" Kerry shouted, pointing.

"Oh, shit!" Carmine cried. "Boss, he's going to kill Vinnie!"

Letting go of Kerry, he started toward his friend, but Vinnie was too far away to do anything.

Kerry pulled his pistol out from his waistband and, balancing himself on his one good leg, took aim at the man with the ax. The roar of the shot stilled the brutal melee going on all around. Blood and brain matter exploded out of the top of the striker's head as he dropped the ax and pitched back onto the pavement. A spreading pool of red spilled from his shattered head.

The battle ended almost immediately. The rest of the strikers turned and ran, leaving the field to Kerry and his men.

Jason Carlew, who had watched the whole thing from his Cadillac, was clearly beside himself with joy. Jumping out of his car, he ran to the front gate to shake each strikebreaker's hand, then rewarded each of the toughs with a bonus of a fifty-dollar bill. He didn't look at the man sprawled lifeless in the gutter, and he didn't ask Kerry about his knee.

JULY 26, 1934, WASHINGTON, D.C.

"Well, John, you don't look any the worse for wear for your adventures in Europe," Senator Champ Dawson told John Canfield on his aide's first day back to work.

"It was quite an experience," John said.

"Yes, the President was quite impressed with your report," Champ replied. "He was particularly taken with your description of the festival in Nürnberg."

"It was much more than a festival, Senator. It was more like mass, controlled frenzy. That rally did something to the people. It changed them in some way. A man who would normally be a mild-mannered, smiling, friendly store clerk would, in the midst of the Party Day activities, turn into an automaton. The people went insane, but they all went mad together. So those on the outside, unaffected by it, began to question their own sanity."

"Then you believe Hitler really does have the German people on his side?"

"On his side? Senator, it's gone far beyond that," John said, shaking his head. "The German people are now merely an extension of Hitler's will."

"Yes," Champ mused. "Well, sometimes I wonder if we wouldn't be better off in *this* country if Franklin couldn't exercise the same power. At least until we get this depression licked."

"You don't mean that," John said.

Champ grinned and squeezed John's shoulder reassuringly. "No," he said. "Of course I don't mean it. We can't save our republic by throwing out our republican form of government."

John laughed. "You've said the dirty word. Don't you remember? It's the President's wish that we start referring to our form of government as a democracy rather than a republic. Democracy makes people think of Democrats. Republic makes people think of Republicans."

Champ laughed with him. "As much as I admire the President, I'm afraid he is pissing in the wind with this one. Democracy? You only find that term in textbooks and a few speeches. Americans have used the term 'republic' for nearly two hundred years; they aren't going to suddenly start referring to this government as a democracy just because that's what Franklin wants."

"Maybe Americans as a whole aren't, but we are. That is, if we want to stay on his good side," John suggested.

"That's true," Champ agreed with a smile. "And I will admit that it's a hell of a lot better to be on his good side than his bad. And speaking of bad sides, did you see the papers yesterday? They settled the strike at MC Motors in St. Louis."

"They settled the strike . . . or they broke it?" John grumbled.

"They broke it," Champ agreed. "The next day the workers agreed to call off the strike and return to work. And get this. Not only did they *not* get the raise they struck for, they agreed to a five-cent-per-hour cut in pay until revenues lost by the strike are made up. Carlew is crediting the labor negotiations of Kerry O'Braugh for the win."

John snorted. "Negotiations? Some negotiations. He killed someone, didn't he?"

"Yes, he did. But more than a score of witnesses, from both sides, swore that he killed the man to keep him from killing someone else. No charges were pressed."

"But he's a criminal," John said. "All the time I was growing up I kept reading his name in the papers, always in conjunction with some underworld activity."

"I don't disagree with you."

"How can he be a labor negotiator?"

"Simple. All he has to do is show up with his goons and break up a strike. After *he's* finished with them, the strikers are more than willing to forget about any grievances they may have. A lot of them consider themselves lucky not only to get their jobs back, but to get out of the confrontation without having had their skulls cracked."

"Tell me, Senator, how come somebody like O'Braugh isn't in jail?" John asked.

"Who knows? Maybe he's skillful enough to just skate around the edges of the law so that he avoids getting caught. Maybe he's bought off enough judges and hired enough police protection to keep him out of trouble. Or maybe he's just grown too big for the system to work anymore. All I know is he can quite literally get away with murder."

John frowned. "Something should be done."

"I was hoping you'd feel that way," Champ said, smiling broadly.

"Why? What do you have in mind?"

"I'd like to launch a little investigation of my own into Mr. O'Braugh's activities. And I want you to head it for me."

"I'd be glad to, Senator," John said. "But what's our mandate for this?"

"Aren't we committed to economic recovery?" Champ asked.

"Yes, sir."

"Well, don't you think that criminal activity such as that perpetrated by Kerry O'Braugh might be detrimental to our economic recovery?"

John smiled knowingly. "Yes, sir, I believe it would."

"Then I think it is our duty to investigate just how

much impact his continued operations are having on the recovery process and to see just what we can do to put a stop to it," Champ said firmly.

"Yes, sir. I quite agree."

"I'm glad you do. Because you, young man, are in charge of the investigation."

"Senator, I'm honored by your confidence in me, but I'm a businessman, not a lawyer or a policeman."

"But you *are* an organizer and a leader," Champ insisted. "If you need lawyers, hire them. If you need private detectives, hire them, too. Get whatever you need"—his face clouded angrily—"but I want Kerry O'Braugh put out of business."

CHAPTER ELEVEN

AUGUST 19, 1934, DELTA, MISSISSIPPI

The sign in front of the little church read:

SUNBEAMS OF HEAVEN
COLORED BAPTIST CHURCH
THE REVEREND THADDEOUS BEASLEY, PASTOR

Several odd-lengthed planks of wood were stripped in along the sides of the building, each plank a different color, indicating that repairs were constantly being made to the structure. The building showed signs of having been painted white at one time, but very little of the original paint was left.

The church sat high off the ground, resting on stone pillars. This was mute testimony that the Sunflower River, which flowed nearby, wasn't always as placid as it was that day. An outhouse behind the church sat directly on the ground; it, apparently, was deemed replaceable.

There was a good-sized parking area as well, but the only vehicles making use of it were two old, dilapidated trucks and four mule-drawn wagons whose teams stood stoically in the morning sun. Compared to the other conveyances, Dr. Andrew Booker's car, a 1933 Chevrolet roadster, was a limousine.

Andy and LaTonya had left Jefferson City, Missouri, early the previous day. At the end of a long, hot day on the road, they had taken a room in a colored hotel in Memphis, then had left long before daylight that morning. That had given them plenty of time to reach Delta before Sunday-morning services were concluded, for Henry Jackson had suggested to Andy that if he came directly to the church before worship was over, he'd get to meet most of the folks in town.

Andy now pulled up alongside one of the wagons and shut off the ignition. After several hours of engine noise the sudden quiet seemed odd. It wasn't totally quiet, though, for singing spilled out through the open windows of the church.

"Listen," LaTonya said, smiling with pleasure. "Listen to that. Isn't that lovely?"

There was neither organ nor piano to accompany the singing, but no instruments were needed for the voices that were blending beautifully in four-part harmony.

"Yes," Andy agreed. "It really is."

"Let's go in," LaTonya suggested. She started to open her door, but before she could, Andy reached across the seat to stop her.

"Wait," he said. "Don't be in such a hurry."

LaTonya looked at him questioningly. "What's wrong?"

Andy took a deep breath, then let it out in a long sigh. "Baby, if you're having second thoughts about all this, now's the time to tell me. Like the preacher says, speak now, or forever hold your peace."

"Are *you* having second thoughts?" LaTonya asked.

"I don't know. Did you see this town as we drove through? Have you ever seen such squalor and poverty anywhere in your life?"

"No, I haven't. But, Andy, you don't have to prepare me for anything. We knew what it was going to be like when we agreed to come down here, didn't we?"

"Yes," Andy replied. "Still, don't forget that what we saw driving through was the *white* part of town. Now, if the *white* folks down here live like that, how must the *Negroes* live?"

LaTonya gazed out the window. "I don't know. But I don't see how it could be any worse." She turned to her husband. "Now," she said forcefully, "I'm going inside that church. Are you going with me?"

Andy smiled at her. "All right." He looked toward the front of the church, then grinned. "Lafayette, we are here."

Climbing out of the car, the young couple hurried across the parking lot and up the wooden steps, then pulled open one of the big double doors at the front of the church and stepped through. The entire congregation was on its feet in song, following the exaggerated arm movements of the song leader down front. Singing so loudly that his voice could be heard clearly over all the others, the music conductor literally jumped from side to side as he exhorted first one part of the congregation and then the other to join in. Finally they reached the end of the hymn, and the leader held both arms up over his head, wiggling his fingers and drawing out the final note until it filled the little church with as much power and majesty as if it were a cathedral organ. Then in one grandiose movement he brought both arms down, cutting the last note off so cleanly that all that remained of the song was an echo.

"Oh, my, that was wonderful. That was truly wonderful, Brother Taylor," an elderly man said, moving to the front. In his late sixties or early seventies, he was about five feet six and slender, even somewhat frail looking, with thick-lensed wire-rim glasses that made his animated eyes appear even larger and white hair that contrasted nicely with his long, black preacher's robe. From Professor Jackson's description Andy knew this had to be the Reverend Beasley. "And you, my children," Beasley continued, addressing his flock, "have never sung more beautifully, nor with more of God's spirit.

Now, brothers and sisters, if you would all take your seats, I have God's Word to share with you."

There was a shuffling of feet, a rustle of clothes, and the squeak of wood as the rough-hewn pews accepted the weight of the congregants.

With the congregation seated LaTonya and Andy were now revealed, standing just inside the back door. Beasley's lined, wrinkled face lit up in a broad smile.

"Welcome! Welcome! Welcome, my children! And you would be Dr. and Mrs. Booker?"

Andy nodded.

"The Lord be praised, brothers and sisters! God has answered our prayers!" the preacher exclaimed, and the congregation responded.

"Amen!"

"Praise the Lord!"

"Praise God!"

"I say the *Lord* has *answered* our *prayers*!" Beasley shouted joyfully, raising his arms and bringing his hand down hard on each word, like a conductor demonstrating the tempo. Again the congregation responded.

"Hallelujah!"

"Praise the Lord!"

"Amen!"

Beasley smiled at the congregants. "Would the ushers please escort the good brother doctor and his lovely lady to their seats of honor?"

Two men got up and walked to the back of the church. Both in their late thirties, one of the men was of average size, but the other was very tall—Andy guessed at least six feet seven inches—and very powerfully built. At first Andy wanted to laugh at the way they were dressed, for both were wearing bib overalls along with a shirt and tie, but he checked the impulse when he realized that the men were making a concession to Sunday by dressing as well as they could. He suddenly felt self-conscious about his tan suit and ran his finger inside his shirt collar, pulling it away from his neck.

As the ushers escorted Andy and LaTonya to their seats, everyone—Professor Jackson among them—turned toward them. Looking at their well-scrubbed and shining faces, Andy got a very vivid image of the name of the church, "Sunbeams of Heaven."

Two chairs had been placed between the front row of the pews and the preacher's pulpit. When the Reverend Beasley had said "seats of honor," Andy assumed he was merely using an expression. But it wasn't an expression at all. These two chairs had been put here just for this purpose.

Andy appreciated the thought, but he didn't like the idea of sitting at the very front. His church attendance had always been, at best, irregular. When he did attend, he normally sat as far to the back as he could get. This was a major departure—and not one he was particularly comfortable with.

Though still fairly early in the morning, it was already very hot, and most of the people in the congregation were using paper fans—courtesy of the local funeral parlor—in an effort to find some relief. As soon as the ushers seated Andy and LaTonya, a young girl brought a couple of the fans over to them. Offering them eagerly, she grinned so broadly that her dimples formed two holes in her cheeks. She was such a pretty little thing that Andy couldn't help but warm to her, and he returned her smile.

"Why, thank you, sweetheart," he said, taking the two fans from her and handing one of them to LaTonya.

The child curtsied, giggled, then hurried back to sit at her mother's side, sliding in under her mother's arm—though her big brown eyes stayed glued to Andy.

"*God's Words!*" the Reverend Beasley shouted, and everyone turned their attention back to the front of the church.

Beasley removed his glasses and took a handkerchief from his pocket, then wiped his face. He put his glasses back on very carefully, hooking them over one ear at a time, and stared at his congregation for a long moment. Someone coughed. Someone else cleared his throat. Another person shifted position, and the pew squeaked. Then all was quiet, the stillness inside the church broken only by the soft whisper of air being agitated by a hundred fans. Finally the reverend began to speak.

" 'Man that is born of a woman is of few days, and full of

trouble,'" the preacher said, quoting from the *Book of Job.* "'He cometh forth like a flower and is cut down. He fleeth also as a shadow and continueth not.'"

Beasley paused for effect, then repeated the last sentiment.

"The Lord says man cometh forth like a flower and is cut down. He is *cut down*!"

"Amen!" several dozen responded.

"Cut down," others said.

"Yes, sir. He be cut down."

"Uh-huh."

"That be the truth."

"He is *cut down,*" Beasley continued. "He fleeth also as a shadow and *continueth not!*"

"Yes, Lord!"

"Amen!"

"Uh-huh. He stop."

"Amen!"

The Reverend Beasley continued with his message, stressing the transitory aspect of life on earth and extolling the glory of the life hereafter. Sometimes his words were barely more than a whisper; at other times they boomed forth like thunder, shaking the rafters and rattling the windows. Throughout his sermon there was constant participation by the congregation, whose "amens," "glories," and repetition of key words from within the reverend's message served almost as a countermelody to the music of the Word so that one would not be complete without the other.

Beasley's eyes danced and sparkled and shot bolts of fire as he swept them back and forth over the congregants. Often he would find someone sitting three quarters of the way back, perhaps secure in believing that he was an anonymous part of the congregation and therefore safe from the Reverend Beasley's penetrating stares. But Beasley would impale him with the power of his gaze, holding him for a long, uncomfortable moment while the hapless parishioner squirmed, no doubt in self-condemnation and recalling every transgression ever committed. Then, as if having granted absolution, the preacher would release his captive, leaving the penitent physically and emotionally drained from the ordeal.

The Reverend Beasley's finger was fully as important as his voice. It would point accusingly at a sinner in his congregation, then straight down with the implied threat of condemnation and eternal perdition, then straight up with the promise of redemption and eternal salvation.

Finally the sermon was over, and the congregation rose as one and began singing "Shall We Gather at the River?"

Holding his Bible over his head, Beasley led the congregation in recession from the church. Puzzled, Andy and LaTonya followed. The parishioners went out across the yard, then down a well-worn path to the Sunflower River. The Reverend Beasley waded out into the river until he was waist deep in the water. There, his robe wafting out around him like a giant water-lily pad, he led the congregation in prayer, then baptized several young people. After the baptisms were completed, the pastor said another prayer, then came up out of the water.

"And now, brothers and sisters," he concluded, "let's bring out those picnic baskets and welcome our new brother and sister into our fold."

Andy was about to go over and greet Professor Jackson when a young woman approached him and asked, "Brother Doctor, would you look at my little girl while they be settin' up for the dinner?"

"Yes, of course," Andy replied. "Why don't you take her over there while I go get my bag?" he added, pointing to a shady spot under a big oak tree.

The woman led her child over, and Andy knelt down to her level. The girl had cut her leg, which had become infected. Pulling out some ointment from his bag, Andy treated the wound. He stood up and was about to return to where he had been when he realized that another patient was waiting for him, and another after that one, and then another still.

With LaTonya acting as his nurse, Andy worked steadily until late in the afternoon, when Henry Jackson and the Reverend Beasley finally stepped in and begged them to give "Brother Doctor"—as Andy was now being called by one and all—and his wife a chance to at least eat some lunch.

Jackson introduced his wife, Doney, who, as head of the church women's committee, had put together the picnic lunch, and Beasley's wife, Evie. The two women spread a red-and-white-checkered tablecloth out on the picnic table, then began bringing out the food: fried chicken, black-eyed peas, turnip greens, potato salad, and sliced tomatoes and cucumbers tossed in a concoction of vinegar, bacon grease, and cayenne. Topping it all off were several pones of golden corn bread.

"Isn't anyone else going to eat?" Andy asked as a filled plate was passed to him.

Doney Jackson laughed. "Heavens, child, don't you know? Everyone else ate hours ago. You've just been too busy doctoring ever since church let out."

"It must be gettin' on to four o'clock," Evie Beasley said. Like her husband's, her hair was snow white. However, where he was very thin, she was quite large.

"So it is," Andy said, looking at his wristwatch. "Matter of fact, it's a quarter till five."

Andy was suddenly aware that everyone in the congregation was staring at him, and he looked around in confusion. The very big man who had been one of the ushers came right over to the table to stare at Andy's watch.

"What's the matter with you folks?" Beasley scolded. "Let Brother Doctor and his wife eat in peace. Big Troy, ain't you never seen a watch before?"

"Ain't never seen no gold watch on a black arm before," Big Troy said. "What's a colored man doin' with a watch like that?"

"He's a doctor," Henry Jackson explained. "He has to have a watch like that in his work so he can count the pulse and heartbeat of his patients. Now, quit staring at him."

Big Troy withdrew, and the others who had been drawn by the novelty of the watch also left.

"Don't pay any attention to Big Troy," Doney said. "He's a good man, but he's not very bright."

Andy smiled. "I guess I'll have to learn not to be so obviously different. By the way," he asked as he took a bite from a chicken leg, "how long has it been since any of these people have seen a doctor?"

"With one or two exceptions, I'd say that none of them have *ever* seen a doctor," Jackson replied.

"Is there a white doctor in town?"

"There's old Doc Waltrip."

"He won't see colored people, though?"

"He will occasionally," the professor said. "But every time he does, he takes a lot of guff for doing it. The white people figure that since he's the only doctor in town, he's their exclusive property." Jackson laughed. "And Doc Waltrip will be the first to admit that we're probably better off because of it."

"Why?"

"He isn't really a doctor. I mean, not in the sense that he actually studied medicine," Jackson explained. "He started out as a self-taught veterinarian, then got into treating people. In fact, most of the white folks in town, if they *really* have something wrong with them, go up to Memphis or down to Jackson."

Andy digested the information along with his lunch, realizing that, as a city boy, he had had no idea just how lacking in what he considered normal services most folks were.

After he had finished eating, Andy began seeing patients again, examining a steady string of them until finally it grew too dark to work.

"Please, Brother Doctor, just one more," an elderly lady pleaded.

"I'm not going away," Andy promised. "I'll be here tomorrow and the next day and the next. You can come to my office . . ." He turned and looked at Henry Jackson. "By the way, do I *have* an office?"

"In a matter of speaking. Your office will be in your house."

Andy smiled. "Then at least I won't have far to go to work, will I?" he asked. He turned to the people still standing around in small groups, waiting to be seen. "Those of you whom I haven't examined, come to my house tomorrow."

"You be a good man, Brother Doctor," someone called from the darkness. "We thank the Lord He seen fit to let you come down here like He done."

"Thank you for your kind words," Andy called back to them. "Good night." Turning to Jackson, he asked, "Professor, do you think you could show 'Brother Doctor' to his house? It's been a long day."

"Your house is right next door to mine and Doney's. In anticipation of your coming, we put in a particularly large garden this year. We've also managed to collect a dozen or so chickens for you, and our cow gives enough milk for us to share."

"All the comforts of home," Andy quipped.

"We do want to make you happy, Brother Doctor," Jackson said with a chuckle as he led Andy and LaTonya back to their car.

Because the houses were right next to each other, Henry and Doney Jackson rode home in the back seat of Andy's Chevrolet. It was only a half-mile drive from the church to the two houses, which sat under a grove of trees about a hundred feet back from the dirt road and were separated from each other by the large garden Professor Jackson had mentioned. Since it was too dark for Andy to clearly see his new home, he positioned the car so that it was illuminated by his headlamps.

The glaring lights washed out all color, making everything harsh white and stark black. Andy wondered if the dwelling would look any more appealing in daylight. Modest in size—more a large cottage than anything else, Andy thought—the house was one-storied with a small front porch, the roof of which sagged noticeably on one end. An old car seat sat on the porch, tilting back jauntily. The best thing he could say about it, Andy supposed, was that it could have been a lot worse.

"Big Troy brought that car seat," Jackson said, breaking the silence. "He thought it would make a good waiting bench in case there were too many patients for the office."

One of the front windows was covered over with boards, and LaTonya asked about it.

"Well, you see," Professor Jackson said, "all the windows in the house were broken out when we started getting it ready for you. We managed to get glass for most but not all of them. The ones we couldn't replace we just closed over so they wouldn't be standing open all the time, letting in rain or, worse, flies and mosquitoes."

"Is there any furniture?" LaTonya asked.

"Oh, yes," Doney said, pride in her voice. "We've got it furnished really nice."

"At this moment the only piece of furniture I care about is the bed," Andy groaned.

"Oh, of course, you must be exhausted," Jackson said apologetically. "Go on inside and get some rest. You need to be fresh tomorrow. You're going to be busy."

"There are matches and a candle just inside the door," Doney put in.

"Matches and a candle?" LaTonya asked weakly.

Doney laughed. "Good heavens, child, you weren't expecting electricity, were you?"

"No, no. I just meant how efficient you were to have everything ready for us," LaTonya said quickly. Andy thought she did a reasonable job of covering her shock, though he knew better.

Saying good night, the Jacksons walked through the garden to their own house, while Andy and LaTonya went inside their new home. Feeling around just inside the door, Andy found a box of matches and a candle on a shelf. He lit the candle, then held it out in front of him, examining the room in the dim, wavering light. This, he assumed, was his office, for there was a table and chair, a couple of shelves, and two wooden benches.

"The bedroom must be that way," Andy said, pointing to a door at the back of his 'office.'

"Well, we'll soon find out," LaTonya said brightly—a bit too brightly, it seemed to Andy.

She led the way and he followed. The door led to a small room that contained an old sofa and overstuffed chair. This, they decided, was the living room. Opposite the living room was a kitchen just large enough to accommodate a small table and an ancient wood-burning cook stove. Off the kitchen was the bedroom, which had a cast-iron, high-sprung bed and nothing else. There was no dresser or chest or even a bedside table. Only the bed.

"Sort of sparse, isn't it?" LaTonya asked quietly.

Andy pointed to the bed. "At the moment, baby, that's the only thing I need."

When Andy awoke the next morning, he lay in bed for a while, soaking in this part of his new world. The walls of the bedroom had a fresh coat of newspapers, while the ceiling was covered with clean cardboard. Rudimentary as the coverings were, Andy had to admit that the jobs were neatly done, and he realized that several people must have worked very hard with limited resources to get the house ready for them.

"Well, what do you know?" Andy said.

"What?" LaTonya asked sleepily, turning toward him and draping her arm across his chest.

"National Prohibition has ended."

LaTonya opened one eye. *"What?"*

" 'Yesterday Utah became the thirty-sixth state to ratify the twenty-first amendment, thus ending the nation's long dry spell.' "

LaTonya sat up in bed and looked at Andy as if he had taken leave of his senses.

"Andy, what in the world are you talking about?" she asked. "That all happened last year. Don't you remember the big party we went to?"

Andy pointed to one of the newspapers that covered the wall. "I know. I was just quoting from the bedroom edition."

"The bedroom edition?" LaTonya looked around at the walls, then gasped. "Good Lord, look at this. We live in a newsstand!"

"I think that's handy," Andy said. "At least the next time you get a 'headache,' I won't be bored."

"Andrew Booker," LaTonya said. She crossed her arms and reached for her shoulders, bunching up the nightgown in her hands and pulling it over her head. Then, nude, she leaned into him, pressing her breasts against his bare chest and pushing her hard nipples into his skin. "When have I ever had a 'headache'?" she asked. Her dark eyes were half closed and smoldered with desire.

Andy grinned at her. "Well, I guess you haven't," he said, his reply a mumble since she was kissing him.

They made love in the soft light of early morning. The springs of the bed squeaked beneath them, softly and almost musically. Their lovemaking was warm, lazy, and intensely satisfying, and when Andy felt himself approaching the pinnacle, he forced himself back, waiting for LaTonya and, in so doing, holding on to the delicious agony of the quest. Finally he heard LaTonya take several sharp gasps, then felt her quiver, and her hands gripped his back. Andy then surrendered himself to the heat that had been pulling at him for several moments. Suddenly there was no newspaper-covered bedroom in a squalid little house in an impoverished Mississippi town. There was only moist, connected flesh and spurting seminal fluid and pulsating sensation that blotted out everything.

Andy and LaTonya were lying in each other's arms when a voice suddenly called through the door. "Brother Doctor, are you folks all finished in there? There be quite a few patients lined up out here, waitin' to see you."

Startled and embarrassed, Andy and LaTonya stared into each other's eyes. Then LaTonya burst out laughing.

"Welcome to Mississippi, Brother Doctor," she said softly, kissing him one last time.

When Andy had a reprieve from patients just before noon, he drove into town. Parking his Chevrolet by the train depot, he glanced over at the fading-black-lettered white sign identifying the town as Delta that hung at one end of the clapboard building. The sign nicely mirrored the town, Andy thought as he got out of the car and ambled toward a green luggage-wagon sitting on the station platform. Two men who looked to be in their early twenties were sitting on the wagon, one skinny and dark-haired, the other fat and blond, and they eyed Andy suspiciously as he started across the platform.

"Boy," the skinny one called, "don't you know niggers can't catch the train on this side of the platform? You better get your black ass around to the other side where you belong."

Andy couldn't bring himself to even glance at them.

"Thank you for the information, but I don't intend to catch the train," he said coolly. "I'm here to pick up a shipment of laboratory equipment."

"That makes it okay, Arlie," the fat one said in a la-di-da tone. "He ain't goin' to catch the train. He's here to pick up a shipment of laboratory equipment."

"Laboratory? Nah, he means *lavatory,* Deekus. You know, like a bathroom. Must be gettin' a shit stool," Arlie replied, laughing. "Now, you just tell me, Deekus, where's a nigger plannin' on puttin' in a shit stool? They ain't no houses down in the Bottoms that can even use a shit stool."

"Hey! Maybe he's plannin' on puttin' him in a commode in that fancy car of his'n," Deekus remarked. "Is that what you're goin' to do, boy? You goin' to put a commode in that there car?"

"Yeah, in the back seat," Arlie suggested. "That'd mean you could just be drivin' down the road, and iffen you had to take a shit, why, you could just stop, drop your drawers, an' then drop a load without ever once havin' to get out of the car."

"Hey, how you reckon a nigger like this ever got a car like that anyhow?" Arlie asked. "I ain't never seen no nigger with a car like that before. Hell, they ain't no white folks in this town with a car like that. How'd you get that car, boy? You done steal it or somethin'?"

Ignoring them, Andy stepped up to the freight window and pulled on the bell cord.

"Clyde! Hey, Clyde, you got you a customer out here!" Deekus called.

"Yeah. A *nigger* customer!" Arlie added.

The shutters opened, and a man's face appeared. "What can I do for you?" he asked Andy.

"This here's the nigger we was talkin' about," Deekus said.

Andy worked at keeping his temper under control. "I believe I can handle this myself," he told the two hecklers. He turned back to Clyde. "Are you the freight dispatcher?"

Clyde nodded. "Freight dispatcher and station manager."

"Do you have a shipment for Dr. Andrew Booker?"

"Just a minute." The station manager took a clipboard down from the wall and checked the cargo manifest. "Yes," he finally said. "Yes, I do. It arrived last week."

"Good," Andy said. "I'm here to pick it up."

"I'm sorry," Clyde said, putting the clipboard back on its nail, "but the instructions state specifically that Dr. Booker must claim this shipment personally."

"I am he."

"You're what?"

"I am Dr. Booker. Those were my instructions that only I could pick up the boxes. I sent the equipment on ahead before I left Jefferson City, Missouri."

Clyde retrieved the clipboard and looked at the paperwork. "Jefferson City. You're right, that's where the stuff came from. Okay, Dr. Booker, if you'll just sign here, I'll start loading the equipment onto a cart."

"Thank you," Andy said as he signed the shipping receipt.

"Hey, boy! If you're wantin' to make us believe that you're a doctor, don't you think you'd better stick a bone through your nose?" Arlie called from his perch on the freight wagon. "Don't witch doctors have bones stickin' through their noses?"

"I seen a witch doctor in a Tarzan movie once," Deekus noted. "He had a bone stickin' through his nose."

Both of them laughed, then Deekus asked Andy, "Boy, how come you ain't laughin' at nothin' we're sayin'? I mean, we're havin' us a real good time here, and you ain't laughin'."

"I don't find you funny," Andy replied without looking around.

"What do you mean we ain't funny? Why ain't we funny?"

Andy turned toward the two hecklers for the first time. "Humor requires a certain level of mental proficiency. As you two are clearly deficient in that commodity, I'm afraid it is an exercise in futility for you to even make the attempt."

"*What?*" Arlie asked, his face mirroring his confusion.

"I ain't never heard no nigger talk like that," Deekus said. "What the hell'd he say, anyway?"

Clyde chuckled as he loaded several boxes onto a handcart. "Fellas, I believe the doctor here just got one over on you."

"Look here, boy. Was you makin' fun of us?" Deekus asked as he stepped down from the luggage wagon and started toward Andy. " 'Cause if you was, why, maybe I'd better just go knock you upside your head a few times."

Suddenly a man in a uniform with a badge pinned to his chest stepped around the edge of the depot. He was big and menacing, and he glared at Arlie and Deekus.

"You two boys want to go on about your business and leave this colored man alone?" he asked.

"This here nigger insulted us, Stump," Arlie said.

"Did he? How?"

"Well, seein' as how you was here, didn't you hear what he said?"

"Yes, I heard."

"Well, don't you think it was insultin'?"

"What I think isn't important," Stump replied.

Arlie sputtered angrily. "Look here, Stump, are you takin' up for this here nigger against one of your own kind?"

"You're not my kind, Arlie. Fact is, I don't know what matter of creature would claim either one of you as their kind. Now, the both of you get the hell out of here and leave this man alone before I run you into jail."

"Come on, Deekus," Arlie said, yanking on his friend's sleeve. "Let's go sit down at the square and watch 'em play checkers."

"Yeah, I'm comin'," Deekus grumbled. As they left, Deekus turned toward the uniformed man. "You better learn who your friends are," he said.

"Yeah," Arlie put in. "And especially what *color* they are."

Stump watched the two men walk away; then, when the loaded handcart was pushed outside of the freight room, he put his hand on the handle.

"You must be this 'Brother Doctor' I've been hearing so much about this morning," he said to Andy with a friendly smile. "I'm Stump Pollard. Why don't you let me help you with that?"

"Thank you," Andy said. "I appreciate it. And I appreciate your timely appearance to deliver me from my situation."

Stump laughed. "You keep on talkin' like that, you're goin' to stay in trouble the whole time you're down here."

"Talking like what?"

"Like that," Stump said. "Deekus was right about one thing. You don't sound like any colored person I've ever heard before. Maybe a little like Professor Jackson, but you're even more highfalutin than *he* is."

"You know Professor Jackson?" Andy asked. Unlocking the trunk of his car, he raised the lid, and they started loading in the boxes.

"Oh, yeah, I know him," Stump said. "He's the one who asked me to keep an eye on you." He eyed all the boxes marked FRAGILE and HANDLE WITH CARE, then asked, "What is all this stuff, anyway?"

"Petri dishes, test tubes, beakers, glass piping, Bunsen burners . . . Some of it's for the practice I intend to establish here. The remaining equipment I shall require for a research project I'm working on."

Stump laughed again. "Professor Jackson said you were a real go-getter."

With the equipment loaded, Andy closed the trunk lid. He pointed at the badge on Stump's chest.

"What are you? A sheriff?"

"I'm the chief of police for Delta," Stump said. "It sounds more impressive than it is. I'm the chief of a three-man force."

It was Andy's turn to laugh. "You don't exactly sound like a—" He stopped himself in midsentence.

"Mississippi hillbilly?" Stump suggested.

"Yes, I guess that was the word I was looking for," Andy admitted.

"I suppose I don't," Stump said. "I have a degree in history from Ol' Miss. I could teach in a high school somewhere for eighty dollars a month, or I could serve as chief of police for a hundred forty dollars a month." He smiled broadly. "I opted for the filthy lucre."

Andy grinned. "I'm glad you did. At least today. I thank you again for coming to my rescue."

"Brother Doctor . . ." Stump paused. "Is that actually what they're calling you?"

"That's what they're calling me," Andy answered with a smile.

"Then I guess that's the handle you're stuck with. But what I was going to say is, don't judge the whole town by those two jackasses. Delta's a decent town with a lot of decent folks. We're coming through some hard times right now, but who isn't? Anyway, if you have any more trouble with either one of those yahoos, come see me. I'll set it right."

"Thank you," Andy said, slipping in behind the wheel. He waved at the police chief as he drove off.

Late that afternoon, after the last patient had gone and while he and LaTonya were unpacking the equipment and setting up his office as well as his laboratory, Andy had an unexpected visit from Stump Pollard.

"Chief," Andy said, greeting him, "is there something I can do for you?"

"Yes, I'm afraid there is," Stump said. "Would you come out here for a moment, please?"

"Sure," Andy agreed.

Stump led Andy to the Chevrolet, then pointed to a long, deep scratch in the shiny paint job on the passenger side of the car.

"Damn!" Andy spat. "Where did that come from?"

"I take it, then, that this is something new?" Stump asked.

"Yes," Andy replied. "Damn. A scar like that can't even be patched. My entire car will have to be repainted."

"It looked suspiciously fresh when I noticed it at the depot," Stump said. "That's why I picked up these two." He pointed to his police car, and Andy saw Arlie and Deekus sitting morosely in the back seat. "They're responsible for it," he said. "I'm as certain of it as I am my own name. I've been holding them at the station, but they've refused to own up to it. So I decided to take them for a little drive."

"I don't suppose they have enough money for a new paint job?" Andy muttered.

"Are you kidding? There isn't a colored person in the Bottoms who doesn't have more money than these two."

Andy stroked his chin and looked at the two men for a long moment. "I need a well dug," he finally said. "If they'll dig a well for me, I won't press charges."

"Did you boys hear that?" Stump asked, leaning over to look in through the back window. "If you fellows dig a well for Brother Doctor, he won't press charges."

"What the hell kind of charges can he place against us?" Deekus squawked. "All we done was make a little scratch on his car!"

Stump smiled. "Ah, so you finally admit your guilt. Well, let me enlighten you boys. If the repair bill is over forty dollars, a charge of willful destruction of property in that amount would be the same as grand larceny. The two of you could go to prison for thirty years each."

"Thirty years!"

"That's right," Stump said. He looked back at Andy. "I'd say a paint job would cost more than forty dollars, wouldn't you, Brother Doctor?"

"It certainly would, by the time I was satisfied with it," Andy agreed, forcing himself not to laugh.

The police chief turned back to his prisoners. "What do you say, boys? You want to dig a well or go to jail?"

"I ain't workin' for no nigger," Arlie growled.

"Me neither," Deekus said.

Stump shrugged and started getting into the police cruiser. "Suit yourself. Guess we'll see you two boys again sometime around 1964."

"No! No, wait!" Arlie said. He sighed. "All right, open the goddamned door. I'll do it."

"Yeah, me too," Deekus agreed.

Stump turned and smiled at Andy. "They're all yours, Brother Doctor."

Andy smiled back. "Thank you, Chief. I'll take good care of them."

CHAPTER TWELVE

AUGUST 29, 1934, BIMINI ISLANDS, THE BAHAMAS

Eric Twainbough stood with his legs slightly spread, flexing his knees to take up the roll of the boat. Charley, his houseboy, was at the wheel up on the flying bridge of the *Katya* as she plowed through a calm sea, leaving a V-shaped wake behind. Two outriggers were dragging, the bait dipping and leaping in the curl of the waves raised by the wake.

Eric turned to face the fishing chairs. One of them was occupied by his son, Hamilton, who was holding a rod and watching the bait with all the intensity that a twelve-year-old could muster. It wasn't the first time Ham had visited Eric alone, but it was the first time he was doing so since Eric and Tanner had been divorced. Tanner had taken Ham by train from St. Louis to Miami, and then the two of them flew over to the island. Eric had tried to get Tanner to stay a few days herself, but she had pleaded important work to be done at the brewery and returned to the mainland on the very same plane she had flown out on.

The second chair was occupied by Guy Colby, a movie director who now considered himself mostly a producer. He had arrived from Hollywood the afternoon before to try to talk Eric into selling him the screen rights to *Stillness in the Line.* Guy had attempted to get out of going deep-sea fishing since he feared getting seasick, but Eric had been adamant. He had already promised his son, and he wasn't going to break his promise. So if Guy Colby wanted to talk, he was going to have to go fishing. Fortunately the sea was delightfully calm, even in the Gulf Stream, and after a short while out Guy conceded to finding deep-sea fishing a very enjoyable experience.

A pair of dolphins executed a graceful leap about one hundred feet off the starboard side of the boat. They were in perfect synchronization, slipping through the water without a ripple, their backs glistening in the sun.

"Look, Papa," Ham said, pointing to the dolphins. "I wish one of those would take my bait."

"No, you don't want to catch a dolphin," Eric said. "They're sailors' friends."

"Sailors' friends? But they're enormous. Wouldn't they hurt me if I fell into the water?"

"No. There've been times when dolphins actually saved a sailor who fell overboard."

"I've heard that about them," Guy put in. "But I never knew if it was true or not. Have you known someone who fell overboard and was rescued by a dolphin?"

"No," Eric admitted. "It's one of those things you have to accept on faith. You know, it always happens to someone who knows someone who knows someone that you know."

"I know what you mean. It's like the story of the man who lost a ring in a lake, then three years later caught a fish, cut him open, and found the ring," Guy said.

"Did that really happen?" Ham asked skeptically.

"Of course it did," Guy answered easily. "I have a friend who knows someone whose friend knows the person that it happened to."

Eric laughed. "There, you've got the picture," he told Guy.

"Do I? Have the picture, I mean?" Guy asked. "Are you going to sell it to me?"

Eric wagged his finger back and forth. "Not so fast. That was a figure of speech." He grinned. "You're a smooth operator, Guy Colby."

"Of course I'm smooth. Why else do you think the studio sent me out here? You have the reputation of being a hard sell. I, on the other hand, have the reputation of being able to handle people like you."

"Sort of like an irresistible force meeting an immovable object," Eric said. He turned and stepped into the cabin, ducking through the hatchway. Opening the boat's ice chest, he called out, "What do you want, Ham? Root beer, orange soda, or Coke?"

"Root beer," Ham answered.

"A root beer for the boy, and two of his mama's brews for the men," Eric said, pulling out one root beer and two Tannenhowers. He popped the caps off, then stepped back through the hatch and passed them around.

"Why don't you want to sell the rights to us, Eric?" Guy asked. "I know it isn't the money. We haven't even talked money yet—and, besides, my production company is prepared to be very generous."

"How long would it be?" Eric asked.

"Until we shoot it?"

"No. I mean how long would the film be?"

"Oh. About an hour and a half, I guess. Maybe two hours—at the very most."

"Let's say it's two hours," Eric replied. "Now, how many pages would that be? I mean of actual script . . . not instructions to the cameras or the set designers or anything like that. How many pages of actual story would there be?"

"That's hard to say. But my guess is it would run from ninety to, oh, maybe a hundred twenty pages."

"Uh-huh. Guy, do you know how many pages there are in the book?"

"Not exactly."

"Three hundred and fourteen," Eric said. "That was in

the printed version. The typed manuscript ran to more than four hundred pages. Now, you tell me how you're going to cut that story from four hundred pages, or even three hundred and fourteen pages, down to a hundred and twenty."

"I think I see what you're getting at," Guy said. "You're afraid we're going to leave the guts of your story out, aren't you?"

"Oh, no, I believe you'll keep the guts. But that's *all* you'll keep," Eric said. "The flesh and bone and *soul* of the story is what you'll leave out."

"Fish, Mr. Eric! There's a fish!" Charley shouted down from the flying bridge in his Bahamian lilt.

Eric looked in the direction Charley was pointing and saw white water where the fish had been, but he didn't actually see the fish. From the angle, though, he knew that it was about to hit Ham's bait.

"Okay, get ready, Ham," Eric instructed. "He's coming at you."

Ham set his half-finished root beer down on the deck. "Papa, would help me, please?" Ham asked in an excited-yet-slightly-fearful voice.

"That wouldn't be fair to you if I landed your fish," Eric replied.

"But if I try and do it myself, I might lose him. And I don't want him to get away!"

"Okay, if you don't mind sharing him with me."

Eric moved around the seat and Ham hopped down. While Eric slipped down into the chair, grabbing the rod, the boy stood beside his father, one hand on his bare leg, the other resting on the butt of the pole.

The line fell from the outrigger, then started racing away from the boat.

"There he is!" Eric shouted. "He just took the bait!" The reel on his rod was spinning furiously.

"My God, look at him go!" Guy yelled.

"You better hit him, Mr. Eric!" Charley called down. "You don't hit him now, he'll run all the way to Cuba. Mr. Guy, get your line in," Charley ordered as if he were a first sergeant giving commands.

Hurriedly, Guy started taking in his rig.

"You ready to hit him?" Eric asked Ham.

Ham's hand tightened on the rod. "You bet!"

"Now!" Eric shouted. He braced his feet against the back of the boat and jerked back hard on the rod. The rod bent almost double.

"Did you feel that, Ham?" Eric shouted gleefully. "We got him!"

Ham yelled and cheered.

"Keep him lined up, Charley!" Eric shouted.

"You don't worry about me," Charley shouted back as he jockeyed the throttles. "I'll drive the boat, you land the fish."

"*We,*" Ham called up to Charley. "You mean *we'll* land the fish, Charley."

Charley laughed. "That's what I meant when I said 'you.' "

"Charley, will you goddammit quit talking and keep the son of a bitch astern?" Eric yelled.

"You want him astern, you got him astern," Charley shot back, maneuvering the boat expertly.

"He's sounding now," Eric said, flicking his gaze to the spinning reel. "He's going way down."

Without being told, Charley began easing the boat back toward the fish, saving the line. When the fish quit sounding, Charley stopped the boat and shifted the engines to idle. They ran so quietly that they could barely be heard.

"He's quit fighting us now," Eric said.

"Has he given up?" Ham asked.

"No. He's just waiting down there for us to make the next move. He's saying, 'Okay, I went deep; now what are you going to do about it?' "

"I don't know," Ham replied. "What *are* we going to do about it?"

"We're going to haul his ass up," Eric said, grinning broadly. "You ready?"

"I'm ready," Ham said, his own grin matching his father's.

"Okay, let's start reeling him in."

Eric put his son's hand on the reel, covered it with his

own, and then started turning, pulling up line, so that they were, in effect, both turning.

"How big do you think he is?" Guy asked.

"Well, we won't be embarrassed to bring him in," Eric replied, "but I don't think he's real big."

"Will he be big enough to hang up and get a picture taken beside him?" Ham asked eagerly.

"Oh, yeah, he'll be big enough for that."

"Boy, I can't wait to show the picture to Mama and all my friends back in St. Louis!"

"Your mama will be real proud when she sees you standing beside this fish, that's for sure," Eric said.

"That doesn't mean anything," Ham retorted dryly. "Mothers are *always* proud."

"Are they?"

"Sure. Don't you know?"

Eric chuckled. "I guess they are," he conceded.

All the time they were talking, Eric was hauling up on the rod, taking up line, and hauling up again. It took almost thirty minutes to get the fish back up to the surface. The creature had been quiet for a long time, but once he neared the surface, he got some life back in him.

About one hundred yards behind the boat and just off to starboard the fish suddenly broke through the surface of the sea, dark blue and silver and shining brightly in the sun. He came all the way out of the water, shaking his head as he did so, trying to spit out the hook that had embedded itself in his mouth. The marlin hung in midair for a long moment, then fell back, sending up a spray of sparkling white water.

"Holy shit!" Guy exclaimed. "That's the most magnificent spectacle I've ever seen!"

"Get the gaff, Charley!" Eric called. "We're bringing him in!"

Charley dropped down lightly from the flying bridge, then got the long, hooked pole. He leaned over the side as the fish came closer, and when it was close enough, he gaffed it. Using the pole as leverage, he brought the marlin into the boat and lowered it. The fish lay on the deck, staring up at them through its large, iridescent eye. It flopped a few times and its sides heaved as it tried to breathe. Finally it lay still.

"Boy, isn't he beautiful?" Ham asked, awestruck.

"Most beautiful fish I ever saw," Eric replied.

"I wish we could throw him back."

"Do you want to?"

"No. . . . But I wish I could keep him *and* throw him back." Ham laughed self-deprecatingly. "But that's crazy, isn't it?"

"No, Ham," Charley said gently, putting his arm around the boy's shoulder. "Maybe it might sound crazy to the folks who ain't never seen a magnificent fish like this. But it don't sound crazy to the folks who have."

"How much you think he'll weigh?" Guy asked.

"He'll go well over two hundred pounds," Charley replied. "Maybe as much as three hundred."

"Have you ever caught a fish this big, Charley?" Ham asked.

Charley looked at Ham and grinned. "Not by myself."

"Well," Ham mused, putting his hands on his hips as he looked down at the fish, "I guess you'd have to say I didn't actually catch this one by myself, either." He laughed. "But that doesn't mean I'm not going to have my picture taken beside him."

That night, after a dinner of conch fritters and sweet potatoes, Eric, Guy, Charley, and Ham played a game of poker on the screened-in porch. The men managed to arrange it so that an unsuspecting Ham won practically every hand—though not without a lot of groans, moans, and accusations of cheating. Finally Charley excused himself to clean up the kitchen, and Eric asked Ham if he wasn't about ready to go to bed.

"Well, I know you and Mr. Colby want to talk some business," Ham said in the kind of understanding voice that indicated adulthood wasn't far off, "so I'll go to bed now. But, Papa, sometime before I go back to St. Louis and start school again, I'd like to sit up all night with you and watch the sun come up the next morning."

Eric laughed. "Sit up all night with me? What makes you think I stay up all night?"

"Because you're always up when I go to bed, and when I wake up the next morning you're still up. Boy, it'll be neat when I'm a grown-up and won't have to go to bed . . . *ever!* . . . if I don't want to."

"Yeah, that's one of the joys of being a grown-up," Eric agreed. "Now, off with you."

"Good night, Papa. Good night, Mr. Colby. Good night, Charley," the boy called toward the kitchen.

He walked across the room toward the stairs, disappearing up them a moment later.

"A kid like that'll keep you young," Guy said after Ham was gone.

"Do you have any?"

"No. I've been married a few times—three to be exact—but so far no kids." Guy was silent for a moment. "It's probably a good thing I never had any," he added. "I'd have been a piss-poor father, and all the women I married would've been shit for mothers."

Eric laughed. "Seems like I've read a little about your domestic life."

"Oh, yeah. Everything that happens in Hollywood is grist for the gossip mills. The person they're picking on the most now is Demaris Hunter. In a perverse sort of way, it's the sincerest form of flattery. That's Colby's Law."

"Colby's Law?"

"The degree of success and popularity one has attained is directly proportional to the amount and inaccuracy of the gossip being generated," Guy explained. "Like right now, for instance. The gossipmongers have linked Demaris with just about every male star in Hollywood. If she did everything they all say she did, she'd have to walk around with a mattress strapped to her back. The truth is, she's quite monogamous . . . in a serial sort of way."

"You discovered her, didn't you?"

Guy chuckled. "Actually, you might say she discovered me. She dropped out of the sky one day. Literally. I was shooting an Alphonso Delavente movie when this beautiful young woman came down in a parachute, practically right on top of me. She had jumped out of a plane to get my attention."

"Evidently it worked."

"I guess it did. Not right away, of course, but eventually. Anyway, she's a very beautiful and very talented woman who's had some tragedy in her life, what with her father committing suicide after the crash and her mother dying when she was young. I just wish to hell people would leave her alone."

Eric studied his companion for a moment. "You're in love with her, aren't you, Guy?"

"What makes you say that?" the producer asked defensively.

"When I found out you were interested in making a picture out of *Stillness in the Line,* I wanted to know about you, so I did some research. Like you said, everyone in Hollywood is grist for the gossip mill, so it wasn't too difficult to find a lot written about you. The hard part was figuring out how to separate the wheat from the chaff. You seem to have a propensity for beautiful movie stars. You've been married to Dorothy Mills, Greta Gaynor, and April Love."

"April Love," Guy snorted. "A press agent's creation, from her made-up name to that phony heart-shaped birthmark she was supposed to have on her ass. Jesus, I don't know. We were married for such a short time that sometimes I wonder if we actually *were* married, or if *that* was part of a press agent's creation as well."

"Your name keeps getting linked with Demaris Hunter."

Guy took a long swallow of beer before he answered. "Yes," he said quietly, "I suppose it does."

"You don't have anything to do with Dorothy Mills or Greta Gaynor or April Love anymore. But you do keep showing up with Demaris Hunter. That's why I think you're in love with her."

"It's really none of your business, you know."

"I know."

Sighing, Guy finally admitted, "Yeah. I'm in love with her. But that's as far as it goes, and that's as far as it will ever go." He looked over at Eric, and Eric could see his eyes shining in the soft light of the sole living room lamp. "And you are the only person on God's earth, including Demaris, that I've ever told that to."

"Don't you think she knows?"

"I don't know whether she knows or not." There was a lengthy pause before Guy spoke again. "Yes, she knows. She has to. But she has her own life to live, and I have mine. And tomorrow she's marrying Ian McCarty."

"How do you feel about that?" Eric asked.

"How do I feel? I feel like shit, that's how I feel," Guy muttered.

Both men were silent for some time after that, just sitting there, looking out over the dark sea and listening to the pounding surf.

"You used to be a screenwriter, didn't you, Guy?"

"Yeah," Guy said, clearly glad that the subject had changed. "But I don't do that anymore. Now I just produce and direct. And mostly just produce."

"Well, if you want my story, you're going to have to do the screenplay."

"Jeez, Eric, I don't know. . . . It's been so long, I don't know if I could do the job. The studio has people for that. Good people."

"I want *you* to do it," Eric said firmly.

"Why?"

"If you wanted the book badly enough that you came all the way down here to see me even though I've already turned you down three times, then you must really like the story."

"I *do* like the story," Guy said. "It's a great story."

"And now that you've met me, fished on my boat, held my kid on your lap, and drunk my beer, I think you might feel that you know a little something about me."

Guy nodded. "I like to think that I do."

"You told me that the screenwriter would have to take out about two thirds of the book, right?"

"Yeah, I'm afraid so. It would be impossible to produce, otherwise."

"I understand. So that being the case, I feel you're the

only one who can cut out two thirds of the book yet still leave the soul intact."

"You would trust me to do that?"

"Yes," Eric said.

Guy drummed his fingers on the arm of the rattan chair, just staring out over the dark sea. "I'll have to reschedule some things, change a few writing assignments," he finally said, more to himself than to Eric. He looked at Eric. "All right," he said, raising his bottle of beer in salute, "I'll do the screenplay *and* I'll direct it. I just hope we're not both sorry."

HOLLYWOOD, CALIFORNIA

The number-one box office draw for 1934 was Will Rogers. He was followed by Clark Gable, then Ian McCarty. Demaris Hunter was in sixth place, right after Mae West and just before Joan Crawford. Demaris and Ian had first met during the filming of *Temptations,* which promised to be one of the biggest money makers of all time because two of Hollywood's biggest stars were in the same picture. When the studio saw a romance developing between their two stars, they did all they could to promote it, feeding the public interesting tidbits of information on a daily basis and rendering weekly reports of how the romance was going until, at last, they were able to release the story everyone had been waiting for: Demaris Hunter and Ian McCarty were about to be married.

The press announcement was the usual gushing pap:

> "How would you describe Ian McCarty?" one fan was asked. "Six feet three inches of gorgeous man," was the reply. For the last three years gorgeous Ian has managed to show up at every premiere with a different beautiful girl on his arm. Many are known to have cast their nets for him, but none have been able to catch him until that dynamite blonde, Demaris Hunter, came along.
>
> Demaris, shedding the last trappings of a failed and miserable marriage via a Nevada divorce, is now as able

as she has long been willing to marry Ian. The wedding will take place on August 30 at eight o'clock in the evening. So many close friends have this handsome couple that the marriage is going to be held on stage at the Royal Theater—where, after the wedding, will be held the world premiere of *Temptations,* the film where Cupid first shot the golden arrow that linked these two wonderful people.

At first Demaris complained about all the press coverage. She hated the idea of newspaper photographers suddenly leaping out at her from behind marbled columns in some hotel lobby or appearing in the midst of a jungle of potted palms in a restaurant. Ian was far more tolerant of the intrusions, explaining patiently that their careers depended upon keeping their names before the public. In fact, it seemed to Demaris as if Ian actually went out of his way to have his picture taken or have a story written about him.

"You know what they say about having your name in print," he joked. "It's only bad if they spell your name incorrectly."

Because of Ian's attitude toward publicity and, of course, the studio's insistence upon it, Demaris learned to put up with it. But she never learned to like it, and sometimes she disliked it more intensely than other times. That was particularly true when the newspapers and the fan magazines wrote untruths about her divorce from Ken Allen, such as the "shedding the last trappings of a failed and miserable marriage" comment.

While it was true that her marriage to Ken had failed, it had not been miserable. The truth was that Demaris still thought a great deal of Ken Allen and probably would have still been with him had *he* not requested the divorce. And Ken hadn't wanted the divorce because he believed any of the gossip about Demaris. He understood the Hollywood game and knew when to listen to gossip and when not to. Neither was it because he had found another woman. Ken loved Demaris and always would.

The reason was much more deeply rooted and basic than that: Ken had not been able to accept the fact that his career was on the decline while Demaris's was racing to the top. It was a matter of manly pride, and it came to a head on the day they arrived at the studio together and found a new guard at the gate. The guard was star struck by Demaris, yet did not even recognize Ken and only let him through on the strength of Demaris's vouching for him.

Ken had laughed about it with Demaris, but it had hurt badly, and he could no longer live with it. He needed a woman who would be an orbit to his sun. He didn't need someone who, instead of being a planet in orbit, blotted out his own bright star. He became surly, began drinking, and finally moved out, setting the stage for abandonment so that Demaris could divorce him whenever she wanted.

It was during the eighteen months that Demaris lived alone that gossip columnists really had a field day. Whenever she was seen at any of the gathering places with any man, rumors of a romance had flown. She was linked with Dick Powell when the two of them just happened to be sitting at the same table at a Hollywood benefit. Clark Gable was next. There was a little more validity to linking her with Gable since they had at least come to dinner together—though it had been arranged by their studios. And, of course, there were constant references to Guy Colby. In that, at least, the reporters weren't too far wrong. The fact of the matter was Demaris did care a great deal about Guy—perhaps even as much as she did about Ken—but he was a part of her past, and she felt that resurrecting the past, even if it were possible, would be unwise.

It wasn't just movie stars she was seen with who attracted the attention of the gossipmongers. One photographer snapped a picture of her talking to a man as she stood clutching her housecoat tightly closed at the neck. The picture ran in newspapers all over America with the caption: "Demaris Hunter's secret love?"

The truth was the man was Demaris's gardener, and the picture cost him his job, for his wife, as taken in as the gullible public, refused to let him return to work for Demaris. Demaris had to hire a new gardener, a Japanese man named Yutake Saito.

"I'd like to see them put Mr. Saito and me together," she had quipped to her friends.

Now that Demaris was about to marry Ian McCarty, the gossipmongers were quieted and the publicists stepped to the forefront. A wedding between two of its major stars was any studio's dream. A wedding that took place at the same time as the opening of the stars' latest picture sent studio executives into a virtual swoon. They were going to milk it for all it was worth.

A thick red-velvet rope strung between polished brass stanchions held back the crowd in front of the Royal Theater. Four huge trailer-mounted searchlights shot their powerful beams high into the night sky while a fifth played its light directly on an enormous billboard that featured a photograph of Demaris and Ian in an embrace, looking into each other's eyes, their lips but a millimeter apart. It was actually a still shot taken during the filming of the movie, and it was advertising the movie—though many thought it was advertising the wedding itself.

Several newsreel cameras were set up on the sidewalk in front of the theater, taking pictures of celebrities as they arrived. Once the celebrities got by the cameras, they were stopped by a battery of the microphones used by the radio reporters doing remote broadcasts of the event. Their reports were going out all across the nation via network hookups, allowing, say, young farm girls in Iowa and shop girls in Brooklyn to lie in their beds in the darkness and listen to the radio reporters describing, with breathless enthusiasm, the exciting scene so far away.

Though the studio had promised Demaris that the wedding itself would be an intimate affair attended only by "a few of your closest friends," the theater was packed. Demaris was sure there were as many people inside the theater as outside, and she was equally sure she didn't know more than one in twenty of those there.

The ceremony was conducted very dramatically and in a stage-trained voice by a well-known preacher who had a large, successful church in Hollywood, on the marquee of which he billed himself unabashedly as "God's Agent to the Stars." Demaris ignored as best she could the fact that what she regarded as a solemn occasion had been turned by studio publicists into a circus. In fact, as she stood listening to her groom recite his vows with loving conviction, she was surprised to find that she was as nervous and as moved as a virginal bride. When it was her turn to say her vows, she felt her eyes well up with tears and could barely say the words above a whisper.

Then the solemnity was over, and at the reception Demaris posed for the usual pictures, such as shoving a piece of wedding cake into Ian's mouth, while the bulbs flashed.

"Demaris, have you heard from Ken Allen? What do you think he's doing tonight?" one reporter, a small man with a pinched face and a bow tie, asked.

"I don't know what he's doing tonight. Why would you even ask about him?" she replied with an insouciance she didn't exactly feel.

"Well, after all, you *have* dumped him for another man. Don't you think it quite possible that he's off somewhere suffering terribly from this hurt you've inflicted upon him?"

Demaris felt a twinge of anger at the barb but was damned if she'd let it show. "No, I don't think that," she said lightly. "I'm sure he's very happy for me, as I would be for him."

"What have you told Ian to ease any apprehensions he may have about you leaving him, as you did Ken?" the reporter then asked.

Demaris wanted to scream at the reporter that she hadn't left Ken, he had left her, but she didn't. She also wanted to shove the cake in the little shit's face, but she didn't do that, either. Instead she smiled prettily and said, "I love Ian, and Ian loves me. I have every reason to believe that this marriage will last."

"You thought that with Ken Allen too, didn't you?" the man persisted.

"Yes. I thought that with Ken Allen."

"And yet here you are, getting married a second time."

"Yes, here I am, getting married again."

"Well, what do you say about that?"

"Sometimes those things happen," she said sweetly while imagining herself grabbing the irritating creep by his bow tie, then taking the cake server and slathering his face with icing.

"Demaris, darling," one of the studio publicity men said, interrupting the inquisition, "I think the photographers would like to get another picture of you feeding a piece of cake to Ian."

Immensely relieved, thinking that this was one of the rare times that she actually appreciated a studio publicist, Demaris smiled cloyingly at the reporter and turned toward Ian.

"Come on, you guys, have a heart," Ian pleaded, putting his arm around his bride. "If I have to taste any more of that crap, I'm going to throw up."

"Just a quick one, Ian!" a photographer shouted.

Ian smiled bravely, and Demaris laughed and stuck another piece of cake into his mouth. Finally it was all over, and the couple ran to the car amid the traditional shower of rice.

There had been all sorts of speculation as to where the happy couple would go for their honeymoon. One published report said they were going up the coast to a quiet hideaway. Another said they had charted a private plane and were flying to a secret spot in Mexico. Still another suggested that they were going directly to Ian's palatial estate, where they had hired armed guards to keep everyone away for a week.

All three stories had been leaked by the studio, and all three were false. The information had been released to conceal the couple's actual plans and ensure them of some privacy. From the studio's point of view it also meant that much more publicity for each story they released—and more publicity converted directly to more box-office appeal for *Temptations.*

Where they actually went—after changing cars three times, finally winding up in a very nondescript Plymouth to put off pursuers—was to Ian's fifty-five-foot yacht, *Prometheus,* which had been adequately stocked with enough provisions to last a week. The couple hurriedly boarded, and

Ian, a competent sailor, explained to Demaris that he was going to take the boat out into Santa Monica Bay and drop anchor.

"Is there anything you want me to do?" Demaris asked as Ian started the motors and eased the big boat away from the dock.

"Not a thing," Ian replied. "I've done this lots of times. This is where I come when I want to be alone to study my lines."

"I don't know much about boats, but this sure is a beauty," Demaris said as she ran her hand over the polished teak railing around the bridge. "I've attended a few parties on yachts, but I've never been on one when there weren't dozens of people on board. How many people will this hold?"

"It has six staterooms," Ian said.

"What a waste."

Ian looked around in surprise. "A waste?"

"Sure," Demaris said. She smiled at him, then pressed against his back, hugging him from behind. "I mean, all those bedrooms when we only need one," she said directly into his right ear.

"Oh, yeah," Ian said, smiling at her. "I guess I see what you mean."

"You *guess* you see? What do you mean, you guess? Honey, you'd better have a clear idea of what I mean, or I'm going to be awfully disappointed tonight." She chuckled, then kissed his neck. "I have to confess, I never thought I'd have been the type to save herself for marriage, as it were, but when you said that waiting would heighten our pleasure when we finally did it, I had to agree with you. Anticipation and all that jazz. By the way, speaking of anticipation, how long before we get where we're going? I mean, now that we're finally going to make love, I'm not really in the mood for a long boat ride, if you follow my drift." She laughed. "Follow my drift. Hey, that's pretty funny, isn't it?"

"It is pretty good," Ian agreed, laughing with her.

"How long?"

"Not long. We're only going about a mile offshore. There's a good place to anchor there."

"Then, if you don't need me up here, I think I'll go down and . . . get ready." She uttered the last words in an exaggeratedly husky voice. "Don't be long," she added.

Demaris kissed Ian passionately, then stepped into the cabin. Stopping just inside the doorway, she smiled appreciatively. The *Prometheus* was more like a house than a boat. The grand salon was very elegant and featured a long white-leather sofa and matching chairs surrounding an exquisitely carved coffee table. Continuing on, she found an equally beautifully decorated dining room and a well-appointed galley. And, as Ian had said, there were six staterooms. It wasn't difficult to find the master bedroom; it was clearly the largest.

Crossing to the dressing table, Demaris went to extra lengths to prepare for Ian. She brushed her long blond hair until it shone, then refreshed her makeup, taking particular care to accent her crystal-blue eyes. She looked around and located her suitcases in a corner of the room, sitting on luggage stands, and rapidly unbuckled them, taking out the nightgown she had bought especially for this night. It was the sexiest nightgown she had ever owned, made of black silk satin with openwork black lace over the breasts and fitting like a second skin.

She slipped out of her clothes and into the nightgown, then turned the covers back and climbed onto the bed. Arranging the folds of the gown just so and spreading her hair out on the pillow so that it was a golden halo framing her face, she lay there, waiting for Ian.

After a while she felt the rumble of engines cease, and it grew quiet except for the sound of the generator that kept the boat supplied with electricity. She could also hear the clanging of a buoy somewhere in the harbor. She heard the anchor chain rattle, then splash as the anchor hit the water. The boat rocked very, very gently.

Demaris's heart began beating with anticipation, and she felt herself growing moist with desire. She twisted her body to show off her curves to their best advantage and stroked her nipples until they hardened and protruded erotically against the silk.

She giggled. *I've got this down pretty good,* she said to

herself. *If the movie business ever goes sour, I can always work as a whore.*

Demaris listened intently for Ian's footfalls. The minutes passed, and she grew tired of holding her body in the awkward position that best accented her curves. Her back started hurting, and she got a catch in her neck from keeping her head in one position so that the hair would look good.

Ian didn't come.

Annoyed and frustrated, Demaris finally slipped out of bed and went to investigate.

He wasn't in the grand salon, the dining room, the galley, or any of the other five bedrooms or three bathrooms. And he wasn't on the deck where she last saw him. Gathering up her nightgown, she climbed down to the engine room to see if he was there. The two big diesel engines were silent, the small gasoline generator was popping away, and there was no sign of Ian. The mystery was deepening. She came back up from the engine room and returned to the salon, concern beginning to gnaw at her.

That was when she saw a small white envelope on the coffee table. She was certain it hadn't been there earlier, when she had first stepped into the cabin. Puzzled, she went over and picked it up. It was addressed to her.

She smiled, relieved. "Oh, so this is it," she said aloud. "We're playing a little game, are we? Okay, I'll play along."

Demaris settled onto the white-leather sofa, close to the table lamp. Opening the envelope, she removed the note.

Dearest Demaris,

Please forgive me for getting you involved in my own personal hell. I should have had the courage long ago to stop this before it went any further. But I've lived with the horror of discovery for so long that I came to you in one last desperate attempt to change . . . no, make that to *save* my life. Unfortunately I realize now that it isn't going to work.

Demaris, my dear, you are a classic case of what they call "rebound." Just before our romance began I had been rejected by the only person I can ever truly love. A couple of people in the studio know the real story, and it was they who suggested that I get involved with you. Actually, "suggested" isn't the proper word. "Ordered" would be more appropriate. They not only ordered that I become involved with you, they orchestrated it.

All the time I was with you, my heart was with my true love, and yet, though I sent impassioned pleas, I was rejected again and again. As I said, I wish I had had the courage to stop all this before it reached this point, but I was weak. And now, Demaris, my dear, I am too weak to go on. By the time you read this, I will be dead. I am taking my own life, for I cannot live the lie of being married to you while actually being in love with Bruce. I saw him yesterday, looking at another man the way he used to look at me, and it tore my heart out.

Yes, Demaris, I am a homosexual. I wish I weren't, but I can't change that fact any more than I can change my height or the color of my eyes. You can understand, I am sure, why the studio would not want word of this to get out. Perhaps you can also understand why they thought that my marrying you might help protect my secret. What neither they nor I understood was how impossible it would be for me to live such a sham.

I ask your forgiveness for drawing you into all of this, and I beg you to have some understanding and compassion for me. Believe me, I have thought about this long and hard, and if there were any other way, I would "let this cup pass from me." But there *is* no other way.

Ian

Demaris was stunned. For the longest time all she could do was sit there, holding the letter in her hand and staring at it blankly. Finally she got up and walked out to the afterdeck and looked over the stern back at the lights of the city.

As she stood there, a gentle breeze playing over her bare shoulders, feeling rushed back into her body with all the force of a volcano.

"Compassion?" she screamed into the night. "You do this to me and you ask me to have compassion? I hate you, you son of a bitch! You egotistical, conniving, queer bastard! I wish I had known what you were planning! I would have pushed you over myself!"

Crumpling up the letter, she flung it over the stern of the *Prometheus,* then sank onto the cushioned seat and wept bitterly.

CHAPTER THIRTEEN

SEPTEMBER 12, 1934, LANGSTON, OKLAHOMA

Shortly after Del and Rubye Murtaugh arrived to claim their farm, they bought a team of mules, getting a good deal on them from a farmer who was giving up. With his new team, Del put in a crop of corn and a crop of cotton. That was four months ago, and the cornfields that by now should have had stalks higher than a man's head were barren or, at best, dotted with sickly brown plants that had grown no higher than a man's knee before they had twisted and died.

The cotton was worse. In one five-acre field no more than fifteen or twenty plants had even taken root, and none of them had produced cotton. The other cotton fields were the same, identified as such only because they were fields in which cotton had been planted, not because they were fields in which any had grown.

It had been a summer of heat and wind and dust. The

dust boiled up behind men and plows and cars, and rather than settling back down to earth, it drifted off to join with all the other dust clouds from all the other men and plows and cars so that the sky grew darker and darker.

Every morning the sun rose at its accustomed time and in its accustomed place, but it couldn't push back the dark. By high noon the sun was still a pale-red circle seemingly struggling to make its way across the sky until eventually it gave in entirely to the darkness at dusk. The nights were even worse than the days, for the moon was never able to break through, making the nighttime landscape one of perpetual blackness.

Even the relentless wind failed to carry away the ugly dark clouds of dust, for what dust it blew away from the local farms was immediately replaced by the dust from other dying farms that were miles away. Farmers joked grimly that if they could hook a plow up to an airplane, they could farm the sky and get better crops than the land was producing.

Finally a night came in mid-September when the wind stopped. It had blown so relentlessly for the entire summer that the people had grown used to the sound and were no longer aware of its banshee howl or the rattle of sand blown against the sides of houses. When it stopped in the middle of the night, the sudden silence awakened Del and Rubye, and they lay in bed trying to figure out what had happened.

"Del, the wind!" Rubye finally exclaimed.

"It's stopped," Del said. He sat up and looked toward the window. "Rubye, the wind has stopped!"

He got out of bed and slipped into a pair of overalls, pulling the bib and straps up over his bare chest and shoulders. Shoving his feet into his shoes, he walked over to the front door. Every night they routinely stuffed rags and papers into the cracks of the doors and windows to keep out as much wind and dust as possible, and Del had to remove them before he could open the door. He walked outside and stood on the edge of the porch, looking out over his farm.

The moon was a brilliant white orb, and the stars were dazzling points of light, seeming even more so than normally because it was the first time Del had seen them all summer. And, ironically, though it was the middle of the night, he was able to see more of his farm than he had seen at any time since he bought it. From horizon to horizon the land rolled in gently undulating waves of silver and black.

Del heard Rubye come up behind him, and he reached back and put his arm around her, drawing her to him.

"I know what it really is," Rubye said in a hushed voice, gesturing with her chin. "I know that all that lying out there is dust and sand, and I know that our farm is under it. And I know how awful it is. But looking at it like this, so silvery under the moon, like drifting snow, I think it's about the most beautiful sight I have ever seen."

As Rubye had said, the beauty evaporated the next morning when harsh reality showed the blanket of silver for what it really was: a suffocating, crop-killing pall of sand. It lay in great drifts against the buildings and alongside roads. Across one field Del saw a long line of black stumps, no more than several inches high, and for a moment or two he wondered what they could be until he suddenly realized that he was looking at a fencerow. The black stumps were the very tops of a long line of fence posts that had been completely buried in the drifting dust and sand.

Del was at the pump, filling the drinking bucket with water, when he heard a car engine. Stopping his chore, he raised up to look down the road, where he saw a rooster tail of dust marking the progress of the approaching car. He was so unaccustomed to the brightness of the sun that he had to shield his eyes to see, but he was able to identify the car. It was a '28 Chevrolet, belonging to his neighbor, Jim Ramsey.

The car pulled into Del's front yard, then stopped, although it had a bad case of postignition and continued to rumble and shake for several seconds after the engine had been switched off. Jim Ramsey thrust his hand out the window to operate the door handle. Then he climbed out of the car, but his wife and two kids stayed inside.

"Oh, Del," Rubye called from behind the front-door screen, wiping her hands on her apron, "why didn't you tell me we were having company?" She pushed open the screen and smiled broadly and waved, calling, "Hello, Jim; hello,

Julia! Won't you and the kids get out and have some lemonade?"

"Thank you for your kind offer, Rubye, but we wouldn't want to impose none," Julia called back through the open window of the car, tucking back a fallen strand of mousy-brown hair.

"Mama, I want some lemonade," one of the children said from the back seat.

"Hush. Mind your manners."

"Why, it wouldn't be a bit of trouble," Rubye insisted, walking on out to the car. "It'd only take a minute."

"Thank you, no," Julia said. "Jim has some business to discuss with your man, and then we'll have to be going."

"Well, you could at least get out of the car and come over to set on the porch with me, couldn't you? Maybe the children would like to run around in the yard a bit and stretch their legs some."

"I suppose that wouldn't hurt," Julia agreed, opening the door. She was painfully thin, and her manner was one of a woman closer to sixty-five rather than the thirty she was.

"Mama, can we have some lemonade?"

"No," Julia said firmly. "And you behave yourselves, or I'll make you stay in the car."

While Rubye and Julia walked up to the porch and sat down on a bench Del had made, Del and Jim went out to lean against the fence that ran around the barnyard. Del's two mules came out of the barn and stood nearby, as if trying to listen in on their conversation.

"I come to see if there's somethin' I got that you might want to buy," Jim said, not meeting Del's gaze. "I can make you a real good price." He pointed to the mules. "I can let you have another team just like 'em for fifty dollars apiece."

"I couldn't work another team even if I had land worth plowin'," Del said. "Anyhow, why would you want to sell your team? How're you goin' to put in a crop next year without 'em?"

Jim snorted. "What crop?" he asked, his voice bitter. "Mr. Tingsley, the fella that owns the land, tells me the farm is worth more to him iffen I don't plant nothin'. I farmed for that man and his daddy for fifteen years, an' now he's runnin' me off. Don't believe his daddy woulda done nothin' like that. But hard work an' loyalty don't mean nothin' to the young Tingsley. All he wants is that government check."

"What are you talkin' about?" Del asked. "What government check?"

"Ain't you heard?"

Del shook his head.

"Seems the government's got it in mind that the trouble with the country today is there's too much crops. They figure iffen there's less crops around, then the price of what crops there is'll go up. That way the farmers'll make more money."

"I guess that makes sense," Del said. "But what's that have to do with a government check?"

"Well, sir, the government signed up a whole bunch of landowners some months back. They're goin' to pay 'em not to grow any crops next year. The landowners is gettin' paid for doin' nothin'."

"Hell, that's the beatin'est thing I ever heard of," Del said, astonished.

"Ain't that the truth? 'Course, the really bad thing is, the government is helpin' out all the landowners, but us tenant farmers who don't own no land, we're left holdin' the bag since we don't get no money unless we can make a crop and take our share. For the last two years there ain't been no crop 'cause of the drought and the wind and the sand, and now next year there ain't goin' to be no crop 'cause the landowners ain't goin' to let us put no crop in."

"Well, what are you goin' to do?" Del asked. "I mean, how're you goin' to make a livin'?"

"We ain't. Leastwise, we ain't goin' to do it here. That's why I'm sellin' out ever'thin' I own. I'm leavin' here. Me an' the wife and kids is goin' to head out to California in a couple'a days."

"I'm real sorry to hear that, Jim. You was a good neighbor."

"I tried to be," Jim said. "Just like I tried to be a good farmer. But goddammit, a man can't fight the drought and the dust and the government and the big landowners all at the same time. He can't . . . I mean, he just can't go on like this, not without . . ."

He stopped and took several deep breaths, and Del realized, with some surprise and embarrassment, that Jim was crying. Del looked out across his dust-covered land to avoid looking directly at Jim. Finally Jim recovered somewhat.

"So, anyhow, that's why I come to you," he said, speaking calmly now that he had regained his composure. "I'm goin' to all my neighbors, all o' them that's goin' to try and stay, that is, and I'm goin' to make them the best deal I can on whatever I got. I reckon I'll always be a farmer at heart, and I'd like to think that some of my stuff was still bein' used."

"Jim," Del said, hooking his thumbs around his overall straps, "I didn't make no crop this year myself, so I reckon you know how I'm fixed for money. I just barely got enough to get what seed and supplies I'll need for next year. But I'd be glad to take a look at your stuff, and I'll buy somethin' if I can. Who knows? If I'm goin' to stay on here, I might need it."

"Thanks," Jim said. "Listen, you own this place yourself, don't you?"

"Yeah."

"Well, then, there you go. Why don't you put in for one of them government checks for not raisin' any crops?"

"I don't know," Del said, running a callused hand through his shaggy brown hair. "It don't hardly seem right to get paid for doin' nothin'."

"What do you mean, for nothin'? You worked hard this year tryin' to make a crop, didn't you?" Jim asked.

"Yeah, I sure did."

"Then you already done the workin' part. Seems to me like you ought to get paid for it, somehow or the other. I mean, the way I got it figured, it all evens out."

Del laughed. "I guess you've got a point. So, where does a fella go to sign up for that government check, anyhow?"

"There's a man from the Department of Agriculture that handles it. His name's Wilbur Stone, and the bank rents him a room to use as his office," Jim explained. "The way I heard it, all you got to do is go in there and sign this little ol' piece of paper where you promise not to raise no cotton, corn, or wheat next year. If you do that, he'll give you a check, right there on the spot. When you walk out of that bank, you'll likely have the money in your hand."

"You don't say?"

"That's the way they're tellin' it. Hell, young Tingsley's already gone and bought hisself a new car with the money he got for not growin' nothin' next year." Jim's face darkened. "He got a new car; me and Julia and the kids . . . we got nothin'."

"I'm real sorry to hear that, Jim," Del said. He put a consoling hand on his neighbor's shoulder. "I mean, I feel real bad about it."

"Listen, don't you go feelin' bad about it. It ain't none of your doin'." Jim forced a smile. "Anyway, I hear tell they's some jobs in California that's so good it makes a body wonder why he ever tried to put a plow in the ground in the first place. And it don't ever get cold and there's the ocean . . . Hell, Julia and the kids is already lookin' forward to it."

"I wish you good luck, Jim. I truly do," Del said.

"We'll make out all right," Jim replied. "You're the one needs the luck, what with tryin' to make a crop on dirt like this." He turned and started walking toward the car. "Julia!" he called, looking over at the house. "Come on, get the kids! We got to go!"

The Ramseys piled back in their old Chevy, and Del and Rubye stood in their front yard, waving good-bye as they drove off.

"I'm sure going to miss them," Rubye said. "They were good neighbors."

"Yeah, that's just what I told Jim," Del said. Then he looked at Rubye and smiled broadly. "But, Rubye, he gave me a piece of information we can sure use. What if I told you I knew how we could get four or five hundred dollars? What would you do with it?"

"Del, I don't like to even joke about things like that."

"I ain't jokin', Rubye. Jim told me how to get the money. Now, if we had it, what would you do with it?"

"What would I do with it? Why, there are so many things we could do with it, I can't even begin to tell. But where are we going to come up with that kind of money?"

He explained the government's policy to her, just as Jim had explained it to him.

"What? You mean all it takes is promising not to grow anything?" Rubye asked, stunned. She chuckled. "Too bad we didn't sign something like that this year."

"I didn't know nothin' about it before I planted this year," Del said. "And, truth to tell, I don't reckon I woulda signed it if'n I *did* know. I was certain I could make a crop out of spit and dust. Well, even fools can learn." He hugged his wife. "Get on your goin'-to-town duds, Rubye. I'm fixin' to see the government man and pick up that check, and you're comin' with me. You know that dress you was talkin' about last time we was in the Emporium? That pink one? I want you to buy it."

"Oh, Del, I couldn't do that! We need so many things."

"We'll have enough money to buy pretty near ever'thin' we need and that pink dress, besides. And I think you ought to get a pretty hat to go with it." He grinned. "I might even get a new hat for myself."

"Oh, Del, are you sure?"

"Don't you think I need a new hat?"

Rubye laughed. "No, I mean are you sure we're going to be able to afford it all?"

"I'm sure, darlin'. In fact, why don't you just make out a list? We'll fill the car with all the things we been needin'. You know what? I might even get rid of this old piece of junk and get us a better car. We're landowners, by God, and we may as well act like it."

"It just seems too good to be true," Rubye said. "Oh, my! If I'm going to be trying on a dress, I had better get a move on it. I have to take a bath. Would you take the tub down and fill it for me?"

"I don't know about that. If I watch you take a bath, I might just forget all about goin' into town," Del teased.

"Then you just don't watch!" Rubye scolded, laughing. "Because I *am* taking a bath, and we *are* going to town."

It was nearly eleven o'clock when Del and Rubye arrived in Langston. Del parked directly in front of the Emporium, joking that that way he wouldn't have as far to carry all of Rubye's packages.

"You just go on in there and start buyin' whatever you need," he said, pointing to the store as he set the parking brake. "Meanwhile I'll go across the street to the bank and see Mr. Stone about signing that paper. As soon as I get that took care of, I'll cash the check, and then I'll come meet you over here."

"Oh, Del, isn't it wonderful to think that at last we'll have a little money?" Rubye asked, her eyes welling with tears of joy.

"It sure is, darlin'. You know somethin' I think I might do? I might ask Mr. Stone if the government has any books on takin' care of the land. Since I won't be able to put in a crop after I sign that paper, I'll just spend the whole year workin' on the land. Maybe if I spread some fertilizer and, say, plant just grass to keep the topsoil down, why, we might have some pretty good land to work on by next year. Yes, sir, this is goin' to work out all right," he declared, feeling an optimism he hadn't felt in a long, long time.

Del kissed his wife on the cheek, then sprinted across the street to the bank. There he was directed to the room in the rear where the agriculture agent had his office.

The door was open, so Del walked in. A relatively small man with a neatly trimmed mustache was sitting behind a desk piled with papers and deed books.

"Wilbur Stone," the agent said, standing up and reaching across the desk to shake Del's hand.

Del looked past Stone at the large-scale map of Logan County that was pinned to the wall behind him. Studying it, Del realized that it listed every farm in the county, though he noticed that the map hadn't been completely updated because his own farm was still listed as belonging to Roger Crawford. The former Crawford farm, as were many of the others, was crosshatched in red.

Looking back at the government agent, Del smiled. "I guess I'm forgettin' my manners, ain't I? My name's Del Murtaugh, Mr. Stone."

"You're a farmer, Mr. Murtaugh?"

Del forced a laugh. "Well, sir, I tried to be, but I didn't have much luck with it, this year."

"Who did?" Stone replied with a sigh. "Have a seat, Mr. Murtaugh," he added, indicating the wooden chair beside Del.

"Thanks." Del sat down and assessed the man across from him, deciding that even though Wilbur Stone was just renting a room here, he looked right at home in the bank because he looked like a banker himself. It wasn't only because of his dark-blue suit; it was his overall look.

The agent took off his wire-rim glasses and began polishing the lenses. "You shouldn't feel bad about not making a crop this year, Mr. Murtaugh. Why, do you know that in 1933, Logan County produced only thirty percent of what it produced in 1932? And though all the reports aren't in yet, I'm afraid it was even worse this year."

"I wouldn't doubt it," Del remarked. "You know, my pa used to say that God was every farmer's partner. And meanin' no disrespect, He sure didn't hold up His end of the partnership this year."

Stone frowned slightly. "I don't mean to be blasphemous, Mr. Murtaugh, but God didn't have anything to do with it. No, sir, I'm afraid it was all our doing."

"Our doing? Whose doing?"

"Mankind's. And the miracles of science and technology."

"No, sir, I can't go along with that," Del said, shaking his head firmly. "Science didn't make the drought or cause the wind to blow."

"Maybe not. Except you have to remember that there have been droughts before and wind before, but never before has all the topsoil blown away. That was mankind's contribution."

"How?"

"It's the steel plow and the gasoline-powered tractor," Stone answered. "You see, Mr. Murtaugh, when farmers first came to this land, the weed and grass roots were so strong that we could barely get a plow down deep enough to turn the ground over. So when we couldn't plow deep enough with the plows we had, we invented new plows, made of case-hardened steel. And when we found that the horses couldn't pull the new plow, we invented the gasoline-powered tractor."

"But that just made life easier," Del protested.

Stone held up his hand. "Hear me out. We then took that new case-hardened steel plow and hooked it to the gasoline-powered tractor, and we pulled long, hard, and deep. Within a few short years we had completely raked up dirt that had lain undisturbed for fifty centuries. When the droughts came, that dirt began drying out, and when the winds came, that dirt blew away. That's what I mean when I say God didn't have anything to do with this, man did."

"I guess I never really thought of it like that," Del said, his brow furrowing.

"Well, don't feel bad about it. Neither did any of the rest of us. At least, not until it was too late," Stone admitted. "But, now, what can I do for you, Mr. Murtaugh?"

"I've heard tell of a check the government's givin' farmers for not growin' any crops," Del replied. "Is that true?"

"Yes, sir, it's true, all right. And if you stop to think about it, why, it's a good thing all the way around. For one thing, it helps keep the price of commodities high enough to make farming profitable. And for another, it will help us recover some of this land. You know, if we keep on scraping off the topsoil like this, year after year, we're going to turn this country into a desert as dead as the Sahara."

Del nodded, impressed. "Yes, sir. Well, I ain't got no quarrel with none of that. And when you put it that way, it don't make me feel too bad about takin' a check for not doin' no work. Sign me up, Mr. Stone, and give me the money. I'll let my land lay by."

Stone smiled condescendingly. "I wish I could, Mr. Murtaugh, I wish I could. But this isn't for the tenant farmers. I've written a letter to the Secretary of Agriculture, explaining as forcefully as I could the dilemma of the tenant farmer and how you are being left out of our agriculture recovery program. I hope we're able to come up with some solution soon."

"Yes, sir, I hope so, too," Del said. "But I ain't no tenant farmer. I own my own land."

"You do?"

"Yes, sir."

"That's funny. I thought I knew every landowner in Logan County."

Del smiled. "Well, I figured I might come as a surprise to you, seein' as how on the map there you still got my farm listed as belongin' to the fella I bought it from."

"Ah, that explains it," Stone said. "What you're saying is you just bought the farm?"

"Yes, sir, I bought it from Roger Crawford this past spring."

"And I've never adjusted my records," Stone said. "Well, then, I'm glad you came in. It will allow me to update my files. In the meantime, of course, I'll be glad to get you a government check, Mr. Murtaugh. As I said, the more land we can get into the soil bank, the more land we're going to recover from this terrible affliction." He turned in his chair to look at the map on the wall behind him. "Now, which one is your farm?"

"That one right there," Del said, pointing to the crosshatched area identified on the map as Crawford's.

Stone's eyes narrowed, and he leaned forward to check the map more closely.

"Oh, my," he muttered. "Oh, my, oh, my, oh, my."

"What is it?" Del asked, a sense of foreboding creeping into his gut.

"You say you bought the Crawford place?"

"Yes, sir. I got the papers. You need the proof?"

"No, I believe you. And even if there was a doubt, I could quite easily verify the ownership by checking the deeds at the county land office." Stone sighed and held up his hands. "Unfortunately, that isn't the problem."

"What are you sayin'? That there *is* a problem?" Del asked, the sick feeling in his stomach growing worse.

"Yes, I'm afraid there is, Mr. Murtaugh. You see, we've already paid the allotment on that farm."

"What does that mean, you've already paid the allotment?"

"Well, do you see the red crosshatching? That indicates

the farms that are already in the soil bank system. According to this map, the former Crawford farm is just such a farm."

"No," Del said firmly, "you've made a mistake. I ain't signed no papers."

"Let me check my records," Stone said. He walked over to a file cabinet and pulled open one of the drawers, then riffled through several folders until he found what he was looking for.

"Ah, yes, here it is," he said after he had examined it for a moment. "It's all right here, in black and white. We've already paid next year's allotment. We paid it to Mr. Crawford."

"Well, what does that matter? You might've paid Crawford, but you ain't paid me."

"Unfortunately, Mr. Murtaugh, the allotment is paid on the land, not on the farmer," Stone explained.

Del digested this fact, then nodded. "I see," he replied, unable to keep his disappointment out of his voice. "Then what you're tellin' me is, I can't get a check from you for next year."

"No, sir, I'm afraid you can't."

Del drummed his fingers on the desk for a moment, then let out a long sigh.

"Well, it was just a thought I had," he finally said. "Truth to tell, I didn't much like the idea of gettin' paid somethin' for doin' nothin' anyway." He smiled weakly. "Since I'm goin' to be on my own, I just hope I make a better crop next year."

"Mr. Murtaugh, I'm afraid you don't fully understand what this means," Wilbur Stone said, putting the folder away and pushing the cabinet drawer closed. "You not only can't collect any money from the government, you also cannot put in a crop. We have a contract on your land. Your land *has* to lay by next year. For the whole of next year your land belongs to the government."

"Oh, I see," Del said in a voice far more hearty than he felt. He stood up. "Mr. Stone, I want to thank you for your time."

"I wish I could have been of more help."

"You've been help enough," Del said, picking up his hat to leave. "You're a kindly man, and I 'preciate that."

Walking slowly out of Stone's office into the bank, Del thought hard about his situation. The future looked even bleaker now than it had when he had woken up that morning—almost as bleak as the view from his front porch.

The little bell on the door tinkled cheerily when Del stepped into the store a short while later. Rubye and the Brocks, who owned the Emporium, were all over by the right wall, near the dress rack. They all had wide smiles on their faces, Rubye because she was shopping for a new dress and Carl and Lucy Brock because in this time of very slow business they were making a sale.

"Hello, Mr. Murtaugh," Carl Brock said. "Mrs. Murtaugh told us about the government check you'd be gettin' this mornin'. I tell you, your pretty little wife's been having quite a time for herself this morning." He laughed. "'Course, there's nothin' will cheer up a woman like buyin' clothes."

"Oh, Del," Rubye said, smiling brightly and holding a dress up in front of her. "Sweetheart, what do you think of this? Isn't it beautiful? I think I like this one even better than I do the pink one."

"Put it back," Del said quietly.

"You don't like it?"

"It's very pretty," Del said, "but we can't buy it. Put it back."

Lucy Brock's smile instantly disappeared, replaced by an expression hovering between despair and resentment. She reached possessively for the dress.

"Okay, Del, if you say so," Rubye said, giving up the dress. She looked back at her husband. "We aren't getting the money, are we?"

"No." Del turned around, saying nothing further as he headed out of the store. He didn't want to look at the face of the store owner, who was already starting to reshelve the substantial pile of items Rubye had selected.

He was leaning on the front fender of his car when

Rubye emerged a moment later and joined him, putting her hand on his shoulder.

"It's all right, Del," she said. "It's not like I need the dress. Really, we didn't need any of that stuff. I mean, we've been getting along just fine without the government check. We'll make a crop next year. I'm sure we will."

"No. We won't make a crop next year or the year after or ever."

"What? Sweetheart, what are you talking about? Why not?"

Choking back his anger and frustration, Del told her what the government agent had told him.

When he had finished, Rubye shook her head in confusion. "But that's illegal, isn't it? I mean, *we* own the land, not the government. Can they really prevent us from growing crops on it?"

"According to Mr. Stone, they can. When you buy land that the allotment's already committed on, it's the same as buying land that has a second mortgage. The mortgage stays in effect, no matter who owns the property."

"Oh, Del, what are we going to do?"

"I've already done it," Del said resolutely. "I just sold the farm, the livestock, and all the equipment on it to the bank. We're goin' to California."

Del had received $450 for the farm and $75 for all the equipment, including the plows, mules, and harness. He owed the bank $150, which they withheld from the check, as well as $35 to the feed and seed store and $25 to the machine shop, both of which he paid right away. He also owed $100 to the Bank of Sikeston, and though he could have paid it off in five-dollar-per-month installments, he wasn't sure how long it would be before he got a job, so he decided to pay it all off at one time. That left $215.

The following day Del drove back to town and took the Oakland to the Langston garage, intending to have it put into condition for the trip. But Henry, the mechanic there, gave it the once-over and shook his head.

"You're plannin' on goin' to California in this thing?" Henry asked in a dubious voice.

"That's what I was plannin' to do, yeah," Del replied.

"I wouldn't want to be tryin' it in this car," the mechanic said.

"I know it's not in real good shape. That's why I brought it in. I want you to fix it up."

Henry's chortle was more a snort than a laugh. "Mr. Murtaugh, 'bout the only way you could fix this car up would be to unscrew the body from the rest of it, drive the old car out, then put a new one under it."

"What's wrong with it?"

"What *ain't* wrong with it would be a better question. To begin with, your crankshaft is bad out of round, 'sides which you got a hole in one of your pistons—but that don't matter none 'cause the engine block's got a crack in it anyway. The transmission is about to fall out, and the back end sounds like it's full of broken glass. Truth is, I don't see how you kept the damn thing runnin' this long."

"What do you think I'd get for it ifn I was to sell it?" Del asked.

"Nothin'."

"*Nothin'?* What do you mean, nothin'? It's got to be worth somethin'!"

"Not as a car, it ain't." The mechanic scratched his nose, and when he did, he left a smear of oil along the side of his face. "You could probably get somethin' for it from Dago Simmons."

"Who's Dago Simmons? I never heard of him."

"He's the fella that runs the junkyard over near Guthrie. I reckon he could make his money back by breakin' it down into repair parts."

Del sighed. "Guess I don't have no choice, do I? All right. I'll drive over to Guthrie."

"I hope you make it."

"What do you mean? That's no more than twenty miles."

"That might be about nineteen miles more'n you got left in this car," Henry warned.

"I drove this car out here from Missouri, and I been

drivin' it ever since. I don't figure it's goin' to stop on me before I get to Guthrie," Del said, more of a challenge to the car than the man.

"I hope for your sake it don't. But I wouldn't make book on it gettin' there."

"Good," Del said in a harsher voice than he had intended as he got back into the car, " 'cause I ain't a bettin' man."

Despite the mechanic's ominous prediction, the Oakland did hold together long enough for Del to get to Dago Simmons's junkyard. However, he was aware, more than ever before, of every squeak, rattle, scrape, and bump in the car. He could hear the lifting of the tappets, the knock of bad bearings, the grinding of the transmission, and the high-pitched whine of the rear end. Finally, mercifully, he saw the small, faded road sign that welcomed travelers to Guthrie. He had made it without breaking down.

The junkyard was on the east end of town. Even without the big sign proclaiming DAGO WILL PAY FOR YOUR JUNK it wouldn't have been hard to find. The five-acre field was stacked high with rusting bodies of old cars and trucks, some of them with windshields that flashed in the sun, others as devoid of glass as they were of paint. In addition to the car and truck bodies there were also large piles of doors, fenders, and hoods, arranged by makes and models, and one area of the yard was completely given over to engine blocks, pistons, and gears. Here and there large pieces of unidentifiable machinery sat, rusting and overgrown with weeds.

In the middle of the junkyard was a wooden shack covered with dozens and dozens of license plates. The multicolored plates were from nearly every state in the union, and the years stamped on them showed that Dago had been collecting them for quite some years.

When Del pulled the wheezing, coughing, thumping car into the junkyard, steam was gushing from the radiator and smoke was billowing from the exhaust pipe. A small man with a big nose and dark eyes came out of the license-plate-covered shack. He was chewing on an unlit cigar, and he started examining the Oakland closely, even before Del got out of it.

"Can't let you have too much," the man said, pulling the cigar out of his mouth and spitting out a piece of tobacco.

"What makes you think I was comin' here to sell?" Del asked—though he knew the answer was obvious.

"Not much else you could do with a piece of junk like this," the man said. "You're lucky it got you this far."

"Yeah, that's what everyone seems to say," Del said with a sigh. "Are you Dago Simmons?"

"That's me."

"Well, you're right, Mr. Simmons. I am here to sell."

"That's a '23 Oakland, isn't it?"

"Yes, sir."

"Uh-huh, that's what I thought. Well, I'm afraid I don't have many calls for parts from an Oakland. Especially one this old. But I'll tell you what I'll do. I'll give you fifteen for it."

"Fifteen dollars? Are you kidding? Fifteen dollars is as high as you'll go? I mean, I'll admit it ain't got much more use as a car, but what about the parts? Surely the parts in it is worth more'n any fifteen dollars?"

"Well, I hope so," Dago said, sticking the cigar back in his mouth and opening the hood. The smell of hot oil assailed them. "I mean, I'd have to make somethin' out of it. And I'd have to have enough to cover my time. Else it wouldn't be worth foolin' around with."

"How about twenty-five?" Del proposed.

Dago closed the hood. "Sorry," he said. "Couldn't do that. Reckon you'll have to take your business somewhere else." He started back toward the shack.

"Wait!" Del said. As far as he knew, there wasn't anyplace else, and he had to sell the car. "How about twenty dollars and that set of wheels over there?"

Dago stopped and looked over at where Del was pointing. "What're you wantin' them wheels for?"

"I'm goin' to build me a trailer," Del said.

Dago smiled and pulled the cigar out of his mouth. "Well, now, maybe we're goin' to be able to do a little business after all. What if I said fifteen dollars and a good trailer that's already built an' ready to go?"

"You have such a trailer?"

"Come here. Let me show you."

Del followed Dago through the weeds, stepping over patches of broken glass and around puddles of oil and grease.

"How 'bout this beauty right here?" Dago asked, pointing to a small, rusty frame barely visible in the tangle of weeds. He reached down into the vegetation and picked up the tow bar, then walked forward, pulling the trailer with him—and enabling Del to see that the "trailer" was actually no more than a tow bar, frame, and wheels. There was no bed, but it would be easy to build one and attach it. The hard part of construction, the running gear and tow bar, was already done.

Del looked the trailer over carefully, then said, "You got yourself a deal."

"Fine. Now, you got somethin' to pull this trailer out of here with?"

"Not yet, but I'm about to go buy me a car," Del replied, remembering a large used-car lot he had passed several blocks back.

"Okay. I'll move the trailer out front by the shed," Dago said. "It'll be waitin' there for you when you get back."

QUALITY USED CARS the sign said. It was strung between two poles above the large lot that took up nearly the whole of a block. Most of the cars were black, brown, dark green, or nondescript gray, but there was one, a canary-yellow four-door V-8 '32 Ford, that stood out like a rose among cabbages. It occupied the position of honor, an elevated platform right on the corner of the lot so that it was easily seen by motorists passing by on either street.

As Del walked over to the Ford, he thought how good it would make Rubye feel to ride in a car like that. But then he saw the $120 price marked on the windshield, and since he had only $230 dollars in his pocket, he knew it would be the height of folly to even look at this car. He quickly walked on, checking out more affordable, practical cars.

But he couldn't avoid the yellow Ford. No matter where

he was on the lot, he found his gaze wandering back to that car. Again he pictured himself and Rubye driving out to California in it, Rubye sitting proudly by his side.

Wresting his gaze away, he quickly opened the door of a '29 Chevrolet, then slid in behind the wheel.

"Yes, sir, that would be a fine car," the car dealer called expansively as he came out of his shed. He walked over to stand by the car. "I can put you right where you're sittin' for fifty-five dollars," he added, patting the fender.

"It's got quite a few miles, doesn't it?" Del asked, looking at the odometer.

"Sure, but she's good for another thirty, forty thousand easy," the dealer insisted. "They never made any better car than the '29 Chevy. This was the last model they built before the market crash, you know, and it was built back when folks were still willin' to pay for quality."

"You sayin' any car built after '29 doesn't have quality?" Del asked.

The car dealer coughed. "No, I'm not sayin' that exactly. I'm just sayin' that these '29 Chevys were awful good cars."

"What about that one over there?" Del asked, pointing to the yellow Ford while berating himself for his lack of common sense.

The dealer smiled. "I can see you've got an eye for fine cars, friend. That's my pride and joy. The best car on the lot. It's only got twenty-eight thousand miles on it."

"Twenty-eight thousand miles, you say? Is that actual?"

"Oh, yes, sir. I'd put my hand on the Good Book and swear to it," the dealer replied. "This car belonged to Elmer Jones. I reckon you knew him, didn't you? He used to own the grocery store down on Main."

"I'm not from Guthrie," Del said.

"Too bad you didn't know him. He was a fine man, God rest his soul. He took sick and died a while back, and his wife don't drive, so she had to sell the car. Told me it really hurt to have to part with it, bein' as Elmer loved it so much."

"Yeah, well, it is a pretty car, all right," Del said. "But I don't need to be lookin' at anything like that. All I need is somethin' to get the wife and me out to California."

"Well, this here Chevy'd probably do that for you," the car dealer said, patting the fender again. "I got maybe a dozen cars'd probably do it. 'Course, with the Ford, there ain't no probably to it. The only thing that'd be on your mind would be gas. Notice I didn't say oil. That car would take you all the way out there without usin' a drop."

Del sniffed. "For a hundred and twenty dollars, it damn sure should."

"You say you got a wife goin' with you?"

"Yes."

"I reckon it all depends on how much you love her. By that I mean how much are you willin' to pay for the peace of mind of knowin' you aren't goin' to be broke down out in the desert somewhere? Seems to me like a hundred and twenty dollars wouldn't be too much of a price to pay to avoid a consequence like that."

Del looked back at the Ford. "Yeah, that's somethin' to think about, all right. Tell me, could you come down off that price any at all?"

"I don't see how I could," the dealer replied, slowly shaking his head. "I mean, I won't be makin' but ten dollars as it is." He stroked his chin and studied Del for a moment. "You're really wantin' that car bad, aren't you?"

Del sighed. "It's a real nice car." He walked over to it and lovingly ran his hand across the smooth, highly polished yellow front fender.

"I'd sure like to see you drive away in that," the dealer said. "Open the door and take a look inside."

Del obediently opened the door.

"Clean as a whistle, ain't it? I mean, if you was to go right down to the Ford place and pick out any model they got on the showroom floor and bring it down here to put alongside this car, you wouldn't find that new Ford any cleaner'n this one."

"No, I reckon not," Del agreed.

"All right," the car dealer said. He looked around as if making sure no one could hear him. "I tell you what I'm goin' to do. I mean, I got a soft spot in my heart—and probably in my head—but I wouldn't want to think of you and your wife tryin' to make it all the way to California in some car that was goin' to break down on you. I'll let you have this beauty for a hundred and ten." He held up his hand. "That means I'm not makin' one cent on this car, but at least I won't be losin' nothin', and I would have done a good deed by givin' Mrs. Jones all the money I made." He smiled. "And I'd be doin' a good deed for you and your missus by puttin' you in such a fine car for so cheap. But you got to swear you won't tell a soul how much you paid for it. I'm goin' to have to raise the price on some of these other cars to make up for it."

"I won't tell anyone," Del promised. He couldn't stop rubbing the smooth fender.

The dealer grinned and put his arm around Del's shoulder. "Come on inside," he said. "We'll make out the papers. Mister, you just got yourself the best deal in Guthrie . . . probably in the whole state of Oklahoma."

The two men walked over to the sales shed, where Del handed the dealer the money and the dealer handed Del the papers and the keys. Smiling broadly, Del climbed into his new car and drove back to the junkyard, where he and Dago Simmons hitched up the trailer to the Ford.

Del drove back home to Langston singing at the top of his lungs and periodically running his right hand over the dashboard and the leather seat cover. Sparkles of sunlight danced across the gleaming yellow hood—like diamonds, Del thought. Driving this car made him feel ten feet tall.

But as he got closer to home, the adrenaline stopped pumping and the intoxicating feeling of excitement began fading. Sobering up fast, he realized how much money he had spent on this car and how little he and Rubye would have left to go to California and start over. He groaned aloud. How could he have been so irresponsible? What was he going to tell Rubye? What was she going to say to him?

He drove the rest of the way in silence.

Rubye Murtaugh had spent the day wandering around their small home, making painful decisions as to what they could take and what they'd have to leave behind. She was standing in the living room, assessing their belongings, when she heard the car pull in. Going over to the front door, she looked out to see Del driving up in what she thought was a brand-new car and felt a sinking sensation in her stomach. She wanted to cry. What had he done? How could he have spent so much of what little money they had left on a car?

Seeing the sheepish smile on Del's face as he got out of the car, Rubye knew that he regretted his act. She sighed. It would do no good to get angry with him now; the damage was done. She would just have to live with it. It did make her all the more certain, however, that she shouldn't tell him about the eleven hundred dollars she had in savings back in the Bank of Sikeston . . . money left her by her mother and father. She had a feeling that the time would come when they'd have an even more desperate need for that money, especially now that she was pregnant—which Del also didn't know about.

"Couldn't you get the old car fixed?" she asked Del, holding open the screen door as he climbed onto the porch.

"The mechanic said it was impossible," Del replied, stepping into the relative cool of the house. "I didn't have no choice, Rubye. I had to get us another car."

"But did you have to get such a . . . such a grand car?"

Del grinned. "It is a grand car, ain't it?"

Rubye merely sighed.

"Well, now, wait. I know you're wonderin' why I bought this," Del said, his tone defensive. "Well, I didn't want to take no chances on us breakin' down on the way to California. Besides which, I got us a real good deal on it, so when we get to California, we could probably sell it and make a little money. Folks are probably lookin' for good cars out there."

"Well, I'm glad to see you got a trailer," Rubye said. "We need to start getting packed. The Ramseys will be over here tomorrow at the crack of dawn, ready to leave. I know that it was Jim's idea that things might go better if we all drive out to California together, once he learned we were planning on leaving, but since they already delayed their departure, I wouldn't want to hold them back any because we aren't ready."

"Uh, yeah," Del said, looking surprised that she wasn't making too much of a fuss about the car even though she was upset about it. "I need to get a trailer bed put on that frame. The bed off the cotton wagon should do. I'll just change into my overalls and get started."

Jim and Julia Ramsey and their children—Charlie, a boy of eight, and Dorothy, a girl of six—arrived just after sunup the next morning. Their car was straining under the load, and Jim got out to check all the tie-down ropes to make certain nothing had shifted during the short drive over. Seeing Del's shiny yellow Ford with a fully loaded trailer hitched behind it, he did a double-take.

"What's this?" he asked, pointing to the car. "When did you get this?"

Del told him the story.

"I don't know . . ." Jim said, looking at the Ford and then at his own jalopy. "You sure you want to travel with me? I mean, we're bound to hold you back, seein' as how our car can't possibly keep up with yours." He laughed ironically. "And to think I suggested that we travel together 'cause your old Oakland was in such bad shape that I was worried about you breakin' down."

"Breakin' down ain't the only reason for travelin' together," Del said quickly. "Sometimes it's good just to have friends along."

"Yes," Rubye said. "I mean, just think about it, Jim. We're going to get out to California and not know a soul. Don't you think it'd be nice to have some friendly, familiar faces around?"

Jim smiled. "You're right. And since you put it like that, why, I reckon we'd be real proud to travel with you."

"How far is it to California, anyway?" Julia asked.

"Near as I can figure, about two thousand miles," Jim replied. He looked at Del. "I was thinkin' we could probably make about two hundred miles a day, which'd put us there in ten days. 'Course, like I say, you could go a lot faster than that. And maybe we could, too."

"No, no. Two hundred miles a day is good," Del said.

Grinning, Jim said, "Okay, then, what do you say we get the first two hundred in before nightfall?"

Del held open the door to the Ford for Rubye, then looked back at Jim and smiled.

"Lead the way."

CHAPTER FOURTEEN

MAY 15, 1935, NEWCASTLE, WYOMING

Eric Twainbough was the only passenger to leave the train in Newcastle. He stood on the platform and watched as the door to the baggage car was opened and his suitcases handed out to a thin old man who, though he looked barely strong enough to hold himself up, actually handled the luggage with ease. The old man loaded the bags onto a four-wheeled cart, then pushed the cart, with one of its wheels squeaking loudly, toward the depot.

Following alongside the luggage cart, Eric told the old man, "You don't have to take them all the way to the depot. I can just take them off your hands right here, if you want."

"You got a baggage claim?"

Eric chuckled. "Not much chance in my getting them mixed up with anyone else's, is there? I mean, since I'm the only one who got off here."

The old man shook his head resolutely. "You got to have a baggage claim," he insisted.

Eric took the baggage claim from his billfold and handed it to the old man, who then checked it very carefully against the tags on the suitcase.

"Give the wrong grip away once," the old man explained. "Fella that really owned it got so mad he threatened to shoot me. Don't plan on makin' that mistake again."

"Can't say as I blame you," Eric said.

"Don't believe I've seen you before," the old man said. "You ever been here?"

"Yes. But it's been a while."

The telephone rang, and the oldster went inside the depot to answer it. Eric smiled. No doubt the man was both stationmaster and porter rolled into one.

Stepping to the street side of the station, the globe-traveling author looked out over the small town. A number of cars were parked on both sides of the busy thoroughfare, and others bustled about, some honking impatiently. Two traffic lights controlled the steady flow of vehicles. On the left side of the street was a restaurant with a big sign proclaiming, "DELMONICO'S, Newcastle's Finest Restaurant Since 1895." A man came out of the restaurant picking his teeth, looked up and down the street, then crossed over to the other side, where he went into a jewelry store.

Eric remembered Delmonico's. Back in '04 it had been where the jewelry store now stood; and back in '04, far from being a fine restaurant, it had been a saloon where you could also get a meal—among other things.

Thirty-one years had passed since Eric's last visit to Newcastle. Then he had arrived from the north, having ridden down on horseback from the high plains country with his two best friends, Marcus Parmeter and Jake Quinn, all three of whom were cowboys working on the Flying E ranch for an Englishman named Rodney Ebersole. Ebersole had given them a couple of weeks off and a fifty-dollar-apiece bonus so that they could go to St. Louis to see the wonders of the World's Fair then in progress.

On the way to Newcastle, where they were to catch the train that would take them to St. Louis, Jake and Marcus had learned that the then fifteen-year-old Eric had never had a woman. Determined to take care of that gap in Eric's experience, Jake had steered them to the town's whorehouse. That same Delmonico's was where Eric had lost his innocence. He had come into Newcastle a boy; he had left it a man.

Eric smiled as he recalled the experience. All his subsequent lovers—and his ex-wife—owed a measure of thanks to the woman named Penny who had taken such good care of him and had awakened him to the mysteries of a woman's body.

Walking back to the depot, Eric found the stationmaster just finishing his telephone call. The old man hung up the phone, then came over to talk to Eric.

"Some damn fool wanted to know what time the next train headin' east was," the oldster said. "I told him that the trains've been runnin' on the same schedule for fifty years. All he has to do is remember what time it was that he went last time. He don't need to call me every time he takes a trip just to see what time the train leaves."

Eric chuckled. Then he pointed to Delmonico's and said, "Seems to me that that used to be a saloon, and it was situated across the street where that jewelry store is."

The stationmaster eyed Eric. "So you *have* been here before—but a long time past, it's plain. Yes, sir, that used to be a saloon, all right. Went out of business with Prohibition. Fact is, the woman who owns the jewelry store now used to work there. 'Course, she's a fine, upstandin' businesswoman now, so she don't like anyone to remind her of it. And, truth to tell, there's not a whole lot of folks around who can still remember. So I say why stir up the past? I guess most of us have somethin' we'd as soon not remember, and Miss Penny has as much a right to keepin' her memories buried as anyone else."

Eric wondered if he had heard right. "Who did you say?" he asked, his eyes wide.

"Miss Penny. Her name is Penny Thurgood, but most ever'one calls her Miss Penny." He paused, then chuckled. "Well, speak of the devil! That's her right now in that there Cadillac."

A long black Cadillac had pulled up to the front of the

jewelry store. The chauffeur hopped out and opened the rear door, then helped a woman out. She was tall, thin, white-haired, and held herself regally as she nodded at the driver. Eric was too far away to see her face, but he didn't have to see it. Anytime he wanted, he could see it in his memories—and in his memories the face would forever be young.

Other memories, these much more painful, came flooding back. He could see as clearly as if it were now taking place in front of him the despair on Marcus Parmeter's face when he had burst into Eric's room at the whorehouse early the following morning, telling him that all their money—their poke, as Marcus called it—had been stolen from their saddlebags, which they had unwisely left at the livery stable the night before. That single act of carelessness had turned out to be the most pivotal event in Eric's life.

"So, is there anything else I can do for you?" the stationmaster asked.

Eric shook himself out of his reverie and came back to the present. "Yes. Is there a bus to Oshoto?"

"A bus? No, nothin' like that."

"How do people get up there?"

"Nobody ever goes," the stationmaster replied. "There ain't nothin' to go to up there."

"You mean Dunnigan's General Store isn't there anymore?"

The stationmaster looked up sharply. "Dunnigan's been dead now, oh, twenty years or more. You knew him, did you?"

"Yeah, I used to work on a ranch near there. The Flying E. Ever heard of it?"

" 'Course I have. You mean Mr. Ebersole's place, don't you? Just about everyone's heard of it. That old man is one of the best-known ranchers in Wyoming."

"*Is* one of the best-known?" Eric gasped. "Are you telling me Mr. Ebersole is still alive?"

"Oh, yes, sir, he's alive, all right. 'Course, he don't get around like he used to. But you couldn't really expect that, seein' as he's way up in his nineties now."

Eric was stunned into speechlessness for a long moment. Finally he said, "I would very much like to see him again. Look, if there's no bus or anything, where could I go to find a taxi driver?"

The stationmaster smiled. "You don't have to go far. Fact is, you're lookin' at him."

"You?"

"Yep. Seemed the logical business to get into. 'Bout the only folks that ever use a taxi around here is them that come in on the train."

"Well, then, will you take me to the Flying E?"

"I'd like to, but I can't. Leastwise not today. I've got four more trains comin' through today, an' I've got to meet 'em all."

"Look, this is very important to me. I could make it worth your time."

"Is Mr. Ebersole expectin' you?"

"No. Why? Is that a problem?"

"Well, sir, it could be. You see, there's so damn many of them oil wildcatters pokin' around on everybody's land that they're gettin' to be a worse kind o' pest than prairie dogs. Mr. Ebersole has his land posted against wildcatters and is offerin' a bounty of a dollar fifty to anyone who'll bring in a wildcatter's hide."

Eric laughed. "A dollar fifty?"

The old man cackled heartily. "Ain't that somethin'? But you see, the bounty on coyotes is two dollars each, and Mr. Ebersole says wildcatters ain't worth as much as coyotes."

Grinning, Eric said, "Well, Mr. Ebersole isn't expecting me, but I'm not a wildcatter, and I did work for him a long time ago, so I don't think he'll shoot me."

The stationmaster stroked his chin and studied Eric for a moment. "You got any identification on you?"

"Identification?"

"Yes, somethin' that tells who you are. A driver's license or a business card or somethin' like that."

"Sure. Why do you ask?"

"If you got some identification, I could maybe rent you a car. I don't like to do this with strangers just comin' in off the train and all, but if you used to work at the Flying E, well, I guess you ain't exactly a stranger. All I've got is a Model A. It ain't new, but it runs just fine. Is that good enough for you?"

"Yes! That'd be swell, thank you," Eric said.

"It'll be three dollars a day."

"You've got yourself a deal."

The stationmaster pulled out a tablet full of preprinted car rental forms and began filling one out.

"Name?"

"Twainbough. Eric Twainbough."

The stationmaster looked up from his form and studied Eric intently. "Say, are you that arther fella?" he finally asked.

"Yep, I'm an author."

The stationmaster smiled broadly and stuck his hand out. "Well, I'll be damned. I'm really pleased to meet you, Mr. Twainbough. *A Time for All Things* is my very favorite book. By damn!" he exclaimed. "Then you *did* live out here, didn't you? I knew when I read that book that you must've been out here at some time in your life. I told ever'body who'd listen to me that sure as a gun is iron, you'd been out here. So, you used to work for Mr. Ebersole, did you?"

"I did."

"Well, I'll be damned," the oldster repeated.

Eric signed the form—which the stationmaster promised to keep as a souvenir—and paid a ten-dollar deposit on the car. Collecting his luggage, he hauled it out to the Model A, stuffed the bags in the car, then drove away. But instead of going north, which was the most direct route to the ranch, he drove due west.

Having the car at his disposal triggered an immediate need to make a kind of pilgrimage. Hundreds of times over the past thirty-one years he had thought about the events that had so inexorably altered his life; now, for the first time since that night, he would return to the scene of the crime. He smiled mirthlessly. An all-too-apt phrase, if ever there was one.

The road west out of Newcastle followed the railroad track. Eric drove for a few miles, until he saw what he was looking for. There, in a desolate spot by a water tank sitting alongside the track, he got out of the car and walked over to take a look around.

The wind was whistling through the telegraph wires and causing the spout on the tank to bump and rattle against the blocks that held it in place. Standing under the tank, Eric put his hand on one of the wooden legs. It was damp from a small leak. He stared up and down the tracks. For as far as he could see in all directions there was nothing but emptiness.

But he wasn't alone. He could feel the presence of Marcus Parmeter and Jake Quinn as clearly now as he had on that night thirty-one years ago . . . the night Eric McKenzie died and Eric Twainbough was born.

He shuddered, feeling gooseflesh rise on his arms. He could remember every moment as vividly as if it had happened yesterday. He could remember sitting in his saddle in the dark of the night with a cold rain spitting in his face, trying one last time to talk Marcus and Jake out of their crazy scheme of staging a train robbery. But Marcus had insisted that getting the several hundred dollars that all the night trains carried in the mail car would be an easy matter since the clerk wasn't about to die trying to defend such a piddly amount. And it wasn't as if they'd be robbing any passengers; they'd just be taking the train's cash—which it could well afford to lose—to make up for the theft of their entire poke from the Newcastle livery stable.

Eric could remember the sound the train whistle made as it drew closer and how the sparks from its chimney looked as they were whipped up into the wet night sky. He could still hear the squeal of the wheels as it braked to a stop under the water tank and the train crew clambered to fill the tank. He could remember his horse stamping its foot restlessly as he waited back in the darkness while Marcus and Jake went to rap on the door of the mail car, the plan being that as soon as the door opened, Eric was to fire a couple of shots into the air to frighten the clerk. Marcus and Jake were to then do the rest.

Eric stared at the track. He could visualize the scene so clearly it was as if he were watching a movie: The mail-car door had slid open, a narrow wedge of light quickly growing to a large one. A man had appeared in the gap, silhouetted by the lamps inside the car, and looked outside. "What is it? What do you want?" he had called.

"Okay, let her go!" Marcus had shouted, and Eric, who was pointing his gun straight up, pulled the trigger several times.

The flashes of light from the muzzle of his gun had painted the side of the express car in a wavering orange. What had happened next froze the scene in Eric's brain so indelibly that even now, over thirty years later, he could call it up for the most minute examination.

"Throw down your money!" Marcus had called.

After that moment everything had gone wrong.

From far inside the car had come the bright flash and loud roar of a shotgun. An instant later Marcus had tumbled backward out of his saddle, his face shot away.

"Let's get out of here!" Jake had yelled. He had actually managed to get his horse turned around before the second shotgun blast—a blast that exploded a spray of blood, bone chips, and brain matter from Jake's head.

Terrified to the point of hysteria, Eric had slapped his legs against the sides of his equally panicked horse and galloped away. Since the train guard had discharged both barrels of the shotgun, he had had nothing left to shoot at Eric, but the passengers had thrust their arms out the train windows and began firing their pistols at the retreating youngster. None of the shots had hit him or even come close, but the flash and roar of their gunshots had added to the overall terror of the night.

Finally, with the train safely out of sight and sound, Eric had stopped and let his horse catch its breath, afraid that if he ran it any longer its heart might burst. But it hadn't mattered that he had safely escaped; all he had been able to think about, all he had kept seeing over and over and over, was the sight of his two friends, lying back there in the darkness with half their heads blown away—a sight that for all of his life was as indelible as if it had been chiseled into his brain.

Until that night he had been Eric McKenzie; that night he had changed his name to Eric Twainbough and fled Wyoming. This was the first time he had been back home in thirty-one years.

Swallowing the lump in his throat, Eric returned to the car and resumed his drive out to the Flying E Ranch.

The Flying E occupied several thousand acres of rangeland just west of Devil's Tower in northeastern Wyoming. The range was fed by the Belle Fourche River, which twisted and turned its way across the property to provide water even to the most remote part of the ranch. The river and good grassland was what made the ranch such a valuable piece of property.

As Eric approached the main part of the ranch, he felt as if he were taking a trip back in time. On his right was what appeared to be the very same bunkhouse where as a fifteen-year-old cowboy he had lived. It was ringed by the cookhouse, smokehouse, corral, granary, machine shed, and the outhouse for the ranch hands.

To the left was the ranch house, a two-story white-frame Gothic complete with turrets, dormers, big bay window, and screened-in porch. It had changed little in the intervening years—except it no longer seemed to have an outdoor toilet. It must have been converted to indoor plumbing as well as been electrified, since Eric also saw electric wires running to the house.

The corral was full of horses, and, as there had been in his time, several wagons were parked outside the barn. Now, however, in addition to the horses and wagons several cars and a couple of pickup trucks were also parked on the place. One of the cowboys who had been standing near the corral walked over to confront the visitor just as Eric stepped up onto the porch.

"Something I can do for you, mister?" the cowhand asked in a voice that was neither friendly nor hostile.

"I'm here to see Mr. Ebersole," Eric replied, stopping to answer the cowboy, a rugged-looking man in his early thirties.

"What about?"

"Just a visit. We're old friends," Eric explained.

"I'll tell him you're here and see if he wants to talk to you," the cowboy said. "What's your name?"

"I'd rather not tell him that," Eric said. "I want to surprise him."

"He don't like surprises," the cowboy said, becoming suspicious.

"Tell him . . ." He broke off. Looking beyond the cowboy, Eric spotted two gravestones. There was something about them, about the way they were lying together . . . He had a feeling about those tombstones, and he pointed to them. "Excuse me. Would you mind telling me who's buried over there?"

"Nobody. Just a couple of cowboys used to work here a long time ago."

"Would they be Marcus Parmeter and Jake Quinn?"

"Yeah," the cowboy said with surprise. "Yeah, that's right." He looked at Eric more curiously now. "Did you know those two fellas?"

"Yes, I did."

"Well, I'll be damned. Except for Mr. Ebersole, who don't ever talk about 'em, I've never run into anyone who actually knew anything about them."

"Would it be all right if I just stepped over there to pay my respects?"

"Sure, mister, go ahead. I 'spect those two old boys'd welcome the company. You say you used to work here. Did you work here with them?"

"Yes."

He turned and walked over to look at the stones, again swallowing back a lump in his throat. Reaching the spot, he read the first grave marker:

MARCUS PARMETER
1881–1904
A Good Hand

Except for the changes in name and date of birth, Jake's tombstone was identical.

Eric stood there for a long moment, wondering again as he had wondered a thousand times before if there might have been anything else he could have done that night, anything at all, that might have stopped them from going through with their idiotic plan . . . and stopped them from getting their heads blown off. But Marcus had been so adamant that they couldn't go back to Mr. Ebersole with their tails tucked between their legs, having gotten no farther than Newcastle before getting themselves "robbed like a bunch of greenhorn tenderfeet from the East." And how could they have known that the train they had chosen to stop that night was actually ferrying a huge money transfer between two banks, resulting in the train putting on hired, professional guards?

"I sure have missed you guys," Eric said softly, staring at the gravestones. His mouth quirked into a lopsided grin. "But I *did* make it to St. Louis, after all. Matter of fact, I made it all the way around the world." The grin faded, and he felt his eyes well up. "I hope I've done you proud," he murmured.

"Who are you?" came a query behind him.

Eric smiled. The voice was high and thin, but the English accent was as strong now as it had been thirty years ago.

Turning, Eric found a very old man standing there, leaning on a cane and clutching a black shawl around his shoulders.

"Hello, Mr. Ebersole," Eric said softly. "It's been a long time since I left with these boys to go see the wonders."

"Eric? Eric, my boy, is that you?" Ebersole asked, squinting hard as if trying to see something of the fifteen-year-old boy in the middle-aged man standing before him.

"Yes, sir. It's me."

"My God, lad! What ever happened to you? And how did you ever let these two fools talk you into doing something as dumb as robbing a train?"

"Have you got a few minutes?" Eric asked with a wistful smile. "It's a long story."

CHAPTER FIFTEEN

AUGUST 15, 1935, JACKSON, MISSISSIPPI

The sandy-haired young man behind the wheel in the truck cab backed into the loading dock, sliding the long trailer neatly into the narrow gap between two trucks that had arrived earlier.

"Come on back! Come on back!" the man guiding him shouted, beckoning him with his hands. Finally the man held his hands up, signaling Richard Edward to stop. "Okay, hold it!"

Richard Edward Parker cut the engine and set the parking brake of his red Reo. He got out and stretched, then walked a few feet away from his truck before he turned around for a proud look back at it. He had just bought the truck, and whereas the lettering on the doors of the other trucks parked at the loading dock proclaimed them to be the property of the Foster Warehouse Company, his truck door said:

RICHARD EDWARD PARKER TRUCKING
Jackson, Miss
B.L. 35,000 lbs

Noticing a spot of dirt on the door—so small that it would be invisible to anyone else—Richard Edward wiped it off with his sleeve. Satisfied, he went into the office of Foster Warehouse Company to turn in the bill of lading and pick up his money for the load he had just brought down from Memphis. The pay was ten cents per mile, and the Memphis trip was figured at two hundred fifty miles. Since independent haulers earned only for time their trucks were actually loaded, Richard Edward was paid just for one way and either had to pick up a return load from somewhere else or "deadhead" back.

An independent hauler made twenty-five dollars for the Memphis-to-Jackson run, compared to the eight dollars a driver for hire would make. But out of that twenty-five Richard Edward had to buy his own gas and oil, come up with the insurance and license fees, and make payments on the truck. Still, even with all that factored in and even deadheading in one direction, which happened more often than not, it was more profitable for him to own his own truck than to drive for someone else.

Richard Edward had bought the Reo truck cab and the Dorsey trailer by combining the money he had saved from three years of driving for other people—starting when he was just eighteen—with his half of the money he and his sister, Rubye, had been left by their parents. There hadn't been enough money to buy the truck outright, but there had been enough to make a down payment, and Richard Edward figured he could find enough hauling jobs to make the monthly payments.

In an average week he'd make as many as three to four trips. Some of them were very hard. Of the two hundred fifty miles to Memphis, for example, less than fifty of them were on paved road, and it normally took about eight hours, one way. But in a time when many people had no jobs, Richard Edward was able to work steadily and make damn good money. He considered himself very lucky.

The Foster Warehouse was located at the extreme right end of the loading dock. Hopping up onto the dock, Richard Edward walked past the big stacks of multicolored salt-lick blocks, by the hundred-pound drums of floor sweep, and around several bound bundles of ax handles.

A big wad of cotton was hanging by a hairpin from the screen door of the office. The cotton had been soaked in citronella and was supposed to keep away flies, but the carcass-covered strips of flypaper that hung just inside the office bespoke the ineffectiveness of the idea. Richard Edward stepped in through the door, the hinges protesting loudly, and looked around. The front door and the windows were open, and two oscillating fans worked hard to move the air, but despite all that, it was still very hot in the office.

There were two desks in the outer office, one used by the secretary, a woman in her forties named Irene, and the other by the warehouse manager, a man of about fifty named Herman. For the moment Herman was at the opposite end of the dock, reading purchase orders to men loading the smaller trucks, called "bobtrucks," preparing them for their delivery runs to grocery stores in and around Jackson on the following day.

Just off the bigger room was a smaller office where Fred Foster, who owned Foster Warehouse, had his desk. He was on the phone when Richard Edward came in, but he waved through the open door, and the young trucker, who rather liked the man, waved back.

The office had a very distinctive and not unpleasant smell of chewing gum, cigarettes, and candy bars. Foster kept them stacked up in wire racks for sale to the warehouse workers at wholesale prices. Mingled with those aromas was the smell from the vase of roses on Irene's desk.

"Did you have any trouble comin' down?" Irene asked. Her southern accent was so heavy that she made two syllables out of the word "have."

"They were working on the streets in Yazoo City," Richard Edward said. "Had to detour several blocks out of the way. A couple of places the tree limbs were so low across the road, I was afraid the trailer wouldn't clear."

Irene slid an envelope over toward him. "There's your check," she said.

"Thanks." He put the check for twenty-five dollars in his billfold, then walked back out onto the warehouse dock. "Ready for me yet, Bill?" he called to a man piling goods into one of the bobtrucks. It was the truck driver's responsibility to get his load out of the truck and onto the dock; that done, the warehouse workers would take over.

"Nope," Bill called back. "Relax a while."

Nodding, Richard Edward crossed over to a pile of hundred-pound-bags of chicken feed, opening a package of Lucky Strike Greens as he walked. He pulled out a cigarette, tapped it on his wrist, then lit it. Glancing at the feed bags, he smiled in recognition. The blue-and-white diagonally striped logo on them identified the feed as a product of Canfield-Puritex Corporation, his father's employer for many years.

Sitting down on top of the feed bags, he pulled an envelope from his pocket. He had picked up his mail at the post office on his way to Foster Warehouse and found a letter that had arrived from his sister, Rubye Murtaugh, in California. Anxious to hear what she had to say, he slit it open and began to read:

August 6, 1935
Dear Richard Edward,

Just wanted to see how you're doing and let you know how things are going for us. I was glad to hear that you've bought a truck. I'm sure it's all going to work out well for you. You always were a hard worker.

I sure wish you could see your little niece, Joyce Ellen. She is the most beautiful baby there ever was, though I could be prejudiced since I'm her mother.

Things are going very well with us now, but we had a really hard time of it when we first got out here. Most people in California resented folks like us, calling us Okies and sometimes even spitting at us and yelling the most awful things. I know now how the colored people must feel back home, for out here we were treated just like colored people.

At first the only work we could get was picking oranges as migrant workers. We had to live in camps and go from grove to grove as each one was picked out. It was hard work and didn't pay very much, and the owners would deduct so much for damages that by the end of the day there'd be hardly any money left at all for the workers. Then, as I got farther along with the baby and couldn't work, it got even worse. Del had to work twice as hard, and I was afraid he was going to get sick.

I think I told you about the nice car Del bought before we left Oklahoma—a yellow Ford that he really liked a lot. Well, we finally had to sell it just to make ends meet. I felt so bad for Del, for he really loved that car, and it broke his heart to have to part with it, but we didn't have any choice.

I didn't tell you all this before, Richard Edward, because I didn't want you to worry. But I can tell you now because things are much better. A couple of months ago Jim Ramsey, the man we came out here with, heard about a job working for someone who owns a gardening service. The job paid real well, and all it entailed was going around and working in the yards of rich people. Jim told Del that the reason the job was open was because nobody (himself included) wanted to work for a Jap. That's who owns the business, a Japanese man named Yutake Saito. Del said that if the job was for real and was actually going to pay as much as Jim said it was going to pay, then he didn't give a d— if he was working for a Jap, German, colored person, or Mexican. He was going to go down and see if he could get the job.

It turns out the job was for real, so Del took it. His boss, Mr. Saito, is a very nice man, very polite and very smart. He and Del get along really well, and since Del doesn't have a car, Mr. Saito lets him bring the truck home to use at night. Mr. Saito's daughter,

Miko, is really good with the baby and has even offered to babysit for her. Sometimes Del drives me around in Mr. Saito's truck to show me the yards he works on. It turns out he really has a knack for gardening, and he takes a lot of pride in making the yards look real pretty. Who'd have thought it? Although I guess raising things is raising things, whether it's cotton and corn or shrubs and flowers.

One of the people Del works for is Demaris Hunter, the famous movie star. I asked Del if he'd get Miss Hunter's autograph for me, but he won't even try because he says he thinks things like that are foolish. He says she's a nice person, though. She lives all alone in a huge house. I guess she's never gotten over the tragedy of having her husband fall off their boat and drown on the very night they got married. He was so handsome, and she is so beautiful, that it must have been like a fairy tale wedding. But I guess he drank too much champagne or something at the wedding. Anyway, it sure was awful.

You can write to me at the address on the envelope, because I think we're going to be here for a while. Del says that if everything keeps going like this, we can even think about buying our own house in another couple of years.

I sure want to hear from you again soon. I'm really proud that you've got your own trucking business, and Alice Hughes sounds like a very nice girl. Be sure and let me know if you get married.

Your loving sister,
Rubye

Richard Edward smiled to himself. *Boy,* he thought, *I can't wait to tell Alice that Del is working for Demaris Hunter. Won't it just tickle her to know that? Guess that'll give her something to impress her friends with.* He chuckled. *Who knows? It might even impress her father.* He chuckled again. *Nah,* he decided. *Gordon Hughes would hardly be impressed by* that.

. . .

That night Richard Edward stood on the doorstep of the Hughes house, smoothing back his hair as he waited for a response to his knock and wondering if it would be Alice who answered. Alice was the youngest of six daughters born to the Reverend and Mrs. Gordon Hughes. A Methodist Episcopal minister, the good reverend was quick to point out that the Methodist Episcopal church was quite a "separate and distinct entity from the Protestant Episcopal Church, which, despite its name, is a little too close to the Roman Catholic church in doctrine, if you ask me."

The minister was staunchly against drinking, though two of his daughters drank, and he was against smoking, though four of his daughters smoked. He had never been to a movie in his entire life and neither had he allowed any of his daughters to do so while they were young enough to be influenced by him.

Alice, who neither smoked nor drank, was a big fan of the movies. She and Richard Edward were sitting on the porch swing when he gave her the news that his brother-in-law actually worked for Demaris Hunter. Alice was suddenly beside herself with excitement.

"Oh, my goodness!" she squealed. "What does she look like? In person, I mean?"

"I don't know," Richard Edward said. "I'm not the one who's seen her. Del is the one who knows her, not me."

"What does he say she's like?"

"According to Rubye, he says she's very nice."

"Oh, Richard Edward, do you think Del could get a photograph of her? You know, a real picture that he took personally, not one that you buy somewhere or that the studios send out."

"I don't know," Richard Edward said. "I doubt it. He probably doesn't want to bother her. Rubye said he won't even get an autograph for her."

Alice groaned in despair. "Oh, how am I going to be able to tell everyone that I know someone who knows Demaris Hunter if I don't even have a picture of her?"

Richard laughed. "You don't know anyone who knows her."

"Well, your brother-in-law does, and I certainly know you," Alice said. "That's practically the same thing, isn't it?"

He slowly wagged his head. "If you say so. So, how about a movie tonight?"

"Yes, I'd love to."

"Good. How about *China Seas* with Clark Gable and Jean Harlow? It's on at the Capitol."

"I'd rather see *Temptations.* It's showing at the Bijou."

"*Temptations?* But we saw that already. When it first came out, remember?"

"I know we did. But that was before I knew that I know someone who knows someone who knows Demaris Hunter. It will be different this time, now that I practically know her."

Richard Edward laughed heartily. "All right, if that's what you want. But we need to catch the first feature 'cause I have to leave really early in the morning. I have a load that has to be to Delta before noon."

Alice jumped up and ran to the front door. "I'll just grab my sweater! I won't be a minute!"

Richard Edward Parker left Jackson before dawn the next morning, hauling twenty-two thousand pounds of assorted freight, bound for Foster's other warehouse in Delta. Some of what the young trucker was carrying was needed for the afternoon delivery runs from that warehouse, making it imperative that he be in Delta by noon.

Hours later, when Richard Edward felt the Indianola Highway change from gravel to paved road under his tires, he knew that he had reached the city limits of Delta. He glanced at his watch and smiled. He had made it in plenty of time. It was only 10:43.

Dr. Andrew Booker waited for the big, red-cabbed trailer truck to pass, then pulled onto Indianola Highway and headed toward the police station. He had no idea what

Stump Pollard wanted with him, but the police chief had sent one of his officers for him, asking him to please come right away.

Andy couldn't say that he and Stump Pollard were friends exactly, but the two men did communicate on a level that wasn't adversarial. As a result they had formed the most effective point of contact there was between Delta's two worlds of white and black. Perhaps because of that the lot of the Negro in Delta had improved considerably in the year since Andy had arrived.

But even with Andy's ameliorating influence, Stump's regard of the Negro could not in any way be considered enlightened. Stump was a southerner, armed with stereotypical southern racial concepts. However, in his treatment of Negroes, Stump had drawn a line that he thought was fair, and he never stepped across it.

One of the reasons Stump tended to treat Andy with a degree of respect was because he found the idea of a black man with Andy's intellectual capacity absolutely fascinating. Andy, of course, knew that that in itself was a racially prejudiced concept. He also knew that Stump wouldn't recognize it as such, so he never mentioned it.

In many Mississippi towns a Negro could be arrested and thrown in jail for such offenses as loitering and public nuisance, which generally occurred when a white police officer was irritated by a black man he thought was being "uppity" or was in the wrong place at the wrong time. Stump didn't do such things and neither would he allow that from any his policemen. Even on more legitimate charges of drunkenness and public disturbance Stump now frequently let the Negro offenders go on their own recognizance or, at worst, let them sleep it off in jail and released them free and clear the next morning. White offenders had always been dealt with this way, but in the past Negroes who found themselves in such a fix could see a simple thing like drunkenness be compounded into resisting arrest, assault and battery, and contempt of court. What might be one night in jail for a white man could become up to three years in prison for a black one.

On a more personal note, shortly after he had arrived in

Delta, Andy had gone to Stump to ask him to persuade the Delta Light and Power Company to connect his house with electricity. Stump had done so. The electricity supplied by DLP, along with the well dug by Arlie and Deekus, had, in Andy's words, "brought his house and office into the twentieth century."

As a result, Andy's laboratory was now functional, and when he wasn't playing the role of "Brother Doctor" to his patients, he was deeply involved in research on a method of classifying and storing blood. His research was being partly funded by the Schillingberg Institute of Medical Research, for though Andy had turned down their position, a request from Dean Moyers, his old Dean of Medicine, had engendered some economic assistance from the Institute. The grant was relatively small, but it was enough to equip his laboratory and provide basic living expenses for himself, LaTonya, and the baby that was due in January.

Andy swung in at the curb, pulling up to the front of the police station. Stump Pollard was nervously pacing back and forth, and when he spotted Andy, he hurried out to the car to greet him, even opening the door for him.

"Brother Doctor," he said, "I'm glad you came. We've got a problem here, and we need some help."

"What kind of problem?"

"I'd rather let Doc Waltrip tell you about it," Stump replied. "He's inside."

Andy followed Stump up the foot-polished concrete steps of the police station, then pushed through the double doors to go inside.

A policeman was behind the desk, reading a newspaper, and he nodded at Andy when he came in. Andy nodded back, then looked over at the cells. Three of the four cells in the police station were occupied, two by white prisoners and one by a black man. The Negro prisoner was asleep, snoring loudly. One of the white prisoners was sitting on his bunk, holding his head in his hands. The other white prisoner was standing at the door of his cell, holding on to the bars. He wasn't a native of Delta, and, as was clear from his expression, he was shocked to see a Negro so well dressed and treated with what seemed like respect by the local police.

"Hey!" the prisoner yelled, pointing to Andy. "Hey, Chief! Who's this fancy-dressed nigger? What's he doin' in here?"

"Mr. Butrum, I suggest you just sit down there in your cell and be quiet," Stump said.

"I want to know who that fancy-dressed nigger is."

"He's the judge who's going to decide your case," Stump snapped.

The man snorted. "The judge? Who you tryin' to bullshit? There ain't no nigger judges in Mississippi."

"We do things a bit differently here in Delta."

"I'll be damned," the prisoner said, suddenly contrite. "Look, Judge, I hope you didn't take no offense to me callin' you a nigger. I didn't mean nothin' by it."

"He's back here, Brother Doctor," Stump said, ignoring the prisoner and leading Andy toward Stump's small office at the rear of the station. When they went in, Andy saw Dr. Waltrip sitting on the end of a small sofa, drumming his fingers nervously on his knee. He stood up when Andy came in and, uncharacteristically, offered Andy his hand.

"Dr. Booker, I'm glad you could come."

"What is this all about?" Andy asked.

"Listen . . ." Waltrip began. He ran his hand nervously through his thinning hair. "I know what you think of me. I'm just a veterinarian, and you think I got no call to be treatin' people. Well, you're probably right, but the truth is, I'm the only doctor the white people of Delta have. I tell everyone who'll listen to me that the coloreds have it a lot better than the white folks when it comes to doctorin'. At least they got a real doctor. Most of the treatin' I do is just commonsense stuff and followin' the instructions in this big book I got called *Our Family Physician.*"

"I'm not familiar with the book."

"Well, there's no reason you should be. It's pretty old, I guess. I bought it off a doctor's widow, down in Jackson. It was published in 1885."

"Eighteen eighty-five!" Andy was horrified. "Dr. Waltrip, there have been a lot of advances made in medicine since 1885. I don't see how that book can be of much help to you."

"Well, like I say, it's mostly common sense and a lot of nostrums," Waltrip admitted. "And, anyway, mostly I just see cuts, bruises, broken bones, colds, and headaches. I figure that if I'm not that much help, at least I'm not hurtin' anyone. And it generally makes them feel better just thinkin' they're bein' attended to."

Andy smiled. "The most important motto of a doctor. 'First, do no harm.' "

"Yeah, well, that's always been my motto. And I know my limitations, and I won't go beyond them," Waltrip said. "Which is why I wanted to see you. I need some help from a real doctor."

"Let me get this straight," Andy said. "You want me to help you with one of your cases? With a *white* patient?"

"Not with one of them, Dr. Booker. With seven," Waltrip replied. "And if we don't do somethin' soon, there'll be that many more before nightfall."

"Seven? How rapidly has it spread?"

"I saw my first case of it, whatever it is, yesterday mornin'. I saw my seventh case about an hour ago. That's when I came over here to ask Stump to ask you for help."

"Brother Doctor, I figure it's to your advantage to get in on this now," Stump interrupted. "If we don't get whatever this is stopped with the white people, it's going to spread down to the coloreds. You know how many colored folks work in white people's homes every day."

"That's the truth," Waltrip said.

"How does the illness present itself?" Andy asked.

"Well, at first I thought it was just a summer cold. Then I thought maybe it was the flu. It starts with a fever, nausea and vomiting, diarrhea, headache, and sore throat. Then there are the severe muscle pains and muscle spasms. But the real kicker is what happens next."

"Paralysis?" Andy asked in a quiet, somber voice.

"Yes," Waltrip replied. "How did you know?" The old man's eyes narrowed. "Dr. Booker, you know what it is, don't you?"

"I hope I don't," Andy replied. "I hope I'm wrong. I'd have to examine the patients, but I'm afraid it sounds like poliomyelitis."

"What?" Stump asked.

"It's also called infantile paralysis."

"Yes. Well, I considered that, Doctor," Waltrip said. "But two of my patients aren't children."

"Neither was President Roosevelt when he contracted the disease," Andy explained. "Children are the most common victims . . . but they aren't the *only* victims."

"How serious of a problem do we have?" Stump asked, his tanned face losing some color.

"Very serious. This is a highly contagious disease, and if we don't take steps immediately, it will spread through this town like wildfire."

"What do we do first?" Stump asked.

Andy thought a moment, then asked, "Chief, do you think you could get the mayor to call a meeting of the town leaders?"

"You mean the city council?"

"Not just the city council. We'll need *all* the town leaders: businessmen, preachers, teachers, anyone whom anybody will listen to."

"The mayor's at his barbershop," Stump said, picking up the phone. "I'll call him over."

No more than three minutes had elapsed when Mayor Joe Butler came racing into the police station. Butler, who was the proprietor of Butler's Hair Emporium, took his job as mayor very seriously—even though the job paid just one dollar per year—and when Stump told him to come right over, Butler came so quickly that he was still wearing his apron.

"What's wrong?" he asked, somewhat breathlessly. Then he noticed Andy. "Hello, Brother Doctor. Don't tell me we're havin' problems with our coloreds?"

"No, nothing like that," Stump answered, then explained the problem, ending with Andy's suggestion that the mayor call a meeting of all the town's leading citizens.

"All right, I'll do whatever it takes," Butler said. "We sure don't want this thing to spread any farther than it has."

"Mayor, don't forget to invite Professor Jackson and the Reverend Beasley," Andy said.

"But they're Negroes," Butler said with a dismissive shrug.

"Yes, I'll concede that," Andy said with a resigned sigh. "But they also happen to be very influential with the colored citizens of this town. And if we're going to beat this thing, we'll need complete cooperation between the white and the black communities."

"Dr. Booker is right, Joe," Doc Waltrip said.

"All right," Butler agreed. "Some folks might kick up a little stink—I mean 'bout us lettin' coloreds come to a meetin' like this—but let 'em bitch. I guess this is much too serious to be worryin' about disturbin' anyone's sensitivities."

Richard Edward Parker had his truck unloaded by twelve-thirty, so he decided to have lunch before starting back to Jackson. Leaving his truck parked at the warehouse, he walked across the street to get a hamburger and some french fries at the Chatterbox Café. There he overheard some of the other diners talking about the big town meeting being called for two o'clock that afternoon.

"What's it all about?" Edna, the waitress, asked the man sitting just to Richard Edward's right as she slid the Blue Plate Special—*"chicken-fried steak, mashed potatoes and gravy, black-eyed peas, and a roll . . . all for thirty cents"* —across the counter to him.

"Beats me," the diner replied, picking up his fork. "All I know is, everybody in town who's anybody is bein' asked to attend. Charley Gaines from down at the mill is goin'. So is Bobby Paterson from over at the bank."

"Elmer Matson, too," one of the other diners contributed. " 'Course, he's the editor of the newspaper, and you'd expect him to be goin'."

"The thing is, they're askin' all the preachers to come, too. That's pretty unusual, don't you think?" the first man asked.

"Yeah, and I heard that they even asked a couple of nigras to come," the second man replied.

"It must be somethin' all-fired important," Edna said.

"Can't be too important," the diner next to Richard Edward commented, as he shoveled a heap of mashed potatoes onto his fork.

"Why's that, Earl?"

"Well, hell," Earl said, grinning broadly, "they didn't ask *me*, did they?"

The meeting, which was held in the city council chambers, was attended by about thirty people, including Professor Henry Jackson and the Reverend Thaddeous Beasley. When the professor and the preacher arrived—somewhat apprehensively, since they had no idea what the meeting was about—they saw two chairs sitting at the very back of the room, separated from the others. They needed no invitation to know that this was where they were supposed to sit. They were surprised, however, to see "Brother Doctor" sitting up front with Stump Pollard, Dr. Waltrip, and the mayor.

After several minutes given over to the scrape of chairs and the buzz of conversation—*"What's all this about?"* and *"Why are them niggers here?"*—Mayor Butler got to his feet and held his hands up for quiet.

"Gentlemen," he said, "I asked all of you here today because Dr. Booker has somethin' to say that you all should hear."

"Wait a minute! Hold it, here!" someone shouted from the audience. Charley Gaines, manager of the feed mill, stood up, jabbing his finger toward Andy as he spoke. "Are you tellin' me we've all come down here to listen to a damn nigger?"

There were some dissenting sounds from others who shared Charley Gaines's opinion.

Stump stood up, his face hard. "Gentlemen, we have a crisis facing our town, and we thought the best way to deal with it would be to call together the leaders of the community. But, Gaines, I can see that we obviously made a mistake in calling you. You don't qualify as a leader, so you don't have to listen to a goddamn thing. Why don't you just get the hell out of here? The rest of us will handle it."

"Now, wait a goddamn minute, Chief! What's this all about?" Gaines demanded.

"I told you, we made a mistake in asking you. Don't worry about it. Just get the hell out, like I said."

"I'd . . . I'd really like to stay, Chief," Gaines said, suddenly apologetic.

"All right. But if you stay, you keep your mouth shut unless you've got something constructive to say," Stump ordered. He looked out over the audience. "And that goes for all of you. This is too important to be listening to any of your bickering bullshit. Begging your pardon, Reverends. Now, Brother Doctor, you want to get up here and tell them what this is all about?"

Andy stood up and looked out over the room. Except for dissertations in school, he had never spoken before a group before. And this was a nearly all-white and basically hostile group. He took a short breath. There was nothing he could do but plunge in.

"Gentlemen, this town is facing a serious outbreak of poliomyelitis. Infantile paralysis. So far it has only attacked a few people in the white community, but if it gets out of hand, it will sweep through this town like wildfire."

"If it hasn't infected anyone but white people, why are you involved?" someone asked.

"Because the polio virus does not differentiate between white skin and black. We are all in this together."

"What I want to know is, why are you doin' the talkin'? Why isn't Dr. Waltrip handlin' things?" another man asked.

"I can answer that," Waltrip said, standing up to face the group. "You folks know I'm not really a people doctor. When I ran into this thing, I knew I'd need help, so I called on Dr. Booker. The fact of the matter is, Dr. Booker is the one who made the diagnosis."

"*He* made the diagnosis?"

"Yes."

"Then we don't even know if it's really true or not, do we?"

"We know," Waltrip said, his face and voice grim. "It's true."

"All right, say it *is* true. I still don't see why you had to ask a nigra doctor for help. Why not ask someone to come over from Greenville or up from Jackson?"

"Because they might not come," Waltrip replied. "And why should they? Like Dr. Booker said, this is a very contagious disease. Suppose a doctor from Greenville came over here and caught it, then took it back to his own town? Then we'd have two towns infected instead of just one. That wouldn't be a very good thing, would it? No, gentlemen, if we're goin' to beat this thing, we are goin' to have to do it ourselves, and we are goin' to have to use the best weapon we've got. And that weapon is Dr. Booker."

"Hell, I never knew Brother Doctor was a real doctor. I thought he was just someone the niggers went to," a man toward the front said.

"He's real," Waltrip said.

"Well, now, if we ain't in a hell of a fix," someone said. "I mean, when a nigra doctor is the best weapon we've got."

"Maybe I can put your mind at ease," Dr. Waltrip said. "About a half hour ago I put through a long-distance telephone call to Dr. Paul Moyers, Dean of Medical Education at Tufts University in Boston. Dean Moyers told me that Dr. Booker was one of the most brilliant students ever to graduate from that school and is extremely qualified to deal with the problem facin' us. You want me to tell you the truth? I think right now I'd rather have Dr. Booker helpin' us than anyone else in this entire state."

"Hell, if Brother Doctor is good enough for you and Stump, he's good enough for me," someone said, and his comment was seconded and then roundly approved by the others.

"All right, then," Stump said. "Let's all be quiet and hear what Brother Doctor has to say."

Andy resumed his talk.

"First, let me tell you about the disease, which is an infection of the central nervous system that attacks the cells of nerves that control the muscles and may destroy or weaken them. After the onset of the initial symptoms—fever, nausea, and headache—paralysis may set in. Most commonly it affects the arms and legs. The muscles of affected limbs can be irreversibly weakened and then begin to atrophy—

shrivel away. Less frequently it paralyzes the muscles that govern breathing or swallowing—in which case the victim must be placed in an iron lung that artificially controls his breathing.

"One fortunate aspect—if one can call it that—of the disease is that it is not progressive. Of those victims whose muscles are weakened, many are never paralyzed, and of those whose muscles are paralyzed, once the virus has isolated itself to a particular part of the body, it will not spread."

"Well, what can we do about it, Brother Doctor?" someone asked.

"Most importantly, we must prevent it from spreading, and it's here that all of you can be of help. Some of the measures I am going to suggest will seem rather stringent. It's going to take the persuasive and coercive powers of each and every one of you to see that all the steps are carried out."

"What kind of steps are you talking about?"

"First, and foremost, the swimming pool must be closed at once. Today."

"Come on, Brother Doctor, you can't expect us to close the swimmin' pool in the middle of the summer," Mayor Butler complained. "Why, you know how important a swimmin' pool is this time of year. Folks couldn't get along without it."

"Oh, I think they can. *My* people seem to manage without one," Andy said, his tone dry.

"How do we know you're not just sayin' that 'cause the colored folks don't have a pool?" Gaines asked.

"Gaines, what he's saying makes sense," one of the others said. "It stands to reason that people swimming in the same water could infect one another."

"All right," the mayor agreed reluctantly. "We'll close the pool. The people aren't goin' to like it, but we'll close the pool."

"Good," Andy said. "And, you preachers, I'm afraid this also goes for immersion baptisms," he continued.

"No, sir, Brother Doctor, no, sir," the Reverend Beasley said, speaking for the first time. "We can't stop the Lord's work for a malady of man." Beasley's protest was seconded by the white preachers present.

"You don't have to stop the Lord's work. All I'm asking is that you not immerse your flock. Sprinkle them," Andy suggested.

"Sprinkle them?" the Baptist minister shouted. "Sprinklin' isn't baptism! It's blasphemy! It says in the book of St. Matthew, chapter three, the sixteenth verse: 'And Jesus, when he was baptized, went up straightway out of the water.' The people I baptize can't rise up straightway out of the water if they haven't been dunked under it."

"Reverend Landers, it also says in that same verse that the Spirit of God descended like a dove and lighted upon him," the Methodist minister broke in. "Now, since a dove doesn't land upon the shoulder of everyone you baptize, that is obviously a metaphor for God's love. And if that can be so interpreted, so can the part about Jesus rising straightway from the water."

"I need no interpretation of the Bible from a Methodist, sir!" Landers retorted hotly.

"Gentlemen, please!" Stump shouted. "We are not here to discuss theology! We are here to save lives!"

"And we, sir, are here to save souls!" the Reverend Beasley shouted back, and he was loudly applauded by all the white preachers.

"All right, all right," Andy gave in. "If you must immerse, immerse. But do it only in an inside baptismal where you can control the cleanliness and the temperature of the water. Cold water seems to bring on the malady. Also, empty the water after you are finished. Don't let it stand, even for one day."

"Brother Doctor, you know our church. We don't have an indoor baptismal," Beasley said soulfully.

"Brother Beasley, you can use our baptismal," the Reverend Landers offered.

"To baptize colored people?" Gaines asked.

"Mr. Gaines, souls have no color," Landers rejoined, and the other ministers, particularly the Methodist, approved the sentiment. "Reverend Beasley, we'll work somethin' out," Landers continued. "You can bring your people down on Saturday mornin'."

"Bless you, Brother," Beasley replied, his eyes growing moist.

"Now, gentlemen, if you have that worked out, may we continue?" Andy asked.

"Go ahead, Brother Doctor. We're listenin'."

Andy smiled. This was the first time since coming to Delta that he didn't feel he was outside looking in. He couldn't help but wonder if the feeling would continue once this crisis was past.

CHAPTER SIXTEEN

APRIL 3, 1936, ST. LOUIS, MISSOURI

Several thousand people were gathered around the Rockwell-McPheeters Aviation hangar at Lambert Field, awaiting the formal unveiling of the aircraft company's latest airplane, the "Windjammer." Though the public had not yet been officially introduced to the Windjammer, many had seen it during its test-flight stages. The Windjammer—technically the RM-435—was not only a seaplane, but was the largest aircraft Rockwell-McPheeters had ever built, fully as large as the Sikorsky S-42 now being used by Pan American for their Clipper flights across the Pacific Ocean. Rockwell-McPheeters had built four of the giant Windjammers, specifically for Mid-America Transport.

A special reviewing platform had been constructed for VIPs, and the invited guests included Missouri's two United States senators, Champ Dawson and Harry Truman, as well as its congressmen, its governor, and the mayor of St. Louis.

Though all the officials were Democrats, they weren't necessarily political allies. Today, however, they had put aside their differences, for the introduction of such a magnificent airplane would be a bold step forward not only for state and city prestige, but for their economy as well.

Many prominent St. Louis businessmen were there for the unveiling. Emerson Electric had supplied the airplane with its radios, while MC Motors had manufactured the fuel and exhaust-manifold systems for the four big engines. Even the St. Louis Steamboat Company, which had been building riverboats for nearly one hundred years, had played a role in the production of the aircraft, for it had designed and built the sleek racing-yachtlike hull. The airplane was equipped with wheels, but the wheels could be retracted and the wheel wells covered, making the hull watertight.

The introduction of the aircraft was turning into quite an affair. Three St. Louis high-school bands were present as was the Men's Glee Club of Jefferson University. *The St. Louis Chronicle* had distributed several thousand tear sheets of its front page, the single sheet making a good souvenir as it had a half-page photograph of the airplane above the fold, with the rest of the front page dedicated entirely to stories about it. It was also good advertising for the newspaper, which, according to a proud announcement in a small box in the upper right-hand corner, had nearly returned its daily circulation numbers back to the peak it had enjoyed before the depression.

"What I don't understand," KSLM announcer Floyd Stoner was saying to Willie Canfield, president of Mid-America Transport, who had just given Stoner a fact sheet on the new craft, "is why MAT would need such a plane? Where, within your airline's network of cities, do you intend to land such a craft? In the Kansas City Municipal Swimming Pool?" Stoner laughed at his own joke.

Willie smiled. "If I tell you now, it will spoil the surprise. Please, have patience for just a few minutes longer and it'll all become clear to you. Now, if you'll excuse me, they're signaling me from the reviewing stand. I have to get up there. But don't go away. I'll answer all your questions after the ceremony."

Before Floyd could respond, Neil Goodman, the radio station's engineer, interrupted.

"Floyd, are you ready?" Goodman asked from his control board, holding a telephone that connected him with KSLM's downtown studio.

"I'm ready," Floyd replied, clearing his throat and stepping up to the microphone.

"He's ready," Neil said into the telephone. "Switch us on my count. Counting. Five, four, three, two, one, now!" He pointed to Floyd.

"Good afternoon, ladies and gentlemen," the announcer began, speaking into the microphone while his voice was amplified out to the waiting crowd, *"this is Floyd Stoner, coming to you directly from Lambert Flying Field in St. Louis, Missouri, where, momentarily, Rockwell-McPheeters Aviation Company and Mid-America Transport will introduce a new airplane."*

He quickly scanned the printed data that Willie Canfield had handed him, then continued, *"The airplane, which they are calling the Windjammer, is, we are told, a four-engined craft capable of landing on land or at sea and big enough to carry seventy-five—yes, I said seventy-five—passengers nonstop for a distance of over two thousand miles."*

The hangar doors rolled open then, and a yellow tractor appeared. A long towing bar was attached to the tractor, and on the other end of the towing bar, just appearing from the shadows of the hangar, was the first Windjammer.

As the size and majesty of the airplane became more apparent, the crowd reacted with oohs and ahs, then broke into applause.

"Hey, look!" someone called. "Look at the airline's name!"

Though the logo's colors were the same, yellow and green, the *M* had been turned upside down so that it was now a *W*. And *WAT*, according to the name written down the side of the fuselage, meant World Air Transport.

"I don't know if I can describe the impact of this sight to you, but I'll give it a try," Floyd Stoner told his listeners. *"The airplane is huge. Perhaps you'll get some idea of just how huge when I tell you that a man is sitting on top of one of*

the big engines, and he's absolutely dwarfed by it. Each one of the engines, ladies and gentlemen, is as large as a big truck, and there are four of them.

"The nose of the plane looks like the prow of a boat, for that's exactly what it is: a flying boat. There's an open hatch just behind the sleek-looking prow, and a man is standing in the hatchway, wearing earphones and talking into a microphone, no doubt giving orders to the other men inside what must be the cavernous interior of this ship.

"The wheelhouse, or pilot's compartment, is located on top of the plane just behind the nose, while the passenger compartment is below. A series of windows—I can count fourteen of them—stretch along the fuselage. The tail is painted yellow and the lettering is green, just as before. But, and here is a change, the stylized wings that used to adorn the letters MAT are gone. In their place are two globes, one representing the New World and the other the Old.

"And now, ladies and gentlemen, Mr. William Canfield, the president of Mid American Transport—or rather, I suppose I should say World Air Transport—is stepping up to the microphone to say a few words. Let's hear what he has to say."

Willie stepped up to the speaker's podium, squinting against the glare of the sun. Brushing his wind-ruffled auburn hair out of his eyes, he looked out over the battery of microphones at what appeared to be a sea of hats, thousands of hats shading the expectant faces of those who had turned out for this event. Beyond the sea of hats, out on the runway, was a twin-engine, twin-tail Starduster just beginning its takeoff. This was Flight 173 for Chicago, Willie knew. The Rockwell-McPheeters Starduster was a twenty-four-passenger airliner that had, along with the Douglas DC-3s, in the last year replaced more than eighty-five percent of the Tri-Stars, Tri-Motor Fords, and Curtis Condors that previously made up the nation's airline fleet. The Starduster was fast, quiet, safe, and comfortable, and was almost daily winning over new converts to airline travel.

But, as Willie had told MAT's board of directors when he first introduced the concept of the Windjammer, "To paraphrase Al Jolson, people ain't seen nothin' yet."

The twenty-eight-year-old entrepreneur cleared his throat and began to speak.

"Governor Stark, Senator Dawson, Senator Truman, Mr. Mayor, esteemed Congressmen, honored guests, ladies and gentlemen . . . Throughout the history of our country St. Louis has been the gateway to America, opening up all points of the compass: east to west, west to east, north to south, and south to north. St. Louis is still the gateway city, but beginning today it is not only the gateway to the rest of America, it is the gateway to the rest of the world."

The crowd applauded politely.

"I am pleased to announce that we have just secured docking privileges in New York Harbor for two Windjammer airplanes. We have also made arrangements with officials in Lisbon, Portugal, to land, dock, and maintain two Windjammers there. As soon as we receive certification, we will begin service with two Windjammers per week departing New York for Lisbon and, of course, two return flights per week from Lisbon to New York.

"In addition, we have secured docking rights in Oakland, California, and landing rights in Honolulu, Guam, Manila, and Hong Kong for our Pacific route. It will soon be possible for a person to board one of our Stardusters here in St. Louis for a flight to New York or San Francisco, where you can connect with the Windjammer. Once you are on board the Windjammer, the world is your destination, for it is now possible for a citizen of St. Louis, by a series of connecting flights, to encircle the globe entirely by air! Around the world in eighty days? We can thumb our nose at that old dream. As of now, there is no place on the surface of this planet that is more than one hundred sixty-eight hours away from any ordinary St. Louisian." Willie pointed to the airplane. "Ladies and gentlemen, I give you the future!"

The crowd erupted with cheers. When the applause, yells, and whistles had died down, the dignitaries were introduced, including Senators Dawson and Truman. They all spoke, keeping their words brief, and after the last speech came the moment the crowd had been waiting for. They were invited to line up for a carefully orchestrated walk-through tour of the airplane, entering through the rear door, then coming out the front. For many it would be the first time ever that they were inside an airplane of any kind, and a few approached the event with some degree of trepidation.

"You sure that thing is tied down good? I mean, it can't suddenly break loose and take off, can it?" a man standing in line asked one of the guides, laughing nervously.

"They aren't goin' to start it up, are they? I'm not goin' to get on it if they start it up," another man said.

Soon all the fears were eased, and everyone stood in a long, orderly line, moving slowly toward the great craft, examining it carefully as they approached.

A smiling stewardess, uniformed in a green jacket and skirt, greeted the spectators as they stepped into the plane, just as she would if they had been passengers.

"Hello, welcome aboard the Windjammer," she said somewhat mechanically. "For your safety, we ask that you watch your step as you pass through the airplane, and stay behind the ropes, please."

Though people were boarding in a steady stream, those who had made it inside were going through so slowly to check the craft's every detail that it seemed to take forever for those approaching on the outside to actually make it inside, and they had to endure listening to the stewardess's same welcoming statement over and over again.

"Hello, welcome aboard the Windjammer. For your safety, we ask that you watch your step as you pass through the airplane, and stay behind the ropes, please."

Many of those in line were clutching the information sheets that had been passed out, and as they shuffled along, they read them, often speaking aloud as if no one else knew what they knew:

"Hey, this thing is one hundred and nine feet long."

"Golly! Listen to this: If somethin' was to go wrong with one of the engines, you could walk down through the middle of the wings to get to 'em!"

"Hey, how about this? This thing'll go a hundred and seventy-five miles per hour. Can you imagine anything this big going that fast?"

"Hello, welcome aboard the Windjammer. For your

safety, we ask that you watch your step as you pass through the airplane, and stay behind the ropes, please."

The airline had hired actors to portray passengers. They sat reading magazines or looked out the windows with as much excitement as if they were looking down on the clouds or talked among themselves just as if hundreds of people weren't gawking at them.

The first compartment the visitors saw was the private "Deluxe Suite." It had a sofa and a coffee table and its own lavatory. A bed was pulled down from the after bulkhead, and a woman in an exquisite nightgown was sitting in the bed, holding a silver-framed mirror while combing her long blond hair. A man, wearing a silk smoking jacket and with his feet in a pair of velvet slippers, sat on the sofa reading a magazine. Breakfast was laid out on the coffee table for this elegant couple as if it had been brought by one of the stewards.

The ladies' dressing room was next. The door was open to show one "passenger" brushing her hair, while another was applying lipstick.

Next the visitors filed into one of the passenger compartments, realizing then that the airplane was actually laid out in a series of compartments, each one separated by a bulkhead. Each compartment had ten seats, arranged in two facing rows of three seats on the left side of the plane and two facing rows of two seats on the right side. Every seat in this first compartment was filled, and the "passengers" looked out the windows, played cards, or read books, ignoring the line of curiosity seekers endlessly shuffling through.

In the next compartment the seats were made into sleeping berths, four berths on the right and six berths arranged in a U on the left. Curtains were drawn closed across the berths as was done on a train. On one berth, however, the curtain was open, and the "passenger" lay propped up on his pillow, reading. The book was Eric Twainbough's *The Corruptible Dead*, fashionably correct as it was just this week number one on the best-seller list.

There were a few more compartments, then a dining room/lounge that could accommodate twenty-five people at one sitting. A few "passengers" were here as well, being served by uniformed stewards. The tables were elegantly set with crystal, china, silver, and candlesticks.

Just before the visitors passed out of the plane they were allowed to climb up a spiral staircase that gave them a quick look at the flight deck. No one failed to be awestruck by the array of instruments, dials, knobs, levers, wheels, and switches that were spread all the way across the panel in front of the two pilots and down each side in front of the flight engineer, navigator, and radio operator.

When finally the visitors exited the front of the airplane, they marveled at the world they were fortunate enough to be living in. After having had their turn at seeing the Windjammer, the visitors began streaming out into the parking lot, where they would pile into their cars to fight the traffic jam on their way back home. Everyone would agree, of course, that traffic was the curse of modern times.

In another part of the airport a custom-built Starduster was being made ready for a flight. Sizewise no different from any other Starduster airliner, this particular aircraft was the Canfield-Puritex corporate plane, recently acquired to replace the Tri-Star that had served the company for so long, and it was fueling up to take John and Faith Canfield back to Washington after witnessing Willie's triumphant launching of his new airplane and expanded airline service.

The Starduster was nearly twice as large and twice as fast as the Tri-Star, even though it had one less engine. Like its predecessor, the Canfield-Puritex corporate plane was all white with a blue stripe just at window level painted along the fuselage. The aircraft's interior was sleek leather and chrome with all the accoutrements required to make it a veritable flying living room.

Aside from every passenger comfort, this craft had the latest state-of-the-art navigational equipment for its pilots, including a radio that could home in on a beacon, enabling the plane to fly through all kinds of weather.

Elsie, the black nursemaid whom John and Faith had hired to care for their baby, Morgan, was already on board the aircraft, tending the infant in his crib. With the ceremony over, John and Faith boarded the airplane, and Faith stopped by the crib and looked down at Morgan.

"Was he a good baby?" Faith asked the nursemaid, though her eyes never strayed from her son's smiling face.

"Oh, yes, ma'am, he was a very good baby," Elsie replied. "Why, I just held him on my lap and let him look through the window at the bands and such. Me and him had us a fine time."

"You were a dear to come with us, Elsie," Faith said. "I don't know what I would have done without you."

"Why, I enjoyed it, Mrs. Canfield. I don't know too many folks, white or colored, who get to ride in such a fine machine like this. I mean, I sit here in this seat and have the servin' lady do for me just like she does for everyone else." Elsie laughed. "And I don't see how she stays so cool and pretty lookin' after doin' all the cookin' and then walkin' around and servin' everybody, all the while we're just flyin' over the clouds."

Faith laughed. "Well, Jeanie was a stewardess for the airline before she took this job. I guess she figures it's real easy cooking for and then waiting on no more than five or six people. She used to have to do it for a lot more."

Senator Champ Dawson came on board then, accompanied by his secretary and a man who had been working as a special investigator for the senator. Champ pointed at the briefcase that the special investigator was carrying, then smiled broadly at John.

"John, my boy," he said, "guess what Carl has in his briefcase."

"The affidavits?" John suggested hopefully.

Champ grinned. "Right on the first guess."

"Senator Dawson, we got them!" John exclaimed.

"That we did, son, that we did. It's exactly what we've been looking for. When those hearings open next week, we'll be ready for Mr. Kerry O'Braugh."

"Where is Senator Truman?" John asked, looking toward the door. "I thought he was returning to Washington with us."

"My esteemed colleague decided to take a commercial flight back," Champ replied.

"Really? Why, for heaven's sake? This has got to be a lot more comfortable. And faster."

"You know how Harry is. He doesn't want to do anything that would even hint at some impropriety."

"Impropriety?"

"Yes, you know, like accepting a free ride on a private plane. Especially one that belongs to a corporation."

"Oh," John said. "I guess I hadn't thought of that."

Champ snorted. "Believe me, Harry has."

"What about you? Does he think you're wrong for flying back with us?"

"No, I guess there's a fine line there, and Harry found it for me. You see, according to him, I'm not flying back as the guest of Canfield-Puritex," Champ said, grinning. "I'm flying back as a guest of my daughter. And grandson," he added, looking toward Morgan's crib. "Elsie?"

"Yes, sir, Senator?"

"Soon as we take off and start flying level, I want you to bring that little fella over here to me. We've got a lot of talking to do."

"Yes, sir, Senator. I'll do that—soon as I'm not scared to walk around."

Jeanie, the stewardess, came walking down the aisle from the cockpit. A very pretty young woman with short blond hair and bright blue eyes, she was wearing a female version of the uniform worn by the pilot and copilot. She shut the outer door, dogged it tight, then started back up the inclined aisle toward the front of the plane, bending forward slightly at the waist to keep her balance.

She smiled at the passengers, telling them, "We'll be taking off in just a few minutes, folks. Better get into your seats now. I'll have coffee ready as soon as we reach altitude."

"You don't even have to serve coffee if you'll just walk up and down the aisle and let me watch," the special investigator quipped. Jeanie blushed, and the others in the airplane laughed.

"Is your belt fastened?" John asked Faith.

"Yes," Faith answered. She looked back toward Elsie and Morgan's crib. "Elsie?"

"The baby's all fastened in, Mrs. Canfield," Elsie called up to her. "I know what I'm supposed to do."

Faith smiled. "I know that you do. I'm just being an overly nervous mother."

John felt Faith's hand reaching for his, and he took it, then looked through the window over the nacelle of the left engine. Unlike the engines on the Tri-Star, which hung down from the plane, these were an intregal part of the wing, curving gently to make as little an interruption in the airflow as necessary. It not only improved the plane's aerodynamics, it made for a much more graceful-looking craft.

John heard the low-pitched whine as the inertia starter began winding up, then the cough as it was engaged. There was a large puff of blue-white smoke from the exhaust, and then the blades of the propeller started spinning, finally turning into a silvery blur. A moment later the right engine joined the left; with both engines running the pilot began taxiing the airplane slowly across the wide concrete apron.

From John's window he could see the huge Windjammer sitting over in front of the hangar, a long line of spectators still waiting to go through for a close-up look. He had examined the airplane quite thoroughly this morning along with the other VIPs, long before it went on public view. The Windjammer was quite an airplane, and John felt that his younger brother could be justifiably proud of it.

More than just increasing business from expanded routes, John knew, the Windjammer and the Pan Am Clippers were going to change forever the way America thought of itself. No longer were events in Europe a week away. Now they were as immediate as tomorrow.

John also knew that President Roosevelt was equally aware of that concept. Roosevelt was the first American president who didn't think in terms of America being a place set apart from the rest of the world. Roosevelt saw the future of Europe and especially of England as being closely tied to the future of the United States. However, there were many isolationists in Congress and the Senate who would, if they could, separate the globe into two halves and send each half orbiting around the sun with never any contact between the two.

The transoceanic airplane would bring such people into the twentieth century. They might kick and scream every inch of the way, but they *would* be brought into the twentieth century.

The low rumble of the two engines changed to a loud roar, and John realized with some surprise that they had already reached the runway and were starting their take-off run. If he hadn't known by any other way, he would have known by how tightly Faith was squeezing his hand. John chuckled, then reached down to put his other hand over hers. She never had liked takeoffs.

CHAPTER SEVENTEEN

JUNE 13, 1936, WASHINGTON, D.C.

Kerry O'Braugh, Carmine Brazzi, and Vinnie Todaro had been subpoenaed by the United States government to appear before a hearing conducted by Senator Champ Dawson and his Economic Recovery Advisory Board. The subpoena charged that Kerry, Carmine, Vinnie, and the Missouri Labor Negotiations Commission were conducting business in a way that was detrimental to national recovery efforts, and Kerry was ordered to appear before the ERAB and show cause as to why he should not be charged in federal court for his activities.

Carmine and Vinnie, though summoned, were not specifically scheduled to appear. But they had been instructed to repair to Washington and hold themselves available to be called. Accordingly, Kerry's two lieutenants had left for Washington by train on Friday morning, June 12. Kerry, having had some business to attend to that couldn't be concluded until late Friday, left the following morning, taking a direct flight from St. Louis to Washington.

It was now late Saturday afternoon, and the thirty-five-year-old crime boss was seated in the plane, looking through the window. The flight had left St. Louis nearly nine hours before, and Kerry was tired—and tired of being confined to his seat.

There was nothing to see outside the window except clouds. They lay beneath him like a great vat of cream that had been fluffed and whipped into swirls and peaks. Occasionally feathers of mist trailed back from the wing tip, carried along for a while before letting go. The propellers, too, would often leave unwinding coils of vapor behind them as the engines droned on monotonously.

Kerry realized it had been some time now since he had seen the ground, and it made him nervous. Turning away from the window, he saw the stewardess walking by, heading toward the front of the plane, and he called out to her.

"Miss?"

"Yes, sir?" she replied, turning toward him and leaning down slightly, balancing herself by holding the seat back just in front of him.

Kerry looked her over appreciatively. From the tips of her fingernails, which were long, perfectly manicured, and glistening red, to the top of her head, she was a knockout. Her figure-defining uniform consisted of a green jacket with yellow trim and buttons and a matching skirt. A campaign cap sitting jauntily on her short, dark hair was also green, with a stylized golden wing coming out of the entwined globes that were the World Air Transport emblem. The uniform was very trim and stylish and represented quite a departure from the nurselike uniforms worn by the stewardesses Kerry had seen on most other airlines.

"Yes, sir?" she repeated. "May I help you?"

He remembered why he had called her over. "Yeah. Listen, I haven't seen the ground in over an hour. How can the pilot tell where we're goin'?"

"Oh, I assure you, we're quite safe," the pretty brunette answered with a practiced smile. "We're flying on the beam."

"On the beam?"

"Yes, sir. You see, a radio station at our destination sends out two letters in Morse code. The *A* is a dot-dash, sounding like 'di-daah,'" she explained, demonstrating. "If the pilot hears that signal, we're too far to the left and must turn to the right. The other signal is the letter *N*, and it's just the opposite of *A*. It's dash-dot. Daah-dit. If he hears that letter, we're too far to the right. Now, if we're perfectly lined up, the dash of the *N* will cover the dot of the *A*, and the dash of the *A* will cover the dot of the *N* so that we get a steady tone. It sounds like, 'daaaahhh,'"

"Amazin'," Kerry said, grinning broadly.

"Isn't it? Science is a wonderful thing."

"No," Kerry countered. "I mean it's amazin' that someone as pretty as you can know such technical stuff."

The stewardess's smile grew even broader. "Well, that's part of my job," she said. "And so is service, which means I had better get back to work. Would you care for something to drink? Coffee, perhaps, or tea?"

"Yeah, a cup of coffee would be nice, thank you."

"I'll be right back."

Kerry watched her walk up the aisle toward the tiny galley. He knew that it was probably necessary that she swing her ass back and forth like that to maintain her balance while moving about in a plane, but he could almost swear that she was exaggerating it for his benefit, knowing he would be watching her.

When she came back a moment later with the cup of coffee, she was also carrying a copy of *Time* magazine. Holding it out to him, she asked, "Would you care to read about yourself, Mr. O'Braugh?"

He stared at her. "Read about myself?"

"This is your picture, isn't it?" she asked.

Sure enough, Kerry O'Braugh's picture was on the cover of *Time*. Beneath the picture was his name and beneath that a short sentence: HIS LABOR NEGOTIATION TACTICS HAVE COME INTO QUESTION *(National Affairs)*.

"Well, I'll be damned," Kerry said, reaching for the magazine. "What do you know about that?"

"You mean you didn't know your picture was on the cover?" the stewardess asked.

"No." Kerry looked up at her. "Tell me, have you read the story?"

"I'm sorry, I haven't," she said. "I just noticed it."

"I didn't think so. I'm sure they don't have anythin' nice to say about me, and if you'd read it, you wouldn't be so friendly."

"Of course I would," the stewardess replied. "Being friendly is as much a part of my job as serving coffee and explaining how the beam works."

Kerry chuckled. "Is that a fact? Well, you're good at it, honey. You're damned good."

"I try to be," the stewardess replied easily. She left the magazine and the coffee with him, then moved away to answer the summons of another passenger.

Kerry turned to page eighteen, the National Affairs section of the magazine, and read the cover story.

> In all his scouring of the nation's economic woes, Presidential pal Champ Dawson, senior senator from Missouri and chairman of the powerful Economic Recovery Advisory Board, has never before examined a real-life character from the underworld. At his ERAB hearing in Washington next week he will be seeing one: tough, one-time bootlegger (and former henchman of Al Capone) Kerry O'Braugh.
>
> Mr. O'Braugh, who calls himself a labor negotiator, has been involved in several strikes, sometimes as advocate for management, sometimes for labor. In every case in which he has been involved there has been violence. That in itself is not particularly noteworthy, for violence has been featured in nearly all the major strikes over the last few years. What *is* noteworthy, and what Senator Dawson will surely want to know, is how Mr. O'Braugh can account for his phenomenal success rate. In every strike in which Mr. O'Braugh has been involved, victory has gone to the side represented by his "Missouri Labor Negotiations Commission."

. . .

Kerry was just finishing the story when the stewardess came back through the airplane, requesting everyone to please extinguish their cigarettes, fasten their seat belts, and return their seat backs to the upright position for landing in Washington, D.C.

About time, Kerry thought to himself. *Another half hour on this thing and my feet'd be permanently asleep.*

Kerry had never fully recovered from the knee injury incurred nearly two years before during the strike against MC Motors. He could walk, but he had to use a cane, and he had a very pronounced limp.

Because of his disability, when the plane landed, he was the last one to get off so as not to hold the other passengers back. As he limped across the flight ramp between the plane and the fence that surrounded the airport, he saw a relatively short, well-dressed man standing patiently by the gate. This was Matthew Quinn, his lawyer.

"Kerry, welcome to Washington," Quinn said, stepping through the gate to meet him. "Do you have your baggage claim check?"

"Yeah, right here," Kerry replied, producing it from his jacket pocket.

"Give it to me," Quinn said. "I'll have someone from the office claim your luggage and bring it to the hotel. My car is just over there. We must get going right away."

"Wait, hold it, hold it! Why the bum's rush?" Kerry asked. "I just finished a long, tough flight. I need to find a bar and have a drink or two."

"I'd rather you not do that. Why don't you just let me have a bottle sent up to your hotel room?" Quinn suggested.

"I'm not the kind to sit up in a room and suck whiskey out of a bottle," Kerry groused. "I'm not a goddamn drunk. It's Saturday night, for Chrissake. I'd just like to socialize a little, that's all."

"I wouldn't advise that, Kerry," Quinn said darkly. "There are too many reporters in this town. If they found you, they could carve you up into little pieces before we ever got before Senator Dawson's hearing. I'm sure by now you've seen the article in *Time*."

"Yeah, I read it on the plane."

"I wish you had spoken to me before you consented to that interview."

"I guess I should've, but you know, the funny thing is, I didn't exactly grant that interview. I mean, when that fella called me, I didn't know he was from *Time* magazine. I thought he was some guy from Dawson's office."

"Uh-huh. And you never thought to say, 'I'm sorry, you'll have to speak to my attorney.' I thought we had that all worked out. You don't talk to *anyone* until this is over with. If you need instructions on finding the toilet, you ask me and I'll ask for you. *You don't talk to anyone.* Now, that's not too hard to remember, is it?"

"Come on, Quinn, I didn't answer anythin' incriminatin'. He just asked a few questions like where was I born . . . that sort of stuff."

"Whatever he asked, he gave you a pretty good lambasting in the article he wrote. I want you to listen to me from now on. I've already convinced Mr. Todaro and Mr. Brazzi that they are to go nowhere and speak to no one until I give them permission."

"Until *you* give permission?"

"That's right. Until *I* give permission," Quinn replied firmly. "After all, I'm costing you a great deal of money, and if you don't do what I say, you won't be getting your money's worth."

"Okay, okay, whatever you say," Kerry agreed. "But it's going to be goddamned borin', sittin' in that hotel room night after night, I can tell you that."

"Here's the car," Quinn said. He smiled. "And don't start feeling sorry for yourself. After the hearings are over, I'll unlock your cage and let you and your friends fly around a bit."

"Well, gee, that's damned big of you," Kerry said sarcastically. "After all, I'm payin' you to keep me *out* of jail, not put me *in*."

• • •

On Monday morning when the hearings opened, the meeting room of the Economic Recovery Advisory Board was filled with reporters, radio microphones, and newsreel cameras. Because Kerry's picture had been on the cover of *Time* as well as in numerous newspapers and magazines across the country, he was recognized the moment he came into the chamber. Dozens of flashbulbs popped while he was being sworn in and took his seat at the witness table.

As soon as Kerry was sitting, Senator Champ Dawson leaned forward to speak into the microphone. "Let the record show that on this day, Monday, the fifteenth of June, in the year of our Lord 1936, there was summoned to appear before this hearing of the Economic Recovery Advisory Board one Kerry O'Braugh. Is Mr. O'Braugh present?"

"Mr. O'Braugh is present, Mr. Chairman," Matthew Quinn replied.

"And I take it you are Mr. O'Braugh's attorney, so he is represented by counsel."

"He is, Mr. Chairman."

Dawson looked up and down the table at the other board members present, then cleared his throat. "All members of this investigation panel being present and the witness having appeared as summoned and represented by counsel, I now call this hearing to order."

A few papers were shuffled, someone coughed, and one of the board members poured himself a glass of water. At the back of the meeting room the door opened and closed, but for the most part all those present were silent, waiting for the hearing to begin.

"Mr. O'Braugh, you have been summoned before this board to testify about your activities with regard to several recent strikes. In particular, I would like to talk about your role as strikebreaker in the MC Motors dispute."

"I'd prefer not to be called a strikebreaker, Senator," Kerry said.

Champ Dawson looked up from his paper and adjusted his glasses on his nose. "You don't wish to be called a strikebreaker?"

"No, sir. I am a labor negotiator."

"A labor negotiator, you say?"

"Yes, sir."

"Mr. O'Braugh, do you know the definition of the term 'negotiator'?"

"Well, yes, sir. A negotiator is someone who negotiates."

Laughter rippled through the hearing room.

"Actually, Mr. O'Braugh, you are correct," Champ said. "Perhaps I should reword my question. What does it mean to negotiate?"

"To settle things," Kerry said.

"Let me read you Mr. Webster's definition," Dawson said, reaching for the topmost book of a stack to his right. "According to the 1936 edition of *Webster's School and Office Dictionary*, to negotiate means 'to treat with others in business or private affairs; hold intercourse respecting a treaty, etcetera; to conclude by treaty, bargain, or agreement.'" Senator Dawson looked up from the book. "Does any part of this sound like anything you do?"

"Well, I . . ." He cleared his throat. "Like I said, I settle things."

"Sometimes permanently," Champ said under his breath.

"Mr. Chairman!" Quinn interjected.

"I apologize for the remark," Dawson replied, though not very convincingly. He looked up at Kerry again. "Mr. O'Braugh, how much money did you earn by 'settling things' last year?" he asked.

"Senator, I was always taught that it wasn't polite to ask a man how much money he made," Kerry replied. "What if someone asked you how much money you made last year?"

"I am a United States senator," Dawson replied smoothly. "What I make is a matter of public record."

"Yeah, well, what I make isn't."

"Oh, but it is, Mr. O'Braugh." Champ turned to his left, and John Canfield, who was sitting just behind him, handed him a piece of paper. "In fact," the senator continued, "when you filed your taxes last year, you made it a part of the public record. This board has subpoenaed your tax records, and they show that you personally earned over one hundred thousand dollars last year. Is that figure correct?"

"Do I have to tell him that?" Kerry whispered to Quinn.

"If that is what you filed, you had *better* tell him that," Quinn answered.

Kerry turned back to the microphone. "Yes, Senator, that figure is correct."

There was a buzz of astonishment among the spectators.

"That is a great deal of money, Mr. O'Braugh. Particularly in these difficult times. You are making more money than the President of the United States. Don't you feel a little self-conscious about earning so much?"

"Senator, I remember readin' about somethin' Babe Ruth once said," Kerry replied, a sly smile on his face. "When someone told him that he was making more money than the President of the United States, he said, 'I'm havin' a better year than the President.' "

The gallery laughed, and Senator Dawson had to use his gavel to restore order.

"Surely, Mr. O'Braugh, you are not comparing yourself to Babe Ruth? He is a genuine American hero, a man all the youth of our country can look up to. Whereas you, sir, are a criminal."

"I object," Quinn said.

"Save your objections, counselor," Champ shot back. "This is a board hearing, not a court of law." The senator shuffled his papers for a moment, then continued, "During your 'negotiations' to settle the MC Motors strike, a man named Marvin Gates was killed, was he not?"

"I don't recall the guy's name."

"I believe you shot him, did you not?"

"Yes, sir, I shot him."

"You don't even recall the name of a man you killed?"

"We weren't exactly friends."

Again laughter rang through the gallery, and again Senator Dawson had to use his gavel to quiet the spectators.

"But you do not deny killing him?"

"No, Senator, I don't deny it. He was about to chop off the head of one of my associates. I had no choice."

"And you just *happened* to have a gun?"

"Mr. Chairman, let the record show that Mr. O'Braugh

was duly licensed to carry a firearm in his capacity as a security guard for MC Motors," Quinn put in.

"So noted," Champ replied. "Tell me, Mr. O'Braugh, is Mr. Gates the only man you ever killed?"

"Beg your pardon?"

"Did you know a man named Tony Fusco?"

"Tony Risco?"

"Fusco, Mr. O'Braugh. Tony Fusco. Do you remember him?"

"I don't recall the name."

"Well, let me refresh your memory. Mr. Fusco owned an automobile repair garage in Chicago in 1923. As were many others during Prohibition, Mr. Fusco was involved in bootlegging. He was engaged in this activity without the permission of one Johnny Torrio, who was at that time the head of organized crime in Chicago. Did you know Johnny Torrio?"

Kerry looked at his lawyer, and his lawyer nodded.

"Yes."

"Did you work for him?"

"Sometimes."

"What was the nature of your work?"

Kerry and Quinn consulted for a moment before Kerry answered. "I respectfully decline to answer that question, Senator, on the grounds that it may be self-incriminatin'."

"Yes, I daresay that it would," Champ said dryly. "Do you know Al Capone?"

"Yes."

"Did you ever work for him?"

"No, not directly."

"What was your relationship with Mr. Capone?"

"I never really liked the son of a bitch."

The spectators broke out laughing, and Senator Dawson waited for them to be quiet.

"I meant, what was your working relationship with him? You said you didn't work for him directly, so what did you do?"

"He was Johnny Torrio's top man. He was pushing, shoving, trying hard to take over control. I worked for Torrio, not Caponi."

"Who?"

"The man you call Capone. His real name is Caponi. We both worked for Torrio, but I didn't work for him."

"Was it Johnny Torrio who ordered you to kill Tony Fusco?"

Quickly, Quinn put his hand over the microphone, then leaned over to whisper in Kerry's ear. Kerry nodded, then responded.

"I stand on the rights guaranteed me by the fifth amendment and respectfully refuse to answer that question."

"Mr. O'Braugh, who is Heavy Hart?"

"He was a colored man from East St. Louis," Kerry said. "He's dead now. He died a couple of years ago."

"Did you know him?"

"Yeah, I knew him."

"Were you friends?"

"I don't know as you'd call us friends. I mean, we kinda moved in different circles, if you know what I mean. But Heavy Hart was a good man. I'll sit right here and tell you that colored man or no, he was a good man."

"He was a known outlaw," Champ Dawson informed him.

"You can be an outlaw and be a good man," Kerry defended. "If you got honor."

"Sir, don't you dare sit there with blood on your hands and talk to me about honor!" the senator snapped. "You don't know the meaning of the word, and I'll not have these hallowed halls—halls that have seen the likes of Daniel Webster and Henry Clay—besmirched by your perverted concept of honor! All I want from you are direct answers. I do *not* want your editorial comment."

Kerry turned to Quinn. "What's this son of a b—" That was as far as Kerry got before Quinn slapped his hand over the microphone. They exchanged harsh whispers; then Kerry nodded and turned back to the microphone. Quinn took his hand away.

"I beg your pardon, Senator," Kerry said contritely.

"I shall let it pass. Now, back to Heavy Hart. Were you and Mr. Hart associates? Did you do business together?"

"I respectfully decline to answer that question."

"Do you recall a man named Eddie Quick?"

"I'm not sure."

"Did he not work for Paddy Egan?"

"I don't remember."

"Surely you remember Paddy Egan, Mr. O'Braugh. You and he fought for control of the St. Louis underworld in the twenties. You *do* remember Paddy Egan, don't you?"

"Yeah, I remember Paddy Egan."

"Do you remember Rana McClarity?"

Kerry pinched the bridge of his nose. Even now, after all these years, it hurt to even hear her name mentioned. Rana was the most beautiful woman Kerry had ever known. He had been in love with her—perhaps would have even married her if Eddie Quick hadn't killed her.

"Mr. O'Braugh?" the senator asked again. "Do you need more time?"

"I'm sorry. What was the question?"

"Do you remember Rana McClarity?"

"Yeah, I remember her."

"Was she your . . . Let me be sure I use the correct mobster parlance here. Was she your 'moll'?"

"She was not my moll," Kerry growled.

"Let me rephrase the question. Did you care for her?"

"Yeah, I cared for her. She was a sweet kid."

"What happened to her?"

"She died."

"Do you know how she died?"

"I don't think it's ever been determined."

"Isn't it a fact, Mr. O'Braugh, that Rana McClarity was murdered? And wasn't she murdered by Eddie Quick?"

"I don't know."

"And, Mr. O'Braugh, did you not then kill Eddie Quick to avenge Miss McClarity's murder?"

Kerry remembered the look of terror in Eddie Quick's eyes when he realized that he was about to die for having killed Rana. *Did I kill the son of a bitch, Senator? You bet your fuckin' ass I did,* Kerry thought. But he answered, "I respectfully decline to answer that question on the grounds that it may incriminate me."

"Senator Dawson, may I ask where this hearing is going?" Matthew Quinn interjected. "You have asked my client all sorts of questions that have no relevancy to his activities as a labor negotiator. We have stipulated that while my client was providing a safe escort to allow the replacement workers to pass through the front gates at MC Motors, it was necessary for him to shoot and kill one of the rioting strikers. But he did so only to save the life of another man. That homicide was justifiable and was found to be so by a St. Louis grand jury."

Champ glared at the lawyer. "I would like to remind the counselor again that this isn't a court of law, it is a board hearing. And as its chairman, I will take the hearing anywhere I feel is necessary in order to provide me with all the information I need about Mr. O'Braugh." He then nodded at the man seated beside him and said, "I will now yield to Mr. Philpot, representing the Department of Labor."

The hearings continued for the rest of that day and throughout the week. Newspapers across the country carried the story, giving it equal billing with such events as the Republican nomination of Alf Landon for president, the capture of Lucky Luciano, the defeat of Joe Louis by Max Schmelling, and the fact that the War Bonus, for which the Bonus Army had marched on Washington four years earlier, was at last being paid.

Then late on Friday afternoon, without ever having called Carmine Brazzi or Vinnie Todaro to appear, Champ Dawson prepared to adjourn the hearings.

"Mr. O'Braugh," the senator began, "while this board has neither the responsibility nor the authority to find you guilty of the specific crimes of murder, robbery, extortion, and a dozen or more other offenses that have been attested to in affidavits and by other witnesses, it is my firm belief that we have proven beyond a shadow of a doubt that you are guilty. And while such a pattern of behavior may be construed as detrimental to the national recovery process, unfortunately we have no power to assess what I believe would be a proper penalty. Therefore, it is with regret that I conclude I am unable to bring you to task for any specific violation. You are of no further use to me, Mr. O'Braugh. Please report to this room Monday morning at nine o'clock, at which time all charges being considered by this board will be dismissed."

Kerry grinned. "It's been a pleasure talkin' to you, Senator." Turning to Matthew Quinn, he shook the lawyer's hand and said, "You were worth every penny."

"I don't know," Quinn said, a puzzled expression on his face. "I don't like it."

"You don't like it? What's there not to like? I beat the rap, didn't I?"

"It would appear so," Quinn said. "But I've known Champ Dawson for a long time. He's tough, and so is that young man he has working with him, John Canfield. It isn't like them to give up this easily."

"Yeah, they're tough, but they also got sense, don't they? They know they can't get me on anythin', so why keep on tryin'?"

"Maybe so," Quinn agreed.

"Listen, how about celebratin' tonight? We'll go out to the fanciest place we can find—you, me, Vinnie, and Carmine."

"Would it be all right if I bring my wife?"

"Yeah, sure, bring her along."

"All right. But, in the meantime, I don't want you talking to any reporters. Don't say anything until after you are dismissed Monday morning. I'm telling you, Kerry, there's something fishy about all this."

"Okay, okay, whatever you say," Kerry promised.

That night Matthew Quinn, his wife, Pamela, Carmine, Vinnie, and Kerry went to dinner at one of Washington's toniest restaurants to celebrate their victory. To make the occasion more festive, Carmine and Vinnie had rounded up three showgirls for the evening for themselves and Kerry, even though Kerry had not asked for one and agreed to it only because by the time he learned of the idea, it was a *fait accompli.*

The group had been seated at a large round table that

the obsequious maître d' made it be known was the most desirable one in the room. Ordering a magnum of the finest champagne available, Kerry waited until everyone's glass was filled, then raised his glass.

"Ladies and gentlemen, I propose a toast to Matthew Quinn, the best damned lawyer in America."

"Yeah," Carmine said, "we sure made that Dawson guy look a dumb ass, didn't we? And all because of Quinn, here."

"I just hope we aren't celebrating too soon," Quinn muttered, lifting his glass with the others.

"Leave it to Matthew to put a damper on any celebration," Pamela said, smiling at her husband. "People don't call him 'The Cautious Old Maid' for nothing."

"Prudence is never misspent, my dear," Quinn said. "By the way, Kerry, I do hope you followed my advice and granted no interviews," he added.

"I didn't talk to anyone," Kerry said.

"That's good, because you are quite newsworthy right now. Aside from magazines and newspapers, your face will be on movie screens all across the country for the next few weeks. The newsreel cameras were getting quite a bit of footage on you."

"Oh, my!" the showgirl who was with Kerry said. "You mean you're going to be in the movies?"

"In a manner of speaking, yes, he is," Quinn answered. "It is not, however, something to be desired. Unfortunately, there's nothing we can do about it."

"Oh, I wouldn't want to do anything about it. I think it's wonderful that you're going to be famous," Kerry's date gushed. "Don't you, girls?"

She had been introduced as Toffee. The other two showgirls were Feather and Fawn. Kerry was sure that the names weren't real; no one would actually name a daughter something like Toffee, Feather, or Fawn.

Toffee seemed thrilled that she was with someone famous. She spent most of the evening leaning against Kerry, positioning herself so that he could feel her breast and resting her hand on his leg just inches away from his crotch. Kerry knew that she would be easy, and he believed if he asked her to make love with him in the cloakroom right now, she would agree.

But it wasn't Toffee who held Kerry's attention. From the beginning of the evening Kerry had been drawn to a woman who was at least twice as old as the oldest of the three showgirls. He felt guilty about it, especially since Matthew Quinn had defended him for this entire week, but he couldn't help it. Kerry was strongly attracted to his lawyer's wife.

Whereas all three showgirls were pretty in a very flashy, almost vulgar sort of way, Pamela Quinn's mature beauty was much more subdued and ran much deeper. She had dark hair, and her eyes were as gray as smoke. And though her clothes weren't as overtly sexy as the dresses worn by the showgirls, she was clearly aware of her beauty and dressed to her best advantage. A slit in her skirt nicely displayed her shapely legs, and her silk taffeta blouse showed off her small but well-formed breasts.

Kerry watched her all evening. When she caught him, she didn't bother to look away. In fact, several times she carefully crossed and uncrossed her legs, showing him tantalizing glimpses of thigh.

"What do you say we leave this place and go over to the Plantation Club?" Quinn suggested after dinner. "They have dancing. Besides, I'm hoping to catch someone there."

"Good idea," Carmine said. "That'll give Toffee and me a chance to rub up against each other."

"*I'm* Toffee. You're with Feather," the girl with Kerry said.

"I don't care if she's Florence Nightingale. I just want to rub against her," Carmine said in a lustful voice, to which Feather purred and posed.

"Matthew, I have to run by the house for a few minutes," Pamela abruptly said. "I think I may have left the back burner on on the stove."

"What? Oh, Pamela, by the time we drive home and then come back to the Plantation Club, Phil will have come and gone. You know I've been trying to catch up with him for weeks."

"Well, then, why don't you go on? You can escort Nutmeg over in a taxi, and Kerry could use our car to run me by the house."

"It's Toffee," the girl said quietly.

"What?"

"My name is Toffee."

"Of course it is, dear. And such a *lovely* name it is, too," Pamela said patronizingly. She looked at Kerry. "You wouldn't mind running me home, would you, Kerry?"

Kerry saw a hunger in Pamela's eyes that was so intense he couldn't believe it. She wanted him as badly as he wanted her.

"Uh, no, of course I don't mind," Kerry said, deliberately hesitating so that his desire to be alone with her wouldn't be blatant.

"Kerry, are you sure?" Quinn asked. "I mean, this is asking an awful lot of you."

"Hey, you got me through the hearin's, didn't you? Don't worry. Just look after Butterscotch for me. Me and Pamela will join you at the club as fast as we can."

"Who's Butterscotch?" Quinn asked.

"I am," Toffee said resignedly. She smiled, shifting over to put her hand on Quinn's shoulder and lean into him. Kerry realized that she could see what was going on even if the others didn't.

The bill was quickly paid, and the celebrants made their way out of the crowded restaurant to the street. Leaving the others to hail a cab, Kerry and Pamela walked around the corner to where Quinn's car was parked.

Other than the directions, they didn't speak a half-dozen words to each other during the whole drive. Finally they pulled into the Quinns' driveway. Shutting off the ignition, Kerry turned and looked easily and confidently across the seat at Pamela.

"You didn't really leave the back burner on, did you?"

"What makes you think I didn't?"

"I *know* you didn't. You wanted me to bring you home because you want me to fuck you."

Pamela laughed huskily.

"My, you do come right to the point, don't you?"

"Am I right?"

"Perhaps."

"Then why are we wasting time out here?"

"Why indeed?" Pamela replied, and she kissed him, sliding her tongue into his mouth for a long, teasing moment before hopping out of the car and hurrying up the walk.

Five minutes later they were lying naked in Pamela's bed, exploring each other with fingers, lips, and tongues. Pamela's hands wandered over Kerry's body, knotting the hair on his chest, moving down across his stomach, grabbing his rock-hard penis. Kerry's hands were equally active as he stroked her buttocks and thighs, then moved over to let his fingers slide through the throbbing, wet crevice between her legs.

Finally they joined. Kerry was on top, plunging, pushing, riding the wild, writhing creature beneath him. At that moment he was no longer aware, nor did it even matter, that Pamela was a beautiful woman. Her mature sexuality was so powerful that it far transcended mere beauty. Pamela soared, sharing with Kerry the waves of pleasure that started deep inside her and burst out of their confines to catch Kerry up in her orgasm. Even as she was moaning his name in climactic frenzy, he was experiencing his own explosive release.

Their pleasure finally spent, they lay together, coasting down from the pinnacle. After a few moments, Kerry groaned, "I feel like shit, you know."

"Why?"

"What kind of friend would fuck his friend's wife?"

Pamela chuckled. "Maybe the friend's wife wanted to be fucked."

"That's no reason."

"And maybe the friend *wanted* his wife fucked."

Kerry lay there thinking about that; then he raised up on his elbow and looked down at Pamela.

"What are you talkin' about?"

Pamela reached down, and her long, cool fingers stroked Kerry's inert penis.

"I suspect that, just about now, Matt is putting it to the little candy girl. Then later tonight, after he comes home, he'll go into great, descriptive detail about it . . . what she looked like, felt like, smelled like, the sounds she made while they were making love. . . ."

"*What?*"

Pamela laughed a deep, throaty laugh. "And I will reciprocate," she said. "Oh, I'll be most descriptive when I talk about how it felt to have your hot, throbbing cock inside me. Sometimes Matthew gets off just lying there in the dark, listening to me talk about it. This should spice things up for us quite nicely for several weeks."

"Goddamn," Kerry breathed. "I guess you learn somethin' every day, huh?"

"Especially if you have a good teacher," Pamela purred, reaching for him to pull him to her again.

"I still don't like it," Matthew Quinn said.

It was Monday morning, and they were back in the Senate hearing room, waiting for what Champ Dawson had said would be the dismissal of charges.

"What do you mean, you still don't like it?" Kerry asked, tired of the lawyer's attitude. "He's going to dismiss us, and we'll all go home. What's wrong with that?"

"Look at the expression on his face," Quinn said.

"What expression? I don't see any particular expression. I mean, he looks like he's deliverin' mail or somethin'."

"That's just what I mean. If we had beaten him, there'd be anger or frustration. I don't see that—not on his face or on anyone else's. And why are the reporters still here?"

"You worry too damn much," Kerry muttered.

Not one word had passed between them about Friday night. Quinn pretended that he knew nothing about what had happened between Kerry and Pamela, and Kerry pretended that he didn't know that Quinn knew. Somehow they managed to carry it off so that it didn't hang between them. It was over . . . like a sneeze.

Senator Dawson banged his gavel on the table in front of him. "If everyone would take their seats, please, I'll call this hearing to order."

The buzz of conversation stopped, and everyone waited

expectantly for the senator's announcement. Champ picked up the paper in front of him and began reading:

"The Economic Recovery Advisory Board is charged with the responsibility of providing advice and recommendations to the President and Congress for the timely recovery from the period of sustained economic depression currently affecting our country. This hearing was convened for the purpose of determining if the activities of Mr. Kerry O'Braugh were detrimental to the conduct of the business of bringing this nation back to economic stability.

"While this board heard testimony and read affidavits relating to a string of crimes up to and including murder that were allegedly committed by Mr. O'Braugh, we have neither the authority nor the responsibility of passing judgment or assessing punishment for such allegations. Therefore, with regard to any specific allegation that this board may have heard, I hereby state that no further action will be taken."

Kerry glanced at Quinn. "What did I tell you?" he said, smiling broadly.

"Mr. O'Braugh, if you please," Senator Dawson cautioned. "I am not finished."

"Sorry, Senator. You go right on," Kerry said, holding up his hands in apology. If the senator wanted to take up a couple more minutes of his time before dismissing the charges, that was fine by him.

"Thank you," Champ replied, his tone ironic. He returned to the paper and cleared his throat before he continued reading.

"This hearing has, however, reached the inescapable conclusion that Mr. O'Braugh's nefarious business activities are detrimental to the continued recovery of our nation. Unfortunately, though this board can find Mr. O'Braugh guilty of such behavior, we are not constituted to assess a penalty. Accordingly, we are withdrawing that charge as well."

Kerry grinned again and turned around to wave at Carmine and Vinnie. Carmine clamped both hands over his head like a victorious boxer.

"Therefore," Champ continued, "this board has resorted to the only option left available and that is to direct that the National Immigration Service declare Kerry O'Braugh an undesirable alien."

"*What?*" Kerry turned to Quinn. "What the hell does that mean?"

Quinn briefly studied his client. "Kerry, are you an American citizen?"

"Well, yeah, I guess so. I mean, for God's sake, I been in this country since I was a kid. That makes me a citizen, doesn't it?"

"Were you ever naturalized?" Quinn asked quickly.

"No. I didn't think I had to be. Doesn't livin' here since I was a kid count for anything?"

"No," Quinn said with a defeated sigh. "So, that's what this was all about." He looked across at John Canfield, who was looking at him. Quinn smiled wanly, nodding a quiet salute. John nodded back. "Mr. Canfield, you are one smart son of a bitch," the lawyer said under his breath.

"What the hell is goin' on here, Quinn?" Kerry demanded.

"Your goose is cooked," Quinn said matter-of-factly.

"Are the officers from the Immigration Service here?" Champ Dawson asked.

"Yes, Senator," someone said from the back of the room.

"Would you come forward, please?" The senator faced Kerry. "Mr. O'Braugh, this board has dropped all charges and specifications and dismisses you from your subpoena. You are free to go."

"What? You mean I'm free?" Kerry asked. His fear turned to huge relief, though he was thoroughly puzzled. He faced Quinn and snickered. "So what was all that business you said about my goose bein' cooked, huh? Guess you can be wrong on occasion. They're lettin' me go."

Quinn sighed. "Wait. It's coming."

The immigration officer who had come forward at Champ Dawson's summons now walked over to the witness table and stood in front of Kerry O'Braugh. The numerous reporters and photographers and the newsreel cameras moved in close.

"Mr. Kerry O'Braugh," the immigration officer intoned, "it is the decision of the United States Immigration Service that, having been declared an undesirable alien, you are to be placed in immediate custody and held until such time as transportation can be arranged for deportation back to the place of your birth."

The color drained from Kerry's face. "Sicily? You mean to tell me I'm goin' back to Italy?" he asked, feeling as though his entire world had just been turned upside down. He turned to Quinn. "You've got to get me out of this! I can't go to Italy! I haven't been there since I was a little kid! Hell, I don't even know anyone there!"

"I'm sorry, Kerry," Quinn said. "My hands are tied. There's nothing I can do for you now."

Kerry slumped in his chair, stunned by this turn of events. Champ Dawson and the young man who had been by his side during the entire hearing walked over to talk to him.

"Mr. O'Braugh," Champ said, "I'd like you to meet my assistant, John Canfield. It was he who came up with the idea and the means to get rid of you."

Kerry stared at John for a long moment; then he suddenly grinned.

"You must be a pretty smart cookie," he said. "Too bad you aren't on my side. I could've really gone places if I'd had someone like you workin' for me."

John chuckled. "You are going places, Mr. O'Braugh. You're going to Sicily."

"Yeah, I guess I am." Kerry sighed. "Well, you know what they say about Sicily, don't you?"

"What's that?" John asked.

"See Sicily and die."

CHAPTER EIGHTEEN

APRIL 26, 1937, GUERNICA, SPAIN

At first glance the Basque peasant pulling the cart seemed to be an old man because his hair was completely gray and his face was very weathered. But a closer examination disclosed that he was not nearly as old as he looked. He had muscular arms, powerful shoulders, and strong legs, and as he had no horse for his cart, the peasant pulled the cart himself. Using the long trace poles as handles, he had placed the yoke around his neck and tied it to the cart with ropes to help with the pulling.

As the cart rolled down the dirt road, its wheels squeaked loudly, and the metal rims threw up little rooster tails of dust. The cart was piled high with bits and pieces of broken furniture and a collection of rags and tattered clothing.

Someone was lying in the cart, and even from the door of the small house-cum-aid-station where she stood watching the approaching peasant, Valentina Lvovna Kosior could see the blood.

"Here comes someone," she called over her shoulder. "It's a man pulling a cart. It looks as if someone is in the cart, badly wounded."

"A Loyalist soldier?" the doctor behind her asked.

"No, I doubt it. It appears to be a woman. Perhaps it's his wife."

"Comrade Nurse Kosior, we cannot take in any more civilians," Dr. Peter Suslov insisted. "As it is, we've barely enough medicine for our own partisans and the Loyalist soldiers. We cannot waste what medicine we do have on civilians."

"How would it be a waste, Comrade Doctor, if we are helping someone?" Valentina asked, trying to keep the outrage out of her voice. "Aren't we here to save lives?"

"We are here to save *Soviet* lives," the doctor said. "And then, if we can, the lives of other International Brigade volunteers and the Loyalist soldiers who are brought to us. We are not here to provide medical attention to every peasant who happens to drop a rock on his toe."

Valentina shook her head heatedly. "You heard the German bombers last night. You heard the sound of the bombs. The villagers were helpless . . . men, women, little children . . . they could do nothing as the bombs crashed down around them. It would be wrong not to help them now. Besides, some day we might treat the person who has some information about Yakov."

The doctor came over to Valentina and put his hand on her shoulder. "Valentina, when are you going to give up on Captain Kosior? You must accept by now that your husband is dead."

"No, I cannot accept it," Valentina said firmly.

"Do you think he would stay away if he weren't dead? Who would not hurry back to such a beautiful woman as you?"

"He could be a prisoner," Valentina suggested.

Suslov snorted scornfully. "A Soviet citizen? A Communist partisan, fighting with the Loyalists for the Republican government? Come now. If the fascist Nationalists captured such a man, do you really think they would make him a prisoner?" Suslov asked. "You know what the Insurgents think of us."

"But Yakov is a doctor."

"So am I. And you are a nurse. But if the Nationalists capture you, they will kill you—no matter that you are a woman and no matter that you are a nurse. Valentina, Yakov is dead."

Valentina sighed. "I know," she finally said in a quiet voice. "My mind tells me this is true." She looked at Suslov. "But you must understand, Peter, that my heart will not let me accept it so readily."

Suslov returned Valentina's gaze for a long, pregnant moment; then he sighed and looked through the door. "All right, go," he finally said. "Go and tell the peasant to bring his wounded woman in here. I will do what I can."

Valentina grinned. "Thank you, Peter! Thank you!"

She ran down the hill from the aid station and out into the narrow road that passed by in front. Reaching the peasant, she spoke to him in Spanish.

"I am a nurse. There is a doctor here," she said. "Perhaps we can help you."

The man pulling the cart stopped and looked at Valentina through eyes that were clouded with pain and confusion. Valentina stepped to the back of the cart to look at the woman. When she pulled the sheet back, she gasped. The wounded woman's intestines, bloated and yellowish-gray, were visible through a gaping hole in her stomach.

"No!" the man shouted. "Leave her alone!"

"Don't you understand? This is an aid station! There is a doctor here," Valentina explained again.

"A doctor?"

"Yes, a doctor."

"What can a doctor do for her now?" the man asked. "She is dying."

Valentina looked at the woman again and saw that her face was contorted with pain.

"He can make her dying easier," she said gently. "We have medicine that will take away the pain."

The man's eyes softened, then filled with tears. "*Sí, por*

favor," he said. "Take away the pain. I do not want my wife to suffer anymore."

"Bring her inside," Valentina directed.

The man scooped his wife up in his powerful arms as easily as if she were a child, and he followed Valentina back into the small house. Moving the woman increased her pain, and she cried out, but he quieted her with loving little noises. The woman found one of her husband's big fingers with her small hand, and she squeezed it hard and opened her eyes, looking trustingly at him.

"Put her there," Suslov said, when the man stepped inside the cool interior. He pointed to a table that at one time had been a dining table for the former occupants of the house. It was now being used as an operating table. When the woman was put down, the doctor was able to see her wound for the first time. He sucked his breath in between clenched teeth, then looked up at Valentina. "What did you tell him we could do for her?" he asked in Russian. "Surely you didn't tell him we could save her."

"No. I told him we had medicine to ease the pain, to make her dying easier."

"We can't even do that."

"Why not? We have morphine, don't we?"

"We don't have enough," Suslov replied. "It would take a great deal to ease the suffering of this poor woman. And for what? She will die, and the morphine we used will be gone. Suppose a badly wounded soldier comes in who might live if we could ease the shock of his pain with morphine. If we use it for this woman, we wouldn't have it to give to that soldier."

"But you must do something!" Valentina insisted.

"There is nothing I can do."

"Please, Peter," Valentina begged. "You must do something!"

Suslov looked at the woman for a long moment, then sighed. "An air bubble," he suggested. "An embolism will end it more quickly. Valentina, it is all I can do."

Valentina bit her bottom lip and looked at the woman. She put her hand on the woman's forehead and brushed the hair back. The woman reached up to take Valentina's hand in hers, and then she kissed it. Tears began flowing down Valentina's cheeks, and she turned her face away.

"That is all I can do," the doctor said again, more softly this time.

Valentina nodded. "Yes. Do it."

"You have something?" the man asked in Spanish. "You have something that will take away the pain?"

"Yes," Valentina replied. "Yes, we have something that will take away the pain."

"God bless you."

"What did he say?" Suslov asked, as he prepared the needle.

"He said God bless us."

"How can people see things like this and still believe in God?" the doctor asked, shaking his head.

"For some a belief in God is important," Valentina replied. "I remember the comfort it brought my mother."

"How long will it take . . . before the suffering is over?" the peasant asked.

"Not long," Valentina promised. "Not long. Your wife, she was wounded last night in the air raid? When the German planes came over?"

"They were Germans?"

"Yes."

The Basque looked at Valentina with confusion. "Why are the Germans fighting us?"

"The Germans are helping the Insurgents," Valentina said. "Just as we Russians are helping the Loyalists."

"If Germany and Russia wish to fight, why do they not fight in their own country?" the peasant asked. "Why do you come here to fight?"

"It is your war. We have only come to help," Valentina explained.

"It is *not* my war," the man said bitterly. "I have no war. I heard the airplanes last night, but I did not think of the war. My wife and I were in bed. It was dark. We worked hard yesterday, I in the fields and she in the house. What do we care for the war? We were lying in the dark, feeling the comfort of each other's presence. This is the way of it for a man and his wife."

The woman groaned once, and the man looked at her. He was silent for a moment, and then he continued to talk.

"There were very many airplanes, but they sounded so far away. Not far in distance—they were only one or two thousand meters high—but they were far. It is hard for me to explain it. . . . What I mean is, they were not in our lives; they were of another world. After all, what do men who fly in such machines know of tilling the soil and tending to sheep?

"I heard the strange whistling sounds as the bombs started down. I didn't know then what the sounds were, but I felt them here, in my heart." He put his hand over his chest. "And I felt a fear . . . greater than any fear I have ever felt. Then, suddenly, there were many explosions all about. The barn was gone, and the granary, and the well, and then our house. When it was all over, there was only the crackling of the fires, the bleating of the sheep, and the sounds of many airplane motors as they flew away. My wife made no sound, but she was bleeding from a terrible wound in her belly."

He fell silent again, and Valentina took his hand and held it, patting it softly. It was a useless gesture, she knew, but she felt compelled to do something—anything!—to help him.

The Basque took a deep breath and started talking once more, as if speaking itself were a catharsis. "What did the men in those machines feel, I wonder? Did they know about us? Did they know when they dropped their bombs that my wife and I were lying side by side in the darkness far below them? Did they care?"

Glancing down at his hands, the man stopped talking.

The silence was growing long when Peter spoke.

"She's dead," he said in Russian.

Valentina reached up to touch the peasant on the shoulder. "It is over," she said quietly. "Your wife is no longer in pain."

The man looked over at his wife, and the tears that had filled his eyes now began to slide down his cheeks. He nodded.

"Thank you," he said, his voice barely audible. "Thank you."

SOMEWHERE OVER THE ATLANTIC

"Weather Station Baker, Weather Station Baker, this is Windjammer Three, Windjammer Three. Do you read me, over?" Willie Canfield asked into the mouthpiece of his headset.

"Windjammer Three, this is Weather Station Baker. I read you. How me, over?" came the crackly voice through Willie's headphones.

Willie made a slight adjustment to the tuner. "I've got you five by, Weather Station Baker. What kind of weather do you have for me?"

"Smooth as silk, Windjammer Three. You could land right here beside the ship and take a swim, if you'd like."

"Thank you for your kind invitation," Willie said dryly. "But I have twenty souls on board who want to go to Lisbon."

"The world is in too big a hurry," the weather ship radio operator said. *"Okay, we have a fix on you, Windjammer Three. You are directly on course, ten miles west of our station. We will turn on our searchlight beam . . . now."*

Looking ahead out the plane's windshield, Willie saw a long finger of light shoot up from the black horizon in front of him, poking at the inky sky.

"I see you, Weather Station Baker," he said. "I estimate that we will be passing directly overhead in zero-four minutes."

"I have you in view now, Windjammer Three."

Willie leaned forward and looked down toward the base of the beam of light. Though it was late at night and most of the weather ship's crew would be in their berths asleep, the ship had enough lights glowing to make it stand out against the black surface of the sea.

Weather Station Baker was the second of three United States Coast Guard weather ships that maintained a constant station, not only to monitor the weather, but also to provide navigational assistance to the World Air Transport flights from New York to Lisbon. Pan Am flights would also be so serviced, but that airline was still working out a reciprocal schedule arrangement with British Overseas Airways for a London route and hadn't yet started their own trans-Atlantic flights, leaving World Air Transport the sole beneficiary of the Coast Guard's facility.

"I've got you, too," Willie replied. "I'm logging passage at oh-two-three-zero, Greenwich mean time."

"Confirm, oh-two-three-zero, GMT."

"Thank you, Weather Station Baker."

"Glad to help out. Keep your feet dry, Windjammer Three. Weather Station Baker, out."

Turning to his copilot, Willie asked, "Johnny, you want to mind the store for a while? I'm going down for a cup of coffee and a break."

"Go ahead, Captain, I've got it," the copilot answered.

Willie took off his headset and hung it on its hook, then pushed the seat back and stood up. He made one last check of the pilot's instrument panel, then another of the panel in front of the flight engineer. Quivering needles in all the gauges told the story of the functions they were monitoring, and in one quick glance Willie could see that everything was behaving as it should.

He climbed down the ladder from the flight deck to the lounge, which also served as the dining room. It was double-compartment in size and furnished with enough tables to feed twenty at one sitting. As Willie had told the Weather Station Baker radio operator, there were twenty people on board the plane, but five of that twenty were the crew—the three on the flight deck plus the steward and stewardess. That left fifteen paying passengers, which meant that, on this trip at least, they could all eat at one sitting.

Eric Twainbough was in the lounge, sitting at one of the tables, drinking coffee and looking through the window into the darkness. Ten years before, Willie Canfield and Rocky Rockwell, the vice president of Rockwell-McPheeters Aviation Company, had flown one of the earliest Tri-Star airliners across the Atlantic. Since Lindbergh had captured the public attention with his solo flight to Paris, Willie and Rocky had decided it would be a good public-relations stunt for both the fledgling airline company and Rockwell-McPheeters Aviation if they would carry regular passengers on their first trans-Atlantic flight. The civilians they had carried were Eric Twainbough, his then wife, and his son.

Willie filled a coffee cup at the Silex, then sat down across the table from Eric.

"A little different from the last time we did this, huh?" Willie asked, smiling.

"That's for sure. We've got a lot more room to move around in, and it's a damn sight quieter. Not that you can't hear the engines," Eric added, "but you can at least carry on a conversation in here."

The lounge was right in the middle of the plane, just over the wings with their four huge engines, two on each side. Despite that, as Eric noted, the mighty roar of the engines was muffled down to a manageable thrumming.

Willie patted on the side panel. "You know what's between this panel and the skin of the airplane?"

"What?"

"Egg cartons."

"Egg cartons?"

"Well, not actual egg cartons. I mean, they aren't little crates that say something like 'farm fresh eggs' or anything like that. But the same people who make regular egg cartons made the soundproofing for us. It's made exactly the same way, only in larger sheets."

"Whatever it is, it does a good job," Eric said. He looked at his watch. "So, what time will we arrive?"

"Nine A.M. local time," Willie replied.

"That's good. I'm booked on a plane scheduled to leave for Madrid at ten-thirty. I guess they're still letting planes through. At least they were the last I heard."

"Yes," Willie confirmed. "The Loyalists and the Republicans have agreed not to bother civilian airliners. But tell me, Eric, why do you want to go to Spain? From everything I hear, it's a very good place to stay away from right now."

"It's my job to go," Eric explained. "I signed a contract with the United Newspaper Association."

"Yeah, like you really need the money," Willie said sarcastically. "Every book you've ever written has made the best-seller list, the movie version of *Stillness in the Line* was nominated for the Academy Award, and I believe I read somewhere that they're going to make a movie out of your newest book."

"Yes, they are. And you're right, I don't need the money," Eric agreed.

"Then why go to such a dangerous place?"

"Have you ever seen anyone make sausage?"

Willie gave the author a cockeyed stare. "Sausage? What's that got to do with it?"

"The way you make sausage is to use a meat grinder. You put all those chunks of pork into the top of the grinder, you add some salt and a few spices, you grind away on the handle, and out comes sausage."

"Yeah, I've seen it," Willie said dubiously.

"Okay, now I want you to think of my stories as sausage. They come out here." Eric held his hands in front of him as if they were poised over the keyboard of a typewriter, and he moved his fingers as if he were typing. "But in order to get the sausage-slash-stories to come out here, something has to go into the top of the meat grinder up here." He pointed to his head. "So, I feed it chunks of pork, in the form of new experiences."

"But you've already seen one war," Willie protested. "Isn't one war enough?"

"In a way you might say I've seen two wars," Eric said. "Because the Russian experience and the Russian Revolution were totally different from the war in the West. And that makes my point. Each war is unique with its own personality." Eric refilled his coffee cup, then grinned crookedly. "Besides, Hemingway is over there. You don't think I'm going to let him get one up on me, do you?"

Willie laughed, then asked, "Do you guys really dislike each other that much? Or is it all publicity?"

"Oh, I like Ernest all right," Eric replied. "He's not a very likeable son of a bitch, but I like him all the same. And I have a tremendous amount of admiration for his work. But, like me, Hemingway understands the necessity of new experiences for the writer."

"Well, I can see the bullfighting, deep-sea-fishing, big-game-hunting experiences. But going to a war when you don't have to . . ." Willie shook his head. "That's what's hard for me to understand. Especially *this* war. I mean look who's fighting. Who do you root for, for Chrissake? You've got Hitler on one side and Stalin on the other. Neither one of them is someone you'd want to invite to a family dinner."

Eric laughed. "That all depends on what you were planning to feed them."

"Is this a private party, or can anyone join in?" a woman's voice asked.

Eric looked around and smiled at the attractive redhead who had just come into the lounge. "Sure 'n there's always room for a wee bit of a bonnie lass like you, Miss McKay," he said in a thick, affected brogue.

Shaylin McKay groaned. "My God, that was absolutely awful," she said. "It's a good thing you're a novelist. You sure couldn't make it as an actor."

"Have a seat, Miss McKay," Willie said. "How do you like your coffee?" He stood up and walked over to the Silex.

Shaylin stared at him, then laughed. "Good Lord, Mr. Canfield. You're the president of the airline, you're flying one of its airplanes, and now you're doing steward duties. Tell me, when you get back home, do you sweep out the hangar as well?"

Willie laughed with her. "Don't think I haven't done it," he said, bringing her a full cup. "I guess I'm just an impatient man. I could make arrangements for other people to do things, but it always seems faster to just do them myself. Anyway, I really like flying, and I'd rather be here than sitting behind a desk. And since I am the president of the company, I can do what I damn well please. Seems to me that that's the only thing of importance."

"I suppose there's something to be said for that," Shaylin agreed.

Willie smiled, then said, "Listen, if you folks will excuse me, I think I'll go back and visit with the other passengers for a bit. Some of them like to talk to the pilot." He laughed. "On the other hand, it always scares the hell out of a few of them to see me back there. I think they're afraid the airplane will fall out of the sky if I'm not up front every moment. But that's a normal response, I suppose, since some of them are not only crossing the Atlantic for the first time, but are taking their very first flight of any kind."

"Well, now that you bring that up, it seems to me that's a good point," Shaylin said, holding up her finger. "I wouldn't like to think of something that needs to be done not getting done just because you aren't where you're supposed to be."

"Ah, don't worry about it," Willie said in an offhanded voice. "I've got Johnny Blake up there. This is only his second flying lesson, but I think he's coming along really well."

"His second flying *lesson?*" Shaylin gasped. Then, realizing he was teasing, she snorted. "*Very* funny."

Willie laughed at his own joke as he disappeared into the rear of the airplane.

Eric watched him go, then observed, "If ever anyone was born to be an aviator, it was Willie Canfield." He looked back at Shaylin. "So, you're off to Spain for the great adventure, are you? Shaylin McKay, female war correspondent."

"Wrong," Shaylin said.

"Wrong?"

"Shaylin McKay, *war* correspondent," she corrected. "The fact that I am a woman has nothing to do with it."

"Really?" Eric replied, thinking that she was in for a rude awakening. "Well, I want you to keep that thought in mind when you're taking a bath in an ice-cold mountain stream."

"You think an ice-cold mountain stream is going to bother me? I've bathed in cold water before."

"With a bunch of men?" Eric asked, eyeing her over the rim of his coffee cup.

Shaylin merely stared at him.

BERLIN, GERMANY

Dr. Sigmund Rosen was in his laboratory at the university, calculating yet again the results of neutron bombardment on uranium atoms. Though his earlier tests had been very promising, Sigmund was beginning to believe that while his isotope enhancement theory was possible, it simply wasn't practical. He was continuing the work, however, just to avoid stumbling over the same path again. It was, as he had explained to his friend Simon Blumberg, a process of elimination roughly akin to finding a needle in a haystack by removing the haystack one straw at a time.

"Rosen," a voice called from the door of the laboratory. Sigmund stiffened slightly. At one time he had occupied a position of great respect in the university. Indeed, those in charge had told him time and time again how honored they were to have a man of his credentials on their staff. Back then he had been "Herr Professor Rosen" or "Herr Doctor Rosen." Now, because he was a Jew, the title of professor had been withdrawn, and he was universally referred to by his last name only.

When Sigmund didn't look up from his work he was rudely summoned a second time. *"Rosen!"*

Stifling a sigh, Sigmund looked up. "Yes?"

The person who had summoned him was a graduate student who was also a teaching assistant. At one time such students fell all over themselves to pay tribute to him, to work for him—just to be in his presence. Now, of course, that was all changed.

The student stood in the doorway with his arms folded across his chest. On his left sleeve was a red swastika armband. On his cheek was a three-corner dueling scar, the nineteenth-century idea of a dueling scar as a badge of honor again gaining popularity among Nazi youth.

"There is a meeting of the staff and faculty, Rosen," the student said. "Herr Doctor Kordt will be lecturing on the Germanic curriculum."

"Yes. I will come in a moment," Sigmund said.

"You will come *now*, Rosen," the student said sharply. "The others are already there. They do not like being kept waiting by a filthy Jew."

Sigmund stared at the unpleasant young man standing in the doorway, wondering when all this had happened. He had never had an interest in politics or the mores of society. He lived in a world of numbers and invisible particles, so intently focused upon his research that he was only barely aware of what was going on around him. He could vaguely remember his friend Simon complaining about Hitler and the Nazis, but he had passed all that off as the dissatisfactions of a man as bitter toward society as Sigmund was indifferent to it.

And yet gradually the environment around Sigmund had begun to change until he could no longer remain indifferent. One by one, many of the older professors at the school were replaced by wild-eyed, unpleasant, loud men. Sigmund missed the old professors. He missed being able to sit in the gasthaus with them, drinking beer and discussing music—or discussing nothing at all, just lost in his own thoughts, comfortable with the silent company.

Reluctantly he stood and followed the student down the hall.

There were nearly two dozen men in the library when Sigmund arrived. More than half of them were new, having arrived in the last few months to implement the bizarre policies of Bernhard Rust, the Reich Minister of Science, Education, and Popular Culture.

Under Rust, all German education had been Nazified. Textbooks had been rewritten, curriculums changed, and teachers hired to promote the ideology of National Socialism. Such courses as "Racial Science" had been added, while philosophy, history, and sociology courses had been either withdrawn or so radically changed to conform to Nazi ideology that they had lost their identity.

Those hired to teach the new courses had been taken on without regard to academic qualifications, for a classical education was much less important than the unquestioning acceptance of National Socialism. A new doctoral degree was created—Doctor of National Socialist Thought—and this degree was given as much weight as any other in academia.

As Sigmund took his seat—in the rear of the room, of course—he looked at the other faculty members. Those who had been there the longest, many of whom had at one time called themselves his friend, avoided his gaze or returned it only briefly, a flicker of guilt passing over their faces. Only the new members looked squarely at him and did so with ill-concealed contempt. These were the ones who made no effort to keep Sigmund from overhearing their frequent anti-Semitic remarks.

Sigmund gazed at Helmut Kordt, noting the so-called academician's new persona. No longer wearing the simple brown suit he normally wore, Dr. Kordt was now dressed in the splashy black-and-silver uniform of an SS *Obersturmbannführer.* Kordt glared angrily at Sigmund as he entered.

"Rosen, your absentmindedness is legend," he said. "However, that is a thing of the past, for I will not put up with it. When I call a meeting, you would be well served to arrive promptly. Perhaps if you knew how fortunate you are to still have a position here, you would be a bit more grateful."

"Yes, Herr Doctor," Sigmund said, mustering up the proper amount of humility.

"Good. Now, we will commence," Kordt went on, squaring his glasses on his nose.

He began his lecture by discussing some of the new courses either being added or replacing existing ones. The new courses were German Physics and German Science, which, Kordt explained, would fit in nicely with the existing classes in German Literature and German Culture. The expanded curriculum was soundly approved by the attending faculty—except for Sigmund Rosen, who said nothing and wasn't expected to.

With the business concluded, the meeting broke up, and the staff began filing out of the library. Sigmund avoided looking at any of the other faculty members and dutifully waited until the last one had passed him. Then he stood up to leave. Only not everyone had left. There was one teacher, Dr. Gessler, still in the library.

Gessler was one of the original professors and had been retained on the university faculty because his political philosophy justified his retention. He had joined the Nazi Party in the early 1920s, when it was still considered by a majority of Germans as a minor, radical party.

As Sigmund stood, Gessler drew even with him and shoved him back into the chair.

"Filthy Jew! Wait until the last!" Gessler said loudly, angrily.

The commotion caught Dr. Kordt's attention, and he turned around in time to see Sigmund sit quickly in the chair to avoid falling. Sneering, Kordt mocked, "What's the matter, Rosen? Did you lose your balance?"

"I'm sorry," Sigmund apologized.

"Just learn your place, Jew," Gessler snarled as he left the room.

Sigmund noticed that all the new members of the faculty were laughing smugly, enjoying the fact that one of the old guard had been the one to turn on Sigmund. But they might not have been so smug had they known what Sigmund knew. While roughly shoving him aside, Dr. Gessler had slipped a note into Sigmund's pocket.

As soon as he was alone back in his laboratory, Sigmund took out the note—which was unsigned—and read it.

> Sigmund:
>
> For your own good, you must leave Germany as quickly as you can! You have been spared the fate of other Jews only because of the work you are doing on a method to develop atomic energy. The Nazis want to use your work to develop an atomic weapon of some kind. As soon as the scientists who are monitoring your experiments feel you have advanced far enough to enable them to carry on with your work, you will be killed, and a weapon of horrific power will be put in the hands of a madman! Destroy your notes and papers, and leave at once. Destroy this note as soon as you have read it. Do not speak to me! It would be far too dangerous for both of us!

Sigmund's heart was pounding. Simon had warned him something like this would happen.

Igniting a Bunsen burner, he held the note over the flame until it caught; then he dropped it into a metal trash can, watching it burn until it was nothing but ash. Next, he unlocked his file cabinet and removed the books containing all his research notes, then began tearing the pages out and burning them one at a time. Finally, when all the relevant notes had been burned and there was no trail left by which another scientist would be able to follow his progression from what had been nothing but an intuitive theory to where he stood now, he was ready to leave. He smiled to himself. What remained in his notebooks were the reams of theorems and equations that had repeatedly led him to nothing but frustrating blind alleys. Let Hitler's scientists follow them into the same blind alleys. Perhaps it would slow anyone who hoped to develop an atomic weapon.

Sigmund took a last look around his laboratory. There were a few things he would have liked to take with him, but he felt it best that he leave everything just as it was so that it would appear that he had every intention of returning. At the last moment he balled up some inconsequential papers and dropped them into the garbage can, effectively hiding the telltale ash. Then, feeling an apprehension greater than anything he had ever felt—or had ever dreamed he would feel—he switched off the light and left the lab.

CHAPTER NINETEEN

JUNE 3, 1937, JEFFERSON CITY, MISSOURI

Andrew Booker put yet another suitcase into the trunk of his car—a brand-new light-blue Plymouth, bought with money he had received from the Schillingberg Institute for his work for them—then turned to his father and said, "Pop, LaTonya and I really appreciate you and Della looking after the boys while we're in Washington."

"Are you kidding?" Loomis Booker said with a grin. "Della was so excited about her two grandsons staying here that she hasn't slept for a week." He handed his son another suitcase. "You and LaTonya just have a good time while you're there, and don't worry about a thing. The boys will get along just fine."

"I just don't want them to be any bother, that's all."

Loomis laughed. "That's the beauty of being grandparents, don't you see? We'll get to keep them for a while, spoil them rotten, and then when you come back from your trip, we can get rid of them."

"I don't see how you can spoil them any more than they're already spoiled," Andy groaned. "But, more to the point, Deon is still an infant and so you always know where to find him, but Artemus is now quite the walker and gets into an incredible amount of mischief."

"Well, what *you* see as getting into mischief, *I* see as discovering his capabilities," Loomis said. "Which I think is a most admirable attribute."

"Yeah, I guess it is. I am pretty proud of him."

"And I'm proud of you," Loomis said, putting his hand on his son's shoulder. "Getting the Spingarn medal for the advances you've made in blood preservation and for your work on blood plasma. And the medal is to be presented by the President of the United States! That's quite an honor, Andrew."

"Hold on, now," Andy said. "I had a part in it, true enough, but so did several others, especially Dr. Charles Drew."

"Who is also a Negro," Loomis noted. "That must have turned a few white heads when they realized that two of the principal developers of blood plasma were, as they say, 'gentlemen of color.' "

Andy chuckled. "I called Dr. Drew and asked if he thought President Roosevelt would serve us fried chicken and watermelon at the awards banquet."

Loomis laughed with him, then grew serious.

"I have to tell you, Andrew, that as big an honor as this is, I am just as proud of what you've been doing down in Mississippi as I am by this award."

"I am, too, Pop. You know, in the beginning I really had misgivings about going down to Mississippi." He laughed. "And when I got there and saw that it was even worse than I had imagined . . . Well, believe you me, I was ready to turn around and come back. In fact, I even tried to convince LaTonya that that was exactly what we should do—but I was going to make it seem like it was *her* idea."

"What did she say about that?" Loomis asked.

Andy grinned. "She wouldn't have any part of it. She was determined to stick it out."

"You've got yourself a good woman, Andrew."

"I know it, Pop. And I'm really glad she held me in there because now I wouldn't leave Delta for any amount of money. I can't begin to tell you how much personal satisfaction I receive from being there. Even from being called 'Brother Doctor.' "

"You *should* feel a sense of personal satisfaction. You've taken a most difficult situation and made it work," Loomis said. "And even the white people credit you with stopping the polio epidemic last summer."

"Well, that was simple enough. All it took was a little common sense."

"And a lot of leadership and the courage to exercise that leadership," Loomis added. "But I'm not the only one to think that. I've got something I want you to see." Loomis chuckled. "I would have shown it to you earlier, but I decided I'd better wait until just before you were about to leave. Otherwise, you might have gotten a swelled head."

"What is it?"

"Come on back into the house for a minute and I'll show you. You're going to have to tell Della and the boys good-bye one more time anyway."

"Okay, Pop, but this better be good," Andy said, looking at his watch. "I'm getting anxious to get on the road."

"You just want to try out that new car, that's all," Loomis quipped.

"It is pretty, isn't it?" Andy said, stepping back to admire its lines. "I can't wait to get back to Delta to show it to the folks down there." He took out his handkerchief and made a swipe across the top of the car, brushing away an all but unseen speck of dirt. "Maybe I should have gotten dark blue instead of light blue," he mused, more to himself than aloud. "Oh, well . . ."

Andy followed his father back into the house, taking one more look back at his car just before he went inside. He walked over to LaTonya, who was in the living room, talking with her mother and putting on her hat to leave. Artemus was standing beside his mother, holding on to her leg and looking up at her with large, soulful eyes. He was fighting hard to keep from crying, but it looked as though he was about to lose the battle. Deon, who was too young to be aware of what was going on, was asleep in his crib.

"The car's all packed," Andy told his wife.

"I'm ready," LaTonya said, making a last-minute adjustment to the veil of her hat. She looked down at her older son. "Artemus, are you going to be a good boy while Mama and Daddy are gone?"

"Yes, Mama," Artemus answered. His voice was quivering.

LaTonya smiled and reached down to pick him up. She hugged him tightly, telling him, "Don't be sad, baby. It's not like we're going off forever. You'll have a nice visit with Grandmother and Grandfather, and we'll bring you back a surprise."

"What surprise?"

"Well, I can't tell you that, can I? If I did, it wouldn't be a surprise." She kissed her son, then set him back down. "But I can tell you that you and Deon will each get a surprise. We'll bring back a little surprise for little Deon and a big surprise for big Artemus."

The child clapped enthusiastically at the announcement.

Loomis, who had disappeared as soon as he and Andy stepped inside the house, now reappeared, carrying a newspaper with him.

"This is last Sunday's edition of *The St. Louis Chronicle*," he said, thumbing through the paper. "I thought you might be interested in an advertisement I saw here."

"An ad?" Andy said. "Pop, you made all this fuss over an ad? Why would I be interested in an ad?"

"Because this is a very special ad," Loomis said. He opened the paper and showed it to Andy and LaTonya.

TO "BROTHER DOCTOR" ANDREW BOOKER
FOR WINNING THE PRESTIGIOUS SPINGARN MEDAL
FOR HIS WORK IN BLOOD STORAGE.
CONGRATULATIONS
FROM THE WHITE AND COLORED CITIZENS OF
DELTA, MISSISSIPPI

"At first I wondered why it was that they placed it in a St. Louis newspaper. Then I realized that they must have wanted everyone in your hometown to know just how well you turned out," Loomis said, grinning.

"Well, I'll be," Andy said. "LaTonya, what do you think of that?"

"What do I think of that?" she asked, tears welling in her eyes. "I think I'm prouder of my man than any other woman in America is of hers."

UNION STATION, ST. LOUIS, MISSOURI

Bob and Connie Canfield stood watching the arriving passengers as they stepped off the train just in from Chicago. In Bob's pocket was the letter he had received a week earlier from his old friend and college roommate, David Gelbman:

> Dear Bob,
>
> Although I've lived in Vienna for so long that I now consider myself more Austrian than American, I've never given up my American citizenship—and with the way things are going in Europe, that may well turn out to be very felicitous. But for right now I've used that citizenship to prevail upon the American ambassador here to allow me to send this letter via the diplomatic pouch, a necessary precaution to keep what I have to tell you from falling into the wrong hands.
>
> My cousin, Simon Blumberg, recently helped a friend of his, Dr. Sigmund Rosen—who is a brilliant physicist—to escape from Germany. You may think the term "escape" a strange one to use, but, believe me, it is increasingly appropriate when it comes to Jews in that country. Anti-semitism has gone far beyond mere state-sponsored prejudice. Being a Jew in Germany is no longer just uncomfortable, it has

become dangerous. Life threatening in Dr. Rosen's case.

I made arrangements for this eminent man to emigrate to America, and I'm now prevailing upon my friendship with you to find a position for him in the physics department at Jefferson University. He speaks English, though with difficulty, but I'm certain that his brilliance will enable him to quickly master the language well enough to be able to teach. However, in all likelihood his principal contribution won't be in teaching, but rather in the field of research.

Bob, what I understand about nuclear physics would fit on the head of a pin, so I don't know exactly what Dr. Rosen has been working on or the significance of his research to the Nazis. But from what I've been able to find out, I do know that it would be disastrous were Hitler able to utilize Dr. Rosen's discoveries. Perhaps you'll get some idea of what I'm talking about if you know that Dr. Rosen and Dr. Albert Einstein work in the same field and have even exchanged research. You can get further clarification on the subject from one of the physics professors there at good old JU. At any rate, the very fact that the Nazis want his research is reason enough for me to keep them from having it.

Please, if you will, meet Dr. Rosen at the train—his ship arrives in New York on June 2, from where he will board a train to Chicago and then catch the Twentieth Century Limited out of Chicago at 10:05 a.m. on June 3—and take him under your wing for a while. He is a very gentle, very wonderful man—though he's about as eccentric as they come. His mind is so crowded with theoretical equations and the like that he sometimes, quite literally, forgets what day it is or where he is. If you see someone getting off the train with a wild bush of hair and a look of total detachment, that will be your man.

Keep your fingers crossed that Hitler will be satisfied with his move into the Sudetenland and his adventures in Spain. I'm afraid, however, that he's going to cause quite a bit of difficulty for quite a few people before his foray is all over.

My love to Connie and the boys—or I suppose I should say men.

David

"There he is," Connie said, pointing toward the far end of the platform.

"Where?"

"There. That must be him." She laughed. "Who else would be wearing a Jefferson University letter sweater from the year 1904?"

Bob laughed with her, for trudging through the crowd was a man with an uncombed halo of graying hair and a faraway look, wearing a green sweater with a red letter J.

"Dr. Rosen!" Bob called, waving. "Dr. Rosen! Over here!" Smiling broadly, he and Connie walked over to greet him. "Dr. Rosen, I am Bob Canfield, and this is my wife, Connie. David wrote us about you."

"David?" Sigmund asked.

"Yes, David Gelbman in Vienna."

"Ah, yes. He is a nice young man." Sigmund began looking around Union Station as if he were searching for someone.

Confused at first, Bob then remembered what David had said about the scientist being an absentminded professor.

"That's a nice sweater you're wearing," he said, unable to keep the amusement out of his voice.

"Yes," Sigmund said, holding his arm up to look at the sleeve. "It belongs to my friend in Vienna. He asked me to be wearing it when I got off the train. I am not sure why."

"So I would recognize you, of course."

"You? You are here for me? I am Doctor Rosen."

Bob laughed. "It's good to meet you, Dr. Rosen. Do you have any luggage?"

"It was checked on through to St. Louis."

"This is St. Louis."

"It is?"

"Yes."

"You don't say. How far was it from New York?"

"Well, about fifteen hundred miles, I suppose."

"Fifteen hundred miles. It would be easier in kilometers, but miles is possible. Let me see. It would be . . . yes, it would be six hundred thirty thousand two hundred seventy."

"I beg your pardon?"

"Revolutions."

"Revolutions?"

"Of the locomotive driver wheel."

Bob glanced at Connie, who was biting her bottom lip to keep from laughing, then back at the professor. "Oh, yes, of course. I don't know why I didn't realize that."

"No reason you should, unless you are interested in such things. But it is quite simple, given that the diameter of the wheel is four feet and that a mile is five thousand two hundred eighty feet." He shook his head. "Why Americans do not use meters is difficult to understand. Perhaps you can help me find Mr. Canfield."

"*I'm* Bob Canfield," Bob said in exasperation.

"Ah, *gut, gut.* I was to look you up," Dr. Rosen said. "Herr Gelbman sent me."

Shaking their heads in bemusement, Bob and Connie led the professor out of the station to their car. They helped their visitor safely into the back seat, then climbed into their car, exchanging a look that said, *This is going to be most interesting,* before pulling away from the curb.

If Bob had been concerned about taking the eccentric Sigmund Rosen to meet Dr. Stephen Wilkerson, head of the Jefferson University physics department, he needn't have been. The conversation between the two men started hesitantly enough—there was the natural reticence of the two scientists, especially Sigmund, and a language barrier in that Dr. Wilkerson spoke no German and Dr. Rosen spoke lumbering English—but they soon found a common language in mathematics and were exchanging numbers as rapidly as others might tell jokes.

"Amazing!" Wilkerson said after a few minutes. "Absolutely amazing!"

"Dr. Wilkerson, will you be able to work with him?" Bob asked.

"Work with him?" Wilkerson asked. "Well, I don't know about that, but I can certainly try."

"Please, just be patient with him," Bob asked.

"Be patient with him?" Wilkerson laughed. "Mr. Canfield, you don't understand. The question isn't whether I'll be patient with *him*, it's whether *he* will be patient with *us*. He is so far ahead of anything I have ever read or anyone I have ever spoken to. When you said Dr. Rosen, I never dreamed you meant *the* Dr. Rosen."

"Oh? Well, I guess I never realized there was any such person as *the* Dr. Rosen."

"But there is, Mr. Canfield, indeed there is. Your making him available to Jefferson University is, in my opinion, as valuable a contribution as any monetary donation you have ever made—and, believe me, I am well aware of your monetary donations to this institution."

"Then I shall leave him in good hands," Bob said, "and trust that you'll see to getting him established, both within the university family and with a place to live. Oh, incidentally," he added, digging into his jacket pocket, "I've opened a checking account in his name to provide him with living expenses until he gets settled." Bob handed the checkbook to Dr. Wilkerson. "Please explain to him how a checking account works." Shaking his head, Bob laughed. "He might be able to delve into the invisible world of atoms and extract the most abstruse theorems, but I swear to you, I'm not at all sure he can balance a checkbook."

"Oh, I'm sure that he cannot," Wilkerson said wryly. "But don't worry. The physics department will assign someone to take care of him."

Bob turned to leave.

"Herr Canfield?" Sigmund called.

Bob turned back and saw, to his surprise, that the newcomer had tears in his eyes.

"Herr Gelbman, he is your friend?"

"Yes."

"You must make him leave Austria at once. He is not safe there."

Studying the doctor's face, Bob saw deep concern. He nodded. "I will try," he promised.

HOLLYWOOD, CALIFORNIA

When the electric bell rang on the soundstage, all conversation came to a halt. Demaris Hunter stood in position, listening to the quiet buzz of the klieg lights. She held her pose.

"Camera!"

"Speed!"

"Slate it!"

A young man with a slate board stood in front of the camera. "Screen Test Demaris Hunter, *Gone With the Wind.*" He slapped the bar down.

"Action!"

"I can think about it tomorrow," Demaris murmured. She put her hand dramatically to her forehead. "It's a new day, tomorrow."

"Cut! Miss Hunter, that is *not* the line," the test director said.

"What the hell difference does it make?" Demaris replied testily. "I'm a thirty-four-year-old woman, not an eighteen-year-old ingenue. I would *not* make a good Scarlett O'Hara. I know it, Mr. Selznick knows it—hell, even Margaret Mitchell knows it. The only reason I'm here in the first place is to feed the publicity mills. Tomorrow there'll be articles in papers all across the country, declaring, 'Demaris Hunter reads for Scarlett O'Hara.' "

"If you know the game, dearie, why aren't you playing it?" the director asked.

Demaris starting walking off the set. "Because I don't intend to do something half-assed," she said over her shoulder. "If I read for a part, I intend to get it."

"We went to a great deal of trouble to make arrangements with your studio to get you to make this screen test," the director called after her.

Demaris stopped. "So what do you want? I showed up and made the test. You've got your film, now use it to show how unsuited for the job I am. I don't intend to give you anything more."

"Oh, dear," the director said in a troubled voice. He put his hands on his hips, then turned and spoke into the great dark maw of the rest of the studio. "Mr. Falcone, what are we going to do?" he asked.

"If this is all we're going to get, then this is what we get," a disembodied and amplified voice replied from the darkness. "Don't worry about it; I'll talk to David. Thank you, Miss Hunter."

As Demaris walked out of the circle of bright light that made up the *Gone With the Wind* set, she heard someone clapping very softly. "Bravo," a man's voice said. "Bravo."

Demaris squinted into the darkness, and the man chuckled.

"Demaris, I know you don't want your fans to see you in glasses, but if you don't start wearing them, you're going to walk right into a brick wall one of these days."

"Guy!" Demaris squealed happily. She held her arms open, and Guy Colby stepped out of the shadows to embrace her. "What are you doing here?" she asked.

"I came to see you read for 'the' role," he said.

Demaris laughed. "Quite a hoot, wasn't it? Wouldn't I make a fine Georgia belle, though?" she asked, laying on a thick southern accent.

"As a matter of fact, I think you'd be wonderful in the role. What's more, I think *you* believe you would, too."

Demaris didn't respond. Instead, she took his arm and said, "Come into my dressing room with me. I have to get out of this dress."

Guy chuckled. "That's the best offer I've had in over a month."

Demaris led him across the soundstage to her dressing room, then closed the door and locked it behind her. "Undo me, would you?" she asked as she presented her back to Guy. She was wearing a very low-cut, full-skirted taffeta dress. One by one Guy opened the snaps, and a moment later Demaris let the dress fall. Then she pushed down the petticoats and stepped out of the shimmering pool of cloth. She was wearing absolutely nothing but a pair of filmy panties. "Excuse my titties, will you?" she joked.

"Why should I excuse them?" Guy replied. "I think they're beautiful."

Demaris smiled at him, then removed a silk dressing gown from a wall hook and put it on. Sitting down at her dressing table, she began removing the stage makeup.

"You're right," she said, looking at her reflection in the mirror while she applied cold cream to her face. "I *could* do the role. To be honest, I would even *like* to do the role. But Selznick would have to make arrangements with my studio for me to take the part. And after what he paid to get Clark, there's no way he could afford me."

"Isn't that the truth? The deal Selznick cut to get Gable is unbelievable," Guy said. "He agreed to give MGM half the profits from the film for the first seven years and twenty-five percent forever after. But, tell me, why are you even reading?"

"You've seen the publicity," Demaris said. She held the cream-smeared tissue in her hands as if she were displaying a newspaper. " 'David Selznick has tested over one thousand women in his search to find the perfect Scarlett O'Hara.' "

"Yeah, every starlet, extra, hopeful, and waitress is reading for the part. Why you?"

"Why Bette Davis? Why Susan Hayward?" Demaris replied. Unpinning the fall of Scarlett O'Hara sausage curls from the top of her head, she picked up a brush and ran it through her shoulder-length blond hair. "Selznick has to show that a few established names have read for the role. Otherwise everyone would recognize it for the gimmick it is. I'm just paying off a debt for my studio, that's all."

"Demaris, how would you like to work with *me* again?"

Demaris looked up, and her gaze locked with the director's in the mirror. "I'd *love* to work with you again, Guy," she said. She sighed. "Who am I kidding? I'd love to work *anywhere* again. The truth is, things haven't been going too well since Ian died. There's been such awful talk. . . ."

Guy shook his head. "Hollywood has a small-town, barbershop-and-beauty-shop mentality when it comes to gossip," he said. "I know. I've been ground pretty fine by those same mills." He put his hand on Demaris's shoulder, and she reached up to take it in hers, bringing it to her lips to kiss it.

"What do you have in mind for me?" she asked.

"I want you to play the role of Leah in *The Corruptible Dead.*"

"That's Twainbough's new book, isn't it?"

"Number one on *The New York Times* Best-seller List as of this week. And I have the rights." Guy smiled broadly. "Eric was so pleased with what I did with *A Stillness in the Line* that I didn't have any trouble at all buying the rights from him."

"He *should* have been pleased. It was nominated for the Academy Award, after all," Demaris said.

"*The Corruptible Dead* will get the Academy Award for Best Picture, and you will get one for Best Actress, if you'll take the role. It's a wonderful part, Demaris. Leah is a wonderful character."

"I have to confess, I haven't read the book," she said. "I don't know anything about the character or the story."

"Well, why don't you come along to Paris with me and I'll tell you all about it?"

"Paris? Isn't that going a little far just to talk about a role?" she quipped.

"Not far at all. I can have you there and back within a half hour. We live in a city of magic, remember?"

When Demaris was dressed, they walked arm in arm to an empty set where *Dancing in France* was about to be filmed. Guy seated the actress at one of the sidewalk café tables, then walked over to a nearby mobile canteen and returned with a couple of Cokes.

"Pretend it's Beaujolais," he suggested, "and we are at Maxim's." Guy held the Coke up, sniffed its bouquet, then tasted. "Ummm," he said. "Yes, I would say this is an amusing little drink, aggressive without being overpowering, and it has a rich, full-bodied flavor with an adequate if not impressive nose."

Demaris laughed gaily, then reached across the table to

put her hand on Guy's. "I'm glad you've come back into my life, Guy Colby," she said softly.

He put his hand on hers. "So am I, my dear."

JUNE 5, PETERSBURG, VIRGINIA

When Sheriff Tomkins came on duty at six-thirty in the morning, he poured himself a cup of coffee, then walked over to his desk. Tossing down his keys, he picked up the night deputy's duty report.

"George," he called, looking over at the sleeping deputy. "Hey, George, wake up."

The night deputy's head was leaning back against the wall, his eyes were closed, his mouth was open, and he was snoring softly. A line of spittle was dangling out of the corner of his mouth.

"George," the sheriff said again, and he kicked at the side of the desk.

"Uhmmph," the deputy grunted, his head jerking forward. He snorted, wiped his eyes, then his mouth. "Oh, hello, Sheriff," he said. "I guess I didn't hear you come in."

"I guess you didn't. I could've been John Dillinger, robbing the place, and you wouldn't have known anything about it."

The deputy chuckled. "That'd be a good trick, wouldn't it? I mean, him bein' dead and all. Did you see I made fresh coffee?"

"Yeah, I saw it," Tomkins answered.

The deputy stood up and tucked his shirttail down into his trousers, then walked over to pour himself a cup of coffee. "Seems to me if I could have fresh coffee for the day shift when they come on in the mornin', they could have some ready for me at night," he complained.

"I see there was an automobile accident this morning," the sheriff said, ignoring the deputy's grousing and reading his duty report.

"Oh, yeah, there was. I mean, it was one hell of a wreck. It was out on the sixty highway. Claude Meechum was out drivin' drunk again. Only this time he smack dab run head on into another car. Got *his* ass killed, too. Deader'n shit."

"What about the other car?"

"Brand new Plymouth," the deputy replied. He took a swallow of his coffee. "Whooee! You can't believe what old Claude done to that Plymouth. Why, it's tore up so bad you can barely make out what kind of a car it was."

"Never mind the goddamn car," Tomkins said impatiently. "What about the people *in* the car?"

"Oh. It was a man and a woman. Killed the woman right out. The man ain't dead yet, but he ain't far from it. They got him over to the hospital."

"What shape's he in?"

"It depends. They're tryin' to get some blood from the hospital down in Richmond. If it gets here in time, he might pull through. Otherwise, he won't make it."

The sheriff picked up his keys again. "Maybe I'd better get on over to the hospital and see what's going on. You hang around here until Jasper gets in."

"Okay, Sheriff. But he better be here by seven. I promised the wife we'd go see her mother today."

"Is that why you were sleeping all night?"

"Come on, Sheriff. That ain't fair. I just dozed off, is all. Hell, I spent near an hour tryin' to get that fella out of his car."

Tomkins made no comment as he left the office. Getting into the police cruiser, he drove slowly out of town toward the hospital, passing the garage where the drunk driver's wrecked pickup truck and the wrecked car had been brought. The deputy had been right about the car, he thought. Only the emblem and the name on the trunk lid identified it as a Plymouth. From the shape of the back window and the bits and pieces of the grille that could be recognized, the sheriff saw that it had, indeed, been a brand-new car. Light blue it was and probably had been quite a pretty little coupe.

Reaching the hospital, Tomkins parked by the emergency entrance, then went inside to talk to the doctor on duty.

"You here to check on the colored man?" the doctor asked.

"The colored man?"

"Yeah, the fella that was in the car wreck last night."

"Yeah," the sheriff said. "I didn't know he was colored, though. I guess I was fooled by the car. You don't expect to see a colored man with such a nice car. How's he doing?"

"Not too good. He's going to die if we don't get that blood here pretty soon."

"Is it on the way?"

"Not yet. They're putting it on the bus at seven. It'll be here by three this afternoon."

"Will he last that long?"

"I doubt it. We've got some of that newly developed plasma. If I could give him that, I could prevent him from going into shock. That would at least keep him alive."

"Well, what are you waiting on?" the sheriff asked. "Give it to him."

"And go to jail?"

"What do you mean, go to jail?"

"The law is very specific, Sheriff. I can't give colored blood to a white person, and I can't give white blood to a colored person."

"Shit!" the sheriff spat. He sighed. "You're a doctor. Is there *really* any difference?"

"None that I can tell."

"Then, goddammit, give it to him. Who the hell is going to know?"

"We have to account for every unit of blood," the doctor explained. "Believe me, the State Medical Board will know. Even if I don't go to jail, I'd lose my license to practice."

"That's a hell of a damn note," the sheriff growled. He sighed. "What's the man's name, anyway?"

"Booker. Andrew Booker," the doctor said. "And if you want to know what's really terrible . . . the man is a physician."

"Is he conscious?"

"No."

Tomkins looked away. "Just as well. If he was conscious,

I'd have to go talk to him . . . and I don't think I could face him."

JUNE 7

Stump Pollard entered his office to the sound of the ringing telephone. No one else was in the office, and the insistent jangling continued as the police chief crossed to his desk.

"Delta police," Stump said with a touch of annoyance as he picked up the receiver.

"Is this the the Chief of Police of Delta, Mississippi?"

"That's right. Chief Stump Pollard. And who might you be?" Stump asked.

"This is Sheriff Tomkins in Petersburg, Virginia. Near Richmond. Um, we've had a bad accident here, involving some residents of your town. Leastwise, their driver's licenses list a Delta address."

A sudden coldness ran down Stump's spine. He was afraid to ask the next question, but he knew that he had to. And he knew, too, what the answer was going to be. What other folks from Delta would have been traveling near Washington, D.C.?

He steeled himself. "Who are they?"

"A fella named Andrew Booker and his wife, LaTonya."

It was as Stump had feared. "I see," he murmured.

"Yeah, well, I thought you ought to know about Booker and his wife so's you can notify any next of kin."

"*Doctor* Booker," Stump Pollard snapped.

"Doctor Booker," Sheriff Tomkins repeated. "Yes, well, I'm real sorry that it had to happen here in my county. Especially since it was one of our local drunks who killed 'em. The best thing I can say is that the drunk son of a bitch got himself killed, too."

"That hardly makes up for losing a man like Brother Doctor," Stump said. "Hell, if his final resting place were here in Delta, we'd have a place of honor for him."

Tomkins made a sound of surprise. "What did you say? You'd have a place of *honor* for him?"

"That's right. You see, he saved the whole town a few years ago. Stopped an outbreak of polio, dead in its tracks."

"Damn," the sheriff said. "Damn, that's too bad. That makes it all the more a shame about the blood."

"The blood? What are you talking about?"

"Well, the ironic thing is, the hospital says they could've saved him if they'd been able to use some of that new blood plasma they had on hand. But Booker being colored and the only blood plasma on hand being for white people, there wasn't anything they could do. They sent for some colored blood from Richmond, but it didn't get here fast enough. I'm sure you understand how that is, being as you're from Mississippi."

"Yeah," Stump said, slowly nodding, "I understand. And you're right about the irony. More right than you realize. Especially considering who he was."

"What do you mean, 'considering who he was'?"

"Well, Dr. Andrew Booker and his wife were on their way to Washington where he was to be decorated by the President of the United States."

"The hell you say," the sheriff replied in a disbelieving voice. "What was he being decorated for? Saving your town from polio?"

"No," Stump replied. He took out a cigarette and lit it before he answered, then squinted through the exhaled smoke. "You know that blood plasma? The stuff that your hospital wouldn't let him have?"

"Yes, but I told you why."

"Oh, yes, you told me why. And I'm sure the hospital considered they had a good reason for it. But the funny thing is, you wouldn't even have any blood plasma if it weren't for Dr. Booker. You see, he's the one who developed it."

CHAPTER TWENTY

JUNE 8, 1937, MADRID, SPAIN

When the train rattled to a stop in the Madrid station, Eric Twainbough hopped down from the flat car. Six weeks earlier he had caught a troop train out of this very station, riding with a bunch of bright-eyed, unshaven boys who sang songs and boasted of what they were going to do to the fascists.

Some of those same young soldiers had now returned, aging twenty years in six weeks. Their once-bright eyes were now flat and listless, their still-unshaven cheeks were sunken and pallid, and their once-smiling lips were compressed in a tight line.

"Eric! Eric! Over here!" a woman shouted.

Eric looked over in the direction of the voice and saw Shaylin McKay waving at him. He picked up his rucksack and started toward her.

"Where have you been?" Shaylin asked when he drew up.

"Linares," he replied. "What are you doing here?"

"I'm looking for a ride downtown. I just got back from Puertollano."

"Are you going to the Florida?"

"Yes. I'm going to try and get another room. I gave mine up before I left. Have you got one?"

Eric smiled. "Let me tell you about my room," he said. "It has a bed."

"A bed? With clean sheets?" Shaylin asked in an awe-struck voice.

"Of course. And just off the room is a bathroom, with a bathtub that has hot-and-cold running water."

"Oohh," Shaylin breathed with a sigh. "I've *heard* of such things, but it's been so long, I can't remember if I've ever actually *seen* one."

"And downstairs from that room is a bar where you can get beer, whiskey, or wine just by holding up your fingers and asking for it. And a dining room where food is served on a plate . . . without dirt."

"I'm afraid I'll have to actually see such a place with my own eyes before I could ever believe that it's real," Shaylin joked.

"Come on," he said, taking her by the elbow and leading her along the station platform, "we'll find us a ride."

Eric soon found a truckload of military supplies and, with the barter of a package of cigarettes, got a spot in the back of the truck for them. He climbed in first, then reached down over the tailgate to help Shaylin up.

The truck pulled away, and they rode quietly for some time. Eric looked through the back of the truck at the shade trees and the sand-colored walls and red-slate roofs of the buildings of Madrid as the Gran Vía reeled out behind them. Because of the nightly shelling of the capital city, the street was pockmarked with shell holes and littered with chunks of brick and plaster and broken glass. They passed bicycles, taxis, horse-drawn carts, as well as other military trucks as the driver sped down the road, using his horn more often than his brakes.

The night before, fascist Nationalist soldiers had attacked in force the communist Loyalist positions at Linares. One young fascist soldier had made it all the way to the opening of Eric's bunker before a Loyalist defender shot him. The Nationalist youth had fallen down into the bunker, where he took several minutes to die. During those minutes he had asked Eric to hear his confession. Eric had sat there in the dark, holding the youth's hand, listening to his labored breathing and hearing his confession, though he understood little of what the boy was saying until, at the end, he heard him beg, "*Perdoneme.*" The youth's plea for forgiveness was followed by a shuddery, life-surrendering sigh.

Eric couldn't stop thinking about the young soldier, dying with a prayer of contrition on his lips. When one thought of bloodthirsty, murdering fascists, a teenaged boy clutching a crucifix was hardly the image that came to mind.

"Eric?"

Eric looked around and saw that the truck had stopped. Only then did he realize that Shaylin must have been addressing him for some time.

"Oh. Sorry," he said. He looked out and saw that they were in front of the Hotel Florida. "I guess I wasn't paying any attention."

"You didn't say a word all the way here. You seemed to be a thousand miles away."

"No." Eric hopped down, then held Shaylin's hand as she jumped from the back of the truck. "More like a hundred."

"Would you like to talk about it over dinner?" Shaylin asked solicitiously.

Eric smiled and shook his head. "No. There's no way I'd waste the chance to have dinner with the lovely Shaylin McKay by talking business. We'll have dinner, but it's going to be a purely social occasion."

"Why, Eric Twainbough. Are you asking me for a date?"

Eric pulled himself up to full height and smoothed his wrinkled and soiled clothes as well as he could. "You're damned right I am," he said.

With Eric carrying both their bags, they went inside the hotel. Shaylin got a room on the floor above Eric's, and as they walked up the stairs, they decided that she would stop by his room on the way down to dinner, after they both had the chance to bathe and put on clean clothes.

It took Eric about a half hour to bathe, shave, and get dressed. Shaylin wasn't down yet, so he stood in the open window of his room and looked out over the rooftops.

Though Madrid was a city at war, it wasn't blacked out. The rebel Insurgents had the city within range of their heavy artillery, and every night they would shoot off several rounds indiscriminately. The citizens reasoned that since shells fell in the city whether it was blacked out or not, why bother to black it out? That having been decided, the Madridians seemed to turn on even more than the usual number of lights, almost as a gesture of defiance.

It was a heavily overcast night, and the many lights of the city reflected from the low-hanging clouds. The effect suffused the city with a soft, red glow. From his window Eric could almost believe that Madrid was a city at peace, and it wasn't hard for him to remember the Madrid he and Tanner had visited fifteen years before.

He was lost in wistful thinking about his former wife when a light knock sounded on his door. Almost relieved by the distraction, Eric turned away from the window, and he opened the door to find Shaylin standing there, smiling prettily at him, her red hair shining brightly in the hall light. She was wearing a green, off-the-shoulder peasant dress belted at the waist with a bright yellow sash. Her shoes and a ribbon in her hair matched the belt at her waist.

"Well, hello," Eric said, his voice reflecting his appreciation of the picture she presented. "Aren't you a bright and pretty thing, though?"

"Thank you, kind sir," Shaylin said, smiling and curtsying. "Are you ready?"

"I suppose I am." Eric pulled the door closed behind him and stepped out into the hall. "Though looking at you, I feel underdressed. I just put on a clean pair of battle togs."

"So did I," Shaylin said.

"Ha! I'd hardly call those battle togs."

Shaylin put her arm through his, then smiled up at him.

"I suppose that all depends on the campaign," she said sweetly.

On their way down the stairs they decided to have a drink before dinner, so they went into the bar first. A loud burst of laughter greeted them the moment they stepped through the door, and when they looked toward the source, they saw nearly a dozen journalists sitting around a long table. The table itself was a veritable forest of empty beer and wine bottles, evidence that the journalists had been doing some serious drinking for quite a while.

"Twainberry!" someone called jovially. "Twainberry, come over here! Join us!"

"Isn't that Hemingway?" Shaylin asked.

"In the flesh," Eric said.

"What's that he's calling you?"

Eric chuckled. "You mean Twainberry? Well, if you know Ernest, you know he is never satisfied with the names people come with and feels constrained to 'improve' upon them. Even his own name often becomes 'Hemingstein.' "

"Come over and join us!" Hemingway called again. "And bring daughter!"

"Would you like to join that motley crew for a few minutes?" Eric asked.

"Sure, why not?"

As Eric and Shaylin approached, Hemingway said, "Pull up a couple of extra chairs there." He was sitting at the head of a table that was also peopled by the likes of John Dos Passos, Martha Gelhorn, Sid Franklin, Tom Delmer, and Virginia Cowles, among others.

"Dos, you remember this old cowboy from our days as a member of Gertrude's 'lost,' don't you? For the rest of you who might not know, this is Eric Twainbough," Hemingway said.

"It's good to meet you at last," one of the other journalists said, extending his hand. "We've all heard of you, of course, and I have to confess to being one of your biggest fans."

"Thank you," Eric said, embarrassed by the open flattery.

"In our Paris days," Hemingway went on, "Twainberry

and I used to spend an entire day sitting in Marcel's Café, knocking back the beers and turning out the words. I was working on *The Sun Also Rises,* and Twainberry was writing . . ." He paused. "What was that opus you were working on?"

"If you're talking about the Paris years, it must've been *A Time for All Things,*" Shaylin answered for Eric.

Hemingway laughed. "So it was, so it was," he said. "Tell me, I sort of lost track. Did it do very well?"

"Yours did modestly better," Eric replied.

"Ha!" one of the journalists exclaimed, laughing out loud. "Ernest, that's probably the only time the word 'modest' has ever been applied to you."

"Unless one is talking about his talent," Shaylin suggested, and again the journalists laughed.

"Ouch!" Hemingway said. "Are you armed, daughter?"

Shaylin held her hands up like claws and hissed like a cat.

"I recommend you don't mess with her," one of the men said.

Hemingway, smiling, nodded in agreement, holding up his hands in surrender. "I concede, daughter, I concede. Truce?"

"Truce," Shaylin agreed.

"Sit down, sit down," Hemingway said. "I'm telling the story of the fight at Casa de Campo."

"Hem saw it all," someone said. "Through binoculars," he added.

"Did you now?" Eric asked.

"I did indeed," Hemingway said. "And, let me tell you, there is a trick to watching a battle through binoculars. You see, the setting sun glints on the lenses, which makes them easily visible to the enemy riflemen. I mean, if you want to be properly sniped, all you have to do is use a pair of glasses without shading them adequately. And those fellas could shoot, too. Their bullets kept kicking up dirt and sand all around me. They kept my mouth dry all day."

"Did you get any pictures?" someone asked.

"Oh, yes, we got a lot of them," Hemingway said. "But

I'm afraid we were too far off from the action for them to show anything."

Hemingway finished his story, and then one of the other reporters told one, followed by another. When they had all had a turn, one of the journalists asked Eric if he had a story to tell. Because he didn't want to talk about the fascist who had died praying, he shook his head no.

"Twainberry is over here looking for his next novel," Hemingway said.

"And you're not?" someone asked in a sarcastic tone.

"I am," Hemingway admitted. "But I'm not going to do like Malraux, who pulled out before the war really started to right some gigantic *masterpiss.* My book will be of ordinary length and totally unfaked." He looked at Eric. "You can understand that, Twainbough," he said. "You write the best goddamned war stuff I've ever read."

"Thank you," Eric said, surprised and genuinely pleased by Hemingway's accolade. "Coming from you, that's high praise."

"Tell us more about your inspection trip, Hem," someone said.

"Yeah, hell, I'm filing my dispatch from what you're saying," another said, and everyone laughed.

The merriment continued, and Eric and Shaylin stayed at the table for a little over an hour before they finally excused themselves and went into the dining room to order dinner. Even in the dining room, however, they could still hear loud bursts of laughter spilling out from the bar at regular intervals.

"They make the war sound almost fun," Shaylin said.

"They're building up their reservoir of stories," Eric explained. "Years from now they'll be sitting in a club somewhere, and when the topic of the Spanish Civil War comes up, they'll tell everything they heard tonight, just as if it happened to them."

Inexplicably, Shaylin's eyes filled with tears. "I don't know if I am going to be very good at this," she said. "I had a rough one this time out. I know, I'm a reporter, and I'm supposed to hold myself outside these things." She sighed.

"But I had a man die right in front of me. He practically died in my arms."

Eric reached across the table and took Shaylin's hand in his. He rubbed it gently, then raised it to his lips and kissed it.

"Being reporters doesn't make us less human," he said. "We can't be exposed to things like that and not feel them." There was another outbreak of laughter from the group of journalists in the bar. "Why do you think people like that—and I'm including myself—find so many things to laugh at in times like these?" Eric asked, nodding toward the bar.

"I don't know."

"Because if we didn't find enough to laugh about, all we would do is cry."

"You guys cry?" Shaylin asked, wiping away her own tears.

"Everyone cries sometimes, Shaylin," Eric said somberly.

"Good evening," the waiter said, coming up to their table and smiling.

Eric released Shaylin's hand and looked up at the man. "Good evening. We don't have menus, so tell us what you suggest for dinner."

"You are lucky, señor," the waiter said. He smiled broadly. "Tonight, as a special, we have some tins of very nice Spam, straight from America."

Eric and Shaylin looked at each other, then laughed uproariously.

The waiter looked pained. "Is something wrong, señor?"

"No," Eric said. "Nothing is wrong. I'm sorry. Don't take it personally. Bring the Spam. We will have a feast."

"*Sí,* señor."

Their food arrived quickly, and Eric and Shaylin said little through their meal.

"You were in Russia, weren't you?" Shaylin asked as they were finishing.

"Yes, I was. Why do you ask?"

"Because I've heard you speak Russian. Besides, you

describe the Russian scenes so beautifully in *Stillness in the Line*."

"Thank you."

"Tell me about Princess Katya."

"What about her?"

"Well, I know she was a character in your book. But was she a real person?"

Eric laughed softly. "You're like everyone else," he said. "Always trying to read people into my books."

"Was she real?"

"Let's just say she was a composite."

"I think what I'm asking is, when you were in Russia, did you know someone like Princess Katya, and were you in love with her?"

Eric drummed his fingers for a few beats and studied Shaylin across the table. He took a deep breath, then let it out.

"Shaylin McKay, you are asking an awful lot from a casual friendship," he finally said.

"Maybe I want more from this than a casual friendship."

"Like what?"

"Like, maybe I would like to take a fifth of whiskey up to your room, jump in bed with you, and fuck like a rabbit."

Eric blinked in surprise at Shaylin's frank pronouncement, and she laughed.

"Do I shock you?" she asked.

"Yes. No. I don't know," Eric stammered. "You're twenty years younger than I am. Is this the way of it with women today?"

"Well, I don't think you'd find anything like it in Emily Post's book on etiquette," Shaylin admitted with a lilting laugh. "But, then, I've never read the book."

"Obviously."

"Look, if you don't want to, I'll . . ." Shaylin started to get up.

"No, wait!" Eric said, reaching across the table to grasp her hand. "I didn't say I didn't want to. I just said I was surprised."

Shaylin snorted. "Surprised? You were shocked out of your mind."

Eric smiled. "I suppose I was," he admitted. He stood up. "Irish whiskey, I suppose?"

"Sure 'n would there be any other, now?" Shaylin replied in a thick Irish brogue.

The overcast sky that had been promising rain delivered during dinner, and returning with Shaylin to his room, Eric found that he had left his window open. The curtains were floating out over the room, lifted by the night breeze, and rain was blowing in through the open window. Shifting the bottle of whiskey he had just purchased at the bar to his left hand, Eric started toward the window to close it.

"No, don't," Shaylin said quickly. "Leave it open. I like to hear it, smell it, feel it. And don't turn on the lights. I like it this way, with just what light is coming in through the window."

"All right," Eric agreed. He held up the bottle. "I've got glasses for this," he said. "Or do you prefer drinking it right out of the bottle?"

Shaylin laughed. "I'm not totally uncivilized, Eric Twainbough. Glasses, please," she said as she began to undo her sash.

Eric had to get down on his hands and knees and look into the back of the cabinet that doubled as a wardrobe to find the glasses. When he did find them he also found that they were so dirty that he had to take them to the bathroom and wash them out. By the time he returned, with the glasses cleaned and the whiskey poured, Shaylin was already naked.

She stood by the bed, waiting for him. Her body was subtly lighted by the ambient light coming in not only through the window, but also over the transom from the hallway outside. Shaylin's breasts were small, firm, and well rounded, and her nipples were drawn tight from exposure to the cool air. At the junction of her legs the tangle of hair curled invitingly. Eric looked at her appreciatively for a long moment before, wordlessly, he extended a glass.

"Thank you," Shaylin said, taking the proffered glass of whiskey.

Setting his own glass down, Eric began taking off his clothes. Shaylin took a sip from her glass, then, clearly impatient, came over to help Eric get undressed.

"I'll get your boots and trousers," she said. "You finish your drink."

By now Eric was as impatient as Shaylin, and when he was fully undressed—and fully aroused—he pulled her to him, hungrily kissing her open mouth with his own and sending his tongue darting against hers. He propelled her toward the bed, then climbed on top of her.

Shaylin received him easily, wrapping her legs around him, meeting his lunges by pushing against him. Eric lost himself in the pleasurable sensations until a few minutes later Shaylin began a frenzied moaning and jerking beneath him. He let himself go then, thrusting against her, until at last he played out his own passion.

They lay together for a long time after that, holding each other but not speaking. The window was still open, and it was still raining. Eric felt the chill of the dampened air as he listened to the raindrops against the windowpane. He listened, too, to the sounds of shelling and shooting and was suddenly transported back twenty years to the last time he had lain with a woman beside him while a war went on outside. Stark images of Katya Lvovna flitted through his mind, images so poignant, images that so filled him with agony over her fate—and that of his unborn child—that he had to immediately suppress them. Finding comfort and warmth in Shaylin's presence, Eric pressed himself tightly against her and finally drifted off to sleep. He never knew that Shaylin kissed him lightly on the cheek, then slid out of bed and slipped silently from his room to return to her own.

Two hours later when the rebel artillery shell exploded in Eric's room, he was sound asleep. He had a momentary awareness of a brilliant flash of light, a loud roar, and a searing pain—then nothing.

• • •

Valentina Lvovna Kosior was dreaming, and in her dream she was back at the labor camp. The commandant of the camp had ordered everyone to build boxes, wooden boxes to be used as coffins, and Valentina could hear the incessant hammering. *Bang! Bang! Bang!*

In her dream she covered her ears, but the noise wouldn't go away. It continued, penetrating her consciousness until she was awake. Then she realized that it hadn't been a dream. Someone was frantically pounding on her door.

"*Valentina! Valentina, wake up!*"

Valentina recognized Dr. Peter Suslov's voice, and she sat up in bed and looked around the dark room. They had just arrived at the hotel this very day, having spent the last months providing field hospital facilities for Loyalist and partisan soldiers.

"Valentina, are you awake?"

"Yes, yes, I'm awake," Valentina called. Groggily, she walked over to the door and opened it. Peter was standing in the bright light of the hallway, looking distressed.

"Get dressed, hurry," he said urgently.

"What is it? What is wrong?" Valentina asked.

"There is an order for all doctors and nurses to report to the Hotel Florida. The Rebels shelled the hotel tonight. Many have been hurt."

Valentina felt her blood go cold. "I'll only be a minute," she promised.

The lobby of the Hotel Florida was a cacophony of sound when Valentina and Peter arrived a few minutes later. There were cries of pain from the wounded and sharp exclamations of condemnation from Loyalist officials incensed by the Insurgents' brutal act of bombarding a civilian hotel. There were the loud, excited voices of those anxious to talk of escapes and close calls from shells that had exploded on their floor or in their rooms but had left them unhurt. But above all else there were the authoritative barks of orders from the doctors and the others in charge who had turned the hotel's bar into an emergency hospital.

Some half-dozen doctors and more than a dozen nurses were working desperately on the bleeding and wounded residents of the hotel. Another, more silent and somber group was laying out the dead. A long line of bloodied bodies lay covered with sheets, blankets, tablecloths, and anything else that served the gruesome task.

"What are you people doing here?" a man with a blood-smeared apron challenged Valentina and Peter when they arrived. "This is no time for sightseeing."

"He is a doctor," Valentina said in Spanish, speaking for Peter as he had not yet mastered the language. "I am his nurse."

The man nodded. "Good, good. We are glad to have you." He pointed to the corner of the room. "Pull a couple of tables together over there and get to work. The orderlies will bring you your patients."

"Yes, Doctor," Valentina answered, and then she translated the instructions to Peter. With the help of one of the orderlies, Valentina began pulling the tables together, while Peter opened his bag and started removing his instruments. As soon as he was ready, he nodded at Valentina.

"Tell them to bring our first patient," he said.

Valentina passed the word on to the orderly who had helped with the tables. That orderly got another to help him, and they hurried toward a redheaded woman in her twenties who was sitting on the floor with the other waiting wounded, clutching the hand of an unconscious man whose belly was covered with a bloody towel. The two orderlies gently lifted the wounded man onto the tables. Peter pulled the towel away to look at his belly.

"What do you think?" Valentina asked.

"I don't know. He has lost a lot of blood," Peter said. He began gingerly cleaning the wound. "But it doesn't look as if there's any major damage to any of the organs."

The redheaded woman, her face streaked with tears and plaster dust, touched Valentina's arm, then asked in Spanish, "Is he going to be all right?"

The woman's accent made it clear that she was not a native. "You are not Spanish," Valentina said.

"No. My name is Shaylin McKay. I'm American."

"I see," Valentina replied. "He is your husband?"

"No," Shaylin replied. "We're both journalists. My

room is one floor above his. When the mortar shells hit, I was lucky enough to be on a floor that wasn't damaged. But from the loudness of the explosions, I guessed that the floor beneath mine was hit, and I went down to see if he was all right. I found his room a shambles. He was on the floor, like this."

"He's going to have to have blood," Peter said in Russian. "Ask the girl if she knows his blood type."

Valentina relayed the question in Spanish.

"No, I don't know," Shaylin said. "But it will be on the identity card in his wallet. We were all told to carry such cards."

"Where is his wallet?"

"In his pants."

Valentina glanced at the patient. "He is not wearing pants," she said.

"Oh! Uh, right. Okay, wait. I'll go back up to the room."

"No," one of the civil guards said, having overheard the conversation. "We have orders to let no one go back upstairs."

"But I must, don't you understand? If I don't, he will die!" Shaylin pleaded. "He must have a blood transfusion, but it can't be done if his blood type isn't known. And the blood type is recorded on his identity card, which is in his wallet in his pants in his room."

A rugged-looking man in his thirties, another journalist from the look of him, Valentina thought, came over then, apparently having heard the distress in Shaylin's voice. He looked down at the bleeding patient and his face paled.

"How is he?" the man asked Shaylin.

She explained about the identity card.

"I'll get it," the journalist offered.

"No," the civil guard said. "It is too dangerous to go upstairs now. There may be unexploded shells."

"That's my friend lying there, dying," the journalist said, raising a clenched fist. "And I'm going up to his room to get his identity card. If you try and stop me, I'm going to take you out . . . or you're going to have to take me out. Now, which is it going to be?"

The civil guard looked over at a colleague standing

nearby. The second civil guard looked at the journalist, then at Shaylin, and then he nodded once.

"Thank you," the journalist said, pushing past them and bounding up the stairs.

It took about five minutes for him to return. During the entire time he was gone, Shaylin held on to the wounded man's hand, begging him in a quiet, desperate voice to hang on.

"Damn," the journalist said when he returned. "It's a hell of a mess up there, I'll tell you. On top of that, there's no light." He held out the billfold. "But I found it."

"Thank God!" Shaylin said. She quickly removed the identity card and handed it to Valentina.

Valentina saw the name on the card, and she gasped in surprise. "This man. He is Eric Twainbough?" she asked.

"Yes," Shaylin answered.

"Is this the famous American novelist?"

"Yes, yes. You've heard of him?"

Valentina looked at the man lying on the two tables. His eyes were closed, and he had no color in his skin. His muscles were slack, and his breathing was slow and labored. This was her father. This was the man her mother had spent a lifetime waiting for . . . the man who had deserted them, even before she was born.

"I have heard of him," she said quietly.

"Valentina, his blood grouping . . ." Peter said urgently. "I must know his blood grouping!"

"It is group B," Valentina said.

"Find a donor, quickly," Peter said.

"Will I do?" Shaylin asked.

"What is your type?"

"AB."

"No, you won't do," Valentina said. She looked down at the man on the tables, the man who was her father, then made a decision. She started rolling up her sleeve.

"What are you doing?" Peter asked in Russian, looking up in surprise.

"His blood group is B; my blood group is B," Valentina replied.

"You can't give your blood to a patient! Where would you draw the line?"

"I will draw the line here. I will give my blood to *this* patient."

"No, I won't let you do it," Peter insisted. "You know the rules."

"If he doesn't get blood he will die," Valentina said sharply. She wrapped the coil around her arm, then picked up one end of the blood-transfer tubing. "Take my blood, or I will drain it onto the floor!" she snapped.

"What is wrong with you?" Peter asked. "You've gone mad! You've never acted this way before."

Valentina caught the look on Shaylin McKay's face as the redhead looked from one to the other as if she could determine what they were so fiercely arguing about in Russian.

"Please!" Shaylin begged. "What is it? What is wrong?"

"*Nada,*" Valentina said, switching back to Spanish. "Nothing is wrong." She stuck the needle in her vein and handed the other to Peter who, with a sigh of resignation, completed the connection. Valentina began opening and closing her hand in a pumping action, and the blood started running from her vein, through the narrow rubber tube, and into Eric Twainbough's arm.

The following afternoon Valentina made her hospital rounds, checking on her patients. Included among them were the people wounded in the shelling of the Hotel Florida who had been transferred to the medical facility. Valentina had delayed as long as possible seeing the one whom she knew would overwhelm her, but she couldn't put it off any longer.

Steeling herself, she entered Eric Twainbough's room. He looked up at her and smiled.

"My friend Shaylin tells me I owe you my life," he said in Russian.

"An accident of birth," Valentina replied. "We both have the same blood type."

Eric chuckled. "An accident of birth, you say? Then I'm awfully glad you were born."

"Yes," Valentina murmured.

Eric stared at her at length. "Please excuse my gaping," he finally said, "but you remind me so much of someone I knew a long time ago."

Valentina shrugged. "I have a very common face."

"You have a very beautiful face."

"A person's looks are of no value to the state he serves."

"I see." Eric smiled. "Nevertheless, you remind me of her."

"She was Soviet?"

"No," Eric said, his voice soft. "Not Soviet. Russian. From St. Petersburg."

"You mean Leningrad."

"No, I don't mean Leningrad. I mean St. Petersburg."

"Perhaps I remind you of her because we both speak the same language," Valentina suggested.

Eric gazed steadily at her. For a moment—but just for a moment—Valentina thought that his eyes were filled with sadness, and she wondered whether he was remembering another time and another place. Whether he was perhaps recalling an evening that Katya had so wistfully described to her daughter—made all the more wistful by the utter bleakness of the gulag—of a ride in a troika jingling with sleigh bells and a festive ball tinkling with the laughter of Christmas celebrants. For a moment—but just for a moment—Valentina considered throwing her arms around the neck of this man, calling him Father and telling him that she was his long-lost daughter.

Then the moment passed, and Eric Twainbough was once again just a stranger, a stranger lying wounded in this hot, close room in a shabby Madrid hospital.

"Yes," he finally said in response to her suggestion. "Yes, I suppose that's it. At any rate, I want to thank you again. Maybe when I'm better my friend and I can take you and the doctor to dinner."

"No," Valentina said, shaking her head. "No, that won't be possible. Dr. Suslov and I are leaving this afternoon. We have been called back to the Soviet Union."

"Oh. Well, I'm sorry to hear that. That means we won't see each other again."

"No. We will not see each other again."

Valentina turned and walked out of the room. She made it all the way to the hallway before the tears began to slide down her face.

CHAPTER TWENTY-ONE

AUGUST 31, 1939, PARIS

"Morgan," Faith Canfield called to her young son. "Morgan, you keep an eye on your sister, now, you hear me? Don't you dare let her get beyond the fence."

John Canfield looked over at the chain-link fence surrounding the patio restaurant at Orly Airport. His four-year-old son, Morgan, and two-year-old daughter, Alicia, were standing at the fence, watching the airplanes take off and land. John watched them for a few minutes himself. A Lockheed 14, its twin engines roaring, was just beginning its take-off run, while a Junkers JU-52, its own three engines ticking over quietly, awaited its turn. Taxiing out to the end of the runway to join the queue was a Douglas DC-3, while loading at one of the gates was a Rockwell-McPheeters Starduster.

John shifted his attention back to the table when his friend Marcel Aubron returned, saying, "I found a waiter and ordered some tea." The legendary Parisian restaurateur shook his head. "If I had such workers in my café, I would go out of business."

"You would never have such people working for you in the first place, Papa," Chantal Aubron teased. "If they do not move from table to table on roller skates, you fire them."

The others laughed.

"You exaggerate, Chantal," Marcel said defensively. "They don't have to wear roller skates . . . they just have to walk very quickly."

"Why are the waiters here so lazy?" his wife, Denise, asked.

"All the waiters here are young," Marcel replied, waving his hand dismissively. "They are probably listening to the radio. They do not believe they can get ten meters away from a radio."

"In America all the young people are listening to Benny Goodman," Faith remarked. "He seems to be the latest craze."

"Oh, I love Benny Goodman!" Chantal said. "I love the —how do you say it?—swing."

"Swing?" Marcel said, making a face. "That is not music. That is noise."

"Oh, but I like it, too," Faith said.

"You see, Papa. Only very old people do not like the swing," Chantal said, laughing. She stood up and held her hands out in front of her, moving her fingers as if she were playing a clarinet, then began swaying her hips.

"Chantal!" her mother scolded. "Stop that! You are being positively indecent!"

"Oh, leave her alone, Mama," Marcel laughed. "She is nineteen, beautiful, and in Paris. Now, I ask you, what can be better than that?"

"Absolutely nothing," John agreed, laughing with Marcel.

"Paris is such a wonderful place to be," Faith said. "I wish we could stay longer."

"Please, do stay," Denise Aubron begged. "You have been wonderful company for us."

"I wish we could," John said. "I really do. But we must

get back home. Canfield-Puritex is buying a lumber company in Oregon, and my father wants me out there when we close the deal." He chuckled. "I told him that this will put us right back where the family started. My grandfather and great-grandfather were lumbermen."

"Oh, I like lumbermen," Chantal said, smiling broadly. She crooked her arm as if making a muscle. "They have big muscles and big shoulders, and they wear shirts like this." Using her fingers, she made a grid.

"Ah! Plaid shirts," Faith said, laughing. "And I quite agree, they are romantic figures, all right. In his youth, even John's father was a lumberjack."

John grinned. "I don't think he quite fits the picture you and Chantal are painting of him. And I certainly can't see him as a romantic figure."

"No? But your mother apparently did," Chantal suggested, which brought more laughter.

A plane roared over their heads, and when it had passed, Marcel asked John, "So, you will be catching the Windjammer in Portugal tomorrow?"

"Yes. It departs Lisbon at four o'clock in the afternoon, and we'll arrive in New York at seven o'clock the next morning."

Marcel nodded. "That is a good deal faster than the ship we met on, no?"

"Yes, well, that includes the differences in time zones, but it's still hard to believe that one can travel from Europe to America so quickly," John said.

"There are some who think one shouldn't," Faith put in. "I read a nice article in *Collier's Magazine* last month by Eric Twainbough, in which he lamented the fact that trans-Atlantic travel has lost its romance."

"And yet he's been one of our steady customers," John pointed out. "He flew the Windjammer when he went to Spain to cover the war there, and he flew it back. And this past spring he took the Pan Am Clipper from Honolulu to Los Angeles to be present for the premiere of *The Corruptible Dead.*"

"I have heard of that movie, but I have not seen it," Chantal said. "It has not yet come to France. Is it good?"

"It's a great movie," Faith said. "And Demaris Hunter does a wonderful job in it."

"Ah," the French girl sighed, "she is my favorite actress."

"And he is my favorite author," Marcel interjected. "Have you read Eric's newest book? It is called *Confession at Linares.* As soon as I finish reading it, I plan to put it on display with his others."

"I haven't read it," John admitted. "But I believe Faith is reading it now." He turned to his wife. "Is that right, dear?"

"Yes, it is." Faith reached into her oversized bag, then pulled out the novel and held it up. "I haven't finished it yet. I've been reading it in snippets while we're traveling."

"What do you think of it?" Marcel asked.

"Well, to be honest . . ." She paused."Perhaps I haven't read enough of it to form a proper opinion, but I'm not enjoying it as much as I thought I would. It seems to me that there is too much, um, message in the story for it to be truly enjoyable. Also, it makes so much of the war in Spain, and that seems rather old hat now that we're facing the prospect of a much bigger war in Europe."

"I'm afraid I must agree with you," Marcel said. "I think that because Eric was in Spain, their civil war took on much more significance than it actually had. Especially when, as you say, all of Europe may soon find itself embroiled in another war with the Germans."

"You are too critical, Papa," Chantal protested. "*Confession at Linares* is much better than Hemingway's *To Have and Have Not.*"

"You read such books?" John asked, surprised that the girl was so well read. "I mean, books by people like Hemingway and Twainbough?"

"Yes, of course. And Steinbeck and Faulkner and Pearl Buck." Chantal's laughter bubbled out. "Do you think I do nothing but listen to swing music all the time?"

"I don't know. I guess I'm just impressed that a pretty young girl would take the time to read such heavy books. That is, I'd have thought you'd have more . . . interesting . . . things to do."

Now it was Faith's turn to laugh. "Chantal, pay no attention to my husband," she said. "Truth to tell, he is barely aware that such books even exist. I'm afraid he's not a very big fan of fiction. If it isn't a financial statement or a political report, John will never read it. In fact, I don't know that he has ever read a novel."

"No? Not even *Gone With the Wind?*" Chantal asked, astonished. "I thought everyone in America had read *Gone With the Wind.*"

John shrugged. "Well, if that's true, you are looking at the one person in America who has not read *Gone With the Wind.*" He turned to his wife. "But for your information, Mrs. Canfield, I have read a novel. I read *Moby Dick.*"

"*Moby Dick*? Pffff!" Faith scoffed. "*Moby Dick* isn't a novel. It's a college assignment."

Their laughter was interrupted by an announcement over the airport public address system that Lufthansa Flight 313 was now loading at Gate 7 for Madrid and Lisbon.

"Well, that's our flight," John said with a sigh, reaching for the briefcase sitting beside his chair.

"I'll get the children for you," Chantal offered, starting toward Morgan and Alicia.

"Come, we'll walk you to the gate," Marcel suggested. While his daughter went to gather the Canfield children, the restaurateur added to John, "You'd better not be late, or they'll leave you. You know how damned efficient the Boche are."

"Careful, Marcel. You're letting your prejudice against the Germans show," John said dryly.

"You must be mistaken," Marcel said, his face feigning shock and his tone wry. "Who could possibly be prejudiced against a country that defies treaties, refuses to pay reparations, and overruns such places as Austria, the Sudetenland, and Czechoslovakia?"

"Ah, you misunderstand them," John mocked in return. "They're just gregarious neighbors, that's all."

"That is all? *You* should try living with them on your border for all these years."

"No, thank you. I'm happy right where I am."

They reached the gate, and John put down his briefcase

and shook Marcel's hand. "Now don't forget. Next summer you arc all coming to the States to be our guests."

"Yes, to the great city of St. Louis," Marcel said, giving it the French pronunciation. "I am very much looking forward to it."

Just on the other side of the gate, on the concrete apron, the Lufthansa JU-52, a swastika prominently displayed on its vertical fin, sat waiting for the boarding passengers. After an exchange of hugs and kisses with Marcel and his family, the Canfields passed through the boarding gate.

A uniformed steward, wearing a red swastika armband around his sleeve, was standing on the ground just outside the door, helping the passengers to board.

"Welcome aboard Lufthansa Flight 313," he said in German as John and his family began boarding.

"Thank you," John replied in English.

"You are British?" the steward asked in quite fluid English.

"We are American," John replied.

"Ah, American. Perhaps, then, you would like to read the English-language edition of today's Berlin newspaper. You will find it in the rack on the left side of the airplane just beyond the entry."

"Yes, thank you," John replied. Entering the plane, he found the newspaper and took it with him to his seat, holding it folded in his lap until after the aircraft had taken off.

When the plane had reached cruising altitude, Morgan, who was in the seat in front of John, got on his knees and watched happily through his window. On the other side of the aisle, Alicia had settled in for her nap on Faith's lap, and Faith took out her copy of *Confession at Linares* and began reading. John finally opened up the newspaper, and he gaped at its headlines.

POLAND INVADES GERMANY!
ATTACK IS CENTERED NEAR HOCHLINDE

Invaders Temporarily Take Over Radio Station
13 Polish Soldiers Killed
as Attack Is Beaten Back

"My God!" John gasped.

Startled, Faith looked across the aisle. "What is it?" she asked.

"According to this newspaper, Poland has attacked Germany. Why on earth would they do a damned foolish thing like that? I mean, this just guarantees that what everyone has been dreading is about to happen."

"War?" Faith asked apprehensively, her eyes widening.

"I'm afraid so." John shook his head. "But I don't understand it. I could see the Germans attacking Poland. That wouldn't be anything new for Hitler. What I can't understand is why the Poles attacked Germany." He shook his head again. "It just doesn't make any sense."

"I wonder why we didn't hear anything about it while we were in Paris," Faith said. "If there has been time for it to get into the paper, the French have surely heard about it by now."

"I don't know. Maybe the French want to keep it quiet."

"Why would they want to do that?"

"To keep down panic? Who knows?"

"Yes, of course, I never thought of that," Faith said. "I mean, if people panicked, there could be a run on the trains, planes, boats, everything. I'm glad we're getting out of here when we are. Especially since we have the children with us."

"I agree," John said. "Our leaving Europe right now seems to be a fortuitous bit of timing."

SEPTEMBER 1, 1939, LISBON, PORTUGAL

When John Canfield returned to the hotel suite after an early breakfast the next morning, his children were still asleep. Faith hadn't wanted to wake them and so didn't go down to breakfast with her husband an hour earlier. Instead she had ordered coffee and sweet rolls to be sent to the room, and on the damask-covered serving table an empty coffee cup sat beside a dainty china plate with the half-eaten remains of a strawberry danish.

Faith was standing at the window, hugging herself and staring pensively out at the harbor. The room's vantage point gave it an excellent view of the giant, four-engined flying boat riding at anchor in the harbor and glistening brightly in the early-morning light. There were two boats alongside the big airplane, one pumping high-octane gasoline into the Windjammer's fuel tanks, the other loading drink and foodstuffs into its galley. The cowling was open on one of the huge engines, and a man was sitting astride the nacelle like a cowboy riding a horse, working on something inside. The nose of the airplane, rising prowlike up from the water, was adorned with a painting of a United States flag, as was the huge tail.

Seeing his wife watching with such intensity, John chuckled and asked, "Is the plane still there?"

"Believe me, I'm keeping my eyes on it," Faith said. "If I hear anything that even *sounds* like a motor starting, I'm going to grab the kids and run down there."

"You needn't worry," John said easily. "I just spoke with Johnny Blake. He's the pilot on this run, and he's going to have lunch with us. I doubt that it'll leave without him."

"No, I guess not," Faith agreed, turning toward her husband. "I'm just nervous, that's all." She walked toward him. "What news have you heard?"

John took her hands in his. "World War Two has begun," he said solemnly.

"World War Two? Oh, John, don't call it that." Faith shivered. "That sounds so ominous."

"Maybe so, but that's what the radio commentators are already calling it," John said. "Anyway, according to Hitler, and I quote, 'An unprovoked invasion of Germany by Poland took place yesterday, and for some hours our forces have been returning fire.' End quote. He also said that he wants to be nothing but the first soldier of the German Reich, so he was putting on the 'uniform that was always so sacred' to him, and he will not take it off until victory or death."

"What's the reaction of the rest of the world? Have you heard?"

"England and France have guaranteed Poland's security, and they have both notified Hitler that if his troops aren't pulled back, a state of war will exist between them."

"Maybe it's just a little incident," Faith said, her voice slightly hopeful. "Maybe the Germans will pull back as soon as they feel they've gotten even."

"Gotten even for what?"

"Well, for the Poles attacking Germany."

"Poland didn't attack Germany."

"But the newspapers . . . We read it yesterday."

"Would you like to know something interesting? According to the so-called official accounts, the so-called invasion occurred on the thirty-first of August."

"Yes, yesterday," Faith replied, nodding. "We read it in the paper on the plane."

"Uh-huh. The English-language edition," John said. "The funny thing is, that edition was actually *printed* on the thirtieth. Twenty-four hours *before* the Polish attack supposedly happened."

"Before?" Faith shook her head, her eyes narrowing. "I don't understand. How can that be?"

"How can that be? It's very simple . . . if you're planning it," John explained. "There was no Polish attack. The Germans faked the whole thing, just to give them a pretext to invade Poland."

Faith's face paled. "My God," she breathed. "It really is the start of war."

TWO WEEKS LATER, POLAND

Max Tannenhower, a former member of the Hitler Youth—and the twenty-one year-old son of the Gauleiter of Hamburg and an Obergrupenführer of the SS—was now a Wermacht lieutenant in the Fifteenth Panzer Corps. He was also a part of Germany's invading army, and on this fourteenth day of operations, he stood with his upper torso jutting through the turret hatch as his tank rolled quickly along a road near Warsaw.

There had been very little resistance thus far, though

the retreating Polish Army had felled all the trees across the road, using them as roadblocks. It wasn't a very successful effort. All the German tanks had to do was sweep around the road, proceeding through the sunbaked fields without so much as a break in their progress. It had been like that since the first day the German Army had moved into Poland. Everyone had thought Poland's army was one of the strongest in Europe, but it had crumbled before the German onslaught.

Max was wearing a headset with earphones and a microphone so that he could speak to the driver and the gunner in his tank. He was aware that he made quite an imposing figure, protruding as he was from the top of the tank. It made him think of a painting he had once seen, depicting Hitler as a knight wearing shining armor and carrying a spear. Of course, Max wouldn't dare compare himself to the Führer, but he did feel a bit like a knight in shining armor—the armor in this case being the tank.

Max liked to imagine what must be going through the minds of the Polish citizens who looked on with fear as the Panzers, the very symbol of Germany's might, swept by them. He turned to look behind and was startled to see that the other two tanks of his platoon were gone. Where were they? He had given them explicit orders to follow him.

"Sergeant Schultz, stop!" Max commanded, shouting into the microphone that stuck out in front of his mouth.

Immediately complying, the driver braked both tracks, and the tank came to such a sudden halt that Max had to hold on to the turret ring to keep from being thrown out.

"What is it, Herr Lieutenant?" Schultz called to him. "What is wrong?"

"I don't see Sergeant Halder or Corporal Lutz," Max replied. "Where are they? They were supposed to be following right behind us." Max removed his headset and tried to listen for them, but he could only hear the sound of his own tank engine. "Turn off the engine," he ordered Schultz.

"Herr Lieutenant, if we stop the engine now, we might have trouble getting it started again," Schultz warned. "I have been experiencing some difficulty."

"Turn off the engine," Max ordered again, angered that

the driver would question him. What good was it to be the commander if one had every command questioned? Surely his father, an Obergrupenführer, didn't have such difficulty issuing orders.

"*Jawohl,* Herr Lieutenant," Schultz said, and the tank engine fell silent.

"Now," Max murmured, "perhaps I can hear the other tanks."

Crawling out of the turret, he walked to the back of the tank, then strained to hear the sound of engines and clanking track that would signify the approach of the other two tanks. He could hear the far-off rumble of artillery and an occasional rattle of small-arms fire, muffled by distance and made hollow by the echoing sound through the trees. Far closer, he could hear wind in the leaves of the trees, but he heard nothing that sounded like tank engines.

The driver's hatch opened, and Sergeant Schultz stuck his head up. "Ah, it is good to get a breath of fresh air," he said, grinning. The easy familiarity lasted only a moment, and the noncom then asked deferentially, "What now, Herr Lieutenant Tannenhower?"

Max pointed to a low hillock a few yards away. "I am going to walk up to the top of that hill and take a look around. Prepare to start the engine again when I give you the signal."

"Herr Lieutenant, I don't think it's a good idea for you to leave the tank," Schultz said. "We are alone. Suppose there are Polish soldiers or partisans here?"

"Sergeant, I will not have you questioning everything I do," Max said sharply.

"*Jawohl,*" Schultz said, duly chastised.

Max jumped down from the tank, then hurried over to the small hill and climbed it. Near the top he stood still and listened. He could actually hear birds singing up here. He smiled to himself, thinking that it seemed somewhat incongruous for birds to be singing in the midst of a war. He could also hear, from the other side of the hill, a babbling brook. He reached for his canteen. Some fresh water would be a welcome replacement for the stale, slightly chlorinated water he had now.

A tree stood just below the crest of the hill. It was covered with bright yellow leaves that almost seemed to glow. The young soldier studied it closely. He didn't know what kind of tree it was, but he wanted to fix the image of it in his mind so that when he returned home to Hamburg, he could tell his younger sister, Liesl, about it. She would appreciate the concept of beauty in the midst of battle.

Max crested the hill, then started down the other side, digging in his heels to keep from descending too quickly. He could see the stream now. It looked clear and cold, and its surface was bejeweled with a thousand sparkling lights. He opened his canteen and began pouring out the stale water.

An old man suddenly appeared from behind a bush. He wasn't in uniform, but he was carrying a shotgun. Max smiled at him. He was just a simple farmer, no doubt, armed only with a fowling piece. Certainly nothing that represented a challenge to an officer in the mighty German Army.

The young soldier raised his left hand in greeting. "Hello," he said.

The man raised the shotgun and pointed it at Max, then pulled back both hammers.

"Nein! Warten Sie!" Max screamed, suddenly realizing that he was in danger. Dropping his canteen, he clawed at the leather flap over his P-38 pistol.

The roar of the shotgun was the last sound Max Tannenhower ever heard.

SEPTEMBER 25, 1939, HAMBURG, GERMANY

In the *Volkischer-Beobachter*, the Nazi Party's official daily newspaper, notices had begun to appear, placed by the families of the soldiers killed in the Polish campaign. In most cases the entry would read: "For the Fatherland, killed in Poland," followed by the soldier's name.

When Karl Tannenhower, grief-stricken over his son's death, had prepared his own announcement, he had felt a sudden, all-consuming anger at Adolf Hitler for having started the war in the first place. To show that he felt it was

Hitler's war and that Hitler was personally responsible for Max's death, Karl had made a slight alteration in the announcement.

For The Führer,
killed in Poland,
Max Tannenhower,
beloved son of
Karl and Uta Tannenhower

Karl had purposely omitted his own party titles, again as a form of protest.

About a week after the announcement had appeared, Karl had learned that Hitler would be coming to Hamburg and wanted to see him. That day had arrived, and Karl was now resigned to what he was sure would be Hitler's anger over the derisive twisting of the memorial notice.

"Karl, I'm frightened," Uta Tannenhower told her husband as she watched him dress in his Gauleiter uniform for the meeting. "What will the Führer do?"

"He will yell and scream for a while," Karl replied. "And he will tell me that I have no right to blame him personally for Max's death. And then he will strip me of all rank and titles and expel me from the party."

"Will you have to go to prison?"

"There is that possibility, of course." Karl took his hat down from the shelf over the closet, then looked at Uta. "Or worse."

"*Worse?*" Uta gasped, putting her hand to her mouth. "Oh, Karl, don't go! Please, don't go!"

"Refuse a summons to see the Führer?" Karl chuckled. "That *would* be signing my own death warrant."

"But I'm frightened."

"Still, he's right, you know," Karl said and sighed. "He isn't responsible for Max's death. I am."

"You? But how? You didn't start the war with Poland."

"Perhaps not. But I have certainly embraced the National Socialist party from its very beginnings. Max was born into it, he grew up in it, he never had the chance to make up his own mind. He went to war because he knew I *expected* him to go to war."

"Oh, Karl! I am so frightened!" Uta cried.

Karl took her in his arms and held her for a long moment, then kissed her reassuringly. Releasing Uta, he gave his uniform tunic a tug and left the house. His driver was standing at attention, holding open the rear door of the Mercedes. Karl nodded at him as he got into the car.

As the limousine rolled majestically through the streets of Hamburg, Karl looked out through the window, thinking back over the high points of his life. Was it about to end here? Had he survived the sinking of the Titanic, the zeppelin raids over London in the Great War, and the street battles of the Nazi party, only to earn such disfavor from Hitler that he might even be executed for treasonable conduct? There was always that possibility, he knew. Mocking someone as powerful as Adolf Hitler was not a very smart idea.

The car arrived in what seemed to Karl undue haste. Knocking on the door of the chancellor's hotel suite, he was escorted inside and found Hitler standing by the window, eating a small cake. He was wearing dark-brown trousers and a lighter-brown uniform jacket, decorated only with the Iron Cross first class and the Nazi emblem of an eagle clutching a wreathed swastika in its claws. Hitler smiled broadly when he saw Karl, and he set the cake down and wiped his chin with a napkin before he extended his hand in greeting.

"Tannenhower," Hitler said, shaking hands firmly. "Tannenhower, it was good of you to come."

"I was summoned," Karl replied.

"Yes, yes, of course," Hitler said, waving that aside. "First, let me tell you how proud I am of your son. No, I should tell you how proud all Germany is of your son. And how touched I was at the tribute you paid me in his death announcement."

Karl was thoroughly puzzled. "I beg your pardon?"

Hitler put his hands on Karl's shoulders. His eyes, Karl saw, were actually brimming with tears.

"Never have I seen loyalty and affection displayed so

movingly," Hitler said. "To say that your son died for *me* . . . to know that he died for *me* . . ." Hitler put both hands together in front of his face as if in prayer, then turned away from Karl and walked back to the window. He moved his hands up to his forehead and was silent for a long moment. Then he pulled a handkerchief from his jacket pocket and wiped the tears from his eyes. Tucking away the handkerchief, he turned around to face Karl.

"I do not know where fate will lead me," he said. "I have chosen a path that will bring Germany to glory or to ashes. The times ahead are going to be difficult, and during those difficult times I must know that I have around me people who will have the utmost faith in me. People like you, Tannenhower. Therefore, I am herewith creating a new position. From this day forth, you will be known as Oberreichsleiter. You will be a part of my innermost circle, Herr Oberreichsleiter Tannenhower. You will share with me in formulating the destiny of Germany . . . and the destiny of the world!"

The new Reichsleiter of Germany settled into the back seat of the Mercedes to return home. Staring unseeing out the window, he cast his mind back over the strange twist of events.

He had gone to see Hitler, frightened of how Hitler might take his subtle—*too* subtle, as it turned out—act of protest and positive he was going to be punished. Instead, he was rewarded by being appointed to one of the highest positions in the country.

And yet despite Karl Tannenhower's new position of power and authority, despite the esteem Hitler obviously felt for him, the meeting had, indeed, been frightening. The words that Hitler had spoken, the words that kept repeating themselves over and over in Karl's mind, playing like a broken record, ate at his soul. *"I have chosen a path that will bring Germany to glory or to ashes,"* Hitler had promised.

"Which will it be?" Karl murmured to himself. "Which will it be?"

ABOUT THE AUTHOR

Writing under his own name and 25 pen names, ROBERT VAUGHAN has authored over 200 books in every genre but Science Fiction. He won the 1977 Porgie Award (Best Paperback Original) for *The Power and the Pride.* In 1973 *The Valkyrie Mandate* was nominated by its publisher, Simon & Schuster, for the Pulitzer Prize.

Vaughan is a frequent speaker at seminars and at high schools and colleges. He has also hosted three television talk shows: *Eyewitness Magazine,* on WAVY TV in Portsmouth, Virginia, *Tidewater A.M.*, on WHBQ TV in Hampton, Virginia, and *This Week in Books* on the TEMPO Cable Television Network. In addition, he hosted a cooking show at *Phoenix at Mid-day* on KHPO TV in Phoenix, Arizona.

Vaughan is a retired Army Warrant Officer (CW-3) with three tours in Vietnam where he was awarded the Distinguished Flying Cross, the Air Medal with the V for valor, the Bronze Star, the Distinguished Service Medal, and the Purple Heart. He was a helicopter pilot and a maintenance and supply officer. He was also an instructor and Chief of the Aviation Maintenance Officers' Course at Fort Eustis, Virginia. During his military career, Vaughan was a participant in many of the 20th century's most significant events. For example, he served in Korea immediately after the armistice, he was involved in the Nevada Atomic Bomb tests, he was part of the operation which ensured that James Meredith could attend the University of Mississippi, he was alerted for the Cuban Missile Crisis, he served three years in Europe, and of course, the above-mentioned three tours in Vietnam.

The saga continues with

THE AMERICAN CHRONICLES

VOLUME FIVE

PORTALS OF HELL

ROBERT VAUGHAN

CHAPTER ONE

June 3, 1940, Saigon, French Indochina

When the port engine on the twin-engined Grumman flying boat exploded, a jagged piece of metal smashed through the left side window, then out the windshield. Something—either the piece of metal or a shard of glass—slashed a deep cut in Jimmy Blake's forehead, and blood started streaming down his face. The fire that followed immediately lit up the inside of the cockpit with a wavering orange glow.

"Shit!" Jimmy shouted.

He looked out the shattered left window and saw flames shooting out the front of the engine and curling back around the nacelle. Oily, black smoke billowed out behind the fire, already so heavy that the wingtip was obscured. Jimmy put the airplane into a severe right crab so that the windstream would blow the fire on the left wing away from the cabin. He also shut off the fuel and feathered the still-spinning propeller. The propeller wobbled to a halt, then sagged slightly downward as the crankshaft began to melt and warp under the intense heat.

"Are we going to crash?" the young Japanese woman seated beside him asked. Although her voice was calm, her hand was shaking as she put a handkerchief to the cut on Jimmy's forehead and held it there.

"Not, by God, if I can help it," Jimmy replied, his blue-gray eyes narrowing resolutely. "I'm only thirty years old; I'm not prepared to die just yet." He hit the red fire extinguisher button for the number-one engine, and a thick white foam began oozing out from the front of the engine. Within seconds the foam did its job, and the fire subsided. "Yeah!" Jimmy shouted, grinning. "Yeah, I got it! I put the son of a bitch out!"

By the time Jimmy corrected the crabbing angle and leveled off his rapidly descending airplane, he was no more than twenty-five feet above the Saigon River, a very busy trade thoroughfare whose surface was dotted with scores of ships, barges, and boats of every size and description. Jimmy knew that hundreds, if not thousands, of people would be on those vessels or standing alongside the river, watching the crippled plane come down. Some might even be hoping to see a crash, but he had no intention of providing them with that show.

He lowered the flaps and hauled the blunt, boat-shaped nose of the Grumman up, slowing it down so that it was hovering just on the point of a stall. Nevertheless, the flying boat still hit the river very hard and sprayed up sheets of water onto the windshield, momentarily obscuring his vision. All the while the young woman held the handkerchief to Jimmy's face, helping somewhat to stem the flow of blood. When the water fell away a second later, the airplane was speeding across the surface of the river, headed for an unwanted rendezvous with a big wooden boat that glared back through the large red eyes painted on its bow. The occupants of the boat—an old man, an old woman, and a young child—unable to do anything to prevent the impending collision, stood on the deck, transfixed by fear, watching the airplane race toward them.

Steering with the water rudder and his one good engine, Jimmy managed at the last minute to swerve away from the boat and head toward the seaplane pier that protruded out into the river from the foot of Tu Do Street. By the time he reached the docking area, his speed had gradually decreased to the point that he had everything under control and was even able to hold the handkerchief himself. He killed the engine and allowed the airplane to float gently for the last few feet until it bumped lightly against the wooden pier, where an Annamese dockworker stood holding a rope, ready to make the plane fast. Not until his aircraft was secured did Jimmy let out a long sigh of relief, running a hand through his sweat-soaked sandy hair, and allow himself to look through the window at the damaged eninge.

It was misshapen and twisted; a big, jagged hole gaped in the nacelle; and the propeller dangled uselessly, canted at a bizarre angle. The sheet-aluminum covering of the underside of the wing was scorched by fire, and the fabric of the control surfaces was burned away, exposing the bare ribs underneath. Just on the other side of the blackened wing was a fuel tank—and if the fire had reached it, the plane would have gone up in one huge explosion. Jimmy breathed a prayer of relief that the thin-gauge aluminum skin had proven strong enough to impede the fire.

It was only then that Jimmy thought of the young Japanese woman beside him, a passenger he had brought to Saigon from Port St. Jacques. She was sitting quietly, not having uttered a sound since asking if they were about to crash.

"Thanks for the first aid, Miss Amano," he said. "Are you all right?"

"Yes, thank you," Yukari Amano answered in a tiny voice. Her eyes were fixed straight ahead, staring through the windshield, and she gripped her Western-style purse tightly, one hand stained with Jimmy's blood.

Jimmy unsnapped his seat belt and harness. "Well, it's over with. We can get out now."

"Yes, thank you," Yukari replied again in the same small manner. She made no effort to move.

Jimmy looked at her curiously. "Are you *sure* you're all right?"

"I . . . I seem quite unable to move," Yukari admitted.

Jimmy chuckled, and his smile creased his rugged face.

"Well, that's understandable. We just came through what you might call a hair-raising experience." He reached for her seat belt buckle. "Would you like me to help you?"

"Yes, thank you," Yukari answered.

Still pressing the handkerchief to his wound with one hand, Jimmy used his other hand to unfasten Yukari's restraint and help her out of her seat. They stepped over the bulkhead of the small door just behind the cockpit and walked through the passenger compartment of the plane. Yukari was short enough to walk standing up, but Jimmy, who was six-feet-two, had to bend to avoid hitting his head as he passed through the cabin. Normally any of Jimmy's passengers would have ridden back here for the one-hour flight from Port St. Jacques to Saigon. However, Jimmy, the sole owner of the small unscheduled air service, had to make money any way he could, so on this flight the passenger seats were filled with revenue-producing sacks and boxes of freight. Even so, he could have made room in the cabin for Yukari, but, as he had informed her when he picked her up, it would be more comfortable for her up front with him. Smiling shyly, she had accepted his offer.

In the course of the flight Jimmy had learned that Yukari, who had been enjoying a three-day vacation at the seashore in the French resort town of Port St. Jacques, was the twenty-one-year-old daughter of Commander Hiroshi Amano, an aviator in the Japanese Imperial Navy. Commander Amano was in French Indochina as a military attaché to the Japanese consulate; because his duty was considered diplomatic rather than military, he had been granted the very rare privilege of being allowed to have his family accompany him. The Japanese consulate had made quarters available for the Amano family on rue de Pasteur, an avenue of well-kept lawns and stately villas. Hiroshi's wife, Yuko, had gasped in delighted surprise when she saw where they were to live: a large, Western-style, high-ceilinged house, cooled by spinning overhead fans and set in the midst of a shaded garden behind twelve-foot-high walls.

That was all coming to a close, though, for Commander Hiroshi Amano and his family would be returning to Japan the next day. It was because they were about to leave that Hiroshi had allowed Yukari to make an unaccompanied visit to the seashore. Hiroshi's wife and sixteen-year-old son were at home making preparations to leave, while Hiroshi would be meeting Yukari on her return from Port St. Jacques.

Jimmy opened the aircraft's door and spotted a Japanese man dressed in crisp naval whites complete with diplomatic braid waiting on the docks. Hiroshi Amano, to be sure, Jimmy thought. Though certainly, like everyone else, Hiroshi had seen the sudden engine fire, he displayed no outward emotion. He stood with his legs slightly spread, holding a small riding quirt behind his back, as he waited stoically for his daughter. Jimmy helped Yukari from the plane, then walked with her as she went to greet Hiroshi.

"Hello, Father," Yukari said in Japanese, bowing politely.

"Was your visit to the seashore pleasant?" Hiroshi asked.

"Yes, Father."

"I am glad. Wait in the car, please."

"Yes, Father." Yukari turned to Jimmy and bowed slightly. Jimmy bowed back, and then Yukari walked over to her father's staff car. The driver opened the back door for her, bowing deeply as she slipped inside.

Hiroshi watched until his daughter was safely inside the car, then turned back to Jimmy. "You are injured?" he asked, switching to English. It was excellent.

Jimmy took the handkerchief down and looked at it. It was blood-soaked. "It looks worse than it is," he replied, putting the handkerchief back. "A cut, that's all."

"You should have it seen to," Hiroshi said. He called over his shoulder to his driver, and the driver, bowing sharply, barked a one-word reply, then hurried off. "I have sent for a doctor," the commander said.

"Thank you."

"It is I who should be grateful, Mr. Blake," Hiroshi insisted. "Your skill as an aviator saved my daughter's life."

"I appreciate your expression of gratitude, Commander Amano," Jimmy answered dryly, "but the truth is, I was trying to save my *own* life. Your daughter just happened to be with me."

"Yes, to be sure. Nevertheless, that was a display of skillful flying on your part. And to show my appreciation, I would like to invite you to be the dinner guest of my family tonight. I apologize for giving you so little notice, but we will be leaving the country tomorrow."

"You're going back to Japan?"

"Yes. We will be flying back. I do hope the incident today hasn't so frightened my daughter that she will be unable to fly."

Jimmy smiled, and his face was filled with admiration. "Your daughter is a very brave young lady, Commander Amano. She didn't show the slightest bit of fear."

"That pleases me," Hiroshi replied. "You will accept my invitation?"

"I am honored by it."

Hiroshi's driver returned then, leading a man in a white suit carrying a small black satchel.

"This man is a doctor," Hiroshi said. "Please allow him to look at your wound."

"Yes, I will. Thank you again," Jimmy said.

The Japanese naval officer bowed, and Jimmy bowed back, then watched as Commander Amano returned to his car. Not until the car was driving away did Jimmy turn his attention back to the airplane. Already it was being unloaded by a couple of Annamese, and it bobbed up and down each time one of them entered or left the cabin. The native workers were wearing only khaki shorts and rope-and-leather sandals, and in their half-naked state it was easy to see how thin they were. But looks were deceiving, because they moved the heavy sacks and boxes with little apparent effort.

The man in the white suit stepped in front of Jimmy and held up his medical bag. *"Bac si,"* he said, and Jimmy recognized the local term for doctor.

Jimmy nodded. "All right, fix me up, Doc. I don't have time for this."

The doctor looked at the wound; then, by gestures, he indicated that Jimmy needed stitches.

"Yeah, well, can you do it here? I've got to look after my plane." Jimmy pointed to the dock. "Here," he said. "Do it here."

The doctor said something, but Jimmy didn't understand him.

"What?"

"He says if he does it here, it will leave a bad scar," a bystander translated for him.

Jimmy laughed. "A scar, huh? Hell, what difference does that make? I wasn't pretty to begin with. Tell him to sew me up."

The bystander relayed the message, and, finding an empty crate, Jimmy sat down while the doctor cleaned his wound, then began sewing it shut. The operation drew a crowd of curious onlookers, and, through the translator, the doctor apologized for them.

"Oh, hell, let 'em watch," Jimmy said. "I disappointed 'em when I didn't crash. They ought to have *some* kind of a show."

The doctor sewed for another moment or two; then he cut the thread and tied it off. After that he put a clean bandage over the wound.

"Thanks," Jimmy said, pulling several bills from his wallet and offering them to the doctor.

The doctor looked at the money, then waved his hands in protest. He spoke to the translator.

"He says the Japanese man has already paid," the translator said.

"Then tell him this is a tip," Jimmy said. "I don't have enough to fix my airplane anyway, so I may as well be generous."

The doctor accepted the money, smiling broadly at his good fortune.

When the doctor left, Jimmy walked back over to his plane, stepped onto the bow, then scrambled up top and crawled between the two engines. The right power plant was undamaged, but the left engine hung in its mountings, grotesquely twisted and blackened.

"What happened, Monsieur Blake?" a man called.

Jimmy recognized André LeGrand's voice and groaned. LeGrand was the chief loan officer for the Banque de Saigon —and the last person Jimmy wanted to see. Jimmy owed the bank twenty-five hundred dollars on his plane. Now he wouldn't be able to make the money to pay the bank until his plane was repaired. And he wouldn't be able to repair his plane until he made some money.

"I had an engine fire," Jimmy grumbled. He managed to

disconnect one of the cowling latches, even though it was warped by the fire. With the latch disconnected he was able to open the cowling and look down on the blackened engine. The smell of burned rubber and oil wafted into his nose. When he saw the fuel line, he let out a sniff of disgust. "And here's the culprit," he added, holding the rubber hose in his hand. "A broken fuel line."

"Such a shame," the banker said, making *tsk-tsk* sounds. "How difficult is it to fix a broken fuel line?"

"The fuel line's no problem," Jimmy said. He pointed to the engine. "But the crankshaft, propeller, cyclinder walls, and pistons are shot. It's going to take a major rebuild, if not a new engine."

"I see," LeGrand said. "And that means what?"

"That means time and money," Jimmy replied. He smiled thinly. "Neither of which I have at this moment."

LeGrand cleared his throat. "What do you plan to do?" he asked.

Jimmy shut the cowling and pushed the fastener shut. It was an automatic move, though in truth the engine was so badly damaged that it made no difference whether the cowling was shut or not.

"I guess the only thing I can do is try and raise enough money to replace the engine," Jimmy said.

"Yes, to be sure," LeGrand agreed. "And while you are about it, perhaps you will be so kind as to raise enough money to pay the note at the bank as well. It is due by noon tomorrow."

"I thought maybe you could give me a ninety-day extension," Jimmy said. "And loan me enough money to make the repairs," he added halfheartedly.

"Yes, I thought as much," LeGrand said. He shook his head slowly and clucked his tongue. "I wish I could, Monsieur Blake. I rather like you, you know. But, unfortunately, one cannot let business decisions be clouded by friendship. You mustn't forget that I have a board of directors to satisfy, and they are not disposed to wait any longer. You do understand."

Jimmy sighed. "Yeah, I understand. And you understand, I hope, that without that extension and the additional loan, there's no way I can pay you. You'll have to take the airplane. And in its present condition, I'm afraid that it's not even worth what I owe you."

"Such are the risks of business," LeGrand said.

Jimmy climbed down from the airplane, then turned around and took one long, wistful look back at it. He sighed. "Okay, there it is. It's all yours."

"There is no hurry. Noon tomorrow will be soon enough," LeGrand replied with a shrug. "I have no fear that you will fly it away. It is too bad that your idea of a Southeast Asia airline didn't work out. But with only one airplane and one pilot the odds were against you."

"Yeah," Jimmy said. "I guess they were."

"What will you do now? Will you fly for Pan Am?"

"Pan Am? Hell, no. I hate those bastards. I guess I'll go back on with World Air Transport."

"Will they rehire you?"

"I'm sure they will. The president of the company, Willie Canfield, is a good friend of mine. And he told me when I left that if this didn't work out, he'd take me back. Although I probably won't get on as captain," Jimmy admitted. "But it doesn't matter. I'm not too proud to fly in the right-hand seat, and Willie knows that."

"I wish you good luck, Monsieur Blake," LeGrand said.

"Thanks."

Jimmy turned and walked away from the seaplane without looking back.

"Monsieur Blake, wait! Don't you want to remove your things from the plane?" LeGrand called.

"I'm wearing my leather jacket," Jimmy answered over his shoulder. "There's nothing else I want."

CHAPTER TWO

June 4, 1940, Dunkirk, France

Sir John Paul Chetwynd-Dunleigh, Earl of Dunleigh and Colonel of His Majesty's Royal Essex Fusiliers, now in active service with the British Expeditionary Force, looked at the glowing dial of his wristwatch. It was 3:15 A.M., and he was at the final defensive position, approximately one-half mile from the beach at Dunkirk. Over the last week almost 340,000 soldiers had embarked from Dunkirk for England. The vaunted Maginot Line, living up to its promise, had not been breached. But it *had* been flanked, and France, which had based its entire defense on those static fortifications, had fallen. With the fall of France the British Army suddenly found itself outnumbered and outflanked. It had no choice but to retreat, though the English Channel had seemingly cut off even that route.

The British High Command had sent out urgent requests to its citizens, asking that they go to France in anything that would float. All England had responded with ships of war, ships of commerce, yachts, fishing boats, barges, and scows.

The channel was packed with thousands of overloaded vessels as the troops were withdrawn. Newspapers in England and in the United States were already hailing it as the greatest strategic withdrawal in the history of warfare.

The end result was that France had been abandoned, and now practically the whole of Europe belonged to the Germans. John Paul had volunteered to stay behind and command the rear guard, thus buying enough time for the troops to withdraw. During the rear-guard action his men fought bravely and well, turning back three separate German thrusts. The fighting had been ferocious, and of the 323 men John Paul had started with, only 141 had lived long enough to get onto the evacuation ship, boarding it just after midnight that morning.

John Paul would be staying behind only long enough to coordinate the final defense with the French officer who was taking over. The major general who was John Paul's immediate superior had informed him that he was being recommended for the Distinguished Service Order with Bar for his heroism. But that didn't mollify John Paul's dissatisfaction. General Halfacre and the British press could paint it any way they wanted, he thought. In his mind the "strategic withdrawal" was still a defeat.

The commander of the French rear guard reached John Paul's position and introduced himself. "Please excuse me for saying so," Major Pierre Aubron said, shouting to be heard over the constant roar of shells from German tanks and field artillery that continued to rain deadly barrages down on the beach, "but you seem awfully young to be a colonel."

John Paul laughed. "If you think I'm young now, you should have seen me when I was five."

"*Pardon?*"

"That's how old I was when I inherited the commission," John Paul explained.

"I thought people who inherited commissions never used them except for ceremonial dinner parties," Aubron said dryly. "What are you doing over here?"

"When the war started, I asked to go into active service," John Paul replied. "I'm afraid I must plead temporary insanity."

Aubron laughed. "Temporary, you say? We will see about that. The last ship is about to sail. If you don't get down there, your insanity could become permanent."

"Some host you are," John Paul joked. "Rushing me off as if I had overstayed my welcome."

They glanced to the east, where the sky bloomed red with the false dawn of repeated cannon flashes.

"I'll come see you off," Pierre suggested.

"What about your men?"

"They have instructions to hold here for thirty more minutes; then they are on their own."

"Feel like a little run?" John Paul asked.

"But of course," Aubron replied, grinning. "After all, exercise is supposed to be good for you."

As the two men started running toward the beach they heard an incoming howitzer round whooshing down out of the blackness. It hit about one hundred yards ahead to the right of their path, and the shell's brilliant flash was followed a second later by the sound of its explosion. They were so used to such things by now that they didn't even alter their run. By the time they topped the last hillock, they were gasping for breath. Despite that, they were stopped short by what they saw.

"*Mon dieu!*" Aubron breathed. "Look at that!"

The beach was well lighted from nearly a hundred fires as trucks, tanks, and motorcars burned fiercely. For every vehicle burning there were at least ten more that weren't, and they stood abandoned on the beach. Most were in perfect condition, with keys still in the ignition, gas in the tanks, and doors open, as if inviting the Germans to drive them home.

John Paul shook his head sadly. "It shames me to see us abandon all this," he said.

"You have no cause for shame," Aubron replied, bitterness in his voice. "Your army has abandoned some equipment . . . my army has abandoned an entire country."

Another shell rushed over them, sounding like a runaway freight train. It plunged into the channel about a half mile offshore and exploded with a roar and a geyser of water.

John Paul spotted a British noncom and called, "Sergeant! Who is the senior officer remaining on the beach?"

The sergeant saw John Paul's rank and came to attention. "Blimey, Colonel," he said. "I imagine you must be."

"I just got here. Who else?"

"That would be our Major Heath down at the edge of the water, sir," he said, pointing toward the surf where a handful of men were getting into a boat. "He's been in charge of loading."

Thanking the sergeant, John Paul and Pierre Aubron hurried down across the beach to the British officer.

"Step lively, lads, do step lively now," Major Heath was saying to the soldiers who were climbing into the boat. "We wouldn't want to be late, now, would we?"

"Major Heath?"

The major turned toward John Paul, and John Paul saw the same look in his face that he had seen in the faces of all the officers he had spoken to during the last three weeks: exhaustion, shock, and anger. But he didn't see defeat, and somehow the major's look of defiance compensated for all the military equipment lying around on the beach.

"Ah, you must be Colonel Sir Chetwynd-Dunleigh," Major Heath said. "I was told you were still here."

"Yes."

"I'm damned glad you made it, sir. You're the last one, you know. And you, Major?" Heath asked Aubron. "Will you be going with us as well? A lot of your countrymen have."

"No, I will be staying in France," Aubron answered. He took off his heavy steel helmet and rubbed his hand across the crease in his forehead caused by the weight of the helmet.

"Major Aubron's men relieved our chaps at the barrier," John Paul explained.

"Good for you, Major," Heath said.

"Yes, well, I should warn you, I told my men they could disperse in thirty minutes," Aubron said. "After that there will be nothing between the Germans and the beach."

"No matter. We'll be gone by then," Heath said. He pointed to a black silhouette lying a half mile offshore. "Do you see that ship? That's the destroyer *Shikari*, and it's the last military vessel of the entire evacuation armada. Once we're aboard her, we'll head for England, and the Boche can jolly well have this bloody beach. No offense, Major," he quickly added.

"Where will you go now, Pierre?" John Paul asked.

"I'm not exactly sure," the Frenchman replied. "My military orders go only as far as the evacuation. After you are gone, I suppose I will try to make it back to Paris. My brother has a café there."

"Really? What's the name of it?" John Paul asked. "When this damn war is over and the Germans have been kicked back to their own border, I plan on returning to France on holiday. I'll come to the café and look you up."

"It is called Marcel's."

"Marcel's? That sounds familiar. Would I have heard of it?"

Pierre smiled. "You may have. Many famous writers have been there. Hemingway, Dos Passos, Twainbough, Gertrude Stein."

"Oh, yes, of course," John Paul said.

"Colonel," the sergeant said, coming down to the waterline. "I've had a final look around. Everyone has come in now."

"Very good," John Paul said. "Get your men into the boat, Sergeant. Major Heath, after you." He turned back to the Frenchman. "Oh, and Pierre, when you get to your brother's restaurant, do put away a bottle of his finest wine for me, won't you? I wouldn't want to be disappointed when I show up."

"I'll pick it out myself, John Paul," Aubron said, shaking John Paul's hand.

John Paul stepped into the shallows and climbed onto the boat. He was the last one to board, and even before he sat down the operator started the boat toward the destroyer. The small outboard motor popped loudly as the boat climbed up one side, then slid down the other of the heavy, rolling swell of an incoming breaker.

Turning, John Paul gave a quick look over his shoulder back at the beach littered with mutilated bodies, strewn with twisted debris, pocked with mortar craters, shells still raining down. . . . If anyone had asked him what hell looked like, he would have replied, "Dunkirk."